The Kingdom of Ohio

The

KINGDOM

of

OHIO

MATTHEW FLAMING

AMY EINHORN BOOKS

Published by G. P. Putnam's Sons

a member of Penguin Group (USA) Inc.

New York

AMY EINHORN BOOKS
Published by G. P. Putnam's Sons
Publishers Since 1838
Published by the Penguin Group
Penguin Group (USA) Inc., 375 Hudson Street, New York, New York 10014, USA •
Penguin Group (Canada), 90 Eglinton Avenue East, Suite 700,
Toronto, Ontario M4P 2Y3, Canada (a division of Pearson Penguin Canada Inc.) •
Penguin Books Ltd, 80 Strand, London WC2R 0RL, England • Penguin Ireland, 25 St
Stephen's Green, Dublin 2, Ireland (a division of Penguin
Books Ltd) • Penguin Group (Australia), 250 Camberwell Road, Camberwell, Victoria
3124, Australia (a division of Pearson Australia Group Pty Ltd) • Penguin Books India
Pvt Ltd, 11 Community Centre, Panchsheel Park,
New Delhi–110 017, India • Penguin Group (NZ), 67 Apollo Drive,
Rosedale, North Shore 0632, New Zealand (a division of Pearson
New Zealand Ltd) • Penguin Books (South Africa) (Pty) Ltd,
24 Sturdee Avenue, Rosebank, Johannesburg 2196, South Africa

Penguin Books Ltd, Registered Offices: 80 Strand, London WC2R 0RL, England

Library of Congress Cataloging-in-Publication Data

Flaming, Matthew.
  The kingdom of Ohio / Matthew Flaming.
    p.   cm.
  ISBN 978-0-399-15560-4
  1. Gifted persons—Fiction.   2. New York (N.Y.)—History—
1898–1951—Fiction.   I. Title.
  PS3606.L354K56   2009   2008046418
  813'.6—dc22

Printed in the United States of America
10   9   8   7   6   5   4   3   2   1

Book design by Marysarah Quinn

This is a work of fiction.

This book is

for my family,

and for

Cheri-Anne Toledo.

The Kingdom of Ohio

CHAPTER 1

THE PHOTOGRAPH

WHETHER BEAUTIFUL OR TERRIBLE, THE PAST IS ALWAYS A RUIN.

When I look back on my childhood, my earliest memories seem like artifacts from a lost civilization: half-understood fragments behind museum glass. I remember the spherical alcohol lamp that glowed like a tiny ghost, ringed with dancing blue flames, which hung over the dining-room table of the house where I grew up. I remember the sweet, oily smell of coal smoke, and the creaking of horse-drawn carriages on the dirt road outside. Most of all I remember the summer twilight over the mountains and how, on certain evenings, just before the sun sank below the horizon, it cast rays so luminous and golden that they felt like a solid, enveloping cloak into which a small boy could simply disappear. An intensity no light today seems to match.

These images appear as snapshots of a vanished world—literally vanished, considering how much has changed between those years and the present day. Since then, airplane flights linking the continents have transformed once-in-a-lifetime voyages into matters of a few hours spent in a comfortable seat. Things like telephones and automobiles, once improbable rarities possessed only by the very rich, are now taken for granted by average people. When I was young, the changing of the seasons was the most important punctuation of life: ancient rhythms that have since been replaced by electric lights that turn night into day, and fragment each day into electronic-precision intervals measured by the punch-clock instead of the almanac.

Now, watching the young men and women dressed in skin-tight leotards rollerblade past the bench where I like to watch the sun sink over the Pacific on these warm Los Angeles evenings, I know that my world no longer exists. It has vanished utterly, and would be incomprehensible to these self-satisfied, bright-faced youths.

Thanks to the genius of human invention, things have sped up until I can hardly keep track anymore: the new-new internet, the new world order, the next big thing that seems to arrive every day (if the newspapers are to be believed). Carried on the tide of progress, we all seem to be fast-forwarding into a future where our memories become irrelevant relics from a useless and discarded past.

Let me be clear: I don't mean to glorify the "good old days," or to condemn the contemporary milieu. Whatever charms the past may have had, I don't believe those bygone times were any better than the present (at least, apart from my own preferences—and I won't pretend to speak for anyone other than myself). Instead, what I'm trying to explain is that I am a kind of dinosaur: a member of a near-extinct species, fumbling with arthritic talons on the typewriter keys as I write these pages.

Several years ago I took a composition course at the local community college. During those sensitivity-laden sessions (where bad prose was miraculously transformed into "challenging work," and cliché into "irony"), the instructor taught us that a story should start by making clear where the narrator stands, establishing the voice. And that's what I'm hoping to do here—only, rereading these last few paragraphs, I see that it doesn't seem to be working. And to be honest, clarity in general isn't one of my strengths these days. So maybe it's best if I begin (again) by simply explaining how it all began.

IT WAS TWO YEARS AGO when the little bells above the entrance to the antiques store tinkled and the door swung open, a sweating delivery man staggering through. I looked up from the book I'd been reading and stood.

"Got a shipment for you," he announced, dropping the packages next to my desk. "Need your signature."

I wrote my name on the screen that he shoved in my direction. "See you around, boss." He gave me a thumbs-up gesture before departing into the brightness of the world outside. I looked down at the three large boxes.

It had been almost a decade since I'd opened my antiques store, and by then it was a reasonably successful business, located in a middle-class Los Angeles suburb. I should emphasize that I didn't start the business because I was ambitious. In fact, I had opened the store for quite opposite reasons: as a refuge, a way of retreating from life. Despite my decades of trying to feel comfortable in the world, I had never really managed to fit into this place (this sprawling California city with its constant noise, its nirvanas of vitamin juice and self-realization—or this twentieth century in general, for that matter). The store was intended to be a place where I could hide, where I could be alone and let the world forget me.

To my surprise, although I didn't have much in the way of a gift for salesmanship or knowledge of antiques, the shop provided me with a modest but healthy income, until a larger, more polished antiques store opened a few blocks away. Since then, to compete, I'd been forced to sell less furniture and more historical knick-knacks. For the most part these were old magazines and books that I purchased in bulk, mainly from estate sales in the Midwest: in-expensive curiosities that might attract casual shoppers who wandered in to purchase a fragment of the past.

Through the small windows of the shop, dusty beams of sunlight illuminated the cluttered interior of the space: the worn upholstery of armchairs, an assortment of Edwardian-era dressing tables with age-silvered mirrors, a curio cabinet bearing a row of ormolu clocks (all motionless, since I couldn't stand the sound of their ticking). Outside, the shapes of palm trees shimmered in the heat.

I slit the packing tape on the first of the boxes and began to inventory its contents. Issues of *Time* magazine and *Life* magazine, covers displaying images of celebration and catastrophe. A newspaper clipping and a small black-and-white photograph that had been taped together fell out of one of the magazines and I stooped to pick them up, glancing at the picture. A snapshot of three people sitting at a table in a bar, two men and a woman.

The next thing I remember was the door swinging open, a young couple entering the shop. I looked up from the photograph, trying to wipe away my tears with shaking hands. The couple stared at me and I stammered something about the store being closed. They hurried away, and I closed my eyes again.

I told myself that the photograph didn't make any difference or change anything. But already I understood that, whatever I might want to believe, everything had changed. All my efforts at forgetting and indifference were abruptly meaningless. Like it or not, I would have to go back and unbury everything. Somehow I would have to find a way of telling this story: of salvaging some fragment from the scrap heap of the past.

It has been two years since then, and I'm still struggling to fit the pieces together. At one time I imagined that I could be a good scholar, but if I'm honest with myself I never was—and, at any rate, I'm too old for such efforts now. Despite my hours spent hunched over library books and staring at the glowing hieroglyph-ics of computer screens, I still can't prove anything.

More than once, in fact, I told myself that writing this story was a waste of time, a lost cause. But in the end, the cunning of desire always triumphs over the cunning of reason. (Or, as Byron put it, "There is no instinct like that of the heart.") So that even after I'd decided to give up, at the least expected of times—sitting in my apartment, watching the electric nighttime silhouette of Los Angeles—it would all come crowding back to me . . .

Well, at least it's a good story. (Of course I'd have to say that, wouldn't I? But really: it is.) It's a story about conspiracies and struggles to reshape the world; about secret wars between men like J. P. Morgan, Thomas Edison, and Nikola Tesla. It is about one of the strangest and least-known mysteries of American history: the existence and disappearance of the Lost Kingdom of Ohio. It is about science and faith, and the distance between the two. Most of all, it's a story about a man and a woman, and about love.

In my imagination, it begins with a day in the heart of winter. I can picture it effortlessly: the gray sky and the leafless trees, the solemn profile of a young woman standing near a riverbank. A whisper of cold on my cheek as I look up to see the first flakes of snow beginning to fall—

But that's not right. That scene comes much later—or, looking at it another way, much earlier. Really, the only place I can honestly begin is in the middle of things, with New York City, in the year 1900. With the construction of the first subway tunnels through the dark bedrock beneath the metropolis, and with a young man so distant from where I sit now that he seems an unrecognizable stranger: a mechanic, an adventurer, and perhaps also a criminal, named Peter Force.

CHAPTER II

THE SUBWAY WORKER

IN THE YEAR 1900, NEW YORK IS A CITY OF MACHINES. IT IS THE biggest Italian city in the world, the biggest Jewish city, the biggest Polish city, and most of all the greatest city of the New World. There is nothing else like it on earth: the accretion of humanity, the burgeoning accumulation of metal and stone and concrete, and sheer, constant motion.

It is a metropolis that is home to both the wealthiest and the poorest people in America, a city full of hope, and hope destroyed. It is a place of furious ambition and simple fury. It is impossible: this is what newcomers think as they walk through its streets.

When Peter Force arrives in New York, stumbling off the train from Chicago with his meager possessions clutched in a burlap sack, he spends his first few days wandering along the boulevards like a drunk, gaping upward at the buildings, terrified and amazed. At the suggestion of a stranger, he rents a room in one of the nameless flophouses at the lower end of Manhattan, where Grand Street intersects the Bowery among piles of refuse. His hotel is a teetering three-story clapboard structure whose rickety walls tremble whenever a door slams. Peter's room is a stall the size of a closet, with a rough hemp net to sleep on suspended near one wall.

During those first nights in New York, though, sleep eludes him. Kept awake by the continual sound of the city outside, he stares at the flickering shadows on the ceiling and listens to the snores of other men in the darkness. Bedbugs itch beneath him, burrowing in the yellowed woolen blankets. Wrestling with insomnia, he thinks of the landscape he left a week ago—the echoing stillness of the western mountains—struggling to connect this recollection with the foreign place where he finds himself now.

Peter remembers clambering up a sheer rock face of granite, pulling himself over a final ledge to collapse exhausted at the top of a cliff. He remembers lying on an outcropping above a twisting, nameless river, staring up at the mindless blue of the frontier sky and the ascending spiral of a hawk. Nights spent sitting across a campfire from his father, the crack and hiss of sap in the logs, sparks rising through dark evergreen branches. These random images returning to him. But none of these things have any place in the present, he reminds himself, listening to the rattle of wagons and omnibuses on the street outside. The rumble of turbines under the earth, burning coal into a fine, black dust that settles over everything.

He imagines the city as a collision of all the forces of human nature, a zoo of poverty and wealth. One-room flats house extended tribes of dishwashers and laundresses and the unemployed, who meet and clash each day in the streets in a Babel of signs and curses and discussion. Electricity and steam push through the earth in layers of pipes and tunnels. In Times Square, moving pictures and tinctographs loom behind garish full-color billboards, the Talking Dog and magic-lantern arcades and restaurants and trinket-mongers crowded together in between.

On his fourth day in Manhattan, as the few dollars he arrived with dwindle to a handful of small coins, Peter makes his way to a recruiter's office where legions of workers are being hired to help build the first subway lines under the city.

This is the setting, the place and time, where I need to begin. The only question is how to get there. How to find a bridge across the span of so many years. And it's hoping to discover such a path that I keep scrutinizing the history books, searching among all those dust-dry words for some hint of the living past.

In 1900 no comprehensive public transportation system existed in New York City. Instead (the historians tell me), most passengers traveled on privately operated horse-drawn omnibuses, which inched along the crowded, ill-paved streets. The few aboveground trains that ran through the city were perpetually overcrowded, their noise intolerable, and the footings of the elevated tracks were a further obstacle to traffic.

Finally, in 1899, after years of debate (and, as the textbooks point out, against the opposition of politicians whose power was bound up in revenues from the omnibus lines), a transit proposal was passed, authorizing the Rapid Transit Commission to build the first segment of the New York subway. A number of powerful financiers almost immediately gained control of these subway contracts, among them August Belmont, Jr., John D. Rockefeller, and John Pierpont Morgan.

On October 27, 1904, the subway would finally open to the public, seventy thousand people riding the new underground railroad on its opening day. This account, which I found in the *New York Tribune*, seems typical, describing how

> indescribable scenes of crowding and confusion, never before paralleled in this city, marked the throwing open of the subway to the general public last night. . . .
>
> Men fought, kicked, and pummeled one another in their mad desire to reach the subway ticket offices or to ride on the trains. Women were dragged out, either screaming in hysterics or in a swooning condition; gray-haired men pleaded for mercy; boys were knocked down, and only escaped by a miracle being trampled underfoot. The presence of the police alone averted what would undoubtedly have been panic after panic, with wholesale loss of life.*

In the years following its opening, the subway would deeply shape the daily and emotional life of New York, becoming a meta-

---

* "Panic in the Underground Railroad," *New York Tribune*, October 28, 1904.

phor for the city's character. In his epic poem *The Bridge*, for example, Hart Crane would describe a subway ride from Times Square to Brooklyn as a journey through hell, writing:

> *And why do I often meet your*
> *visage here,*
> *Your eyes like agate lanterns—*
> *on and on*
> *Below the toothpaste and the*
> *dandruff ads?*[*]

But at the beginning, before all these things, came the seemingly impossible task of shifting aside tons of bedrock to make this miracle possible. Employment on the subway crews was backbreaking, heartbreaking, an almost unimaginable labor. Nearly unnoted in the history books, beneath the rock of Manhattan, twelve thousand nameless men were hired to perform the work of Hercules for twenty cents an hour, ten hours a day.

I read this and close my eyes, trying to re-create the scene (as if somehow I could return to watch it happening, a time traveler perched in a time machine). I imagine the young man who calls himself Peter Force joining the group of ragged applicants outside the office of the New York Drilling Company. The gray autumn sky, the swaybacked brick buildings. The sudden disorientation and loneliness that comes over him: a brief sensation of watching himself, like a distant stranger, fumbling to fit his gestures into the imagined shape of this new life.

---

[*] Hart Crane, *The Bridge* (Paris: Black Sun Press, 1930).

I picture young Peter Force, waiting in line, trying to convince himself that this is how a new life might begin.

THE RECRUITER looks him up and down. For a moment the recruiter's eyes linger at the fading bruises on Peter's face. He looks away.

"You got no experience." The recruiter has already decided— he is a thin, red-faced man with an angry rash up the backs of his legs. The office where he sits is cold, the chill wind whimpering through chinks in the window framing.

Peter shakes his head. "I've been in mines before. Some might get nervous, down there. Not me."

The recruiter scribbles on a piece of paper. "Take this. Give it to the secretary."

"Thank you."

"Don't thank me." He waves Peter away as the next man enters the office, a lumbering giant with his hat in his hands. Peter glances at the paper but can't decipher the scrawl. Outside the office, he hands the slip to a secretary who perches on a tall stool behind a pulpit-desk. The secretary accepts the paper and barely glances at it before tossing it on the floor. He opens a ledger and writes something.

"Name?"

"Peter Force."

"Age?"

"Twenty-three."

"Crew B, Canal Street tunnel. Tomorrow morning at eight. Your foreman is Josiah Flocombe." He looks up.

Peter nods mutely.

"You're paid Fridays. Next."

Dizzy with the suddenness of his employment, Peter nods again and descends the stairs to the street.

And the following morning, his breath steaming in the chill November air, he walks to the subway-works. Outside the rough wooden fence surrounding the excavation site he stops for a moment, hands in his pockets, hesitating.

Around him the streets are filled with a silver mist that fragments the city into a series of disconnected details: the tangle of wrought-iron fire escapes, indistinct shapes of hurrying pedestrians, sidewalk vendors beginning to open their stalls, a knot of beggar children encamped in an alleyway around a smoldering trash-can fire, the sound of horses' hooves, shouts, and the rumble of carriage wheels . . .

Inside the construction site, a line of workers are clambering out of the tunnel excavation. A reddish light is shining from somewhere underground and, silhouetted in this glow, wreathed with swirling clouds of stone-dust, each figure seems to be on fire. At least, this is the unsettling thought that comes to Peter as he watches—a vision that stays with him for a long moment, despite his efforts to blink it away.

More and more often, in recent months, he has been troubled by images like this: men plunging from cliffs, bodies torn apart beneath the impact of bullets, limbs slashed by invisible knives. But these are just meaningless daydreams, Peter tells himself. He has never put much faith in intuition or visionary stuff, has always been more comfortable with cautious reasoning and careful judgment.

And gradually, as he shakes his head, the normal world returns. Inside the construction site the workers rack their tools in wooden trestles before breaking off into little groups. They pull wrapped packages of bread and cheese from their pockets for the morning meal, smoking cigarettes twisted together with scraps of newspaper.

Peter takes a deep breath. He knows what he's doing here, he reminds himself, and has more experience with this work than most men. Still his heart is pounding with the painful self-consciousness of being watched as an outsider as he steps through the gate.

He finds the foreman—a stocky man with weary pouches beneath his eyes and thinning orange hair—sitting on a mound of rubble, a flask pressed to his lips and his head thrown back, fervently as if in prayer.

"Are you Josiah Flocombe?" Peter asks.

The other man lowers his flask and wipes his mouth on his sleeve, regarding Peter with one bloodshot eye. Beneath this silent scrutiny, Peter looks away. Somewhere underground, pushing up through the soles of his feet, he can feel the throb and crack of drills eating into rock.

Finally, at a loss, he decides to repeat the question. "Are you—"

"I am," the foreman interrupts. "I am that Josiah Flocombe. And who are you?"

"Peter Force," Peter says.

"And what do you want, Peter Force?" Flocombe demands.

Growing up on the western frontier, a territory populated largely by crackpots, wanderers, and persons too eccentric for regular society, Peter is no stranger to odd characters, but something about the foreman—a certain gleam in his eyes, behind their pinkish glaze—still unnerves him. He tries to choose his next words carefully.

"That recruiter said—"

"Don't talk to me about the poxy, shit-for-brains recruiter!" Flocombe sits up straighter, his stare redoubling in reddish intensity.

"I only meant—"

"Listen to me, Peter Force." The foreman's voice drops to a whisper, forcing Peter to lean into the alcoholic haze of Flocombe's breath. "There's something rotten in this project. It begins at your recruiter's office, and goes up from there. So—"

With a groaning effort Flocombe pushes himself to his feet and stands, wavering unsteadily. Peter takes a hasty step backward, out of the foreman's reach. "So best we understand each other now. Are you with those men? Or with me?"

Peter takes another step away from Flocombe, struck by the unpleasant thought he might be working for a madman—a category that seems to encompass half the population of New York with its mobs of mumbling beggars, every street corner marked by a preacher shouting at the moon.

"Well?"

Peter's lifelong sense of caution answers for him: "I'm here to work."

This seems to satisfy Flocombe. He nods, the intensity of his stare evaporating into exhaustion. He runs a hand through his hair. "Well, then. You ever dug before?"

"No." Peter shakes his head. "Done some blasting, though. Silver mines."

Flocombe spits on the ground. "Not much blasting here. We use pneumatic hammers, picks, shovels. Handwork, you understand?"

"Yes."

"You will." The foreman's face is now unreadable. "Follow me."

Peter follows Flocombe across the construction site to where a makeshift shanty, built from discarded boards and packing crates, has been erected against the side of a building. A fire is burning inside, a tin pipe through the roof belching smoke. He trails the foreman through a low doorway into a space that feels more familiar than any other that he has seen in New York— two bedraggled men sitting on split barrels by the small coal fire, piles of gunnysacks, rows of tools, soot-darkened wood: a scene interchangeable with countless others from his frontier days. While Flocombe rummages through the equipment stacked in one corner, Peter tries to wrestle down the sense of vertigo this recognition brings. That life is over, he reminds himself, done with and in the past.

"There's a lamp." The foreman hands him a paraffin lantern, its glass charred nearly opaque with use. "You want to buy gloves?"

"Gloves?"

"They'll cost your first week's pay."

Peter hesitates, clutching the lantern. "All right."

The foreman looks away. "Better if you don't," he says gruffly. "The skin'll come off your hands anyway. With the gloves it's only slower and hurts worse. And the glove will stick when your blisters burst."

Peter nods.

"All right. You'd better light now."

Peter kindles his lantern with a coal from the fire—the glowing ember tracing an arc like a momentary shooting star in the dimness of the shack.

"Put the lantern on the rack by the gate before you go," Flocombe instructs. "The guards'll search you every night when you leave. Sometimes in the morning as well."

The first of these facts is unsurprising to Peter: in the silver and copper mines he has known, desperate workers sometimes tried to supplement their wages by stealing equipment. "In the morning too? Why then?"

The foreman stares at him. "Not everyone wants this project to happen," he says shortly, then turns away. Trying to digest this statement, Peter follows Flocombe into the morning gray. The sound of traffic, the early smells of bread baking, sewage, smoke. They descend into the tunnel-works, ducking under the broken girders and plumbing that protrude like teeth around the maw of the hole.

The half-finished subway tunnel is thirty-five feet wide and twenty feet tall, a dark corridor downward. The excavation is lit by widely spaced lanterns whose orange flames cast shifting shadows on the jagged rock walls. The floor underfoot is covered with out-croppings and rubble: the only clear space is near the center of the tunnel, where rails for a handcart have been laid down. And the air under the earth is a heavy, living thing, the continual roar from dozens of echoing hammers drowning out thought and speech. Beside Flocombe, Peter stumbles and the foreman catches his elbow, steadying him.

At the end of the tunnel, Flocombe stops and says something to Peter, his lips moving silently. Peter shrugs helplessly, and Flocombe shrugs as well—gestures to another man, his back turned, drilling at the wall with a pneumatic hammer clutched to his chest. He points to the side of the tunnel, and Peter follows him to where a second hammer is resting.

Peter watches as the foreman explains with exaggerated motions—a lever for speed, a valve at the base of the air hose that snakes away down the tunnel. Then Flocombe hands the tool to Peter and is gone, back toward the surface.

Uncertainly, he shoulders the hammer—it has a leather harness that wraps around the waist, binding it to the body. It is an unwieldy machine, powered by a coal-driven steam donkey chugging away somewhere above. The pressure hose that leads toward the engine on the surface can come loose with dreadful force, the metal fittings smashing ribs and teeth. The head of the hammer is a blunt chisel blade, scored deeply by the rock. Taking a breath, Peter braces himself and sets it against the granite wall.

When he starts the hammer, its vibration nearly knocks him off his feet. It jars his bones like beans in a rattle, making his vision swim. He glances over at the man next to him—a head shorter than himself and broader, teeth clenched, given entirely to the work. It seems impossible to last a full ten-hour day at this, Peter thinks, let alone come back for another and another. But he leans into the hammer and tries to clear his head except for the rock, its crevices and crystalline structure. Darkness and the roar of hammers like a forge beneath the earth. The next breath and the next.

AT A CERTAIN POINT, Peter realizes that he's lying on his back and that the other man is stooped over him, the hammer unstrapped. He doesn't want to move, but the man slaps his face and pulls at him until he is standing. On wobbly legs, Peter allows himself to be led out of the tunnel into the sudden morning above.

After the incessant roar of echoes belowground, the relative quiet of traffic passing and open air is startling, incomprehensible. Near the mouth of the tunnel Peter pulls away from the man and leans against a stack of scaffolding planks. The sun bright and distant in the pale winter sky. The other man stands next to him, hands in his pockets, breath steaming in the chill air. He says something that Peter doesn't hear, his lips moving soundlessly.

"What?" Peter knows his voice is too loud but has no way of quieting it.

"You first day?" the man shouts back.

Peter nods. Since arriving in New York he has avoided conversation, secretly afraid that the intimacy of being known by anyone in this place will make his new life real in a way he isn't ready to accept, but the other man seems intent on being friendly.

"I been here six month." He grins at Peter.

"Six months?"

The other man nods. "Six month on the subway crew. What is your name?"

"Peter."

"Paolo. You are from where?"

"Idaho."

Paolo shrugs. "I don't know about that."

"Where you from, then?" Slowly, the sounds of the world are beginning to return. The back of his head hurts, and reaching up Peter feels a wet spot near his ear. When he looks at his fingers they are red with blood.

"Roma."

"Italy?" he guesses, half recalling a long-ago school lesson.

"Yes." Paolo smiles. "I came here twenty years ago, when I am twelve."

Both men stand silently for a moment.

"You can go back to work?" Paolo asks. "Or you want water?"

"Water."

Peter follows the Italian to a corner of the construction site, where a broken pipe trickles into a barrel beside the wooden fence. Paolo hands him a metal cup and he drinks. The water tastes acrid, like copper.

"How long you have been here?" Paolo asks.

"New York?"

"Yes."

"A week." It takes Peter a long moment to calculate this, and when he does the figure doesn't bear any resemblance to the scattered span of hours that have passed since his arrival.

"When I am here one week, I start work on the bridge."

"The bridge."

"The big one. You don't know?"

Peter shakes his head.

"I will show you, someday."

Peter nods. "Thank you. For helping when I—"

"Don't worry. Everyone does this, the first day."

Peter nods again, looking up at the rising walls of buildings, the distant blue pull of the sky. The smallness of his presence in this place.

"Now," Paolo says.

Peter follows the Italian back into the pit. Somehow, despite having fainted, the din of the tunnel seems less overwhelming now, the weight of the hammer more bearable. He is about to start the machine when Paolo taps his arm, motioning for Peter to put the hammer aside.

"Tomorrow," he shouts into Peter's ear, barely audible, and then points to the handcart. Peter nods and begins to load the broken rock.

THE DARK of the city, after work. As Peter follows Paolo out of the tunnel and into the dusky evening aboveground, he stumbles, half drunk with exhaustion, feeling the grit of crushed rock chafe against his skin. Near the gate of the excavation site a group of men has assembled; Paolo crosses to join them, motioning for Peter to follow. He stands silently as the Italian does a round of introductions: "Jan"—a giant man with the face of a battle-scarred Viking. "Michael, Tobias"—smirking brothers, lean and wiry. "Saul"—bald with a barrel chest and massively callused hands. "Stephen, Hans . . ."

They all have the same look about them, Peter notices. Beneath a film of grime each face is strangely alike, taut and tired, blinking shortsightedly away from the subterranean realm. And he realizes that his expression must match theirs—a thought that brings with it a detached sense of wonder.

"Peter. From Idaho." Paolo slaps his shoulder.

"Welcome," one of the brothers—Michael—says, his greeting echoed in turn by the others.

"So," the other brother, Tobias, announces, "my brother and I are headed for Malarkey Hall. Marie Le Boudoir is dancing tonight." He winks at the group in general. "You boys care to accompany us?"

Paolo shakes his head. "My money is spent before I make. Give Marie my love."

"My pockets are empty." Peter shrugs apologetically, thinking of a warm bed and the bone-deep ache all through his body.

"How long've you been here?" Tobias asks.

"Week, two days ago."

"You're in a boardinghouse?"

"Ropehouse." Peter glances around, at the emptying streets and the confusion of New York twilight, wondering if he'll be able to find his way back to his lodgings.

Tobias nods. "I've lost a few nights' sleep in one of those bloody hammock-nets myself. Come, then—we'll call this a welcome gift."

"I—" Peter begins, thinking to excuse himself, but the other man anticipates his move.

"Come. You'll hurt in the morning, sleep or no—as you will for the next week. Isn't that right, Mikey?"

"True enough." Tobias's brother grins. "I'd not an unbruised muscle in me my first month in the tunnels."

"Go," Paolo says, clapping him on the shoulder—and relenting, Peter allows himself to be led.

Around a corner and another corner, Peter soon realizes that he is lost. Tobias and Michael trade jokes; one of the brothers produces a flask of whiskey, which they pass between the three of them as they walk. At first, Peter has the sense of tunneling deeper and deeper into an endless maze—a suspicion that grows when he spots what seems to be the same sidewalk vendor for the third time. Just as he's about to ask if they're walking in circles, the street ends and he finds himself gaping upward at the brilliance of Times Square.

Lights flash everywhere and above the square he sees steam-powered messenger dirigibles *putt-putt*ing in narrow circles, advertisements spelled out in colored lights on the underside of each balloon: *P. G. Eustis Playing Cards, $17.50 per gross, Used on Burlington Route RR; Acme Folding Boat Co., Miamisburg, Ohio; Be Brilliant and Eminent! Use Cosmo Buttermilk Soap—*

They jostle through the crowd down a set of steps to an underground tunnel, lit by crackling electric filaments on the tilework walls. Lining the tunnel is a kind of baroque summary of the past and present age in novelty form, with marquees for one attraction after the next—and it's all there: kinetoscope shows, exhibitions of Man and Nature featuring Lady Jewel, Champion Egg-Hen of the World, the Alligator Girl, the Talking Dog and Two-Headed Serpent, lectures on the subjects of Aeronautics, Magnetospherics, Psychology and Phrenology, genuine tintype pictures of Bryan's Oration and the World's Fair, boxing demonstrations, cockfighting, hashish parlors with dimmed lights, a miniature galaxy of detritus and vice.

Malarkey Hall proves, on arrival, to be less a hall than an alcove, a door near the center of the tunnel where miniature stalactites of nicotine and coal dust have accumulated overhead. Inside, the single room of the Hall has been done up to resemble an English pub. Thick oak beams hold up the ceiling, above rows of mismatched tables and chairs that seem to have been plundered from the sitting rooms of various flophouses. At one end of the room is a low stage with a crudely painted backdrop, intended to represent a Far East harem. The brothers push their way toward the front, where, somehow, a table stands empty amid the raucous crowd. Peter stumbles into a chair behind them, dodging a wave of beer sloshed from one of a dozen raised glasses.

Michael snags a mustachioed waiter by the arm and shouts something into his ear, and the man vanishes into the throng. The Hall is dimly lit by paraffin, shadows playing along the walls. A spotlight consisting of a gas flame between polished mirrors directs a sudden beam onto the stage and Peter turns as a roar of approval sweeps the place, mugs and pitchers clashing over tables. A young woman in frilled petticoats minces across the platform and launches into a drama that involves a key dropped into her bodice for safekeeping, only to slip . . .

He notices that she has dark hair, slender hips, and an open sore beside her mouth before he's distracted by other things: layers of clothing peel away to reveal small, milky breasts and pink nipples, stomach, thighs—until finally the key is discovered, wedged intimately some distance below its original location. Cheers and howls in the smoky air as she extracts the key and flourishes it overhead. The waiter reappears and sets down three glasses of clear greenish alcohol, one of which Tobias pushes toward Peter. Another skit begins, revolving around a mosquito and two young ladies of tender and much-exhibited flesh.

"Marie always comes on last," Michael shouts into Peter's ear over the din of the room, leaning across the table.

There is a ritual that goes along with the clear drink, Peter discovers, sugar melted in a spoon. Imitating the brothers, he sips the liquor: it tastes bitter, like something dredged out of a cave. Soon his head is swimming, flickers of color at the periphery of his vision.

"Absinthe." Tobias smiles and taps the glass. Peter sees, in a moment of lurid detail, that both his front teeth are false, a stained porcelain bridge.

Peter nods. For a moment, sitting there in Malarkey Hall, he has the terrifying sensation of being misplaced in his own life. He remembers one of the engines that he glimpsed at the subway excavation site: the interlocking of its gears, the mindless regularity of its lurching motion, the steam hoses leading away into underground darkness. An image that feels at once frightening and strangely reassuring. Belatedly he realizes that the others are waiting for him to say something.

"Been here before?" he shouts, trying to make conversation.

"Practically grew up in here," Michael yells back. "My brother too. Tobias here is always saying we should go west, try our luck on the frontier, but—"

"An honest man has a real chance out there," Tobias interrupts. "Not like this place." He spits on the floor. "The bosses run this town."

Peter opens his mouth to respond but Michael interrupts him.

"Look"—he points to the stage—"Marie." They turn as the lights dim and, to a rising thunder of boots that makes the floorboards quake, the final act, dazzlingly blond, already half naked, sashays into the spotlight.

The woman onstage is wearing a nearly transparent shift that doesn't hide her body so much as stylize it: the thin fabric clings to the outlines of her breasts, the swell of her hips and pubis, revealing a landscape of soft curves and pale-dusk skin. She descends from the stage and seats herself on the lap of a balding workman in the front row, squirming against him. Takes the man's hand and guides it upward, over her breast. The hem of her dress rides up on her thighs. Her victim groans, and along with half the audience Peter finds himself shutting his eyes in sympathy, imagining the softness and hidden warmth the other man is feeling—

At this point, or near it, the evening comes unraveled in Peter's recollection. There is a second round of the clear drink, and then a third, Tobias laughing, the cold brilliance of the nighttime stars overhead. There is the memory of fumbling through his pockets for coins somewhere in an alleyway. A strange room, the heat of a woman's body. And then afterward, lying in her arms, remembering the Idaho mountains and crying senselessly, not knowing why.

CHAPTER III

THE REALM OF
THE MACHINES

AT THIS POINT, IT WOULD BE NATURAL IF YOU STARTED TO
wonder about where my information is coming from. If you started
to think: *Where the hell is he* getting *this stuff, anyway?* Certainly
it's true that my footnotes haven't kept pace with these events. And
really, there would be something admirable about such a studious
insistence: a certain heroism in the reasonable resolve to stop reading if the proper citations don't appear.

Unless, that is, you've decided all of this is fiction: the sugar
filling between "once upon a time" and "happily ever after," a
harmless story whose only necessary evidence is itself. More than
once, to be honest, I've thought about claiming this excuse myself.
(An understatement: I've spent *years* trying to convince myself.)
But the fact is, this isn't fiction.

No: these are the facts.

At least, the sparse facts I've been able to assemble. The
problem is, despite my research, I keep falling short on support-

ing evidence—at least, the kind that can be corroborated in books.

For example, take the history of young Peter Force: in the New York Subway Museum, he is depicted in exactly one photograph.[*] There, in black and white, we see a young man of medium build, with shaggy brown hair and a startled expression, standing among a row of subway workers posed in front of an excavation site.

In addition to this photograph, these are the other facts I've been able to confirm about Peter: that he was born in 1877, the only child of James and Eliza Force, somewhere in the scrub-desert wilderness that would become New Mexico.[†] That his father, James Force, was a surveyor. That his mother, Eliza, died near Boulder, Colorado, when Peter was five or six years old,[‡] and that shortly afterward James Force moved with his son from the New Mexico region to the town of Kellogg, north of Coeur d'Alene.[§]

Finally, I learned that in the autumn of 1900, apparently less than a week after the death of his father, Peter left Idaho for New York City, where he found employment in the subway

---

[*] Library of the Metropolitan Transportation Authority Subway Museum, New York, catalogue #IMG-1900-3994, captioned "Subway Workers at Canal Street, December 1900."

[†] Birth certificate registered with the South-West Territory Settlement Trust Office in Santa Fe; in fact, the birth certificate was filed nearly a year after the fact (June 1878) but delays of this nature were not unusual at the time.

[‡] *Red Mountain Gazette* (Colorado), September 30, 1883, obituary column.

[§] James Force is listed as an employee of the Hercules Mining Company of Wardner, Idaho, on August 13, 1884; however, there is some uncertainty as to the accuracy of these accounting records.

construction works.* These are the paltry results of my months spent scrutinizing records and grappling with computer search programs.

They tell me that we're living in an information age, but none of it seems to be the information I need or brings me closer to what I want to know. In fact (I'm becoming more and more convinced) all this electronic wizardry only adds to our confusion, delivering inside scoops and verdicts about events that have hardly begun: a torrent of chatter moving at the speed of light, making it nearly impossible for any of the important things to be heard.

Sitting at the desk in my apartment, below my framed poster of a Lewis Hine photograph (my one real attempt at making this concrete cube "homelike"), I can't help but think that all this stuff about *facts* (in the footnote sense) is overrated anyway. I wasn't a scholar growing up, but I remember learning that Christopher Columbus was a hero, and that the Civil War was about slavery. Now I'm told that Columbus was a "hegemonic exploiter" and that Mr. Lincoln's War was fought primarily for economic reasons. In other words, even though more facts are instantly available than ever

---

* In fact, no record of Peter's journey to New York exists (that I know of). However, on November 14, 1900, the following entry appears in the County Registrar's Log of Kellogg County:

> *Death of James Force, Surveyor, reported by his Son. Thrown by a Horse that spooked from an Explosion. Left no Estate & no widow.*

(*County Registrar's Log of Kellogg County*, 1889–1900, vol. XXIV, courtesy Coeur d'Alene Historical Society.) Less than two weeks later, on November 26, Peter's name appears in the employment ledgers of the New York Drilling Company, beside the notation: "White Male, Aged 23 yrs., 2nd C[rew]" (from the 1900–1906 personnel roster of the New York Drilling Company, courtesy MTA Subway Museum, New York).

before, they also seem to be less *factual*, shifting between one momentary vogue and the next.

Again, I must make it clear that I do not intend to condemn the modern age. If nothing else, the food is breathtaking; the bounty of the supermarkets these days, not to mention the miracle of microwave cooking, still leaves me amazed. Also the TV game shows are wonderfully entertaining (not to mention their willingness to stand by a single correct answer for each question: *Wheel of Jeopardy, Price It Right*, the last bastions of absolute truth). But if the facts themselves can change over time, I can't bring myself to worry too much if some of my details are missing their footnotes—or to believe that any number of footnotes, or facts, can supply the answers I'm looking for.

"Peter Force joined a subway excavation crew in 1900"—that's the part I can document, but how did these moments feel, and what did they mean? Because even if no record of these things ever existed, when Peter first entered the subway construction site he felt and thought *something*.

In fact (I've come to realize), it's these ordinary moments, unmarked and unremembered, that are the substance of our lives. For example: almost every day, over the past nine years, I've left the antiques store in the evening and walked down to the bus stop. Among these thousands of unrecorded walks, I can recall, at most, three or four: all the others have slipped, unnoticed, from my recollection, despite the fact that they unquestionably happened. This is why—I tell myself—even if the details of this history are not certain, they still come closer to the truth than the recorded facts alone.

At the same time, I admit that although our private memories (like works of fiction) may endure without the agreement of anything outside themselves, at the moment when we try to make our recollections into stories the world begins to matter. By weaving memories into a sequence, they also become joined inextricably with time and history (which is to say, with the memories of everyone else).

And maybe this is why, despite my own convictions, I find myself searching the records and history books for proof. Why I'm trying to piece together whatever scraps of evidence remain, while imagining the unremembered days of young Peter Force: how it might have been. The clamor and agony of the subway tunnels, evenings with the other men from the excavation crew, drinks and conversation in a cheap saloon. Exploring the neighborhoods of New York, solitary and turning at random down unknown streets. Renting a tenement room. Breakfast, dinner. Gradually, finding the rhythms of a life.

PETER WALKS through the city with Paolo in the winter darkness after work. His body protests every step, but the Italian has insisted that this excursion is special, so Peter limps along beside the other man. He has been on the subway crew for two weeks now, and although the other crewmen have told him it gets easier, each day in the tunnels still feels like a span of torture. His shoulders are raw with welts from the hammer's harness, the palms of his hands a mass of oozing scabs. Then they round a corner and it comes into view, impossible, and Peter forgets the ache in his back.

"There—" Paolo gestures up at the obvious: the leviathan of metal and light that floats over the river, ethereal in the shadows. The Brooklyn Bridge. Peter has never seen anything like it: inhuman in scale and symmetry, the arc of a stone's throw captured in stone and steel.

"You worked on that?"

"I was a welder. Very dangerous—the more dangerous, the more they pay. Good money, fifty cents an hour but . . ." he whistles through his teeth. "You hang with a rope, underneath. Every night I dream about falling."

Peter shakes his head, struck dumb. There is something about the bridge that tugs at him like a magnet: an idea made concrete in all its perfection, compromising nothing.

"You like?"

Peter nods.

"Me, I like the view better before the bridge."

In his mesmerized state, Peter doesn't answer.

"Tell me," Paolo asks, "what is it like, Idaho? Is very different from here?"

Peter closes his eyes, picturing the concrete chasms of New York and the wilderness canyons of Idaho, trying to imagine what terms of comparison might even be possible.

He remembers how, after leaving the New Mexico landscape of his childhood, his first impression of that frontier had been a world of air and abrupt abysses, of rivers white with glacial rapids and gnarled pine trees whose roots clutched bare stone. Riding the narrow-gauge railway into the mountains with his father, each tunnel and twist of the track had seemed steeper and more improbable than the last. Out the train-car windows, the towns they went through were huddled in ravines so narrow that merchants had to crank up their storefront awnings to let the locomotive pass. It was dark when they arrived at their destination, the town of Kellogg, at the end of the line.

Kellogg was four dust-paved streets of clapboard houses. Evergreen-carpeted mountain walls framed the town, converging on a sheer granite cliff that loomed above the boardinghouses and saloons like a warning finger of the earth itself. Beyond this crag and down the other slope were the mines, the rows of dormitories where the miners lived, and the scraped-bare place around the pit.

James Force rented a room for himself and his son in the home of a middle-aged widow named Mrs. Deagle. There, beneath the rafters of Mrs. Deagle's attic, the two Forces spent evenings sitting by the flickering light of a candle, listening to muffled voices through the floorboards as the widow entertained one of her gentlemen admirers.

James Force was not a talkative man. The things he knew— facts about rocks, hidden faults in the earth and shear distances— were a silent understanding, beyond words. His efforts at explanation were scraps of history and images that never knit together into a whole. "With your mother we ate better. On Friday she'd make biscuits," he might say, and then trail off, staring into the candle flame. Sometimes they spent whole days without speech, these silences broken only when Peter's father would stop to point out a small secret: a mouse watching from the rafters, or the smell of certain pine trees, whose bark had the scent of butterscotch candy.

Peter remembers this, and the hours spent alone while his father was in the wilderness, working as a surveyor. The evenings of sitting at the long table in Mrs. Deagle's parlor beneath the unsteady lamp flame, thumbing through the pages of an old atlas while he waited for his father to come home, thinking about the names of impossible faraway places: Dalmatia, England, Tuvalu.

He remembers standing alone beneath a pine tree in town, watching the sun set over the mountains: the vast wreckage of clouds in the dying western sky, orange and vermilion. A brief splendor beyond the distant peaks, fading toward night.

Now, standing beside Paolo in front of the Brooklyn Bridge, he wonders how to convey some sense of this to the other man—but doesn't have the right words, or maybe it's too soon to say such things.

"I knew everyone in town. Weren't more than five hundred men in the county."

Paolo nods, not really listening. "Look here," he says, and unshoulders the bulky parcel he has been carrying. With elaborate care, the Italian unwraps a battered black box the size of a human head.

"What is it?"

Paolo holds up an impresario's finger and flips open a catch, folds down a door and pulls a lever, causing a snoutlike appendage to appear at one end of the box.

Peter whistles appreciatively. "A camera. This yours?"

"My wife nearly kills me when I bring this home. But always I have wanted one. You want to look?" He extends the instrument to Peter, who peers where the other man indicates and sees an image of the bridge, upside down and hazy, floating in the viewfinder.

"You going to take a picture?" He has never touched a camera before and hands the box back to Paolo nervously.

"Of this? No—is too expensive, the photographic plates. But I like better the way the world looks through this. Like a painting."

Peter nods, understanding that the other man has revealed something private. They stand in silence.

"Come," Paolo says finally, collapsing and rewrapping the camera. "Let's eat. I am freezing here."

A LOST FRAGMENT of memory, returning unexpectedly. Peter remembers that he had been nine years old when his father woke him early to meet the morning train.

In the half-darkness of Mrs. Deagle's attic Peter had dressed quickly while his father watched. James Force's usually reserved expression was lit with silent anticipation, Peter saw, and his heart caught in his chest. Together they left the house and walked through town toward the station, the forested mountain slope beyond the row of shops and houses tinged with pink with the rising sun.

The Kellogg train station was a single room beside an uneven wood-plank platform that ran along the rails. A ragged, red-faced family with a stack of derelict luggage was waiting for the train, and Peter and his father sat with them in the bare little room, nobody speaking, until the locomotive with its string of weathered coaches groaned to a halt outside. While the other family climbed aboard, Peter followed his father to the luggage car at the back of the train. As Peter watched, the porter handed down a suitcase-sized wooden box, which his father cradled carefully in both arms.

Back at the widow's attic James Force set the box in the middle of the floor, then carefully pried open the lid with a crowbar. Inside, wrapped in a nest of wood shavings, was a glass globe the size of Peter's head, along with two coils of wire and a white ceramic platter.

"What is it?" Peter asked.

"A filament bulb and socket."

"What does it do?"

"Makes light."

"How?" From past experience, Peter knew it was unlikely for his father to answer one question, let alone two in a row, but today James Force seemed to be in a rare talkative mood.

The elder Force scrutinized his son. "Shouldn't you be getting to school?"

"No, sir." Peter looked back at his father, trying for an innocent expression. The minister's wife would be giving lessons in the church basement today, but as with all her students, Peter's attendance was sporadic at best, and the prospect of spending a full day with his father made it almost not feel like a lie.

Finally James Force nodded. "You might learn more here, anyway. Sit down."

Peter climbed onto the cot at one side of the room and his father sat beside him, opening the envelope that accompanied the package.

He handed Peter the sheaf of pages. "Read this aloud."

Peter squinted at the smeared print. "The Edi-Edison evac-evacu—"

"Evacuated vacuum bulb," James Force finished, taking back the letter. "Study your reading. That's important."

"Yes, sir." Peter looked down at the floor. A moment later, though, his curiosity got the better of him. "Who's Edison?"

"A magician."

Peter gaped. "Really?"

"Not really. An inventor, though. He made this." James Force tapped the glass globe. "The first filament bulb was born the same year as you."

For the remainder of the morning and the afternoon that followed, Peter helped his father examine the contents of the box and listened while James Force read the pamphlet detailing the Edison bulb. Finally, as the sun was beginning to sink outside the attic windows, James Force repacked the bulb into the box and straightened.

"Going up to the mill now." He pulled on his jacket. "You carry that, follow along."

Peter lifted the box, staggering beneath its weight. "What's at the mill?"

"Where the electricity is."

They made their way to the outskirts of town, where a rough trail ran along the creek, into the hills and toward the mine. Above the path a canopy of evergreen branches extended out over the rushing water. The ground was uneven and several times Peter stumbled, nearly dropping his burden, his stomach clenching at the thought of the delicate glass object inside. If this worried James Force he gave no sign, walking steadily ahead of the boy.

After a time they reached a place where the trail climbed a steep canyon, the creek racing downward in a series of flume-white waterfalls that turned the blades of a waterwheel attached to a small, asymmetrical mill house.

A broad-shouldered man wearing a threadbare brown suit came out and shook hands with Peter's father.

"This is Mr. Kerry," James Force told his son. "He runs the hydroelectric plant for the mine. He's letting us use some of his current tonight."

Peter nodded silently, feeling overwhelmed by the barrage of new words and Mr. Kerry's scrutiny.

"Been wanting to see one of these bulbs in action myself,

James." Mr. Kerry clapped the elder Force on the shoulder. "Glad I can help."

Peter sat down on a log outside the mill house and watched as the two men set to work. They placed the ceramic bowl—the socket fixture, Peter remembered it was called—on a tree stump and ran a copper wire out from the dynamo attached to the water-wheel. Next came a period of adjusting connections, testing the line for voltage, readjusting, and technical discussion.

At a certain point during this tinkering process Peter noticed that a small group of men were standing quietly behind him, watching the proceedings. From their dirty faces, helmets, and lunch pails, he recognized them as miners. A few minutes later another pair of men appeared, trudging toward town, and stopped along with the others to observe his father and Mr. Kerry work.

Peter had started to fidget with the evening chill and thoughts of dinner when his father finally straightened and crossed toward him.

"All ready." James Force beckoned to his son. "Come see."

Peter climbed to his feet and followed his father over to the tree stump. With both hands, James Force lifted the glass globe and gently lowered it into the socket—and abruptly Peter found himself blinking against a wash of yellow light.

Glancing around, he saw that an audience of several dozen men had gathered in the growing evening shadows, their hardened features glowing in the illumination of the Edison bulb. In each of their expressions was a kind of wonder, a feeling that drew Peter's own gaze back toward the light.

Beyond the circle of brightness cast by the bulb, the Idaho mountainside rose in a silhouette of forest toward the deepness of night sky. The river rapids rushed in the darkness. A vast, untamed landscape, and in it, this pocket of seeing. Peter felt his father's hand descend on his shoulder, a reassuring weight, and looked up.

"Sir?"

"Hm?"

"How does it work? The electricity?"

James Force was silent for a moment. "Nobody knows." His voice slow and thoughtful. "It's everywhere, though. What makes everything move."

They watched the steady brightness of the bulb, occasional drops of spray from the rapids falling like cold sparks on Peter's cheeks and forehead.

The stillness of the moment was broken by a derisive snort from the crowd of watching miners. Peter and his father both turned as a stocky, balding man stepped forward, arms crossed on his chest. Peter had seen him in town, usually arguing with someone, although it took him a moment to remember the man's name—Lucius Newton. Someone who worked with his father, but not one of his father's friends.

"What's this, then?" Newton demanded loudly. "Looks like a waste of time, you ask me."

"No need for you to spend your time at all, Newton." James Force shrugged mildly.

"Looks to me like you're wasting all these men's time. Distracting 'em with useless gadgets and the like." Newton approached the light, reaching out to touch the glass, then drew his finger back with a hiss.

"Should've warned you. Some of these gadgets can bite." James Force's words drew a chuckle from the crowd. Newton wheeled to face them, glaring, and the laughter stopped. "Any case," Peter's father continued, "they're here by their own choice. Last I heard, we're all free men."

Newton made a kind of spitting sound and turned away. As he did, his foot caught on the wire leading to the Edison bulb and he stumbled, nearly falling, jerking the light off the tree stump. The glass shattered on the ground, darkness descending instantly. Newton straightened.

"Look what you did. Could've broke my neck." He bared his teeth at James Force. The hand on Peter's shoulder tightened, but his father said nothing. Newton glanced down, and for an instant Peter imagined that he saw a smile on Newton's face.

"One of these days, boy," Newton said, his voice quiet and conversational, "your daddy's going to go too far." Peter stared back at the other man, not knowing how to answer. Then Newton wheeled and stalked away into the night.

The crowd of onlookers slowly began to disperse. Peter turned back to where the light had been. Now the wilderness night, the sound of rushing water, and the distant stars overhead were unbroken, as if they were the only things that had ever existed. But when Peter closed his eyes, for a moment he could still see an afterimage of the electric brightness: as if this light had somehow become part of himself.

Standing in the gray New York morning at the mouth of the subway tunnel, some flicker of this memory comes back to Peter. Beside him Tobias shifts from one foot to the other, rubbing his hands in the morning cold, while Michael and Saul wait resignedly, the four of them lined up with all the other workmen from the Canal Street crew.

In front of where they stand outside the excavation, three men wearing white laboratory coats are making adjustments to a hand-cart laden with machinery. The wheels of this cart are fitted to the temporary tracks along the center of the subway tunnel, but it bears no resemblance to the wooden barrows that normally carry out rubble along these rails. On the cart, a row of dials and switches are mounted above a bank of canister-shaped batteries, thick wires leading to a set of antennae that two of the men are in the process of adjusting. The third man is struggling with a large filament bulb at the front of the assembly that, unlike its twin at the back of the cart, refuses to light.

Peter scrutinizes this operation, trying without success to make sense of the equipment, before turning to Tobias. "They do this every month, then?"

"Ever since I've been here, they have." Tobias scowls. "Head-quarters inspection, they call it. Supposed to take no time at all, but there's always some problem with their damn machine. So we have to wait and freeze while they do their tinkering."

"What are they looking for?"

"Who knows? Making sure the tunnel's sound, they say. But devil knows why they need that monstrosity."

"Quiet down there!" Flocombe shouts, and Peter glances over to see the foreman glaring in their direction from the head of the line. The rank of subway workers shifts restlessly, a handful of snowflakes drifting from the overcast sky, their collective breath forming a brief, dissipating cloud of steam.

He looks over at the excavation that has come to define the border of his days. Near where they stand, at its mouth, it's not much more than a deep trench occupying half the width of the street. Above it, a row of heavy girders spanning the trench forms a skeleton that will eventually be paved over again; a row of iron spikes marks the outline of where the train platform will stand. Toward the end of the block, the trench dips deeper, becoming a tunnel that resembles a rough cave, with unfinished rock walls and ceiling. For an instant, then, Peter feels a tug of homesickness for the Idaho wilderness, for the smallness and comprehensibility of that distant world.

"—been here since six, not a bite of breakfast, and now this." This fragment of conversation, whispered between Saul and Michael, drifting back to Peter's ears.

A flicker of brightness catches the corner of his vision and he turns to see the filament bulb on the cart come to life for a moment beneath the hands of the man in the lab coat, before going dark again. A vague recollection, from that long-ago day beside the mill house with his father, or from one of the other times when James Force could afford to indulge his interest in gadgetry, comes back to him.

"The contacts," he murmurs, half to Tobias and half to himself. "Could be the socket contacts are dirty." Without thinking he starts to step forward, but finds Tobias's restraining hand on his arm.

"What are you doing?" Tobias hisses. "For God's sake, don't go helping them, you prancing nincompoop!"

"Why not?"

"Because they're bloodsuckers, all of them." Tobias shakes his head impatiently. "We break our backs for stale bread and a flophouse room, just to make them rich. Those men are no friends for the likes of you and me, boy-o."

Peter opens his mouth, but before he can think of a reply the glass bulb on the cart blossoms into yellow brightness. With a low rumble the three men wheel their equipment into the tunnel. Strangely unsettled, he watches the light recede into the gray distance, and disappear.

OVER THE WEEKS that follow, without realizing it, Peter falls into the rhythm of life on the subway crew. Although the work is always backbreaking, it becomes gradually less unbearable and his days assume a predictable shape: rising before dawn, the hours of labor, home for a dinner of bread, hard cheese, and pickles.

He rents a room in a tenement apartment, a space he shares with two taciturn, seldom present Polish dockworkers, and apart from the necessities of life and weekly rent, his wages from the subway permit the occasional extravagance: beers with Paolo, Michael, and Tobias, or a meal at the cheapest of restaurants. He begins to feel as if he has been digested by the city, a tiny creature burrowing through the bedrock bowels of the metropolis, like the tiny creatures said to inhabit the bodies of other, larger organisms.

This routine is abruptly shattered on a cold afternoon during Peter's second month on the subway crew when one of the steam donkeys screams, lurches, and shudders into silence. A surge of pressure tears down one of the hoses leading to the pneumatic drills while the others go slack. The arms of the man holding the drill break with a brittle sound that is heard throughout the cavern. The worker drops to his knees, staring at his splayed wrists in disbelief, and the other men let their tools fall and rush toward him. The door of the foreman's shack bangs open and Flocombe lurches out.

Unlike the others, though, Peter remains frozen where he stands, just outside the tunnel entrance. Since his arrival in New York, something about the engines has fascinated him, making him slow whenever he walks past one of the jealously guarded machines, and now the wail of metallic distress echoes through him. He starts toward the silent engine, wisps of black smoke still rising from its stack. Beside the steam donkey, Flocombe is already haranguing the two shovel-men who feed the machine coal.

"What the hell'd you do?"

"She just stopped—"

"Like that—"

"These things don't just stop. You know this monster is worth more than the two of your fancy hides?"

"I swear, we was just here an' then—"

"And now, goddamnit, I have to file a goddamn report, call the mechanic—and wait till he hears, eh? You know he hates coming down here—"

"Can't you fix it, Boss?"

"Fix it?" The foreman swigs from his flask and glares at the two workers. "You think I'm some kind of professor?"

Standing unnoticed beside the machine, Peter kneels beside the engine and leans forward, studying the interlocking jigsaw of its gears and hoses.

"And what're you looking at, then?" Flocombe's voice jolts Peter back to himself.

"I—"

"You don't touch the damned thing, understand?"

Peter nods and watches the foreman stomp away. Around the construction site the other crewmen have broken off into little groups, standing around the coal stoves, stamping their feet and smoking cigarettes. He allows his eyes to drift over the engine.

"Here it is—just quit." Peter wakes, as if from a dream, to these words and turns to find Flocombe and another man standing a few feet away. He clambers to his feet, strangely embarrassed—as if caught in some act of intimacy—his legs stiff from crouching too long.

"So? Let me look." The foreman's companion is a short, heavy-set man with protruding ears and a melancholy expression, the filigree of veins on his nose mapping out years of drink. This is Klaus Neumann, one of the four mechanics employed by the sub-way project to maintain the engines that are slowly hollowing out the space beneath Manhattan. He pushes past Peter, eyes only on the inert piece of machinery, and scrutinizes it for a moment. Leaning forward, he mutters to himself and runs his hands over the curve of the boiler.

Flocombe clears his throat, swaying slightly. "Er—is it bad, then?"

Neumann straightens and glances, annoyed, at the foreman. "Bad? No, not bad," he says, his English marked by a thick German accent. "Give me half an hour." The mechanic extracts a rolled oilskin from his satchel, which he unfurls to reveal an assortment of tools. Glancing around, he notices Peter for the first time.

"Who is this?" he demands.

"One of my men. A sharp one." Flocombe shrugs. "He's been staring at the damn thing like it was a woman, since it broke."

"Like a woman, eh?" Neumann gives Peter an appraising glance and then makes a small gesture toward the machine. "Can you see what is broken here, boy?"

Peter shakes his head. The engine is vastly more complicated than any of the crude devices that he tinkered with, beside his father, on the Idaho frontier: the baroque landscape of its parts a message coded in some incomprehensible language.

"Look harder," the mechanic insists. Feeling foolish, like a small child being taught a lesson, Peter stares at the intestinal tangle of wheels and gears. The cold winter wind cutting into his hands and face, his soaked and muddy shoes, the burnt smell of the air. He glances at Flocombe, hoping to be dismissed—but the foreman turns away, toward the steam donkey. Without thinking, Peter follows his gaze.

Then suddenly, like an image snapping into focus, he sees a small wheel out of place in the midst of the tangled metal—given by a logic that he cannot describe. He points.

"There?"

The mechanic furrows his brow and stares at Peter. He shakes his head.

"Yes," he says, "this is it." He looks at the foreman, then back at Peter. "What is your name?"

A MONTH LATER, as the year lurches to a close, winter wraps the city in an icy grip. At eight o'clock on a Thursday night, Peter and Neumann sit in McGurk's Suicide Hall, cheapest of cheap dives by the river. For reasons that Peter has yet to discover, McGurk's is the mechanic's haunt of choice: in part, perhaps, for its abundance of loose women, where a roll in the hay will cost little enough to go unnoticed, or at least unremarked, when Neumann's wife counts his pay. But more significantly, Peter thinks, because the place seems to express some need of his mentor's for anarchy and oblivion. Some urge or dark pull, exerted by the clamor of the city itself, that Peter has felt as well but has fought against, more out of instinct than any clear reason.

They sit on the narrow second-floor balcony that looks onto a central shaft that runs the four-story height of the saloon. Leaning over the balcony edge to watch the barroom below is a perilous maneuver—the danger of falling inconsequential next to the hail of tobacco-wads, phlegm, and even glasses that patrons on the top-most floors enjoy hurling at those below when the opportunity arises—but the show on the ground floor is worth the risk: whores in pancake makeup flirt with sailors at the bar, pickpockets ply their trade, brawls break out at the rate of two or three an hour. Neumann sits silently, staring into his drink, a noxious mixture of alcohol, benzene, turpentine, and cocaine sweepings that cheap saloons by the river sell under the name of "smash," gnawing his thumb. It is, Peter has come to understand, the closest that his mentor comes to relaxed: this near-stupor that descends on him in the evenings.

Over the past weeks, Peter has been initiated into a world that he struggles to understand, working as Neumann's assistant. Already he has learned to interpret the grunts and silences that make up the taciturn mechanic's vocabulary: requests for tools, points to observe. The principle of a machine's functioning compressed into: "See there?" and a jerk of the thumb.

What lessons the German has to impart are given in single sentences. "You must look at the whole machine first. Understand?"

Displacement, compression, power—Peter has begun to grasp these things, an understanding that begins not in the brain but in the guts. In this age before standardization, each machine is a unique creature, displaying properties unlike any other. Small things: different bolt sizes, gauge of wiring, the number of turns around each terminal. It seems to Peter more like they function through an improbable science of chance than any calculated mathematics. Their constancy both an article of, and reason for, something like faith.

Already his days on the excavation crew in the tunnels have begun to seem like a distant dream. And mysteriously—in a way that neither Peter nor Neumann can explain—he has a knack for the work. Although he never feels like he *knows* what he's doing— more that something *knows through him*—by the end of this first month with Neumann, Peter is sometimes able to see, as quickly as the older man, what must be done to fix the broken engines that pass through the workshop.

Now, as Neumann gnaws his thumb pensively—his mind elsewhere from the stomach-churning brew—Peter, who has stuck to the watered beer that McGurk's dishes out, surveys the place, head spinning slightly. Since his apprenticeship to the machines, he has begun to see mechanics everywhere: a hidden physics to the movement of the whores from one man to the next, the sudden hushes that will descend on the room as a dozen different conversations converge on the same pause. A mathematics that—it strikes him— must be guiding his own actions as well, even if he can't yet see why or how.

A waiter with elaborately greased sideburns and a dirty apron passes the table and Neumann gestures at him.

"Another." Neumann taps his glass.

The waiter does something that might be an attempt at a friendly smile. "That's five cents."

Neumann spills the coins onto the table and Peter glances at his own near-empty mug.

"One for me as well." He counts out five pennies, which the waiter collects with a practiced sweep of his hand. The waiter departs and Neumann sets his pipe down, extracts a tobacco pouch from his pocket, and tamps a wad of shag into the meerschaum. Peter looks away, at the cloud of tobacco and cannabis smoke that curls toward the blackened ceiling of the saloon, twenty feet overhead.

"You have finished with the book?" Neumann asks, puffing on his pipe.

After their first week together the mechanic had silently offered Peter a stack of battered secondhand volumes, which, in his tenement room, he has dutifully grappled with during his evenings after work. And in theory, Peter tells himself, he wants to learn all of it: to be admitted to the inner sanctum of the mechanical sciences, where the mysteries of the world are explained, an ambition that has begun to grow in him since his arrival in New York. In practice, though, reading has never been one of his strengths, and whatever secrets the books may contain seem to be locked behind a wall of boredom. His main recollection of Neumann's latest offering, a treatise called *An Investigation of Various Gear-Shapes and Their Properties*, is of repeated losing battles to stay awake.

He nods. "Yep. Not sure if I'm worth much when it comes to book learning, though."

"You must try harder." Neumann glares at him. "All the world, it is in books."

"I'm working on it." And it's true; gradually, Peter finds himself needing to sound out the words less often, the pages going by faster.

"So? Good." The mechanic reaches into his satchel and Peter's heart sinks as two more books emerge. He takes them, scrutinizing the titles. *Differential Conversion and Its Several Principles in the Ratchet-Driven Flywheel*. Peter stifles a sigh. The second volume, though, seems more promising.

"*The Pilgrim's Progress from This World to That Which Is to Come*, by John Bunyan," Peter reads aloud. "What's this—"

"Ssh!" Neumann gestures for him to put the book away. "Not in here." The mechanic glances around, oddly abashed. "Is only for amusement. If you have time."

Peter nods, sliding the books into his lap.

Neither says anything for a moment. A burst of noisy laughter from somewhere downstairs.

"Any news about the tunneling?" Peter asks.

The waiter returns and sets down their drinks, sloshing stray drops onto Peter's coat. After he has departed, Neumann shrugs. "They are crazy."

"Who?" This isn't the first time the German has hinted that he disapproves of the way the project is being managed, though he has never detailed his sentiments on the subject.

"The engineers. Edison, they say, leads the planning." Neumann shrugs again and bites his thumb.

"Thomas Edison?" Like everyone else, Peter knows about the wizard of Menlo Park from countless newspaper articles, snippets of conversation, and tall tales. This, however, is the first time he has heard that the man who invented the filament bulb and the talking machine is connected with the subway. "Edison's a genius, isn't he?"

"Perhaps."

"Have you met him?" Peter sits up, his heart beating faster. In these last weeks a new pantheon has taken shape in his imagination, centered on the men who invent the devices that he repairs. Among these figures, he knows, the greatest are Edison and his archrival, Nikola Tesla: the two giants who are remaking the world with their inventions.

"Only once I met him, when they bring all of the mechanics to his laboratory."

"Really?" Peter stares at Neumann, impressed by this unexpected proximity to greatness. "What was he like?"

"Edison?" The mechanic puffs on his pipe. "They say he used to collect stray dogs and electrocute them. When I go to his lab, I carry a gun. I never trust men such as this." Neumann grimaces, revealing a row of teeth that—even in this age of routine dental abominations—make Peter cringe, a disaster of mossy stumps, misalignment, and decay. "They are all crazy. See here."

Neumann pulls a greasy sheet of paper from his pocket and smooths it on the table, wiping it through a puddle of beer as he pushes it toward Peter.

It's a crude drawing in three-dimensional perspective done in black ink: a skewed grid of lines, echoed in four layers. It takes Peter a long moment to know what to make of it—then finally he sees. The lines that make up the top layer of the grid form the shape of the subway routes as they will look in their completed state. "The subway tunnels?"

Neumann nods. "The complete plan. Arrived today."

"Do they really mean to dig four levels?"

"It seems to be."

"For separate lines?" Neumann doesn't respond. "I thought they were excavating only one level—this must be a mistake. Why would they need four levels? And all the same lines?"

The mechanic glances around and leans forward, motioning for Peter to do the same. Peter bends toward Neumann, trying not to flinch at his mentor's breath. "I believe"—the mechanic whispers, tapping the paper—"these tunnels . . . I believe there is a *secret meaning in their shape.*"

PETER FORCE in the living room of his apartment on the Lower East Side. The space is quiet, his roommates absent for the night. In one corner an iron stove pings softly, the decrepit furniture, the rusty washbasin and strings of drying laundry, tinted brown with the light of an oil lamp beside Peter's chair.

He looks up, glancing between the burlap curtains to see heavy white snowflakes spiraling downward over the narrow streets. Turning back to the book in his lap, he traces the lines with his finger: *Some men by feigning words as dark as mine, make truth to spangle and its rays to shine.* The phrases like falling snow, slow and heavy with a cadence of their own. The strange vastness of these sentences beginning to make him realize—even more than the widow's old atlas—the scope and strangeness of the world.

A GRAY AFTERNOON in January, just beyond the turning of the year. Peter sits alone on the cobblestone walkway by the East River. This has become his habit in recent weeks: to sit and watch the water. He scrutinizes the muddy current and the smudged skyline of Brooklyn on the other shore, with its smokestacks, chimneys, and water towers, as if trying to make out some distant shape—

Something that the city is trying to tell him: a sense of hidden purpose, hidden meaning that waits for him around every turn, vanishing just as he arrives. . . .

Out of the corner of his eye, he sees a woman weaving unsteadily along the embankment. Suddenly she collapses to the ground. He turns away, hardened by now to sights like this. When he looks back a few minutes later, she is still lying motionless among the heaps of soot-stained snow. Seized by a random altruistic impulse, Peter climbs down from the ledge where he's sitting and cautiously crosses toward her, offering his hand. She is a young woman, he sees, her eyes fixed blankly on some object in the distance. Weakly, she takes his hand and he helps her to stand.

"Are you all right?" he asks.

"Nonce," she murmurs, clutching his coat. "Thank God. You saved my life."

"What?" Startled, he tries to disengage himself from her grasp. "You've got me mixed up with someone else. Name's Peter."

She blinks, then shakes her head confusedly, releasing his arm.

"Are you all right?" he repeats. "You need help?"

"I—no—" she starts to turn but hesitates, passing a hand over her eyes.

He looks away, feeling suddenly awkward, following a pigeon's ascent as it wings upward over the waves.

"I—" she stumbles over the words. "Thank you for helping me."

He looks at her more closely. She is wearing a dress that might once have been expensive, decorated with petticoats and other frilly things that Peter can't identify, but which is now so torn and bedraggled that it's hardly more than a collection of rags. Her face is pale and narrow, framed by a tangle of black curls. And she is beautiful, he realizes, feeling an odd lurch in his chest. Not so much any one thing about her, but something about how the pieces of her face work together. Still, at the same time he can see the need in her gaze, like that of every other beggar and con artist in New York.

"It's nothing," he says, taking a step away. "I was just watching the river."

She nods and glances around again nervously. "I wonder if—" She stops, and then, as if with an effort, starts again. "Though you do not know me, I have a favor to ask of you."

He waits, poised to leave.

"Perhaps," she ventures, "there is somewhere we could sit?"

"I—" Peter hesitates. He has never been one to fall for a pretty face: when he needs a woman's company, visiting a whore has always seemed easier than the entanglement of less clearly defined intimacies. But there's something strange about her, he thinks: she speaks like something out of a book, or a rich foreigner. And although his common sense warns against it, he finds himself nodding without exactly knowing why. "There's a German restaurant, the Kramler, not too far—"

Unexpectedly, her cheeks flush red and she looks down at the cobblestone walk. "I must be candid," she murmurs. "At the moment I am without the means even for a glass of wine."

Peter is unnerved more by her embarrassment than by the admission, which he's been expecting. But he's also relieved to discover what she's after: a small handout, the kind of thing that he is asked for a dozen times each day.

"That's all right." He nods. "My pleasure, and all that."

She nods, still not meeting his eyes. Remembering the few

manners that he knows, Peter offers his arm—she takes it, and they start to walk.

As he feels the slight weight of her hand on his sleeve, and hears the clatter of horses' hooves and the foghorns of barges on the river, he experiences a jolt of something like déjà vu. And with this, the image comes to him of a vast machinery closing in around him. A system of invisible wheels and gears that, now started, will not cease or let him go until some final purpose has been achieved.

CHAPTER IV

THE LOST KINGDOM

I HAVE TO SAY, I'M AMAZED AT HOW WELL THIS IS GOING. IT'S ALL falling into place more smoothly than I ever expected. Of course, I haven't reached the hard parts yet. But for the moment, the actual writing itself—the *story* part of this history—is surprisingly easy. It's just a matter of making everything sound like it came out of a book. And that, for once, is something I know how to handle, since during the last forty years I've felt more at home in literature than in life.

And funnily enough, I think the writing lifestyle suits me. I've almost abandoned the antiques store, opening it once or twice a week. Instead, I walk through the streets now, and in the evening (after watching a few episodes of *Dollars and Sense* or *Your Money or Your Wife!*) I sit at my typewriter, and type.

And telling the story is easy. It's just deciding which parts to include, finding a space to fit them all in, that gives me trouble.

For example, once upon a time there was a place called the Kingdom of Ohio. (Probably, I should have mentioned this sooner—but better late than never, I suppose.) The Kingdom of Ohio, sometimes called the Free Estate Latoledan, has become a fragment of forgotten minutia by now. In most history books it is less than a footnote, glossed over even among academics. But however improbable and ridiculous it may seem, the Kingdom existed. It was real.

The Kingdom of Ohio is documented and visible (with the help of a little squinting and imagination) in the notes, indirect references, and scraps I've assembled over the years. It is an untold chronicle that parallels the early history of America itself: and without understanding that story, I've come to believe, it is impossible to understand this one.

To SUMMARIZE, the history of the Kingdom began in 1774, when the fledging Continental Congress of the United States was making plans for their impending war against England. To raise funds for this effort, representatives of the Congress decided to sell territory on the American frontier to wealthy Old World families. Ultimately, this scheme was short-lived (the objections of Peletiah Webster, a retired clergyman from Philadelphia, were typical when he argued that selling the land would "be like killing the goose that laid an egg every day, in order to tear out at once all that was in her belly").* Before the plan was rescinded, however, a single transaction was completed: a minor member of the French nobility named Henri Latoledan purchased 30,000 acres "west and south of Lake Erye [*sic*] extending to the water's edge for a dis-

---

* Peletiah Webster of Philadelphia, as quoted by Payson Jackson, *The National Land System, 1785–1820* (New York: E. B. Treat & Co., 1910), p. 16.

tance of thirty-six Surveyor's Chain lengths,"* from one of the Continental Congress's secret agents in Europe.

A charcoal sketch that I found, drawn by the Jesuit parson Gide Baddaneau, seems to be the only surviving image of the ancestral Latoledan family castle in France. It depicts a long, low house in the Spanish style with tile roofs, an arched stucco colonnade, and wrought-iron balconies. Gazing at this drawing, it's easy to imagine chickens, dogs, and children wandering through the outer hallways beneath threadbare tapestries. Creeping vines pry at the window catches. Inside, the house is furnished with tables and cabinets simply and solidly constructed by local craftsmen, the gilt inlay of a few heirloom antiques burnished into near-invisibility by the passage of time. This is the world that Henri Latoledan and his family abandoned (almost before the ink on the land deed was dry) for one of the wildest and least understood places on Earth.

Although I've tried, the reasons for this departure are difficult for me to imagine. Perhaps Henri understood that winds of change were beginning to rise in France, which in a few years would sweep men like him toward Paris and the guillotine. Perhaps he chafed against the limited prospects available to an impoverished noble family in a forgotten corner of the rural countryside, far from the Sun King and Versailles. Or perhaps it was the spirit of adventure, pure and simple, that moved him.

Whatever the reason for the Latoledans' migration, the place where they arrived, and where the Kingdom of Ohio began, was a

---

* *Journals of the American Congress, 1774 to 1788*, vol. 3, courtesy Smithsonian American Archives. The actual transaction was completed by Silas Deane, a blacksmith's son from Groton, Connecticut, who was one of the Continental Congress's secret agents in Europe and, later, the first foreign diplomat of the United States.

territory virtually unknown to European eyes. At the time, the Midwest region was

> a silent, somber land, without history and without memory except for the tales of explorers and traders who had followed Indian trails to their scattered camps. . . .
>
> [J]ust four settlements marked the long course of the Ohio River. . . . [Among them was] a colony of French émigrés dancing minuets on a puncheon floor and trying to forget the wilderness around them; this huddle of barracks on the river bank was as unlikely a settlement as ever came to the American frontier. *

Possession of this uncharted territory was a morass of conflicting claims and insupportable titles. England had conquered "New France" and most of Acadia, a territory encompassing modern-day Canada as well as the area around the Great Lakes. At the same time, the Spanish court in Madrid claimed ownership of both Alta California and also "all lands . . . from the Arctic pole to the Antarctic pole . . . west and south from any of the islands commonly

---

* Walter Havighurst, *Wilderness for Sale: The Story of the First Western Land Rush* (New York: Hastings House, 1956), pp. 53–54.

known as the Azores and Cape Verde,"* a hypothetical kingdom spanning virtually all of North America. In the midst of these chaotic and overlapping declarations of empire, practical control of the frontier belonged to the real occupants of the land: the Miami and Chippewa tribes, the Shawnee and the Eel People.

When, after a three-month voyage, Henri Latoledan and his family reached the land he had purchased, his first act was so outlandish as to almost defy explanation. In 1776, only weeks after the Declaration of Independence, he issued a document titled the "Latoledan Proclamation of Sovereignty," in which he declared his patch of wilderness to be a separate nation, sending one copy to the British House of Lords and another to the Continental Congress.†

Although in many ways Henri was an impulsive and perhaps even foolish man, it would be an injustice to ignore the breathtak-

---

* This territory was granted to Spain by Pope Alexander VI, writing in a papal bull on May 4, 1493 (a decree commonly known as *Inter Caetera*). This document was issued in response to Columbus's arrival in supposedly Asiatic lands in 1492, which threatened to destabilize relations between Portugal and Spain, the two great seafaring powers of the world, which had been competing for possession of African territories. The papal decree effectively granted possession of Africa to Portugal, and possession of the Americas to Spain; this document was the legal basis of Spanish claims to ownership of British Columbia and Alaska as late as 1819.

† The British copy of the proclamation survives in the Royal Archives; it is dated July 19, 1776, and reads in its entirety:

I, Henri Georges-Fevrier Latoledan, do hereby Absolve my Allegiance to the laws of any Nation or Power excepting only those of God Almighty, and do Publish and Declare the Rightfully Purchasede Territory called Estate Latoledan in perpetuity shall be Governed only by Myself and my Heirs, unfettered by none other on Earth. Should You wish to receive Us in the Spirit of Friendship we will gladly Accept your Alliance. Should our Rule be challenged, we shall Defend our Land as is the Right of all True Nations.

ing bravado in this act of envisioning his handful of ragged settlers as the beginnings of an empire. Still it may also have been a carefully calculated decision, as historical circumstances conspired to make such a gesture (just barely) possible.

Before the American Revolution, in both Canada and America, generous land grants allocated vast territories to wealthy European nobility, which these colonial patrons ruled in a quasifeudal fashion.* These precedents for Henri's vision were reinforced by the timing of the Latoledan declaration, which placed the Continental Congress in a painful bind: if they contested Henri's right to self-government, how could they legitimately sever their own ties with England? Perhaps because of these complications, the Latoledan proclamation went unanswered—and therefore, effectively unchallenged.†

One of the most surprising aspects of the Kingdom of Ohio is the simple fact that the settlement survived its first few, very hard, years. Similar early expeditions to the wild country around the Great Lakes, many of them larger and better equipped, failed due to disease, famine, or the attacks of Native American tribes.

No documentation remains to describe the earliest history of

---

* This past remains with us in the form of family names imprinted on the palimpsest of the American landscape: for example, those of Lord Baltimore (English), Kiliaen Van Rensselaer (Dutch), and Lord Detroit (French), among others.
† The sovereignty of the Kingdom went similarly unaddressed by the British government. On September 3, 1783, the signing of the Treaty of Paris brought the Revolution to an end. The treaty specifically set forth that all British territory south from the middle of the Great Lakes and their connecting waters, and east from the Mississippi, should belong to the United States. Although no specific language in this document addresses the issue of the Kingdom, it is important to note the careful terms in which the ceded territory is described: "all Territories and Lands subject to the [British] Crown," it reads—a phrasing that left ambiguous the matter of whether the treaty applied to the Free Estate.

the Kingdom—but somehow, the Latoledan settlement persevered. According to family oral histories, Henri instituted a kind of communal feudalism: the settlers of the Kingdom were given tracts of land to farm and provided with the minimum necessities of life by the Latoledan family. In exchange for this support, one quarter of each family's harvest was tithed to the Latoledans.[*]

Apart from clearing the woods to plant fields, and building cabins for themselves (activities which must have consumed nearly all of the settlers' energy), Henri directed the efforts of his colony into the construction of an outpost at the mouth of the Maumee River, which he named Toledo. During the years after the founding of his settlement, Henri commissioned the construction of the five buildings that formed the town: a church, a ballroom, a meeting hall, a general store, and the Latoledan family home.

Six years after the colony was established, Henri's son Mathieu married Héloise Chantilly, one of the maids who had accompanied the family from France.[†] That same year, David Latoledan—Mathieu's son, Henri's grandson—was born.

In March of 1784, Henri Latoledan was riding with his valet near the shores of Lake Erie when his horse spooked and threw him. Taking a bad fall, Henri was knocked unconscious: the valet carried him back to the family house, where he died, probably from internal injuries. He was forty-eight years old.

During his lifetime, Henri had (astonishingly) seen his dream of a kingdom in the American wilderness become a reality. From

---

[*] Daniel Yoder, *An Account of the Ohio Region Told by the Common People of That Area* (Milwaukee: Barlow & Sons, 1908).

[†] This union, of course, represented a crossing of social boundaries that would have been unthinkable in European society at the time—providing a hint of how much life on the frontier must have transformed the Latoledan settlers.

a struggling band of settlers, the Free Estate had grown into an established outpost on the frontier, trading goods with settlers along the Ohio and Maumee rivers as well as with local Native American tribes. Toledo was now a town marked on most maps of the region, comprising thirty houses, four stores, a church, a tavern, and a blacksmith. Cut off from the outside world, the town of Toledo and the Free Estate were (along with Fort Detroit) the cultural and mercantile capital of the western frontier.

This is what I've pieced together concerning the early years of the Kingdom of Ohio. This is where (if beginnings ever really exist) all of this began. But still I find myself at a loss, thinking about how to put the jigsaw pieces of history together: how these events came to echo through the lives of two young people walking along a riverbank in New York. A man and woman, as they enter a nondescript German restaurant and seat themselves beneath the heavy beams of the low ceiling.

I CAN PICTURE the moment so vividly that it feels, sometimes, closer than the roar of traffic outside my window. How she leans across the table and says:

"Cheri-Anne Toledo."

There is sawdust on the floor of the restaurant, the air is dense with the smell of sweat and hops. Thick-ankled waitresses wrangle tankards of beer between the tables. The introductions now completed, they sit silently for a moment, regarding each other. Studying the awkward, angular beauty of her features Peter decides that she must be around twenty years old.

"So you wanted to talk?" he asks finally.

She nods and sips the red wine that the waitress brought out, along with a plate of dark bread and pickles, which she has been visibly restraining herself from devouring.

"I have a tale," she says, "that defies common sense and perhaps even belief. In fact, I considered inventing some other story to explain the favor I will ask."

It takes Peter some time to untangle this statement. He nods and she closes her eyes, swaying slightly in her seat.

"But listen," she continues, "and I will tell you the truth, as simply as I can.

"For all my life, I have been fascinated by theories of science. In the laboratories of Europe I spent years studying physics and mathematics, hoping to glimpse the shape of the universe and its laws. Some years ago, working with a man named Tesla, I undertook a project—"

"Nikola Tesla?" Although Peter had decided to just hear her story without commenting or getting involved, he can't stop himself at this point. "You know Tesla?"

"I did." She hesitates. "Perhaps he would not know me now." An uncomfortable expression crosses her face and she looks down at the table. "Our goal was the construction of a device to transport men instantaneously from one place to another. I—"

"Wait—" Peter finds himself interrupting again. "I'm a mechanic"—he is startled to hear himself say these words, by the loftiness of his new title—"and I can tell you that's impossible."

"Impossible?" She smiles humorlessly. "Of course. But would not electricity have seemed like an impossibility a hundred years ago? The idea of harnessed lightning?"

"Maybe so." He nods. But the fact is, he thinks, she's obviously lying, or maybe just plain crazy. "Then tell me how it's done."

She looks down at the half-eaten plate of food between them. "You are a mechanic?"

He nods.

"Perhaps you have heard of Leibniz's concept of the monad?"

Peter shrugs noncommittally.

"Well, from there it is a simple enough idea, at least in principle. If the world is composed of unitary particles, and if one of these particles were somehow split, then the two halves, however far separated, might still resonate together, being fundamentally entwined. Given this fact—"

To Peter, her words quickly become a maze of bewildering detail and technical speculation that extends in every direction, seemingly without end. The few questions that he manages to ask lead only to more questions, more complexity that makes his head spin. And soon, he stops really listening: she rests her elbows on the table, cupping her chin, her face close to his. Her eyes are bright and flickering and he can smell her breath, sweet and heavy with wine. She sketches rapid diagrams on the dirty surface of the table between them, lines crisscrossing into nonsense.

"—existence of diallel gravitational-field lines," she is saying, "that emanate from every entity. In the case of the Earth, they emanate radially from its center, providing a conduit for combined particle and vibratory flow beyond the speed of light—"

Finally, he raises his hands. "Stop. Stop, please."

She takes a deep breath and falls silent, leaning back in her chair. Her face is drawn and even paler than before, the light in her eyes unsteady. She takes a sip of her wine and passes a hand across her forehead.

"You've lost me," Peter admits. "But you were telling that story . . . ?"

She nods. "I was. And pardon if I am unclear." She sips the wine again, then continues in a rush. "Although I told you that the device we were building was a means of instantaneous transportation, the truth is that Mr. Tesla and I never completed the work. We were close—very close, perhaps. But when I finally did attempt its practical use, before all the necessary tests had been performed, an accident happened.

"To put it succinctly—have you heard of the Royal House of Toledo?"

He shakes his head, and she nods, looking away, her eyes abruptly wet. She angrily wipes the almost-tears away, and Peter experiences a brief moment of admiration—her performance is as good as anything he's seen in a penny theater, he thinks.

"Suffice to say, my family and I were under attack. It was my intention to use the device to remove our attackers. But somehow I miscalculated. The machine exploded, destroying my home and family."

"But you escaped?" Peter prompts, momentarily caught up in the strangeness of the situation and of her tale.

"I escaped. At first, when I awoke in a park, I did not know where I was or what had happened. But finally it became clear to me."

She leans forward conspiratorially, gesturing for Peter to do the same—and as she does, knocks over his glass of wine, the ruby liquid flooding the tabletop and dripping into his lap. Flushing with embarrassment, she leaps to her feet, the motion toppling her own wineglass. An awkward interval of stammered apologies and clumsy mopping ensues, which Peter watches with mingled confusion and disbelief. When the mess has finally been cleared away and a surly waitress has replaced the drinks, they lean together again, the drama of the moment somewhat diminished.

"I was saying," she whispers, "I believe that the explosion somehow hurled me through time itself, so that I awoke seven years after the night my family perished."

She falls silent and they lean apart. Neither says anything for a moment. Around them the hubbub of the restaurant, a burst of laughter from a nearby table.

Wondering how to respond, Peter is at a loss. Her story is easily within the bounds of raving-lunatic territory, but, seated across the little table, she doesn't look deranged. In fact, she seems nervous but alert and clear-eyed, waiting for his answer.

"Guess I don't know what to say." He shrugs helplessly.

She nods, as if accepting a sentence. "You do not believe me."

"Would you?"

"Perhaps not. And what proof can I possibly offer that would convince you? My story, I know, offends common sense—but look." From her pocket she carefully withdraws a battered scrap of newsprint. Smoothing it on the table, she pushes it toward Peter—who suddenly recalls Neumann making this same gesture. Unfolding the brittle page, torn from the *Boston Post-Intelligencer* of August 26, 1894, he reads:

TREACHERY IN TOLEDO

Federal Investigator Reginald Pimsleur confirmed yesterday that both Louis Toledo and his daughter Cheri-Anne were killed by the explosion that destroyed their family home in Toledo, Ohio. Although unable to verify the cause of the explosion, Mr. Pimsleur informed a

crowd of reporters that the disaster
resulted from the treacherous attack provoked by Mr. Toledo against
the troops of Capt. Harlan of the
United States Army. At the time,
witnesses

Here the article ends abruptly in a torn edge. But the text is almost beside—or rather, below—the point: above the article is a small line drawing captioned "Louis Toledo & His Daughter," depicting an ugly man with a distracted look on his face, and a young woman. Peter looks up at the girl seated across from him, then down at the scrap again. And, yes, he thinks, it could be her: the same sharp, delicate features, the same dark curls.

"This you?"

"Yes."

"This is from seven years ago."

She doesn't say anything.

Peter hands back the article and she tucks it into her pocket— this best, and only, real evidence that she has been able to find during her days of research in the newly built public library. Days during which she learned how dramatically the world had changed over the last seven years, an industrial revolution transfiguring open countryside into metropolises overnight—or would it be metropoli? she wonders. For a split second, the image of a gigantic beehive flashes in front of her: a ceaseless, bustling insect activity, multiplying wax hexagons toward the heavens, self-important top-hatted drones stopping mid-flight to confer—Pollen up ten percent last month, old chap, have you heard?—Yes, magnificent outlay from the daffodils, give my regards to the queen—

She closes her eyes, wondering what is wrong with her, thinking things like this.

Peter leans away from her, rubbing his hands over his face.

He knows this is the point when he should make his excuses, slip her a nickel, and escape. He wants to be practical, to hold true to the rational commandments of his new profession. But for no good reason, and against his better judgment, he finds himself also wanting to hear more of her story.

"Supposing all of this is true. You said you needed something from me?"

With an effort she brings herself back to the present, making her eyes soft and looking up at him through lowered lashes. "I am a stranger here," she murmurs, "I know no one. Walking today, I became faint and fell. And when you were kind enough to help me . . ."

In fact, for a dizzying moment, she cannot remember why she is here, in this seedy restaurant, confessing herself to this shabbily dressed, unshaven stranger. It was only something in his expression, as he watched the birds wing upward over the river, as if transfixed by the physics of their flight, that made her imagine she might—

"You need a place to stay, then?" he asks roughly.

She nods and gazes at him—like a moonstruck cow, she thinks, hoping she doesn't look as ridiculous as she feels.

"And you have no money? Nothing?"

She nods again.

The thought occurs to him that this all might be an elaborate hoax: that if he agrees to help her, he'll wake up in the hands of her accomplices—thickset men with low brows who might already be lurking outside. He glances around, knowing that he'll see nothing, and sees nothing. Only the low ceiling of unfinished beams, the crowded tables, and, beyond the thick windowpanes, the smudged silhouette of the city. Dark columns of smoke rising toward the darkening winter sky—the faintest suggestion of shape and order in the mass of buildings and boulevards that fuse together, tilting downward into night.

For a long moment, the demands of reason and faith crowd together inside him. Then abruptly he reaches a decision. Not because he believes her story—but maybe because there's something in her face that intrigues him. Maybe because he is lonely. Or maybe, most simply of all, because he has been waiting for something, and suddenly something has arrived.

"Can't take you to my rooms," he tells her. "I don't live alone, and no guests allowed. But if a roof is what you're looking for, you can stay in the mechanics' garage tonight." He stares at her, afraid to hear her say no, hoping that she will.

"Thank you," she says. And gives him a look of gratitude that—for a moment—makes him feel, despite his misgivings, that maybe he has made the right decision after all.

I PICTURE the two of them rising to leave the German restaurant—but however much I want to follow, I realize that I'll have to leave them there. Because writing these last few pages, I've been plagued by the sense that I'm forgetting something. I've tried to ignore the feeling—because really, I tell myself, it doesn't matter. The important thing here isn't the distant past, or my present: the important thing is what happened in New York. Still, I can't shake the idea that I'll be missing a crucial piece if I don't finish telling the history of the Kingdom of Ohio.

Because although it's not the story I sat down to write, I can't seem to get around the idea that it needs to be told, even if you already know all of this. Because, if nothing else, it seems to me that these things should be recorded somewhere. So that someone besides you and I might read this and remember.

In 1785, the Northwest Territory was divided into separate regions* that were eligible for eventual statehood. With this news, the value of land on the frontier doubled overnight. Taking advantage of this development, in a remarkably circular turn of events, Mathieu Latoledan (now head of the family) reached an agreement with two land speculators—Joel Barlow, an ex-minister, and his partner William Playfair, the former manager of a vaudeville show and convicted horse-thief—to lease small farmsteads in the Kingdom of Ohio on the markets of Europe.

In 1789, when the farms went on sale, it was a good time to advertise American real estate in France—for this was the summer when, as M. Fénelon, archbishop of the church, informed the king, all of France was "simply a great hospital, full of woe and empty of bread,"† and on July 14 a mob streamed through the streets and razed the Bastille. For the fearful Parisians, America represented growth, profits, and security. Barlow and Playfair did a brisk business, selling farmsteads for 1,000 livres each. Their brochures described the tracts of land, claiming that no other territory in the United States

---

* The Indiana, Ohio, Michigan, and Illinois territories.
† François de Salignac de la Mothe-Fénelon, archbishop of Cambray, writing in a letter titled "Fénelon to Louis XIV: Remonstrances to This Prince on Certain Aspects of His Administration." As a result of this impertinence, the archbishop was confined to his family estate for the remainder of his life.

> offers so many advantages. . . . It is the most salubrious, the most agreeable, the most advantageous, the most fertile land which is known to any people in Europe . . . with vast fields of rice, which nature here produces spontaneously. Hogs in this region flourish in the woods without care, multiplying a thousandfold each year or so. Maple trees drip sugar in the forests . . . a swamp-plant in season yields stalks which function as candles.[*]

Four hundred shares of land on the Latoledan estate were sold: for their money, the settlers would receive fifty acres in a ninety-nine-year lease, a cow, seed corn, and an ax. The French colonists were, of course, disappointed on their arrival in Ohio. Picturing America, they must have thought of the clapboard towns of New England, but as one historian writes: "on October 19, 1790, the flatboats swung inshore and were moored to stumps on the [Maumee River] landing. The French pilgrims looked at paradise. What they saw was a high, steep bank, then a square of cleared land ending in a frame of forest. . . . The French had traveled four thousand miles to this new Eden."[†]

---

[*] Havighurst, *Wilderness for Sale*, p. 152.

[†] Ibid., pp. 156–57; and yet, despite the skepticism of Havighurst, I can't help but imagine that this arrival must have held some wonder for the French émigrés.

I picture the dark banks of the river rising above the waters of the Maumee, stained orange and silver by the sunset. It is Ohio autumn, trees silhouetted

However these immigrants took their first sight of the Kingdom, their arrival was a blessing for the Latoledans. The new French

---

against the sky, the flitting of fireflies and bats. The air is still warm and humid: it is a country of thunderstorms that make the sky turn purple and the trees thrash their branches like hysterical worshippers in the wind.

On the clumsy wooden barges, the French say little to each other: all they can do is gaze around in bewilderment, in silent expectation. One of the settlers, a former baker who speaks a little English, has asked the captain of the boat when they will arrive: "Afore dark, I'd say," the bewhiskered riverboat man in his stained jacket replies, spouting a stream of tobacco juice between his teeth into the passing water. *"Il ne sera pas longtemps maintenant,"* the baker relays to his fellow travelers. They watch the wilderness unfold.

When they arrive at their destination, they do not even know it at first. A rough dock of hewn logs stands on the western bank of the river, so low to the water that it seems from a distance like nothing more than a collection of the fallen trees that float now and then downstream. The polesmen set their rods against the current and slowly the two barges turn toward the shore, edging finally against the dock with a rough grinding sound. The captain and two mates jump overboard, lashing the vessels to iron hooks in the dock pilings with ragged hemp ropes. Overhead, the sky is fading to deep purple, stars and a silvered crescent of moon visible in the arcing void. Somewhere in the wooded hills a wolf calls, and then another and another. The Frenchmen shiver.

"Take the cargo ashore," the captain tells his passengers. "They'll come for you; or if not, you've but to walk west. You'll see the fields either side." The Parisians regard him blankly in shock or simple incomprehension. "Here." The captain picks up one of the parcels of luggage sitting on the deck—a battered wooden suitcase tied with twine—and thrusts it into the arms of one of the men, gesturing toward the dock. The Frenchman, sporting extravagant Gaulish mustaches that extend nearly to his ears, looks at the parcel in his arms, at the captain, at his fellow settlers who are exchanging worried glances. "Go, damn you!" The captain shoves him and he stumbles back.

Catching his balance, he understands and drops the package to the deck of the ship, where it splits open, spilling manteaux, tricots, cuteaux, and various meager *petites objets* across the planks and skidding into the river. "No!" The mustachioed Frenchman rolls his eyes in fear at the wilderness where the captain is pointing. "Is not possible—*C'est pas possible! Il n'est pas rien ici, c'est pas correct! Vous-vous-ils ont nous dites que"*—a complaint that is cut short by the click of two hammers being cocked back, the double-barreled short musket, river pirates' weapon of choice, resting gently in the captain's hand.

settlers helped to clear the Latoledan land, built houses, and spurred trade. Equally important, their shared cultural background had the effect of consolidating the distinct identity of the Kingdom. Describing the inhabitants of the Kingdom (as compared to the essentially English Yankees), one historian notes that the French settlers

were of the old European block:
they duplicated on North American

The settlers go. They carry the few possessions that have survived the trip with them from the boats onto the shore, where they are stacked on the docks. When they are finished and assembled on dry land, the captain—musket still in hand—and his crew reboard the boats. "That way," the captain points with the gun, west. And the polemen bend to their task, the barges drifting away from the shore and starting down the river. It is not until the boats are out of sight that the French begin to take stock of their surroundings. Before this they cannot look away from the receding shapes, each holding the silent hope that perhaps this is all a mistake, a *jeste fantastique à la mode américaine.* That any minute now the barges will turn back and transport them to the Eden that they were promised.

When the boats are gone, the settlers calculate the shape of paradise. A rough wooden dock with pilings that are little more than raw-hewn tree trunks, a wooden shed (empty save for a few wood shavings), and a rutted dirt road leading away between the trees, the green and gold of autumn foliage shading into black beneath the pale moonlight. They wait and wait—and finally, when no one comes for them, load their meager possessions onto their backs and begin to walk. It is slow going: in the darkness they trip on cartwheel tracks and potholes, stumble over drifts of leaves. Some of the women begin to cry and some of the men as well. Another wolf calls in the distance. At this moment, they are the most isolated people in the world: in a wilderness four thousand miles from home, mapless, deceived.

Finally, however, they round a bend in the path and see before them the trees opening onto mown fields. The sight of the first shabby barn along the road is more than God's original miracle. Hysterical, ragged, they start to run, scattering dropped clothes, kitchen utensils, portraits behind them unheeded—and then they see the town and the sputtering yellow glow of a paraffin lamp in a window, most welcome of all things on this earth.

> soil the pre-reformation peasant so-
> ciety of the old world. . . . Their
> lives consisted of a series of ritual
> acts such as being born, becoming
> of age, marrying, begetting, dying,
> each of which, properly performed,
> brings its satisfactions and its
> reward. . . . Into this unchanging
> world, there comes bursting the
> hurly-burly of the English man of
> business. . . . He is in a hurry. He
> wants to get things done. He has
> ends to gain. . . . That object is one
> comprehended only remotely by
> the peasant.[*]

In 1812, while British and American gunboats battled and sank each other on the Great Lakes, Mathieu Latoledan died of a "coughing sickness" and was succeeded by his son, David Latoledan. When David assumed the throne he was twenty-seven years old. When he relinquished it in 1872 he was eighty-nine, and during his lifetime the Kingdom would achieve its greatest period of glory, making the Latoledan family among the five hundred richest in North America.

David's father, Mathieu, had been an odd combination of frontiersman and aristocrat. Although he had spent most of his adult life in the New World, he could still remember the old family estate in France. David, on the other hand, never saw France as a

---

[*] Arthur Lower, *Colony to Nation* (Toronto: Longmans, Green, 1946), pp. 66–68.

child, and, growing up in the Ohio wilderness, he had learned a pioneer's sense of entrepreneurial independence.

For David, the difference between running a business and governing a country lay solely in the titles men used. Understanding that in the modern world wealth was power, he pushed for the Kingdom's economic growth above all else, striking deals with the United States that helped to fill the family coffers at the expense of the Kingdom's political autonomy. He sold territory in the Free Estate to foreign investors, and gave land to the Pennsylvania Railroad Company as part of a deal to construct rail lines to Toledo (although due to financial difficulties the route was never completed).

Such concessions to the United States helped promote rapid development in the Free Estate, as in the years following 1816 the Ohio country was transformed by intrepid industrialists from a wilderness into an endlessly profitable source of raw materials to fuel American enterprise. In 1820, David changed the family name from Latoledan to Toledo (after the capital city)—"it has an American sound," he explained in a letter to a friend in Philadelphia.[*] This action was not without basis; in the political climate of the United States during the late nineteenth century, newfound nationalist sentiment ran high and foreign origins were a source of suspicion.

Of his two children, David took a great deal more interest in his older son (and presumed heir), Claudius, than in his younger offspring, Louis. From an early age, David groomed Claudius for

---

[*] In fact, this letter itself appears to be lost but is cited in a second letter, this one written to a third acquaintance by the original recipient of David Latoledan's correspondence, Edgar St. Simone, of Boston (St. Simone-McLelland Family Archive at Boston University, correspondence file, 1820).

the throne and involved him in the daily operations of the Kingdom; Claudius practiced his mathematics by calculating shipping
prices down the Maumee River, and at harvesttime supervised the
gathering and storage of the corn. At the age of fifteen, he was sent
to Oxford for his continuing education and remained in Europe for
the next six years before returning to Ohio to take part in the administration of the Toledo family's concerns.

Louis's childhood was rather different, and far more typical of
a young man of his social standing: sent to boarding schools in
Boston for most of his youth, he felt little connection with Ohio or
the Free Estate. After graduating from secondary school, Louis was
sent to McGill College, in Montreal, where he studied for a bachelor of letters. Kept distant from the business of the Kingdom, his
interests turned to the arts—specifically, he became an admirer of
the Romantic poets and landscape painting. At McGill, he concluded his graduation speech with the words "I can think of no
more heroic example of all that is good and true and manly, that
to which we ought all aspire, than that of Percy Bysshe Shelley."

In 1837, in an effort to gain recognition for his tiny empire,
David held a festival to celebrate the sixtieth anniversary of the
Kingdom (in reality, it was the sixty-first), to which he invited
wealthy families from Boston, Philadelphia, and New York, as well
as the governor of Ohio, several congressmen, the Prince of Wales,
and President Andrew Jackson.

Preparations for the event were extensive, and David spared no
expense to give the impression to his guests that they were being
entertained by a head of state every bit as legitimate as the crowns
of Europe. Two dozen musicians and more than a hundred cases of
champagne were imported from New York, and a baker and five
chefs from Boston. Although the Prince of Wales himself declined

to come, the British Consul of New York, Lord Charles Porpington, bore the prince's greetings to the festivities and drank champagne with David by the banks of Swan Creek in a gazebo lit with oil lamps that had been strung from the trees. In a letter to the prince, Porpington wrote: "There is something magical about that place which, for all its roughness, will always remain wonderful to me."[*] However, neither President Jackson nor any member of Congress attended or made response to the event at all.

Over the following decades, the political and practical significance of the Kingdom diminished rapidly, even as its wealth increased. Culturally and politically, the identity of the Kingdom was fading fast. As one historian put it, life within the Kingdom

> had long since become identical to that of the surrounding United States. Its effective borders shrank steadily in the face of growing U.S. settlement and influence. . . . By 1865, the Kingdom was essentially reduced to the Toledo family themselves, their mansion and grounds, and the businesses in their immediate vicinity, which made much of being "by appointment of the Crown." It had contracted to a rough square, six city blocks on each side.[†]

---

[*] Charles Porpington in a letter to the Prince of Wales, July 16, 1837 (courtesy British Royal Archives, London).
[†] Daniel Yoder, *An Account of the Ohio Region* (Milwaukee: Barlow & Sons, 1908).

In 1866, an aging David Toledo stepped down from the practical administration of the Kingdom to let Claudius, then thirty-seven years old and still unmarried, assume the reins of power. For reasons that are not entirely clear—perhaps feeling that his brother's dilettante existence, wandering the salons of Paris and London, was a discredit to the family—Claudius asked Louis to return to Toledo in 1867, creating a sinecure post for him with the title of "Minister of Social Advancement."

Moved by the lofty sound of this office, Louis returned to Ohio and began a number of cultural ventures including the founding of the Toledo Symphony and the Toledo Museum of Art.*

On May 10, 1869, the transcontinental railway was completed, the two coasts bound together by a golden spike driven into the ties at Promontory Point, Utah. In practical terms, under the competent guidance of Claudius, the Kingdom of Ohio was wealthier and more prosperous than ever before. Symbolically, however, I can't help but see this event as a final nail in the coffin of the Free Estate. Around the tiny Kingdom, the United States had grown together and closed in on all sides, sealing off any possible route of escape.†

---

* Surprisingly, considering the inexperience of their author, these endeavors were moderately successful. Although the Toledo Symphony closed its doors due to financial difficulties in 1895, the Toledo Museum of Art remains open and "is one of the most important and influential cultural institutions in the Midwest" (this from *Toledo Rocks! A Visitor's Guide to the Greater Toledo Metropolitan Area*, published by the Toledo Board of Tourism, 1981—although the "importance" of this museum, consisting of four small rooms, should be measured alongside the source of its inspiration, the Louvre).

† An equally significant moment in the demise of the Kingdom occurred in 1885, when Claudius's carriage overturned down an embankment, killing him instantly. Upon his death, Louis Toledo ascended to the throne, and his inexperience at governance unquestionably contributed to the continued decline of the Free Estate.

Finally—to conclude this brief history—in 1894, the United States government finally put an end to the upstart frontier empire. A division of U.S. Army troops marched into Toledo, sparking a battle that would cost dozens of lives and culminated in a fire that destroyed the Latoledan mansion. According to all reliable accounts, the last two remaining members of the royal family perished in this blaze.

SHE SITS on a wooden stool in a corner of the subway workshop, huddled beside the feeble glow of the stove. Her breath steams in the cold air of the room, windows opaque with frost—the dingy space and the barn of machinery beyond abandoned on a Friday night, gathering shadows pushed back only by the glow of embers through the iron grate. She watches silently, feeling helpless and out of place, as the mechanic sets a pot of water on the stove to boil.

"Make us some tea," he clarifies. "Can't light a lantern, the company has guards that patrol . . ."

She murmurs words of gratitude, surveying the workshop as Peter bustles back and forth.

"Have you worked on the subway long?" she asks, awkwardly trying to make conversation.

"Couple months now." Feeling suddenly at a loss for what to do or say in her presence, he distracts himself with tugging the window latches more securely shut and banking the coals of the fire. Finally he forces himself to sit on an overturned bucket at the edge of the fire's glow, acutely aware of the distance between their bodies. "So, you're from Ohio?"

"Yes. From Toledo, to be exact."

"I've never been to Ohio. Grew up in Idaho. Ever heard of Coeur d'Alene?"

"A silver town." She tries to imagine the place, vaguely picturing endless forest and wild men on horseback. "I remember reading about it in the newspaper. I think it was called a town of lost money and loose women." She smiles at him—then realizes her own tactless clumsiness and looks away, cheeks flushing.

"Maybe so." He stares down at his scarred boots. "Doesn't matter much, anyway. All in the past now." He pauses. "What about you? What was it like, growing up in Ohio?"

"Pleasant. It is a beautiful place." She closes her eyes, a weight of exhaustion descending over her like a heavy woolen cloak. At this moment she feels utterly alone: she feels as if she is floating in a void, both her memories and these present surroundings more distant than the moon.

"And what you were saying about that House of Toledo?" He leans toward her, struggling to put together a question that might give him some clue about who she is, what she's looking for—anything, really. "That's your family?"

"Yes. It was my family, the royal family of Ohio. My father was Louis Toledo, the king."

Peter opens his mouth but then realizes the obvious next question doesn't exist, or maybe there are too many of them. The pot on the stove starts to rattle and he rises, wiping off a pair of metal mugs with his sleeve and adding dried leaves from a rusty canister. He pours the water and hands her one, and she clasps the hot drink with both hands, letting the steam bathe her face.

"And, this . . ." Peter trails off. After the German restaurant, when they first arrived here, he had imagined what might happen between them, two strangers in the New York night. But now, the small distance between where they sit feels like an impossible chasm.

"This place you grew up," he tries, "it was in the woods, in the wilderness?"

She shakes her head. "By the time I was born, the woods had been cleared and become farmers' fields. I spent my early years in Ohio, and then, after my mother's death when I was eleven, I was sent first to a boarding school in Connecticut, and later to Europe for several years." Phrases that sound somehow unreal in her own ears, describing an imaginary person.

"And what was Tesla like?" Peter asks. He still doesn't believe her story, but he has stopped thinking of it as a lie, exactly. Instead, he has begun to regard her words more like a tall tale, along the lines of the ones his father sometimes told, the legends of Paul Bunyan and Johnny Appleseed.

"Difficult. Brilliant. Egotistical—perhaps with justification." Maybe she blushes a little, but it's hard to tell: the light in the workshop is dim, the ghosts of traffic flickering through the ice-fogged windows. "I must thank you again for helping me."

"It's nothing."

Then neither of them says anything for a time, each wrapped in separate silence.

"We should get some sleep," he says finally.

"Sleep sounds like a paradise to me."

"I—" he hesitates. "I have to sleep here as well, you know. The equipment . . ." Which is not entirely a falsehood.

She nods and he rises.

"There's a couple cots in the back, and blankets. I'll get them."

Peter leaves the workroom for the dim expanse of the machinery barn beyond. There, leaning against the door and surveying the dark shapes of engines and furnaces, he feels a weight of weariness and nerves. Although he'd been eager for her company a few hours ago, now he wishes that he could be alone to collect himself, to digest her story—this fairy tale of lost worlds, famous inventors, and an impossible journey through time, all more than he can comprehend or even think clearly about, at this moment.

Avoiding her face, he sets up the two cots, one at either end of the workroom. As she climbs into bed her dress shifts upward, revealing the shapely curve of her calves, and Peter's heart catches for an instant. Noticing the direction of his gaze she averts her eyes, her cheeks burning, and quickly covers herself with the dusty blanket.

Peter does the same and they both lie staring up at the ceiling in silence. The passing lights of wagon-lanterns and omnibuses, diffuse through the frosted windows; the dull, flickering shadows of machinery cast by the stove's faint glow. The sound of slushing wheels, the white noise of the city—till, sooner or later, they sleep.

CHAPTER V

THE GREAT TRAP

THE MORE WE STUDY, THE MORE WE DISCOVER OUR IGNORANCE.

It was Shelley who wrote this, and although I never felt much kinship with that poet, I think he got this right. During these last decades I've lost count of the hours that I spent reading history, studying the why and how of the things that took place before and after our time together. And none of it, really, explains what happened in those moments.

I picture you standing beside me in the dining room of a great house. The growing fear in your face, the way you wouldn't meet my eyes but stared instead at the polished parquet floor. The stifling tension between us and my sense that you were about to speak, just before the butler entered with the silver coffee service on a tray . . .

Even while these memories draw me in, they're also painful to relive. Maybe that's why it feels easier, some days, to lose myself in daydreams about a more distant past.

Recently, in the public library, I found a book containing a portrait of Henri Latoledan by the Italian painter Cipriotto.* It depicts a swarthy man with wide cheekbones and unruly black hair; wearing a velvet doublet and a short cape, he stares out of the painting with impenetrable eyes, seeming equally impatient with the artist recording his likeness and the viewer regarding it.

Studying this image (after I smuggled the book home from the library—easy enough with a baggy coat and a bit of senile mumbling), I tried to imagine what it must have been like, for those first settlers who arrived in the wilderness that would become the Kingdom of Ohio. Sitting in my apartment (the room silent except for the avocado-colored fridge wheezing in one corner), I picture how they would have staggered to the edge of the lake that was their destination. The last of their wagons had shattered an axle in the woods days ago, and their possessions were piled on rough wooden platforms that they dragged behind them.

While the women kindle campfires and unload sacks of flour and haunches of dried meat, the men hang sheets of canvas from the trees to form canopies, groaning as they lift their arms, their shoulders and palms locked from hours of gripping the sledges' weight. It is evening, fireflies dancing beneath the dark branches and out over the water.

When he has seen that all the motions of making camp are under way, Henri Latoledan steps away from the labor to visit his wife. He finds her seated in her tent, perched on a clothes chest and being fanned by her young chambermaid. Henri eyes the girl's ripe curves before extending a hand toward his wife.

---

* "M. Henri Latoledan," by Giacometti Cipriotto, as reprinted in *Portraiture in the Era of Louis XIV*, Stefan Gaston, ed., George Mason University Library Series, 1966.

She rises and they walk together in silence away from the half-built camp, to a point where the small waves of the lake lap a pebbled beach. A wall of oak and beech trees, ancient and immense, stands guard like a motionless army drawn up at the water's edge, extending unbroken into the distance. A pale three-quarter moon has begun to climb in the sky, and the chirping of crickets fills the air. The hem of her long dress trails in the dirt and catches on twigs. In a moment of emotion, Henri takes her hand.

"There," he tells her, gesturing toward the forest. "Even as I told you it would be. One day soon a castle for you will rise here, and a new village."

"But Henri. But really . . ." She shakes her head, wondering as she has done every day since their departure whether this might be an elaborate nightmare, sent by God as some kind of test. They stand silently, side by side in their mud-stained velvet, surveying the horizon. Then he turns.

"Now I must see to the camp." He leads her back to her tent and checks the progress of the settlers—of his people, as he has already affectionately come to think of them: a motley band of brave or foolish souls from the village in France, a few more adventurers from the seaport in Marseilles, and a knot of silent Acadian trappers whom he persuaded to join the expedition in Montreal. In all, some fifty men and women in the trackless wilderness. Henri is not even certain they have arrived at the place described on the deed and crude map in his saddlebag—but it does not matter, he reminds himself. Here, anything is possible.

The encampment is going up well, he notes. Already the evening meal is cooking, the perishable baggage stowed away. A boy who worked as the fishmonger's assistant in the old village has set baited lines in the lake and his valet is tending to the horses. Hefting an ax, Henri sets to work chopping limbs from a fallen tree for firewood. Splinters cling to his beard and the front of his ruined doublet. One of his blisters bursts, dribbling pale fluid.

He thinks that he has never been happier.

The former town barber passes by, carrying his basin and shears, and Henri calls out to him.

"Tell me, what do you think of our new home?"

The barber shakes his ponderous head, grinning nervously. "It doesn't look like France, my lord."

"No, it doesn't. Here, give me your bowl." Henri snatches the shaving basin and places it over his head, rapping the dented brass with his knuckles. "To protect myself from the wood chips," he explains. The barber watches, wide-eyed. Noticing this look, Henri laughs.

"Take good care of it, my lord," the barber says reproachfully. "I'll wager there's not another like it for six hundred miles. And even in America men will need their beards shaved and their hair cut." He glances affectionately at his scissors.

"Not America." Henri shakes his head and leans on the ax, looking out over the water. "This is something else. . . ."

At home in my apartment I imagine these scenes while cars zoom by on the freeway overpass that arcs a dozen feet outside my window, making the glass rattle with each truck that goes by. Sitting in my armchair below the shadow of a wilting potted fern, I push aside the plastic trays from my microwaved dinner and watch as night falls over the city. Overhead, only a handful of pale stars are visible through the haze. And I'm struck by the thought that

Henri Latoledan (and young Peter Force, and you) would have glanced up at these same points of light, and how maybe this is all that binds us together now: these lonely fires in the sky, a million light-years away.

"AND WHAT is this you're trying to do here?"

Cheri-Anne turns from the window of the Ohio mansion, to find her tutor tapping the sheaf of papers that she handed him ten minutes ago. She leans across the desk to study the line of equations he indicates with his silver pen.

"That . . . oh." Seeing the mistake, she crosses out an exponent and rewrites it outside the parenthesis. "It should be like this. You see?"

"Hmm." He glances up and meets her eyes with a blue stare of somewhat unsettling intensity. She looks away. "I thought so." He smiles indulgently at her before resuming his study of the formulae.

Cheri-Anne gazes out the window again. The sunlit room where she takes her lessons is on the second floor of the house, and has a view over the garden to the shimmer of the great lake in the distance. Yellow spring light, the color of parchment paper, tints the harp on its stand in one corner, the shelves of books, the desk by the windows where they sit.

Covertly she glances at her instructor and wonders how long he will last. When Mr. Coulter had been hired to replace his predecessor, she had been delighted—more, she admits ruefully now, by his looks than by his qualifications. Increasingly, though, she finds herself chafing at the glacial pace of study that he insists upon. Outside, the small white triangles of sails glide silently over the horizon of the lake.

Mr. Coulter clears his throat, picks up his glasses, polishes them, and affixes them to his perfectly straight nose. "Well." He shuffles the pages of her work and takes the glasses off again. "I understand the math, but my dear girl"—he chuckles—"honestly, I can't make head or tail of what you're trying to do. These equations simply don't work."

"Yes, exactly!" She realizes that her voice is too loud and lowers it. "You see? They're both true *and* false—or rather, it seems impossible to demonstrate they are either."

He nods patiently. "Yes, but obviously they're false. The problem is just in the way that you've written your maths."

"But—" She struggles to find a way of explaining this most recent inspiration that kept her awake and sitting at her desk all through the previous night, filled with racing thoughts until dawn. "It seems to me there is some paradox about the numbers themselves in this proof. As if"—she struggles for an analogy—"as if I were to tell you: 'The next sentence is true. This sentence is false.' You see? There is a fundamental inconsistency. And here"—she points at the paper—"given this class of recursive formulae, there must also be a set of recursive signs for which . . ." She gazes at him, hoping she has conveyed some inkling of the beautiful, self-annihilating, logical perfection she imagines.

"That's simply gibberish. My dear girl, mathematics is not about word games." He frowns and runs a hand through his blond hair. "You simply can't do this sort of thing. Now, then." He hands the papers back to her and turns his attention to the primer they have been working from.

She accepts the thin sheaf and holds it protectively against her chest, studying the movement of Mr. Coulter's hand and feeling her cheeks prick with red. Maybe he is right, she thinks; maybe she is only fooling herself with these ideas. After all, who would seriously listen to the wild daydreams of a seventeen-year-old girl from the provincial Midwest? Still, she tells herself, she will send a letter to Professor Riemann anyway—more as a gesture of defiance against the invisible walls around her than in hope of a response, as all her previous letters to Göttingen have gone unanswered.

"Now, then," he continues, "why don't we try a few more interpolations?"

She exhales a shaky breath. "We've already done the interpolations." Her voice sounds sulky in her own ears, a petulant child. With an effort she reins in her emotions. "Perhaps we might try something new?"

"Now, now, Miss Toledo." The tutor smiles indulgently. "You still make mistakes, and you know that practice makes perfect. Perhaps next week we can try some more advanced material."

Finally he leaves and she stands with a sigh, wishing that she could loosen her corset. Her neck and shoulders hurt. She paces in circles around the room until the maid arrives with a plate of finger sandwiches and tea, her usual refreshment between lessons.

"Cook told me you'll be having a new gown for the ball next Friday," the maid chirps, bright-eyed. "Is it true?"

"Yes. I will." She pictures the monstrosity of taffeta and ruffles the tailor insisted upon, wincing inwardly. Trying to make her look like a fancy layer-cake that some tedious, well-bred young man from a Boston family will bite down upon. And that is all I am to them, she thinks with a surge of anger and something like desperation: a well-trained confection of ribbons. Even to her father, with all his vague romantic ideals—an ornament to be polished and bartered, for the continuance of the Toledo dynasty.

"And it's true there's lace up the sleeves, brought all the way from France?" the maid burbles.

"Yes. It is true."

"It sounds lovely," the servant girl sighs, pouring the tea. And when she has departed, Cheri-Anne stands motionless beside the desk, where steam from the lavender bone-china cup rises to disappear in a shimmer of air, distorting a tiny patch of the yellow afternoon world outside the windows.

Sipping her tea, she thinks about the equations dismissed by Mr. Coulter. What she imagines with these formulae and the paradox they demonstrate, about some fundamental *imperfection* within mathematics itself—the right phrase coming to her now, belatedly—has a feeling of simple, fierce rightness that brings a nearly physical stab of longing. She absently lets one hand wander over her breasts, down to her thighs, the touch like a stranger's through the layers of dress, petticoats, and corset. If only, she thinks—but then doesn't know how the sentence should, or could, end.

On the mantelpiece, the gilt ormolu clock chimes and she opens her eyes. In a few minutes her harp teacher, Mrs. Hammond, will arrive. She looks out the window again and feels an abrupt and overpowering sense of frustration at the confining elegance of the music room around her, the impossible gulf between herself and the white sails in the distance, the smallness of her life.

She puts down the teacup, hot liquid sloshing over the saucer. The walls and ceiling close in on her, pushing the breath from her body. She pictures a series of disconnected, violent images—the murder of Mrs. Hammond, the metronome's needle quivering in the shrewish old harp teacher's eye socket. The maid screaming in terror, servants running from the mansion as it is engulfed in flames—

Squeezing her eyes shut, she searches for calm. None of this matters, she tells herself. This place is only temporary, a passing obstacle between herself and the world where she belongs: Paris, London, New York, the cities where great ideas are explored in famous laboratories.

But when she tries to picture Paris, she finds that her memories of the few days she spent in that city have grown faded from over-use, like the faces of coins fingered into vague impressions. The size of its gray buildings and boulevards, the glimpse of a cathedral through the curtains of a moving carriage.

She has not left Ohio since she returned from Europe two years ago, kept at home by her father's inept and clinging protectiveness. From below, she hears the butler, Nonce, open the front door and Mrs. Hammond's shrill greeting. Not much longer, she thinks. She opens her eyes, plastering a smile on her face in preparation for the harp teacher's arrival. And she imagines herself far away from here, stepping off a train in New York, onto the stage of real life.

SHE RECALLS THIS NOW, sitting in the subway workshop. It is morning and the fire in the stove has died during the night, her breath steaming in the chill air. Beyond the dirty windows the shapes of New York are a dim jumble.

She shakes her head and shivers, fighting the tug of these memories. Even while her recollections of this Ohio-that-might-have-been offer a reassuring familiarity that she craves, they are also freighted with a growing sense of peril. Because how can these things belong to the same life, she wonders—feeling herself tilt toward hysteria—these recollections, and the dingy room where she now sits? And for the thousandth time in the past week, she struggles against the terrifyingly obvious conclusion that she has simply lost her mind and slipped into some kind of delusion.

She remembers waking up in a park and not recognizing her surroundings. She remembers waking up and finding herself in an impossible place, where the Kingdom of Ohio has nearly been forgotten. An impossible world, where seven years can disappear without a trace.

Where, ever since her arrival, the boundaries between things seem to be blurring more and more: the diminishing distance between herself and every other lunatic woman who begs on street corners for pennies, the distance between reason and something else, older and darker . . .

The mechanic stirs in his cot and she glances over at him, seeing his face as if for the first time. Sleeping, he looks younger and more vulnerable, the prematurely weathered creases around his eyes smoothed away, a lock of brown hair falling across his forehead. For a moment she has the impulse to bend down and touch his cheek but quickly checks herself, vaguely shocked at even thinking such a thing. He is only a helpful stranger, someone who happened to be nearby when her endurance ran out. Silently she watches as he groans and sits up, fumbles to light the stove and begins to make tea. They eat breakfast in near silence, both of them awkward and unsure of how to act in the other's presence.

"So what are you going to do?" Peter finally asks.

"I suppose I am still trying to decide myself." She looks away from him, a wave of panic rising in her chest as she contemplates again the overwhelming dimensions of her situation. One step at a time, she tells herself, clinging to the vague plan she has formulated over the last days, the slender hope it offers like a life raft in an angry ocean. Form a hypothesis, construct an experiment, search for verification. She silently recites these words to herself as a mantra against the terrifying unknown.

Then she draws a shaky breath and offers the mechanic a shaky smile. "There are certain errands I must attend. But if I may impose on your generosity, I hoped that I might spend one more night here?" She blurts the question, stumbling over her words.

He hesitates, then nods. "Guess that sounds all right."

"Thank you. I only wish I knew how to express my gratitude."

A number of impossible suggestions in this regard flash through Peter's mind, most of them featuring the memory of her exposed legs from the night before.

Feeling uncomfortably conscious of his gaze and the space between their bodies, she finishes her tea and stands. For a moment they look at each other, neither knowing quite how to part ways.

He opens his mouth—but before he can speak, she is gone, the door banging shut behind her.

FOR A TIME AFTER her departure, Peter sits in the workshop trying to make sense of what she has told him and to put his thoughts in order. Outside, he can hear the clang of engines and the shouts of the excavation crews—unlike the mechanics, the rock men work seven days a week. On other mornings, similarly unoccupied, he might have gone out to talk with Paolo, or listen to Tobias and Michael trading jokes, but today the thought of doing so seems like a burden. He feels strangely distant from the life of the city that unfolds on the other side of the clapboard walls. As if he has been imperceptibly enveloped by the private world of her story, like the shimmering curve of a soap bubble's wall.

Shouts of traffic and the clamor of pedestrians from beyond the workshop door. He blinks away these wandering thoughts and glances up at the battered wall clock—only half an hour has passed since she left, but it seems like days. Thinking about her, Peter can see clearly enough what's happening: how she's using some tall tales and her pretty face to buy his generosity. He can see this but, to his dismay, he realizes that he's falling for it anyway.

Suddenly overcome by the need to be somewhere else, and disgusted by his own gullibility, Peter stands and pulls on his coat, crossing to the door. Outside he hesitates, then starts walking toward the tip of land called the Battery, where the East River meets the Hudson.

It is a long walk and he chooses it deliberately, hoping that the cold and distance will help clear his head. It is a foggy winter day and he thinks of how the arc of water beyond the Battery will be shrouded in gray, enclosing the city and making the metropolis feel somehow intimate, all sounds muted by the waves. This is what I need, he thinks, and pushes through the crowd, hands in his pockets.

A dozen blocks later, though, he stops. What if she returns while he is gone and, not finding him there, disappears forever? Worse yet, what if she's discovered by the company guards and tells them how he'd let her stay in the garage, a clear breach of regulations? He tries to tell himself these worries don't matter and to keep walking, but they only come crowding back. So despite himself, he finally starts back toward the workshop.

Approaching the construction site, Peter notices a cloud of ugly black smoke rising from somewhere inside the subway-works. One of the engines broken again, he thinks, his heart sinking. Then a clamor of shouts erupts from behind the wooden fence and he breaks into a run. As he nears the gate a crowd of workmen comes surging out toward him, surrounding a knot of struggling figures.

Peter cranes his neck trying to peer through the mob. With a start he sees that one of the men at the center of the melee is Tobias, his shirt torn and face bloodied, being pulled along by three burly company guards. Shoving forward, Peter grabs the nearest workman by the arm. "What's happening? What happened here?"

The workman—one Peter hasn't met before—grins stupidly. "The boy went crazy. He starts yelling, smashing them machines."

Abruptly Tobias wrenches himself free and wheels so he is almost facing Peter, his arms outstretched. "They're killing us!" he shouts. "You see? They're—"

Then the guards are on top of him, wrestling him to the ground. The crowd of workmen falls back as two uniformed policemen appear and join the fray. As Peter watches, Tobias is dragged off into a waiting police wagon. The doors are slammed behind him, and abruptly as it started the whole incident is over. The wagon rumbles away, the crowd slowly disintegrates into knots of muttering conversation.

Peter stands outside the construction-site gate, gazing after the departed wagon. All of this has been too sudden, too distant from his earlier private thoughts, for him to comprehend. He feels a hand on his shoulder and turns to find Paolo standing beside him.

"Paolo, what——?" He looks at the other man helplessly.

Some inner struggle is briefly visible on the Italian's face. "It is a brave thing," he says at last. "A stupid thing, and brave."

"But why? What did Tobias do?"

"You don't know?" Paolo smiles sadly. "Tobias and his brother, always they have been full of ideas. They hate the rich bosses, the capitalists." He shrugs. "So now he decides to do something."

"But——" Peter shakes his head, struggling with this idea and trying to reconcile the memory of Tobias's laughing face with the shouting, furious figure of a few moments ago. "Why start smashing the engines?" he asks. "Seems to me like they make the work easier."

Paolo regards him silently. "Sometimes I think rich men build machines so we become more like the machines ourselves," he says finally, then walks away.

PETER SPENDS the rest of the day fidgeting in the workshop. He tries to pass the time by working on a broken pneumatic hammer, but is so distracted that his efforts only damage it further. Turning Paolo's words over in his head, he remembers what Tobias said weeks ago about the managers of the subway project—*bloodsuckers, all of them.*

He has always been distantly aware of the very rich—the mine owners in Idaho and then, immeasurably wealthier, the royalty of this city—but until now he'd unconsciously assumed that such people existed on a separate plane from his own. Now the realization that these worlds might somehow be connected, perhaps one and the same, fills him with a kind of wonder and outrage.

He thinks about this, and then about her—whether he'll see her again, what it might mean if she does come back. In a dim way, he almost hopes that she won't reappear. Things would be simpler like that, he decides; although he can't say why, there would be a mysterious completeness to their brief acquaintance if it simply ended like this.

In the evening, after the excavation crews have left, when someone taps on the door Peter experiences a moment of disappointment as he opens it to find her standing outside. Beyond the workshop, silver twilight is fading into darkness. As he lets her in, he sees that she is pale and drawn, unsteady.

"How"—he stumbles over the words—"how are you?"

"Tired."

Awkwardly, he ushers her to the stool beside the stove and she sinks down onto it. He sits across from her as she leans toward the iron grate, staring at the coals, blank exhaustion on her face. The jangle of nervous energy in his chest makes it hard for Peter to stay still. Realizing that he is staring at her, he forces himself to look away. For a few minutes neither says anything.

After a time she draws a breath and straightens. "Forgive me. It has been a difficult day." She fumbles inside the folds of her skirt. "I have something for you."

Peter accepts the small book that she offers, noticing the expensive weight of the leather binding. "What's this?"

"It was written six hundred years ago, by an Italian named Dante Alighieri." She smiles at him. "As a girl I was never fond of it. Since arriving here, though, it has been very much in my thoughts."

Peter looks away from her and turns to the first page, reading

Midway upon the journey of life
I found myself within a forest dark
For the straightforward pathway
had been lost.

Beneath her gaze, he becomes conscious of how slowly his finger moves across the lines of text and stops.

"Thank you," he says, hoping she can't see how strangely this gift has moved him. It suddenly occurs to him to wonder where the book might have come from, if she's really as penniless as she claims. After a moment, though, he decides not to ask—not now, at least. "Maybe I've felt that way myself."

"Within a dark forest . . . ?"

"Something like that."

She studies his face, caught off guard by his statement and the previously unconsidered possibility that she and the mechanic might have something in common, although they clearly come from different worlds and speak different languages.

He closes the book and sets it aside on one of the workbenches, among the tools and oily rags, then looks up and meets her eyes. This time, after a moment, she is the one who looks away.

"You hungry?"

"Yes." She nods, the emptiness in her stomach too acute for her to listen to the shreds of her dignity that remain. She watches as he unwraps a paper parcel containing a loaf of coarse bread and a wedge of cheese. He rummages in a drawer and finds a rusty knife, which he wipes on his trouser leg before cutting two portions and handing her the larger.

They eat in silence. She forces herself to take small bites, glancing up at him occasionally. Each time, she catches him watching her with a questioning look on his face, and each time he looks away.

Outside the workshop a car backfires, and she jumps.

"What's wrong?"

"It's nothing." She shakes her head, settling back onto the stool. "Only nerves." For an instant, she has a vision of herself as she must look to the mechanic: a young woman with tangled hair and grimy features, sneaking, frightened, and alone—and she feels a surge of hatred for this pitiful person who wears her face. A moment later, though, as she leans closer to the fire's warmth, these battering fears recede by a few degrees.

"Nerves?" He peers at her. "What's got you nervous?"

"I—" she stops, draws a breath, and forces herself to continue. "Ever since I arrived here—since I traveled through time—I have been afraid."

"Afraid of what?" Peter leans toward her, feeling a jolt of excitement even as he recognizes this as more evidence that she's lost her mind.

"I hardly know. Nothing, really." She shakes her head. "Everything. Sometimes it has seemed to me as if I am being watched and followed. At other times it feels as if I simply do not belong here. As if my presence were an offense against the laws of nature in some way." She bites her lip, staring into the fire.

In fact, sitting in the warm enclosure of the dingy workshop beside the mechanic, these words sound faintly ridiculous in her own ears. She is startled to realize how much this setting and this man have come to feel familiar—a reaction, she reminds herself, she cannot afford to trust.

Peter leans back and tries to digest all of this. Yet again he finds himself at a loss, not because of the basic craziness of her story—lunacy is common enough—but because she doesn't act like a crazy person. Even though he doesn't know much about high society, the way she carries herself and her speech seem more like something out of a ballroom than from an asylum. And if she is rational, he tells himself, there should be some set of words that will make everything come clear. But what those words might be, he can't begin to guess.

"But people don't travel through time." He shakes his head. "Have you thought maybe you're wrong about all this? That maybe you imagined it?"

"Of course." She looks away, wondering why his disbelief—exactly what she herself would feel in his place—still wounds her.

"Couldn't you go to the police? They might help somehow?" Even as he offers this suggestion, Peter recognizes the impossibility of the idea; hard to imagine any kind of authority taking her seriously, even discounting the notorious abuses and unreliability of the city police force.

"I am inclined to doubt they would believe me." She smiles humorlessly. "Besides which, my family was never a favorite of the government of this country."

"What do you—" He leans back, trying to digest this statement. "What do you mean?"

"Our situation was always politically precarious. My father managed to win the sympathy of Grover Cleveland, but"—she sighs wearily, gazing into the fire—"he always had a gift for choosing the wrong horse. When Harrison was reelected as president, he promised to solve the 'Ohio Problem,' as they described my family and the Kingdom."

Peter frowns. "But Cleveland won."

She turns to peer at him, a startled expression on her face. "No. You are wrong. If he had won the election, I probably would not be sitting here now."

For a moment their gazes lock and he feels a shiver of something like electricity run down his spine. Then Peter looks away, confronted again by the basic fact of her craziness as he remembers his father's enthusiasm for "Uncle Jumbo," the plainspoken Democrat who would drive the elitist Republicans out of Washington, where they had held sway since the Civil War, bringing prosperity to the workingman. How his father had grieved when President Cleveland declined to run for a third term against McKinley, who sits in the White House now.

Neither of them says anything for a time. The fire on the stove crackles and collapses in a swarm of sparks.

She looks at his hands, callused and stained, and tries to picture him at work in the subway excavations. She thinks of the endless labor he has been part of, clawing through bedrock beneath the weight of the city, and shudders.

At the same time, there's something about the tunnels that makes her feel strangely drawn to them. To the darkness and stillness of the safe, unchanging world underground they will represent, once they are completed. And then a possibility occurs to her, an idea of such staggering scale that for an instant all the terror and uncertainty of her present situation briefly vanish, swept aside by sheer scientific curiosity. She has to restrain herself from jumping to her feet. Struggling to keep her voice level, she turns to Peter.

"Mr. Force, I am grateful for all you have done already. But I wonder if I might ask for one thing more—a small thing."

"And what's that?" Money, he thinks.

"To see the subway tunnels."

Startled, he glances at her—she stares back at him innocently. Despite this, Peter feels a jolt of paranoia. Recalling the guards outside the construction site and the daily searches, he remembers the rumors he's heard about attempts to sabotage the subway project: a rash of mistimed explosives and broken machines, blamed on the schemes of the omnibus-line owners, anarchists, or maybe— here Peter stumbles, recalling the chaos of a few hours ago—the work of men like his friend, like Tobias.

"Why do you want to see them?" he asks. "Not much to look at down there."

She tries to match his bland tone. "As a scientist, how could I not be curious?"

Her eyes and face are somehow urging him to agree—but with an effort, he shakes his head. "Workmen come early, and no visitors allowed. Besides, it's dangerous."

"Then you won't?"

"Can't."

She nods and looks back at the fire. He feels the withdrawal of her gaze as a physical loss. The dark curtain of her hair swings forward, obscuring all but the line of her profile. With this movement something tumbles from the neckline of her dress and Peter catches a glimpse of silver, a pendant on a chain that she conceals again before he can see it clearly. He begins to form a question about the necklace—which, like the book, doesn't make sense if she's truly a vagrant here—but she speaks first.

"Mr. Force, may I say something to you in confidence?"

He waits, feeling poised on a knife edge.

"Have you considered that the subway excavations might serve some larger purpose?"

"What?" The word escapes Peter before he has a chance to think, as Neumann's slurred voice comes back to him: *a secret meaning in their shape* . . .

"Think of a bird in flight, Mr. Force, trying to land on a moving train. Again and again, the rushing motion of the train sweeps it from its perch. This would be the exact problem encountered by a time traveler."

"What do you mean?" he asks weakly.

"In the same way that an aeronaut or sailor must contemplate his eventual point of landing, a traveler through time would have to do the same." She realizes how flimsy all of this must sound to him—but of course, she reflects, he is already convinced that her whole story is insane, so what more harm can be done?

She forces herself to continue. "If you were to travel to the past or the future, what would stop you from materializing inside a wall, or in front of a galloping horse? You would need to somehow find a safe place, an anchorage that would remain secure."

"So you think the subway diggings . . . ?"

"Perhaps. It is only a thought that came to me, just now."

For an instant Peter remembers the strange objects that have been uncovered in the excavations, like the enormous unidentifiable bones unearthed by the crew on Broadway—but this is madness, he reminds himself, shaking the thought away. "But there'd be trains in those tunnels. Sounds even more dangerous than a horse or a wall?"

She nods—because he is right, of course, she sees. Still, somehow, she can't quite abandon this idea, and the image of the silent excavations continues to tug at her.

That night, as they repeat their awkward bedtime ritual, he finds himself unable to believe her but also unable to completely disbelieve: her fantasy is so elaborate, so complete. It is like a game she is playing, he thinks, or a contest of wills between the two of them—to see who will drop their defenses, look away, and blink first.

Even so, Peter reminds himself, lying in his cot and listening for the sound of her breathing, it's also a game that's gone far enough. Insanity aside, there's something that strikes him now as too convenient about their meeting and her interest in the tunnels. Because isn't this exactly the kind of story a saboteur might use, to find a way in?

The only way to find out, he decides, is to show her the tunnels and watch how she acts. If she tries something, he'll be on his guard. And if she's just plain crazy—well, tomorrow, after the tunnels, he'll make his excuses and they'll go their separate ways.

COLD, and the sound of dripping water.

Peter's breath steams in the air and he shoves his gloved hands deeper into his pockets. Beside him she trembles, hugging her arms across her chest. Glancing over, he sees that she is more unearthly pale than ever, an unsteady brightness in her eyes. Together in the early darkness of Sunday morning, before the arrival of the excavation crews, they stand at the rough mouth of the subway tunnel on Canal Street.

Piles of dirty ice crunch underfoot, and icicles hang from the silent motor that drives the pneumatic hammers, Peter notices with a frown, ravaging the delicate lungwork of the bellows. The buildings and near-empty streets shine pearlescent with the dawn that has just started to glow in the east. He strikes a match with numb fingers and lights the two lanterns, adjusts the wicks, and silently hands one to her. Once again he tells himself that no harm can come from just showing her the place—and, clutching this reassurance, he leads her into the bowels of the earth.

He holds the lantern aloft, casting swinging beams of light over the rock walls, the makeshift wood pilings, and heaps of rubble. A few steps behind, she stumbles against an outcropping of stone and falls forward. He manages to turn and catch her before she hits the ground. Her lantern shatters, glass tinkling into the cavern silence.

She gasps and clings to him for a moment. Then both remember their sense of propriety and step apart. "I—" Peter swallows, mouth suddenly gone dry. "When I started, I fell all the time."

She nods, starting to answer—then all at once, she feels a hidden thronging in the air around her. A sense of presence, somewhere overhead. Her scalp tingles, a shiver running through her body.

Back. This word whispered into her ear, and she wheels to find its source—only underground gloom, jumping lantern shadows on the rough walls. A moment later, though, she hears another whisper, this time farther down the tunnel, almost inaudible, then another—

"Do you hear that?" She grips the mechanic's arm again, her fingers digging into his biceps.

"Hear what?"

She shakes her head. Something is down there, in the tunnels: she knows this with a sick certainty. Something without shape but infinitely hungry, a swarming multiplicity. A part of her brain is screaming at her to turn and leave now, before it is too late—

"You want to go on?" Peter asks.

Taking a breath, she tries to gather her courage. These thoughts and fears are only irrational fantasies, she reminds herself. Listening to them would be a sure sign of delusion. She nods.

"Yes." The word sticks in her throat.

He offers his arm and she takes it more conventionally. Slowly, their way illuminated only by a single lantern now, they continue into the pit.

It has been some weeks since Peter ventured into the tunnel-works, and he is startled to see that already the diggings have changed shape and grown. Neumann told him that the excavations had been expanded and hastened, but until now he had not appreciated how much. Along the length of the tunnel that leads down Canal Street, the beginnings of new side shafts have appeared at right angles to the main excavation, sloping downward. The longest of these new tunnels is still less than ten feet long—but remembering the sketch that Neumann showed him, Peter sees what they will become: a subterranean grid expanding through the city, echoing the matrix of streets above in the dark bedrock of New York.

She stares at the walls of the cavern, up and around. A swarming buzz fills her head, making it hard to think.

"Do you know what they plan here?" she whispers. "To what final destination the tunnels will extend?"

Peter nods and kneels to draw with his gloved finger in the frozen stone dust on the cavern floor. "Four stacked layers. All the same, see? Here"—he points—"Canal Street, Broadway, Seventh Avenue . . ."

She does not respond but something prompts him to look up at her. She stands rigidly, pale and trembling, staring into space.

"What is it?" he asks.

"Four layers." Her voice is a distant whisper. "And there will be trains running along all of them?"

"Only the top one. The sublayers are just access tunnels, not big enough for a train." In fact, Peter thinks, recalling the diagrams, the bottommost excavations will hardly be large enough for a man to crawl through, narrow passageways reserved for future genera-tions of the city's infrastructure—pneumatic tubes, telegraph wires, and the like, according to Neumann.

"So this is it," she murmurs, "the great trap . . ."

"What?"

But she ignores him. She feels the invisible presence around her, even nearer than before, straining to break through the surface of the air. She has to go—some part of her realizes these thoughts are irrational, but even more clearly she knows that if she stays, something terrible will happen. She turns and takes a staggering step toward the tunnel entrance.

"You all right?" he asks. "You look sick."

"No, I'm fine." She takes another step and almost falls. He hur-ries to support her, and together they start toward the surface.

"I'll take you to the workshop," Peter finds himself saying, despite his earlier resolution. "There's bread, tea—"

"No." Impatient with his solicitude, she pulls away from him as they emerge into the light. She feels feverish with urgency now: there is so little time, she thinks, and it takes all her willpower to stay where she is.

"Thank you for your offer, and all you have done for me al-ready. But I must go, I have already waited too long. . . ." She turns to him, wondering if he has understood anything. After all, she tells herself, he deserves some explanation. Despite the differences between them, the mechanic is a good man: his company and generosity have kept her alive and sane these past few days. Looking at his serious face, she feels a nameless welling in her chest, and again finds herself inexplicably longing to touch him.

And I could tell him, she thinks, that—

But in the end, of course, nothing. Such sentences always end in silence, no matter how they may begin—indeed, this is the very essence of fate: that which we never quite manage to say. So she looks at Peter, and forces herself to smile. "I must go," she says. "I hope I will see you again someday. Good-bye, and thank you for everything."

She starts to walk away, a slight figure in the morning gray. Watching her go he feels a kind of tearing inside his chest and tries to speak.

"Wait," he says. "Stop—"

But she does not wait or stop or look back, and he realizes that he has been discarded. And though he might have run after her, seized her arm and tried to persuade her, this isn't his character. So he puts his hands in his pockets and watches her walk away: through the construction site, into the city.

CHAPTER VI

THE SORCERER

I'VE SPENT MY SHARE OF HOURS SITTING IN LIBRARIES AND wrestling with textbooks on mathematics and physics. But despite my efforts, the truth is that I never had much talent for those subjects. Still, there's one small insight that occurred to me years ago, and that has haunted me ever since.

It goes like this: Draw a series of dots on a piece of paper. Each of these marks, in itself, represents a one-dimensional point. But regardless of the number or position of the dots, it's possible to draw a single line that passes through all of them, connecting them into a single two-dimensional shape.

Next, draw any number of additional lines. Again, in the second dimension, each scribble is a separate object. Moving into the third dimension, though, it's easy to picture a single solid (a cube, a cone, etc.) that contains all the lines within its volume. These exercises demonstrate the relationship between one dimension and the next: that is, each higher dimension creates a unity out of objects that seem unrelated in the dimension below.

Now consider the universe in which we live—the third dimension—and its relation to the fourth dimension, time. From where we stand the world is a jumble of disconnected perceptions, dimly linked by cause and effect. (I've read, for example, that each atom in our bodies once existed in the fiery heart of a star—but, sitting in my bachelor apartment, so much distance lies between me and that stellar origin that I can hardly imagine, much less really *believe*, the connection.)

Seen from the fourth dimension, though, everything would be different. These separations of time and space would cease to matter, as each object became one with its origins and future incarnations. From the other side of time, our separate, far-flung paths through the world—yours and mine—would finally come together. From that perspective, we would be part of a single perfect shape. We would be stars.

Of course, much as I wish for it, from where I sit this kind of vision remains impossible. All I have is the memory of the last time I saw you: looking at your stricken face in the darkness, understanding that you might be about to die, that I might have been the one who killed you.

And with the pain of that recollection comes a brief glimpse of the future. Before this is over, I've realized, I'll have to go back. The doctors—not to mention the shooting pains in my chest—tell me that I'm running out of time. So while I still can, I'll have to make one last visit to the crooked streets where it all happened between us. However much the prospect terrifies me (almost as much as the thought of not returning to the scene of the crime), I understand that I'll have to go.

So I've begun to make my preparations. I've closed the store and started speaking to a chirpy blond real estate agent about selling the shop and the apartment. (The memory of that plastic office and her plastic smile—when did the young learn such fierce artificiality?) And meanwhile, sitting at home, with an episode of *Family Secrets Live* playing on the television, I'm trying to reassemble the pieces of the past. It's getting closer, beginning to take shape—that's what I tell myself, studying the history books and the old photographs. Most of all I keep returning to the newspaper article I found in the antiques store along with the photograph, the one that I first read those years ago. From the *New York News-Digest* of January 16, 1901, clipped from the bottom of page 2, it says:

ASSAULT AT THE WALDORF

Gravest tragedy for the world of science was narrowly averted yesterday when an unidentified woman entered the residence of Mr. Nikola Tesla at the Waldorf-Astoria Hotel and set upon the inventor with a knife. According to police, Mr. Tesla, renowned for his discovery of new electrical motors and dramatic experiments, subdued the woman before contacting the proper authorities. Although shaken, the inventor was unharmed and accompanied police officers to the station where his assailant is now held. Exclusive *Digest* sources have revealed that, when asked for her name, the woman identified herself as Cheri-Anne Toledo, daughter of Louis Toledo of Ohio.

Mr. Tesla would not comment on the event other than stating, "I do not, nor have I ever known this woman." Mr. Tesla refused to answer further questions on account of his distraught and nervous state. The police are currently investigating the particulars of this case.[*]

Sitting in my apartment, I wonder what you would have made of it all: your sad laugh, or regretful shrug. And I wonder at how it comes to me so clearly, imagining the way it might have been. A young woman, shivering beneath the meager protection of a threadbare gray shawl, walking through the streets of New York toward the concrete fortress of the Waldorf-Astoria. The woman alone, and the approaching shadow of the man she is going to meet: a scientist who emerged from the impoverished countryside of eastern Europe to become one of the most famous individuals in the world. This is the man who was, for a time, known as the "Sorcerer of Electricity," and yet ended his life penniless and alone in a cheap hotel, tormented by madness and forgotten by the world.[†]

---

[*] "Assault at the Waldorf" in the *New York News-Digest*, January 16, 1901. A nearly identical article appeared in the *New York Post-Times* on the same day.
[†] Throughout his life, and with increasing severity, Tesla was prone to obsessive phobias, hallucinations, and fits of irrationality. As he would recall in his autobiography:

. . .

TESLA'S LABORATORY is a grand stage of a room. A single large space on the second floor of a nondescript warehouse south of Houston Street, it is dominated by the massive spiral transmitter that stands at its exact center: a wire-wrapped metallic cylinder fourteen feet high, from which crackle forth, at Tesla's command, tongues of electrical fire. The windows of the lab are hung with heavy velvet curtains to better allow the inventor (he employs no assistants) to observe electrical phenomena. Around the sides of the room stand four neat worktables bearing stacks of notebooks, batteries, and tools. In one corner a pair of armchairs, a coffee table, and a cabinet of liquors stand arranged on a threadbare Turkey rug. In the opposite corner of the laboratory is a leather fainting couch, where the inventor now lies.

Tall, gaunt, and pale, his lashes flutter as he mutters to himself in a mixture of German, English, Latin, and Serbian: indistinct words between languages. Six inches from his forehead as he sleeps is the blunt point of his Shadowgraph Ray emitter—in common terms, the barrel of an X-ray machine.

He wakes, opens his eyes, and pushes the Shadowgraph aside. Picking up pen and paper from the low table next to the couch, he

---

In my boyhood I suffered from a peculiar affliction due to the appearance of images, often accompanied by strong flashes of light, which marred the sight of real objects and interfered with my thoughts and action. . . . When a word was spoken to me the image of the object it designated would present itself vividly to my vision and sometimes I was quite unable to distinguish whether what I saw was tangible or not. This caused me great discomfort and anxiety.

(Nikola Tesla, *My Inventions: The Autobiography of Nikola Tesla*, Ben Johnson, ed., originally serialized in *The Electrical Experimenter* magazine, 1919.)

begins to sketch. The *mass anchor*—he half remembers this phrase from the dream—a huge, rough block of stone. A series of three small levers matched by three radiating spokes from a wheel. A pair of funnel-shaped magnets somewhere on the left—and that's all he can remember. He squeezes his eyes shut, hoping for some further detail, but nothing comes. He draws a breath and slowly stands. Tesla crosses to the console at the base of the spiral trans-mitter, throws a switch, and the humming that filled the room fades, receding into the walls as the lights on the Shadowgraph go dead. He leans, for a moment, against the console. As usual, he is tired.

He is always tired. But rest is a luxury that he cannot afford: there is too much to be done, too many frontiers to be forced open. This is why he limits himself to four hours of sleep a night—less, sometimes, but never more. For a moment he experiences a surge of anger at the injustices that surround him. The fluorescent light, the practical electric motor, long-distance power transmission over copper lines—all of these have been his inventions, and every time he has been robbed. Because I trusted too much, he rages inwardly, because I dared to dream of more than mere profit—

But this anger, too, he reminds himself, is a waste of time. With the iron discipline that he has practiced all his life Tesla forces himself to be calm. Straightening, he turns back to the table and examines the sketchbook. Each page bears a part of a diagram, fragments of the thing that has eluded him for so long. It is still more empty space than not, the barest suggestion of a shape—but he can feel its presence in the air around him, tantalizing, grow-ing closer, as slowly, year by year, he dredges it from the depths of sleep.

A wave of dizziness hits him, and he sways on his feet. Closing his eyes, Tesla leans against the table and suddenly remembers the moment, nineteen years ago now, when these dreams began. The moment of his first great invention, when something in his memory seemed to come unstuck.

He recalls how, after convalescing from a long illness, he had walked with his friend through a park in Budapest, where he had been working as a junior employee at the telephone exchange. The two of them had been discussing some inconsequential thing and enjoying the sunset. The sinking sun painted the sky orange, silhouetting the domes and orioles of the city. At a bend in the path, a group of little girls were playing jump-the-rope, laughing and chanting nonsense rhymes, while their mothers sat on a bench nearby.

As his eyes fell upon them, a passage from Goethe's *Faust* came back to him, and with it the vision of a rotating wheel of fire. It took him a moment to realize what it was: and when he understood, he fell to his knees with a cry and began to draw in the sand with a twig while his friend watched. There in the dirt, he sketched out a diagram of the motor that would earn him the acclaim of the world when he presented it before the American Institute of Electrical Engineers two years later. The simple, perfect secret of alternating-current electricity, which he had been studying ever since his undergraduate days.

And afterward it was as if this vision had opened a floodgate in his mind. That night, for the first time, he had seen the grail he has been pursuing ever since. In his dream Tesla had glimpsed an endless, shadowy row of inventions waiting to be discovered, and at its end a perfect, final machine. A device to tear a portal through the fabric of time itself: to free mankind from the tyranny of life, with its meager span of years. An idea of breathtaking audacity—and yet, he tells himself, not impossible. This is the machine he has been dreaming about ever since.

Now, as an incantation, he whispers the lines of Goethe that accompanied his first vision:

> *See how the setting sun, with ruddy*
> *glow,*
> *The green-embosomed hamlet fires.*
> *He sinks and fades, the day is lived*
> *and gone.*
> *He hastens forth new scenes of life*
> *to waken.*
> *O for a wing to lift and bear me on,*
> *And on to where his last rays*
> *beckon.*

And despite the fact that he is an avowed atheist, with these words Tesla finds himself thinking, as if in a moment of fervent prayer: Whatever Powers may exist, please let me find this one thing. A moment later, though, irritated with himself for this lapse into superstition, he opens his eyes and shakes his head.

A red droplet falls onto the notebook page, and, reaching up, Tesla realizes with a sense of irritation and disgust that his nose is bleeding—this has been happening to him more and more in the past year. He tilts his head back, shuddering at the metallic tang in his mouth, and stanches the flow with a white handkerchief.

When the bleeding has finally stopped, Tesla busies himself. He brews a pot of coffee using a Bunsen burner and efficiently consumes it; washes his face, buttons on a fresh collar, and places a dab of cologne behind each ear. He regards himself for a moment in the mirror—elegant as always in his suede boots, tails, cane, top hat, and gloves—before descending to the street. Hailing a horse-drawn cab, he directs the driver to take him uptown, to the World Club, where he has recently become a member.

The World is dark, all wood paneling and leather, steeped in nearly a century's worth of patriarchy and wealth. The club occupies the first three floors of an old brownstone, stolid and anonymous: on the first floor are the library, the sitting room, and the refectory, while the second floor houses the bar and "club room," where members drink, dine, and smoke cigars. The third floor contains the kitchens and the servants' quarters.

The cab pulls up at the door—"Fifteen cents, sorr," the driver says, turning to face his passenger. Tesla regards the cabbie's sagging jowls with distaste, and imagines for a moment that he can smell the sourness of the other man's breath. All his life he has disliked contact with others' flesh and has an almost obsessive fear of bacteria, once telling a friend: "I would not touch the hair of another person except, perhaps, at the point of a revolver." Now, he shudders and slides the woolen rug from his lap, handing the coins forward with his fingertips.

"Thank you, sorr." The reply of an automaton, the inventor thinks, climbing out of the cab and crossing the sidewalk. As he mounts the steps, he absentmindedly wipes his gloves with his handkerchief. A liveried valet opens the door for him and he enters.

On the second floor of the club, Tesla sinks into an armchair and orders his customary buttered roll and four cups of coffee from a hovering waiter. While eating his breakfast, he leafs through a copy of the London *Times*, glancing occasionally at his pocket watch. He allows himself fifteen minutes of this leisure before summoning the waiter again.

"Another coffee," he murmurs, "and my mail."

Sipping the fifth cup, he surveys his correspondence. Tesla has his professional mail forwarded to the club from the Waldorf—a more civilized setting, he thinks, in which to conduct business. His rooms at the grand hotel are luxurious, but despite the eagerness with which he sought them—suites at the Waldorf are in short supply, and Tesla has always been an avid social climber—he now finds that he spends less and less time there. Although the maids visit daily, the odor of his own body has begun to pervade the place: the damp smell of his own discarded skin and hair thick in the velvet curtains and upholstery. The smell disgusts him, and though rationally he knows that the lab must be the same, somehow the tang of electricity in the air masks the whiff of mortal decay.

Flipping through his letters, Tesla finds notices from assorted charitable societies, an invitation to perform at a symposium on Electrical and Parapsychophysical Phenomena, a bill from his tailor, a bill from the Waldorf, and a letter bearing a Boulder, Colorado, postmark. Puzzled by this last item, he opens the envelope—and finds inside another bill, for the overdue rent on a horse stable in Colorado Springs.

The inventor frowns. He can clearly remember the boredom and inconvenience of that miserable mountain village, where he had conducted a series of high-elevation experiments last autumn, but can recall nothing about a stable. No, Tesla decides, discarding the letter: it must be some feeble attempt at fraud, or simply an outright mistake. His own memory, after all, has never failed him.

He turns to the invitation to the symposium. For a moment he contemplates it—then, with a sudden violent motion, tears it to pieces, which he deposits in a pile beside his now empty cup. He takes a deep breath. It maddens him, that to support himself in something resembling style he is forced to give these public demonstrations on a regular basis.

The requests for his presence onstage are frequent: he is a virtuoso showman, dramatic and eloquent, the most sought after of all the inventors and scientists who tout their discoveries on the stages of every great city of the world. And there is a secret part of him, a part he despises, that loves the breathless attention of his audience. The thunder of applause as he strides before the curtain with electric flames shooting from his fingertips and head, brandishing his fluorescent tubes like rapiers. But at the same time, the daylight part of himself knows that these performances are base, they are low; they are *acting*, one rung up from prostitution. They are circuses of electricity for the drooling masses, and he is the trained beast on display. Stand on your hindlegs, like so, for the crowd, Sorcerer—

But all these worries will soon be unimportant, Tesla reminds himself, searching for calm. When the time comes, none of this will matter. And he shivers, feeling suddenly cold despite the two fires that crackle in the stone fireplaces. A certain brittle ache that has crept into his bones in recent months.

Secretly, he wonders whether this grippe might not be connected to the Shadowgraphs. Despite the fact that all the inventors involved in roentgen research have assured the world that no harm can come from the rays, now and then doubts creep up on him. The power of these rays, their penetrating force—might they not affect the body in some secret way, altering the invisible currents of blood and breath? But whatever the consequences, he knows that he cannot stop using them.

He has never been one to spare himself in the pursuit of science, and the way they stimulate his dreams—nothing else has come close, neither opium nor liquor nor any of the other tinctures and potions with which he has experimented. Although Oliver Lodge and the other inventors who have begun tinkering with X-rays grasp the basic mechanical principle, none of them—all fools, Tesla thinks—has understood their true potential.

That potential, which Tesla alone seems to perceive, is why he chose the name "Shadowgraph," a term first used by Kierkegaard in *Either/Or* to describe "sketches derived from the darker side of life . . . woven from the tenderest moods of the soul." It is for these effects that Tesla now spends at least an hour each day sitting under the X-ray machine, bathed in its invisible radiation, allowing the Shadowgraphs to peel away the film of waking consciousness so that he can glimpse the truth that hovers just beyond his grasp on the other side.

He glances at his pocket watch again—a quarter to ten. He snaps shut his satchel and stands. Time to go.

Refusing the valet's offer to hail a cab, he steps down onto the sidewalk, adjusting his hat against the January wind and turning up the collar of his coat. At the corner, he stops short as a horse-drawn phaeton swerves narrowly around a hand trolley, slushing up sheets of icy mud. Overhead a messenger-dirigible chugs past, a monstrous tangle of smokestacks and iron flanges. Glancing over his shoulder, he turns onto Broadway.

Like most major thoroughfares of New York, Broadway is a morass of carts, omnibuses, automobiles, and wagons that jostle together in the street, and the sidewalks are packed with vendors, pedestrians, pickpockets, and beggars. Yet despite all this, a space free of elbows, phlegm, and insult opens itself before the lean monochrome figure of the inventor in his tails and top hat, a silent acknowledgment. Ignoring the chaos of the city, he strides down the street, in the direction of the Waldorf-Astoria.

STANDING IN THE half-darkness behind a fold of curtain, she listens to the silence of Tesla's rooms and tries not to breathe. Around her, the space is empty, its stillness punctuated by the soft ticking of a mantelpiece clock.

Although she has spent days imagining the difficulties involved in reaching this place, her passage through the Waldorf and into the inventor's suite had been almost disappointingly easy. In the grand lobby of the hotel, surrounded by potted palms and rich Oriental rugs, it had taken nearly all of her courage to approach the dullest-looking of the uniformed bellhops. But despite her ragged appearance, with the note she had forged on a scrap of Tesla's letterhead scavenged from a dustbin behind the hotel, a few murmured words of French and her best impression of royal hauteur, the bellhop was persuaded. He showed her to this room, unlocked the door, and, with a lascivious wink, departed, leaving her alone to survey the space.

Wandering through the immaculate luxury of the suite, she tried to imagine its occupant. The rooms felt ghostly and unused, the only signs of habitation a stack of letters on the nightstand, a row of identically laundered suits hanging in the closet, and a clinically clean razor beside the bathroom sink.

Briefly, she let her hands run over each of these things, trying to conjure the presence of the man she remembered, or at least—an inward twinge—imagined that she remembered. The dark sheen of his hair, his sharply Roman profile and gaunt cheeks, his eyes that never rested for longer than an instant on any one thing. But despite her efforts, the trace of Tesla's life here eluded her.

The paranoid thought occurred to her that she might be in the wrong suite altogether. She crossed back to the bedroom and inspected the stack of letters, discovering that they were indeed addressed to the inventor. Her eyes fell on the date written at the top of one page—January 15, 1901—and she felt a wave of nausea. Another reminder of the impossibility of her situation, of the rational conclusion she still struggled to avoid: that she had simply lost her mind.

But Tesla was the one person who might be able to explain everything, she reminded herself. And if he cannot answer . . . a possibility too terrible to contemplate.

She closed her eyes, remembering an evening, years ago, when she had walked with the inventor along the manicured garden paths outside her father's mansion. In total, Tesla had spent less than six months in Ohio, under the patronage of Louis Toledo, and while there kept largely to himself and his own experiments. Even so, that time still seemed like a magical interlude to her, a blossoming of scientific possibilities she had previously hardly imagined.

On that evening, it had been sunset and overhead the sky glowed with surreal perfection. They had walked side by side, she in her blue working dress, he tall and angular in his black suit. In the dying light, the roses lining the path were shaded from deepest red to rust, the sunset a vast cliff of orange clouds towering miles high above the gardens and lake.

She looked up at the shadowy planes of his face and wished, for a moment, that she had some way of photographing this: that some film existed which could capture these colors. In theory, she thought, it should be possible to develop a color-sensitive film; it would simply be a matter of layering different gelatins, each responsive to a different spectrum. And maybe, she mused, someday . . .

"See how the setting sun with reddish glow, the green-embosomed hamlet fires," Tesla murmured, his English formal and faintly accented.

"What did you say?" She turned to him.

"Ah, nothing. Only a line from a poem that suddenly came to me."

She nodded and they walked on in silence, along the garden path.

"And when will we reveal," she asked at length, "what we have been building in that basement?"

"What you have been building," he corrected. "I have only lent a few ideas. You know my real research lies elsewhere." Tesla gestured sweepingly. "What we have worked on together may conquer distance, but the adversary I wish to defeat is time itself."

"Of course." She smiled at him and then looked away, thankful for the concealment of dusk. So strange, she thought, the choices of the heart. That it should be this man, with his arrogance and melancholy moods, who affected her so. A response that she had carefully hidden from both her father, who would never approve of the match, and from Tesla himself, because if he knew, she reflected, it would all be over in an instant. I would cease to be a peer and become only another woman to be avoided.

With an effort, she pushed these thoughts away and turned her attention to the progress they had made over the last few weeks.

The moments of almost godlike exaltation when, after struggling for days with a problem, the solution became clear in a flash of simple, blinding *rightness*. The feeling was an addiction, and like her mentor she found herself more and more forgetting to sleep and eat, forgetting the world in its pursuit. Sometimes she was almost frightened by what was happening to her—but at the same time, she realized, nothing could have induced her to give it up.

"In any case," Tesla continued, "the device should not be made public until you have proven that it works. That is, if it ever does."

"Then you are still skeptical?"

The inventor shrugged. "Whatever my opinions may be, hearing the whispers of Washington, I fear your research may be interrupted." He stopped, turning toward her. "Although I pray it does not come to that." Tesla's forehead creased briefly and, despite herself, she felt a small surge of happiness.

She tried to match his tone. "I am grateful for your concern."

For a moment they stood awkwardly facing each other—then he nodded and stepped away.

"It is late. Good night, mademoiselle. Sleep well."

"Good night, Mr. Tesla." A small, unnamed hope collapsed inside her.

As always, that night they had not embraced, or even touched. The inventor continued down the garden path, and after a moment she had turned and started to walk in the opposite direction, back toward the mansion.

Now, in the stillness of Tesla's overheated room at the Waldorf, she remembered this—and then her heart skipped a beat at the sound of footsteps approaching in the corridor outside. Trying to remain calm, she slipped behind the heavy curtain to wait, trying not to breathe.

TESLA OPENS THE DOOR and cautiously steps through. In the hallway, he'd heard, or imagined, a rustling sound inside—but the room seems undisturbed and empty. The overstuffed armchair and couch of the sitting room, the cold fireplace and cut-crystal ashtray on the end table, appear untouched. Only—the inventor sniffs delicately—the smell is wrong: a whiff of something like an alleyway.

For a moment, Tesla considers leaving to get help, then reminds himself that he has ways of dealing with intruders. Locking the door behind him, he crosses into the bedroom and his fastidious gaze lights upon the nightstand, where a stack of letters stands slightly askew. He starts toward the dressing room, and then another rustle, nearby, prompts him to wheel as she half falls out from her hiding place.

They stare at each other. Taking in her ragged dress and tangled hair, the feverish pallor of her features, Tesla takes a step backward. For her part, she abruptly wants to cry. She struggles to control herself, searching for a flicker of recognition on his face.

Finally, after what seems like hours, she forces herself to speak. "It's me."

He stares at her silently.

"I almost died waiting," she says. "Thank God you are here."

He takes another step away. His mind is racing. His first thought is that she might be a spy, sent by Edison or Marconi or another competitor. But this is something else, he decides. Some wretched woman who has decided that she is in love with him, most likely. He has been the recipient of such advances before and, if anything, this disturbs him more than the idea of industrial espionage.

"What do you want?" Tesla demands. Avoiding sudden movements, he backs up to put half a room between them. "Who let you in?"

"I tricked the porter—and I do apologize. Only, I had to see you, I—" The words tumble out in a rush. She finds herself laughing, near hysterical with relief. Soon everything will be answered, she thinks, it will all be over. "I am being watched, you see."

"Who sent you?" The inventor scowls at her.

"Do you really not recognize me?" Her voice cracks. "How is this possible, how—" She shakes her head, initial giddiness suddenly replaced by despair.

A madwoman, Tesla thinks with an inward shudder. He imagines the contagion of her sickness swarming invisibly through the air toward him. Fumbling behind his back, he pretends to search through his pockets for a handkerchief. While his hands are out of sight he reaches inside his left sleeve and nudges a lever connected to the device concealed near his wrist. A small nozzle swings out to rest beside his thumb. He shakes his head. "Should I? Because I do not."

"Then tell me about this," she says, raising a piece of paper. It is a sketch of the machine from his dreams, he sees with disbelief.

"Where did you get that?" Shocked, he takes a step toward her. The stench of her proximity makes his head swim. "Tell me, where? It was not in this room."

"Nikola, please." She stares, silently pleading, opening her arms to him. Gritting his teeth, he reaches out as if to meet her embrace. Then, when she is only a step away, he flicks his thumb over the lever.

Her eyes go wide as the device attached to his wrist ejects a mist of chloroform in her face. She coughs, chokes, and tries to stumble away, but it's already too late. Her body goes limp, collapsing into the inventor's arms, and then—as he steps hastily away—to the floor.

Tesla stands there for a moment, regarding her motionless shape. At the sight of her face, he experiences an odd tug of almost recollection: as if he has seen her somewhere before—although where, he cannot place. But this is impossible; his memory has always been perfect. Shrugging the sensation away, he goes into the washroom to throw out his soiled gloves and repeatedly wash his hands.

WHEN HE IS satisfied that the last traces of her touch have been cleansed away, Tesla straightens his collar and steps back into the sitting room. As he slides a cigarette out of the slim silver case in his pocket, lights it, and exhales twin streams of smoke through his nostrils, he is annoyed to discover that his hands are shaking. He crosses to the desk and lifts the telephone receiver, but before Tesla can ask the operator to be connected with the police there is a knock at the door. For an instant the inventor hesitates, trying to calculate how long the effects of the chloroform will last. Long enough, he decides. He replaces the receiver in its cradle and pulls the bedroom door closed, concealing the girl's motionless figure, then straightens his jacket and crosses to admit his visitor.

The man that Tesla lets into his chambers is nondescript, of average height with brown hair, wearing a rumpled brown suit. A miserable specimen, Tesla thinks, but this is one reason he was picked for his present role. Smith is his name, or at least the name that he has chosen to use.

"Good morning," Tesla says. "Would you care for a drink?"

"Gin and tonic, if you don't mind." Smith sinks, uninvited, onto the couch.

Frowning at this obvious weakness, the inventor goes to the liquor cabinet and efficiently constructs the cocktail.

"So," he says, handing the other man his drink and stubbing out his cigarette. "We have some business to discuss."

Smith nods. "The work continues. They're digging six days a week now—the first level is almost complete."

Through the tall windows behind the couch the sun is shining in Tesla's face, making Smith appear as a glowing silhouette, clothed in light. Something about this image disturbs him. *Omen. Harbinger*—these words come to the inventor's mind unbidden—the figure of a man consumed by brilliance—but it's just nerves, he reminds himself, the aftereffects of the woman's unexpected appearance. He crosses to the window and tugs the curtains closed, then sits across from his visitor. "And have they found anything?"

"Some old plumbing, that's all. But there's this—" Smith removes a small notebook from his coat pocket and tears out a page, sliding it across the table to the inventor. Tesla glances at the scrap, instantly committing it to memory, and then tucks it into his pocket.

"This is the complete plan?"

Smith nods and gulps his drink. "That's it—no doubt about it."

"It's as I expected, then." Tesla steeples his fingers and crosses his legs, trying to interject a conversational tone into the encounter. He hates all this deceit and spying—not for moral reasons but for aesthetic ones: because he should be above requiring such tools, because it entails working with individuals whose language and manners are ugly. "It's typical of Edison, don't you think? The approach of brute force."

The other man shrugs. The round lenses of his glasses glint with stray reflections, turning his face into an eyeless expanse of pasty skin. "Whatever you say."

"Tell me, what is his mood like these days? Does he seem anxious to you? Confident? Satisfied?"

"Couldn't tell you. Don't see him much, personally—there's a dozen managing assistants above me. Don't get me wrong, though. I'm your man." He gestures with his notebook. "This was only finalized yesterday." Smith drains his glass and sets the empty tumbler on the table, eyeing it regretfully.

"I understand." Tesla sighs and massages his temples for a moment, then freezes as he hears a faint movement behind the closed door. He sits very still, listening—but there is only silence. With an effort, he forces his attention back to the man in front of him. "There is no need to stoke my enthusiasm, Mr. Smith. Your work has been entirely adequate."

"Well, good. But there's a small problem."

"And what is that?"

"Well . . ." Smith pauses and eyes the inventor's elegant figure before continuing. "This is getting dangerous for me. Risky. Security's been tightened around the lab."

"And therefore you want more money," Tesla concludes. "Has it ever occurred to you, Mr. Smith, that the work I am performing—that we are performing—is a service to all mankind?

Some persons, in your place, would consider material renumeration to be beside the point."

Smith laughs a short, unpleasant laugh. "Speak for yourself, Professor."

For a moment, Tesla considers speaking his mind—or better yet, simply throwing out this gluttonous oaf—but an instant later remembers himself. At this point, time is too much of the essence for a replacement to be found. Withdrawing an envelope from his pocket, he hands it to the other man with his fingertips.

"Next time, there will be something extra for you—provided that the information you have given me today is accurate."

"It is." Smith pockets the envelope, visibly restraining himself from examining its contents. "By the way," he asks, trying and failing to sound indifferent, "exactly what are you looking for down there?"

"That," Tesla says coldly, "is not your concern. All you need do is inform me if anything unusual is found in the tunnels, or shows up at the lab." The inventor rises to his feet. The other man does the same.

"Give my regards to the boys at Menlo Park." Tesla does not offer his hand.

Forcing a smile, Smith nods and the inventor ushers him out. When he is gone, Tesla picks up the telephone and informs the concierge that the police are needed in his rooms. Then he settles back in his chair again, closes his eyes, and thinks about the past and the future.

CHAPTER VII

THE BRIDGE

YESTERDAY WAS MY BIRTHDAY—NOT THAT THE EVENT HOLDS MUCH significance anymore. For the last decade, each turning of the calendar has meant the same thing: a steady progression from *old* to *older.** In the afternoon, carrying my stack of frozen dinners home from the supermarket, I passed a vacant lot where a new apartment building is being built. A group of shirtless construction workers were resting in the shade outside, laughing and talking. I smiled and nodded at them; they fell silent, staring stonily back at me. For a moment I felt hurt by their reaction. Then I caught my reflection in a shop window and remembered why. From where they sat, in a private world of youthful camaraderie, I was an unwelcome intruder from the wrong end of life: a reminder of still-distant mortality.

---

* Of course, in these days just after the millennium, it seems like almost everyone is feeling something similar: abruptly aged by the realization that rounding this chronological corner, which we'd all secretly hoped might make everything new again, changed nothing. That history's teetering pile of days only kept growing, the mistakes of the past still as present and near as they've always been.

As I shuffled away, I realized that I could hardly blame them. Some mornings nowadays, after the forgetting of dreams, the gray-haired ghost in the mirror is an unpleasant shock even to me.

Of course, the most significant ways I've changed over the years since our time together go far deeper than the simple brutalities of old age. Rather, they are the result of hours spent studying history, of the shelves of books read and community college courses endured, alterations measured not in wrinkles or infirmity but in the drift of despair and hope, conviction and disbelief.

Still, despite all this, I can't shake my unfashionable, old man's notion that the self is something more constant than postmodern thinkers claim. That, despite all the ways in which we change over time, and the passage of memory into forgetting, somewhere, in each of us, some essential thing remains the same.

For me, more than anything else it's a certain sense of bewilderment that has always been the common thread of my days. This feeling of surprise at the strangeness of the world, of not quite fitting in. That sensation was most acute, I think, when I arrived in Los Angeles three decades ago. During those first months even the most ordinary things (passing cars, the sheen of a plastic fork, my own shocked face in a mirror) would leave me stunned with wonder and despair.

Now my bags are packed and I'm making preparations to leave this city. And that old feeling of disorientation is back, stronger than ever.

In part, this is a result of the unexpected news that I'm a millionaire. During the last ten years, apparently, the little retail space where the antiques store is located has gained enough value that I thought the real estate agent had lost her mind when she told me what I could expect to get. The problem (already a point of tension between us) is that I'm not interested in being rich. At this point in life, wealth seems more like a burden than a blessing.

Even more than this news, however, it's the past that has me off balance these days. Walking alone through the city streets, I'll start thinking about you and all the ways it could have been different—and then suddenly find myself, as if just woken up, baffled and blinking on some honking street corner, or standing in a fluorescent supermarket corridor, or sitting alone at the dark little bar near my apartment, at a loss for what I'm doing in this ill-fitting world of unknown faces and chaotic shapes, where all that makes sense are my memories of a vanished time, and you.

THROUGH THE AMBER LENS at the bottom of Peter's glass, the saloon contracts around him into a jumble of figures and voices—a scene that hardly changes when he lowers the whiskey and leans back, gazing drunkenly around.

This is the Harp Pub, an Irish saloon near the river, where men from the subway crews sometimes meet. There are six of them gathered now around the battered wooden table: Peter, Paolo, Michael, and three others from the subway crew—Saul, Jan, and a blond man whose name Peter never heard, or has forgotten. Around them the space is crowded with the noise and heat of other drinkers, the air thick with grease and paraffin smoke.

"Here's to Tobias," Michael says, lifting his glass for the twentieth time of the evening. He wobbles to his feet, nearly upending the table, and raises his voice. "A more shit-for-brains, scum-toothed, clockslob sneak of an arsehole brother who'd puke"—he pauses for breath—"who'd puke in his own beer and drink it with a grin, did a man never have!"

"Tobias!" Peter and the others echo, raising their own glasses. Michael drains his whiskey and collapses back into his chair, angrily wiping a hint of wetness from his eyes.

"Damn," he mutters, "damnit."

Peter looks away, at a loss for what to say. Since their arrival here, Michael's toasts have become progressively more incomprehensible and vulgar, and Peter—along with his companions around the table, he guesses—is still struggling to understand what it means.

Gazing up at the low ceiling overhead, Peter recalls the look on Michael's face when he'd knocked on the subway workshop door, two hours ago now. The absolute emptiness of Michael's expression when he'd delivered the news that his brother, Tobias, was dead. An accident in his cell, the police had said.

Now, with the room reeling around him, Peter remembers this—and it's not his place to judge, he reminds himself, if this is what Michael needs. If these obscenities can somehow substitute for, or speak, his grief.

Michael raises his glass again and starts to slur: "To that twat-sucking, dog-fucking, piss-drinking, pus-bleeding, sewer-reeking b-bog Irish disgrace of a . . ."

They drink, and drink again, each of them and the pub itself growing steadily more unsteady with the noise of other conversations, comings and goings, interruptions and digressions, liquor spilled or misplaced or both, the fumes of cheap cigarettes, a third bottle of whiskey opened and emptied—

A waitress passes their table and Michael lunges at her, shouting for another round while behind him Paolo tries desperately to signal "No" with throat-slashing gestures. The new bottle of whiskey arrives. Michael lurches to his feet, this time actually upsetting the table, which overturns in a crash of shattering glassware, so that the other occupants of the pub—or at least those at nearby tables—turn to stare. Michael lifts the whiskey bottle over his head. "Come!" he cries. "Come, this way—" And ignoring the onlookers, and the protests of Saul and Paolo, he makes for the door of the pub, leaving Peter and his companions to trail behind, mumbling apologies to the waitresses as they go.

They exit the Harp, ducking between the Scylla and Charybdis of teetering beer barrels and a horse-drawn carriage emerging from the neighboring stable yard as they reach the sidewalk. Michael is storming ahead, bottle hoisted aloft, down the street and around the corner.

"We must stop him, yes?" Paolo grabs Peter's arm.

Peter nods, concentrating on putting one foot in front of the other. In some distant part of his brain, he understands that Paolo is right—but another inner voice is whispering to keep going and follow Michael into drunken wreckage and madness. Because she is gone, out there in the city somewhere, in the vastness of the city without him.

She is gone, and now Tobias is gone, Peter thinks confusedly, focusing on the cobblestones underfoot. Paolo says something and Jan says something else that he doesn't hear. He thinks of Tobias's laughing face and pushes the memory away. Because he is, and she is, only a stranger in the chaos of the world.

In his coat pocket, he feels the weight of the book that she gave him. He has been carrying it since, although each time Peter has tried to look inside, he's found himself frustrated by an impene- trable wall of words: a tangle of text that only hints at a hidden landscape of meaning, beyond his grasp.

With a burst of drunken inspiration, he pulls out the book and opens it at random, moved by the notion that maybe now, through the mechanics of chance, the text will reveal some answer to—

"*And wouldst thou think how at each tremulous motion trembles within a mirror your own image,*" he reads, slurring slightly.

"What is that?" Paolo demands.

Peter shakes his head, returning the book to his pocket. "Nothing."

Michael rounds another corner, and, following him, suddenly they find themselves facing the East River, the nighttime-shadowed symmetry of the Brooklyn Bridge overhead. Michael stops at the low railing that edges the dark current

"This one"—Michael coughs, chokes, then continues—"this is for you, Toby. Always said we could—we'd cross this. This bloody river. Make our fortune out west."

In a moment of clarity, through the whiskey-laden tangle of his thoughts, Peter realizes that they're looking eastward over the water. But that's not important, he realizes, the important thing is this moment, this night, this—

"This drink's on me," Michael mumbles. "I miss you, Brother."

He uncaps the whiskey and upends it, liquor gurgling into the water below. Peter and the others stand silently. When the bottle is empty, Michael lets it drop. It makes a small splash, and leaves a ring of silver ripples, which disappear almost before they have formed.

Paolo puts his arm around Michael's shoulders. Michael bows his head.

Peter closes his eyes. A crowd of emotions knot in his stomach: most of all, sorrow for the loss of Tobias, sorrow for the strange woman who wandered across his path for a few days, and the suddenly aching memory of everything he left behind, coming here—and also anger at this weight of the past that keeps finding him each time forgetting seems within reach. He looks up at the bridge, searching for the sense of calm that came to him the last time he visited this place, with Paolo.

Abruptly he is seized by a need for action: as if the right gesture could cut through the tangle of grief that aches inside his chest. A longing for the clarity of open space. Before he quite knows what he is doing, Peter crosses to the bridge and starts to climb.

Straddling the bundle of cables that arcs upward to the central support towers of the bridge—the twined metal thicker than a man's torso—Peter pulls himself forward. Thirty feet up, pressed against the steel armature, he cannot find another handhold and stops. Remembering himself, he looks down. Traffic passing, the dark water of the river—a chasm of air to swallow his falling body. His heart begins to pound and he reaches out for a protruding bolt to steady himself. As he does, his foot slips and he loses his balance, sliding backward. Managing to catch himself, he clings there, panting and dizzy with fear and adrenaline.

For a long moment he hangs motionless, realizing the craziness of what he's doing. With a great effort he forces himself to raise his head and look up at the rise of the bridge, fighting the fingers of panic that have gripped his legs and stomach.

From below, he faintly hears Paolo and the others shouting:

"—crazy!"

"Careful, what are you—"

These words float up to him, and Peter takes a deep breath, willing himself to think clearly. This is not so different, he tells himself, from the cliffs he scaled in Idaho. He closes his eyes and presses his forehead against the cold skin of the bridge. Another breath, and another. He decides that he's ready to start back down.

Except that suddenly, before he can do so, he feels himself cupped and pushed upward again. He tries to pause, to consider this, but his body will not obey, hands and feet finding purchase with a skill he doesn't recognize as his own.

The others are still calling to him, but as he ascends their voices change.

"—almost there! Steady—" he hears Michael shout.

"That the way—" This from Paolo, encouragement taking the place of warning, as if somehow his ascent could repay, in some small part, Tobias's death. He continues to climb, emptying his mind of everything except physics and points of leverage, momentum and gravity's contract.

Finally, exhausted, hands cut and numb, Peter reaches the top of the bridge tower. Two hundred feet above the river, buffeted and invisible in the nighttime wind, he looks out at the lights of the city below. The drift of barges toward the bay, the lights from a thousand different windows blinking on and off to reveal the ciphered lives of a hundred households' movements, waking and sleep.

As his breathing and pounding heart slow, Peter looks downward to see his companions standing at the foot of the bridge, waving their arms and jumping around each other in a kind of drunken dance. He watches them, and then turns back to the silhouettes of New York.

Surveying the city, the thought comes to him that the metropolis is like a single gigantic machine. The city is an impossibly complex mechanism of betrayal and justice, and he and its other inhabitants are counters moving through its channels, units of a supreme calculus that allots each in turn their fate. And if this is true, he thinks, then his presence here must be more than an accident: there must be some kind of purpose to it all that he can't yet recognize or comprehend.

He sits there, unseen and all-seeing, for a long time. Finally, when the cold grows so intense that he can't stop his teeth from chattering, he starts back down. It's only during his descent that he begins to wonder: if New York is an immense machine, what kind of engine could power a device of such scale?

CHAPTER VIII

THE FINANCIER

THREE DAYS AFTER HER ARREST, THE NEW YORK CITY POLICE
Department released a woman calling herself Cheri-Anne Toledo
into the custody of Peter Force.[*] In itself, this was an unusual
occurrence. Under normal circumstances, even if Tesla had decided not to press charges, as a presumed madwoman she still
would have been confined in one of New York's public asylums:
Throgs Neck, Arkham, or Bedlam.[†]

---

[*] The terse entry in the police logbooks simply reads:

> #19010115-84: *Charges dropped by N. Tesla, suspect released into custody*
> *P. Force.*

(Courtesy New York Police Dept., 5th Precinct Blotter, January 18, 1901, approx.
page 65, New York Police Department Historical Society, New York.) The case
number (#19010115-84) refers principally to the date; case numbers were as-
signed chronologically so this case number reads: year (1901), month (01), day
(15), the eighty-fourth case logged.

[†] Names that still have the power to terrify, and with good reason. In 1901,
particularly in the United States, mental illness was the subject of superstitions

Less than twelve hours later the police would be called again, this time to arrest two individuals matching the descriptions of Force and Cheri-Anne, at the mansion of the financier John Pierpont Morgan.

Why was she released from jail? And why was she taken to visit the financier? To be honest, I don't really *know* the answers (and of course the history books have nothing to say on the subject) but it's easy enough to guess. After all, what would it have taken for Morgan to orchestrate these events? A murmured suggestion, an offhand mention to some lieutenant, is all that would have been necessary.

But then, who was John Pierpont Morgan? None of my textbooks seem to agree. According to some, Morgan was the epitome

---

dating back to the Middle Ages. Although at the time, across the Atlantic in Germany and Austria, a revolutionary new understanding of the psyche was beginning to develop in the works of Freud, Krafft-Ebing, and others, these theories had barely reached the academics of America, much less the judicial system. Lunatics were believed by police, legal authorities, and common folk alike to be criminals; insanity was seen as a kind of moral failing.

Because of this, the mentally ill were objects of fear and loathing. They were locked up in either prisons or mental hospitals that were, if anything, worse than the prisons. The "treatment" that patients received at these hospitals was founded on the notion that, since madness was a moral lapse, the insane needed to be punished until they saw the error of their ways. They were doused with freezing water, confined in cages for the public to jeer at and scold (often in churchyards on Sundays, as examples to the faithful of the effects of sin), beaten, starved, electrocuted . . . .

Even before I found your photograph and began writing this, I'd spent my share of sleepless nights tormented by the thought of such a fate. How could I not? After all, I'd landed in Los Angeles (in the Land of Psycho: psychotherapy, psychopharmacology, psychobabble), the Mecca of madness and its experts. It wasn't long after my arrival, when I was still living on park benches and under beachfront piers, that the experts found me: a progression of social workers, their faces lit with bland compassion, intent on human salvage. Later, when I'd started to "recover" (that is, when I'd found an apartment and a job—because there are some things from which we never really *recover*), I escaped from their clutches, but I continued reading about the subject. And although I never found any answers in those books, I long ago became acquainted with the territory of madness and its history.

of robber-baron capitalist villainy: the "boss croupier" of Wall Street, a financier who bent the course of America's development to the "psychopathology of his will,"[*] he smashed unions, attacked the common man, and crushed his competitors.

Yet at the same time (other historians argue), Morgan championed the growth of the United States, funneling billions into the construction of roads, bridges, and manufacturing plants. He acted as a Federal Reserve Bank before one existed, struggling to end the brutal expansion-contraction cycle that racked the country with depression. And on two occasions, he saved the government of the United States itself from bankruptcy.[†]

Of Morgan, the photographer Edward Steichen wrote that "meeting his gaze was like looking into the lights of an oncoming express train."[‡] This was a fairly typical remark. In portraits he is a fortress of a man, eyes shadowed beneath the brim of his top hat, overgrown eyebrows arching like Gothic vaults. Though Morgan stood over six feet tall and weighed over two hundred pounds, his most prominent feature was without question his nose. Deformed with rhinophyma, the uncontrolled growth of sebaceous tissue, it was (as one wealthy New York widow wrote in her diary), "a Cyrano nose of vast blue oozing glands[,] a hideous deformity."[§] A drooping walrus mustache hangs over his mouth.

Morgan is inarticulate, a man of few words: his British partner,

---

[*] Jean Strouse, *Morgan: American Financier* (New York: HarperCollins, 1999), p. x.
[†] After the first of these incidents, in 1895, President Grover Cleveland asked Morgan how he had managed this colossal feat. "I simply told [the financial interests of Europe] that this was necessary," Morgan replied, "and they did it" (Frederick Lewis Allen, *The Big Change: America Transforms Itself, 1900–1915* [New York: Harper and Brothers, 1952], p. 119).
[‡] Edward Steichen, *A Life in Photography* (New York: Doubleday, 1963).
[§] Diary of Margot Asquith, November 13, 1911.

Edward C. Grenfell, reported that he was "an impossible man to have any talk with. The nearest approach he makes is an occasional grunt." When questioned, he is notoriously terse and direct with his answers: asked to predict what the stock market would do, he replied, "It will fluctuate."* As a financier, he is ambitious, patient, and insightful—yet seems to possess no particular genius. Nothing that he does is noticeably flamboyant or innovative, apart from the sums involved. Through what seems to be luck more than any particular brilliance of strategy, he finds himself in a position unique in the world, his smile or scowl able to send Wall Street into a frenzy of confidence or despair.

And from his throneless position of command—his famous glass-walled office overlooking Wall Street—Morgan realizes, perhaps better than any other, the fragility of the world: the tide of tumultuous forces that threaten to disrupt the too-short moments of peace and prosperity. Around the corner, with the next unwise transaction or overextended bank, John Pierpont sees the shadow of the next great depression, war, or famine . . .

Given these things, he has come to think of himself as the world's protector. All his life Morgan has observed the behavior of financial markets. He has survived cycles of expansion and contraction, price wars and panics. In the face of such unpredictability, Morgan has decided, the only way to keep the economy on track is to control it completely.

MORGAN STANDS in his office at 23 Wall Street, surveying the world that he commands. If there are physical locations on earth where

---

* *New York Times*, December 20, 1912.

power is woven into the very substance of the air (the Oval Office, the throne room at Versailles, the Forbidden City), this is one of them. Situated at the end of the floor farthest from the front door, guarded by phalanxes of bookkeepers, junior partners, lawyers, and the finest finance men in the world, it is a place of dark wood and quiet. Shelves of ledgers and reports bound in somber brown leather stand along the walls. A thick carpet muffles footfalls. A globe with the names of countries inlaid in gold rests on the plain oak desk that dominates the room, an everyday object suddenly potent with symbolism.

The only piece of art in the office is a framed drawing in charcoal pencil: da Vinci's sketch for the Mona Lisa. This, along with the windows opposite the door, are the only overt evidence of the power that is concentrated here. The windows are extraordinary: an entire wall of them with only the thinnest strips of lead joining the smaller panes together—no other structural support, an engineering marvel. They had to change the plans for the entire building, half completed, when Morgan announced that he would move in here and that he wanted such windows.

Morgan stands with his back to the door, gazing outward. A massive man, tall and wide. His hair and drooping mustaches are salt-and-pepper gray. Pouches hang beneath his eyes. His nose is an obscenity.

Outside, the city bustles. Up and down Wall Street march bankers, delivery boys, and secretaries in starched collars—carriages and horseless carriages fill the way. Pillars of gray smoke rise toward the overcast winter sky. Looking at the chimneys, Morgan muses that it all must be symbolic of something, the smoke and smokestacks—as, for that matter, must the buildings and carriages and so forth.

But of what, he can't be bothered—doesn't have patience—to consider. *Things should be what they are*, he thinks—or perhaps thinks is the wrong word: rather, knows—*and leave it at that.* The smokestacks are smokestacks, the smoke the residue of coal and oil. This is why—he glances over his shoulder at the da Vinci sketch above the mantel—he has always had such a deep appreciation for art. The paintings and illustrated manuscripts that fill his home please him because they exist without trickery or complication. This is why he founded the Metropolitan Museum, currently under construction, with his own pocketbook.

Idly, he muses on such things. Then the man seated on the other side of the desk clears his throat and Morgan turns back to the business at hand.

"That's all right, Mr. Morgan," the other man drawls. "No response is necessary." Without asking, he takes a cigar from the box on Morgan's desk, grinning at the financier. Morgan regards him coldly. His visitor's name is James "Bet a Million" Harrison; he is the owner of the Union Pacific Railroad, and a minor competitor of Morgan's.

"You sure gave me a run for my money," Harrison continues, leaning back in his chair and lighting the cigar. "But as I told you six months ago, I wanted your railroad and, by God, I wasn't going to stop till I got it."

Morgan sighs. "Mr. Harrison, you seem to believe I wanted to keep the Northern Pacific out of your hands for some personal reason." He lowers himself into his chair. "However, let me assure you that is not the case."

"Then why'd you turn down my offer to buy you out?" Harrison exhales a cloud of smoke. "I offered a fair price."

"It was a fair price." Morgan concedes. "I refused, Mr. Harrison, because you have already bankrupted a dozen companies. For the public good, an essential piece of infrastructure like the NP cannot be entrusted to such irresponsible care."

Harrison leans forward, his face darkening. "And you suppose that you can decide what's for the public good? Just like that?"

"Yes." Morgan closes his eyes, feeling for an instant unutterably weary and alone. "Just like that."

"I'll be—" Harrison shakes his head, then chuckles bemusedly. "Well, anyway, the NP is mine now. When you saw what I was doing, and chased up the price of that stock, there wasn't a banker in town who'd help me." A note of genuine admiration enters his voice. "None of 'em wanted to interfere in your business." He grins. "Except the one."

"Yes. The Schwab brothers." Morgan scrutinizes the other man's reaction as he mentions this name. For the briefest of moments, a flicker of fear crosses Harrison's face—but he recovers quickly, the smile returning.

"That's right, I guess you heard by now. They floated me that extra capital I needed. So as of yesterday, Mr. Morgan"—Harrison's cigar goes out and with exaggerated leisure he relights it—"as of yesterday morning, I own fifty-one percent of the old NP. Despite your efforts."

"That is true," Morgan nods. "You own fifty-one percent of the Northern Pacific Railroad. You have also caused me a good deal of trouble and expense, Mr. Harrison. Fortunately, my brokers are selling NP stock short as we speak. That should be enough to recoup our costs when you dump your shares on the market."

"When I dump my—?" An incredulous expression crosses Harrison's face. "Why would I? That damn railroad's mine, understand? I intend to keep it."

"Because while you and the Schwab brothers were buying stock in my railroad, I found it more convenient to buy out the Schwabs." Morgan opens a desk drawer and withdraws a folder. "We acquired a controlling interest in their bank yesterday."

Harrison's features go slack, the cigar dangling, forgotten, in his hand.

Expressionless, Morgan flips through the contents of the folder for a moment, then slides a sheet of paper toward the other man. "Sign here, please."

"What—" Harrison blinks dumbly and shakes his head. "What's this?"

"In your haste to acquire the NP, Mr. Harrison," Morgan rumbles, "I believe you agreed to some rather unfavorable terms with the Schwabs. It says here"—he gestures at the folder— "that the balance of your loan can be called in with a notice of twenty-four hours. The document in front of you now is such a notice."

Harrison stares at the typewritten page, the color draining from his face.

"You owe me thirty-six million dollars, Mr. Harrison." Morgan climbs to his feet. "As a lump sum, due in cash or securities tomorrow."

The other man doesn't answer, his face shading from white to ashen gray.

After a moment Morgan sighs. "I take your lack of response to mean you are unable to raise that amount."

Harrison nods, looking up at the financier like a mouse transfixed by a hawk's stare.

"Believe it or not, Mr. Harrison, I have no interest in ruining you." Morgan nods toward the office door. "See Mr. Perkins. He has drawn up a payment schedule that covers our costs without destabilizing your other operations, or the market."

Harrison stumbles to his feet. "But—but why—?" He shakes his head helplessly.

"Why have I decided to offer you terms? Because your bankruptcy would not serve the public good." Morgan turns away from the other man, toward the windows. "Good day, Mr. Harrison." A few moments later, he hears the door slam behind him.

Glancing upward, the pale stone of a building against the sky reminds Morgan suddenly of a certain, precise, white-slatted bungalow on a hill with a palm tree next to it, near the banks of the Nile, a few miles from the ancient ruins of Luxor. He had rented the bungalow with his first wife, Amelia, for their honeymoon; she had died there in his arms, coughing herself to death and racked with the spasms of tuberculosis. The first love of his life, dead before their vows were ever consummated.

He thinks of this, dispassionately noting his own momentary grief over having ignored her doctors' insistence on absolute bed rest, as a fact to be filed away for future reference. Morgan remembers this, then brushes away these clinging fragments of the past. He has always prided himself on his clear-eyed perspective and awareness of his responsibilities to society, his freedom from regrets and nostalgia.

There is a soft knock at the door.

"Enter," Morgan barks.

A secretary in his early twenties timidly pokes his head into the office. "A Mr. Thomas Edison for you, sir."

"Edison? Send him in."

. . .

DESPITE THE SHELVES of biographies and historical treatises written about Thomas Edison, one crucial detail is nowhere recorded: the moment when the great inventor lost his soul.

If one had to guess, it probably happened at some point after Edison, already famous for his work on the telegraph, opened his research laboratory in Menlo Park and turned his attention to the development of small-scale, practical electric light. At the time, gas lamps and candles were used in private houses (society aesthetes preferred candles, complaining that gaslight made diamonds look dull), but city streets and big public spaces had already started to be illuminated by arc lights, which sparked a brilliant discharge between two carbon electrodes. Arc lights were too intense for domestic use, however, and after the inventor toured a Connecticut arc-lamp plant he became fixated on the idea of subdividing electrical energy into smaller units.

The following years of Edison's life were consumed with the struggle of this project as the inventor worked literally around the clock, sleeping in snatches under his desk, until his own wife and children hardly recognized him. It was during this period that he first met J. P. Morgan, and that the financier became the primary backer of the newly founded Edison Electric Light Company, supplying millions in capital and acquiring a majority stake in the venture.* It was Morgan who arranged for the 1881 Paris Exposi-

---

* The significance of the relationship between Morgan and his partners and the Edison project can hardly be overstated; for example, as one historian points out, "the meetings of the directors of the Edison Electric Light [Company] were regularly held in Morgan's office." (Matthew Josephson, *Edison: A Biography* [New York: John Wiley & Sons, 1959], pp. 292–93.)

tion to be lit by Edison's system in the first large-scale public dem-
onstration of the filament bulb, and also Morgan who paid for
Edison's first two lighting installations in New York: one at the
offices of Drexel, Morgan & Co., and the other at a private residence, 219 Madison Avenue, the financier's home.*

But after the success of the filament lightbulb, and his subsequent invention of the phonograph, some subtle, essential thing
had changed for Edison. Perhaps it was the fame and publicity of
being heralded as America's "most valuable citizen," followed everywhere by newspaper reporters. Perhaps it was the betrayals by
friends and business associates, hungry for a share of his wealth
and glory. Perhaps it was a casualty of the drawn-out electrical war
Edison had been forced to fight against Tesla—a rivalry that had
been inevitable even before he rejected the younger inventor's
alternating-current electrical system.[†] Edison had always been

---

* Of course, Edison's early installations were hardly free from complications. The
electrical system at Morgan's office cost nearly four times the original estimate
and, more embarrassing yet, the system in Morgan's mansion was a disaster. The
steam-powered generators installed by Edison's engineers beneath the stables at
219 Madison Avenue belched noise and smoke in such great quantities that
neighbors two blocks away complained. After numerous delays, the engineers
solved these problems by installing rubber supports beneath the generators, lining the engine housings with felt, and digging a trench across Morgan's yard to
funnel the smoke through the chimney of the house, away from the neighbors.

And even after these difficulties were overcome, problems remained. To celebrate the completion of the system, Morgan held a reception at his home to show
off the electric lights to four hundred of his closest friends. Just before dinner, a
loose connection set papers on the financier's desk on fire, filling the house with
smoke. As the bejeweled ladies and tuxedoed men fled into the evening street, it
began to snow: the crowd of New York's elite watched in silence as Edison's lamps
exploded and went dark one by one, the delicate glass bulbs shattering in the heat
of the flames.

† In fact, the silent technical war that took place between 1888 and 1920 was
fought mainly between J. P. Morgan and his partners, who backed Edison's DC
electrical system, and George Westinghouse, who backed Tesla's AC system. Dur-

suspicious of theoretical scientists like Tesla, while Tesla was contemptuous of Edison's plodding trial-and-error approach to research, and their relationship was defined by their antithetical natures: Edison the practical, Tesla the overwrought genius; Edison the small-town boy, Tesla the polished European.

Still, Edison could never think of those endless cruel experiments that he and his assistants had conducted in order to discredit the rival inventor's work, without wondering if that was the point when some unnoticed but important part of himself—call it a

---

ing this time, a common tactic of these rival groups was to publish advertisements attacking the technology promoted by the other: the Tesla AC system was condemned as being dangerous and unreliable, while the Edison DC system was labeled as outdated and inefficient.

Still, over time, the two inventors themselves were increasingly drawn into the fray. For example, as one biographer of Edison notes, "In the presence of newspaper reporters and other invited guests, Edison and [his assistant] Batchelor would edge a little dog onto a sheet of tin to which were attached wires from an AC generator supplying current at 1,000 volts," to demonstrate the perils of the AC system (Josephson, p. 347), and he helped to arrange for the world's first electric chair to be powered by one of Tesla's generators.

For his part, Tesla—who had once hoped to work with Edison—responded with contempt for the other inventor's work, writing: "If Edison had a needle to find in a haystack, he would proceed at once with the diligence of a bee to examine straw after straw until he found the object of his search. . . . I was a sorry witness of such doings, knowing that a little theory and calculation would have saved him ninety per cent of his labor" (*New York Times*, October 19, 1931).

By 1920, Tesla's system—which had a vastly greater range of transmission and higher efficiency than the Edison generators—had prevailed, and remains the basic technology still in use today. Unfortunately for the inventor, to secure a merger that would stabilize his ailing company, George Westinghouse was forced to ask Tesla to give up his royalty rights to the AC system. Tesla responded by telling him, "The benefits that will come to civilization from my polyphase system mean more to me than the money involved. Mr. Westinghouse, you will save your company so that you can develop my inventions. Here is your contract and here is my contract—I will tear both of them to pieces . . . ." In doing so, the inventor relinquished ownership of what was arguably the most valuable discovery in modern history. (James O'Neill, *Prodigal Genius: The Life of Nikola Tesla* [New York: I. Washburn, Inc., 1944], pp. 80–82.)

sense of wonder—had slipped away, leaving him just a tired, aging man with a mind full of machines.

Standing in a corner of Morgan's living room, on an autumn evening in the year 1897, his back to the luxurious furnishings and the crowd of party guests, the Wizard of Menlo Park briefly considered these things. But all of it was nonsense, he reminded himself. One hundred percent pure nincompoopery, a waste of time and energy.

As he turned from the window Edison's gaze fell on a gilt-framed mirror, and for an instant he hesitated, struck by the mechanics of the moment. Light from the candles in the chandelier overhead, angling downward through the crystal facets and reflected off the mirror's surface, to be absorbed by the eye and reconstructed by his brain into the image of an elderly man with bushy eyebrows, pale blue eyes, wearing a rumpled white linen suit: his own reflection, transmitted instantly from the modest flickering of a half-penny candle overhead.

If there were only a way to use light as a means of sending information at this speed, Edison thinks, a kind of instantaneous Morse code—he shook his head, making a mental note of the idea.

In the background of the mirrored image, the room behind him was a swirl of color and motion, men in evening coats and bejeweled ladies gathered together, their lips moving soundlessly.

Edison's hearing had started to disappear when he was twelve years old, an aftereffect of his bout with rheumatic fever, and had slowly grown worse since then. Most of the time, at the lab among his assistants, blackboards and sheets of drafting paper could substitute for speech well enough that he hardly noticed the handicap.

At certain rare introspective moments, Edison was even glad for the affliction that had driven him to pursue his self-taught education, shutting him off from the foolish noise of everyday life. It was only at times like this, during his infrequent appearances at social events, that Edison became aware of the silent chasm between himself and the rest of the world

For a brief instant he pictured the cellar of his parents' house, where he had built his first workshop after being taken out of school—too backward for ordinary lessons, his teachers had said. There in the basement, the shelves of chemicals stored in old milk jars, purchased with the money he earned selling newspapers at the village train station. The sense of discovery he had felt with those early experiments, unlocking new worlds in that quiet space beneath the floorboards.

He shrugged the image away and turned to face the bustle of the financier's soiree. A diamond-encrusted dowager was hovering near his elbow, Edison noticed, indistinct murmurs issuing from her mouth. He nodded politely in response, picturing a device like a windmill strapped in front of her lips to capture the wasted energy of her speech. If enough people would wear such things, he thought, a city could power itself. Call it a fashion accessory of some kind.

Glancing around, he spotted his secretary, Tate, approaching through the crowd, trailed by the young reporter who had been accompanying Edison for the past few weeks. Waving in their direction, the inventor stepped away from the old woman, interrupting her commentary in mid-sentence.

"Been a real pleasure, talking like this." He smiled amiably. "Have to do it again soon. You take care."

Ignoring her response, he crossed to stand beside Tate, gripping his shoulder and whispering—at least, he hoped it was a whisper—into the other man's ear. "Think it's about time for us to leave, don't you?"

As usual, instead of answering aloud, the secretary reached for Edison's wrist, tapping out his reply in Morse code: a technique that the inventor had taught all of his closest assistants.

Talked with Morgan, Tate quickly spelled out. *He wants to see you.*

The inventor stifled a sigh. "You realize how many experiments I've got waiting at the lab? All we need, see, is a good solid escape plan. Now, if you examine those windows—"

Tate shook his head, tapping impatiently. *After. Follow me.* As the secretary began threading his way through the crowd, Edison reluctantly trailed him across the room, navigating the crowd of air-displacing mouths, through a doorway into a smaller parlor.

As he entered, Morgan looked up from the green velvet sofa where he was sitting beside his wife Fanny and waved the inventor toward an overstuffed armchair flanked by a pair of large ceramic elephants. Edison lowered himself into the seat, dimly aware of Tate and the journalist hovering somewhere behind him.

"Mr. Edison." The financier inclined his head. "Enjoying yourself this evening, I hope?"

Edison sat silently while Tate tapped out Morgan's question on his shoulder, staring at one of the painted elephants and trying vaguely to calculate the cost of its manufacture. Quarries for the raw clay, factories to make the raw paint, transport of materials, labor expenses, packing and unpacking costs for the voyage across some ocean to this house . . .

Tate finished his Morse-code translation of Morgan's question and the inventor looked up, smiling. "Of course, Mr. Morgan.

Mrs. Morgan. Wasn't for your kind hospitality I'd just be alone at the lab."

"Tell me," the financier continued, "are you working on any new experiments at the moment?"

The secretary relayed Morgan's words in Morse, adding his own postscript of *Think commercial application!*

Edison swallowed the lecture on his new bifurcated ratcheting screwdriver that he'd been preparing to deliver, casting his mind over the dozen-odd projects under way at Menlo Park. "Well, for one, been playing with those new roentgen rays."

"The device for seeing through men's bodies?" Fanny, Morgan's wife, joined the conversation for the first time. "Does it actually work?"

"Yes, ma'am."

Fanny winced and Edison realized with a surge of annoyance that, as usual, he was talking too loudly. Trying to quiet his voice, he continued. "They do. Been experimenting with a new kind of screen that I'm calling a fluoroscope. It'll give much more detailed pictures than previous models. Might have some interesting business possibilities. Medical applications, whatnot."

Morgan shook his head. "These rays may be an interesting toy for scientists, but hardly of practical significance."

Edison wrestled down the objection on his lips. It was all so much easier, he thought, before everything had become tangled up in worries about money and business. When his time had still been his own, without obligations to various consortia, contractual commitments, the interests of financial backers, and an army of assistants to manage: that long-gone era when it was just the inventor alone in his workshop, penniless and free to do as he chose.

"And who is this gentleman?" Morgan gestured at the young reporter. "I have met Mr. Tate, but I do not think we have been introduced, sir."

"Oh, him? This here's George Lathrop. Says that he's planning to write some stories about me."

"How fascinating. What kind of stories?" Fanny asked, sounding bored. Edison had met Morgan's second wife only once before—she seldom appeared with him at social functions, and it was common knowledge that whatever affection may once have existed between them had long since faded into mere courtesy.

The inventor blinked away an initial plan for a device for detecting emotions—call it the sensograph, measure the heart rate and so forth; although with the world being how it is, nobody would want such a thing—as Tate finished relaying Fanny's words.

"Well—" Edison shook his head, grinning at the strangeness of the world, "they ran the first story in the Hearst papers last month. 'Edison Conquers Mars,' I think it was called. Ray guns, time machines, all that. Nearly busted a rib when I saw it." He glanced at Morgan, expecting a laugh, but the old walrus was silent, brow furrowed.

"I wonder if you could tell me, sir," the financier said at length, "your honest assessment of the possibility of such a thing being achieved. Of travel through time, I mean—apart from in the pages of penny fictions . . . ?"

The inventor tugged at a lock of his hair uncertainly. Until this moment he had never seriously considered the subject, but Morgan was clearly expecting an answer. And really, Edison, thought, who knows the limits of human ingenuity? It turns out that it's possible to inscribe sound waves in wax and make dead matter remember living speech. Wires can be strung across the ocean, allowing conversations between continents. Men can fly and tread beneath the sea. This is an age of great discoveries, the morning of the Century of Man: when regarding himself in the mirror, Man found himself to be more like a god than he had ever before imagined.

A valet glided into the room, offering an assortment of crustacean cakes in a *sauce hollandaise* on a silver platter. The inventor popped one into his mouth and chewed thoughtfully, briefly investigating the anatomy of the arthropod with his tongue, before answering.

"Why, I'd estimate it to be possible. After all, it could maybe take a hundred years before the secret of time travel is discovered. But when it is . . ." He paused, enjoying the rapt attention of his audience as the financier and his wife, secretary and reporter, all leaned toward him.

"Well, then," Edison continued, "couldn't our visitors from the future travel back in time to the present with their device? Thus guaranteeing, if you see my point, the eventual arrival of a time machine if such a thing was ever invented. In fact, I'll tell you, I wouldn't be too surprised if travelers from the future arrived in Central Park tomorrow."

He peered at Morgan, wondering what the walrus—calculating, subtle walrus—was thinking. In general, scientifically illiterate men like Morgan bored Edison. At certain moments he even despised Morgan for being a money man, born rich and pampered. But he also knew that soirees like this had to be endured in exchange for the things that Morgan could provide: the favors and funding necessary to power his invention factory. And whatever else might be the case, Edison reflected, the walrus wasn't afraid to think big—to think about changing the world.

The financier leaned back on the sofa and sipped his sherry.

"And tell me, Mr. Edison, how would you locate these time travelers if they arrived?"

A decade ago a question like this would have sent the inventor scrambling for a book and slide rule, but since then countless newspaper interviews have accustomed him to answering with quips and certainties plucked from thin air. Tate finished tapping out the question on his shoulder, and Edison shrugged. "Seems to me—if you want to catch a bigger mouse, build a bigger mousetrap."

The financier frowned. "What do you mean, sir?"

"Well . . ." Edison drew a deep breath, closing his eyes.

For years he had been telling people that genius was ninety-nine percent perspiration—but privately he knew it was the other one percent, the inspiration, that made all the difference. And maybe it was the thought of the mining experiments he had started in the New Jersey hills, or his recent work on the kinetoscope—the mechanical challenge of framing a single fixed point of reference among a blur of still photographs, to make an image from the past return to life—or maybe it was simply the weight of Morgan's silent stare. But sitting in the financier's parlor, a sudden half-formed insight, and with it a tingle of long-absent wonder, came to Thomas Edison.

He met Morgan's gaze. "I hear," he said, struggling to modulate his unheard voice, "that down at Tammany Hall there's talk of building a new underground railroad."

For a moment the financier's eyes widened and it seemed as if he was going to ask something further—but then stopped himself, glancing around as if the thick folds of the velvet curtains over the window, or one of the tall gilt cabinets, might contain some hidden threat. Through the doorway, the tinkle of glasses and the sound of laughter.

"I do not wish to discuss such things now, Mr. Edison," Morgan said. "But come by my offices, someday. I would enjoy the opportunity to speak with you further, at your earliest possible convenience."

The inventor realized that he was being dismissed and stood. "Certainly. Mr. Morgan, Mrs. Morgan." He turned away, followed by his secretary and the reporter, wondering if Morgan actually believed what he'd said—whether he believed it himself, for that matter. Probably not, he decided. Just a bit of fun, a kind of parlor game. Still, thinking of the intensity that had appeared on the financier's face, Edison couldn't help feeling a thrill of unsettled excitement as he made his way across the living room toward the buffet.

Now, four years later, Edison recalls that conversation as he enters the financier's office and seats himself before the expanse of Morgan's desk. Briefly he pictures those moments, and the countless conversations he has had with the financier and his associates since then, like a current passing through a maze of electrical circuits. Each word a tiny fluctuation in amperage, individually insignificant but together causing unpredictable cascading voltage effects, aberrations in the behavior of the machine—

Effects that, Edison still suspects, may be an exercise in craziness. The planning of the subway tunnels as a point of safe anchorage, leading to a few known exits that can be monitored for any incursion. The endless scheming—all of it is speculative in a way that causes deep misgivings in Edison's practical nature. He toys with a loose bit of thread trailing from the chair's upholstery and tries to meet the financier's gaze.

"Well, Mr. Edison. I expect you have some news for me . . . ?"

"Sir . . . ?" The inventor inserts his ear trumpet: he remembered to bring it this time, and with its help, and by leaning close to the financier, some semblance of conversation is possible. Still better, Edison realizes, might be a device like a telephone speaker, worn over the ears—but before he can pursue this thought further, Morgan is repeating himself more loudly.

"—*some news for me!*"

Edison pauses, licking his lips. Not for the first time, he considers telling the financier that this whole adventure is a fool's errand. But that itself would be another kind of craziness, he reminds himself, not to mention bad business: upsetting a man who could ruin his career with an offhand remark. Besides which, since those magical years of the lightbulb and the phonograph—Edison thinks with a sense of uncharacteristic despair—none of his other projects have come to fruition. Alongside the failure of his experiments in mining, motion photography, and a dozen other directions, their lack of results on this effort is just one more dead end among many.

He clears his throat. "Well, yes, though it's far from conclusive—"

"I understand."

"In fact, it's hardly anything." Seeing Morgan's scowl, the inventor hurries ahead. "Only, there seems to be a woman the police arrested for attacking Tesla." He smiles briefly at the thought. "Apparently she claims that she traveled through time."

"Is that all?" The financier leans back in his chair, swiveling away from Edison.

"Well, yes. And that she claims to be a woman who died seven years ago."

"I see," Morgan rumbles. "So it is not certain."

"No." Edison shakes his head quickly. "Like I said, only a small thing. But enough that we should maybe . . ."

"Be cautious, yes," the financier finishes for him, leaving the words that both of them are thinking unspoken—*that the time travelers may already be here. Anywhere. Given the benefit of perfect understanding, insinuated where they* know *with the certainty born of some future perspective, that they will not be found . . .*

Morgan closes his eyes, massaging his temples. "And the subway tunnels? Has there been anything . . . ?"

"No, nothing in the tunnels. But"—the inventor brightens, seizing at one of the few meager shreds of evidence that he hasn't been completely mistaken—"apparently she told the police a certain subway worker could vouch for her."

"And do you believe we should pursue this matter?" Morgan presses.

"Oh, well . . ." Edison glances up at the walrus, common sense and self-preservation battling inside him. "I wouldn't know. Could be just a madwoman. Probably nothing, come to think of it."

"Perhaps so." Morgan rises. "Thank you for the news. I will make the necessary arrangements and keep you apprised of any further information."

"Sir . . . ?"

"—of any further information!"

Edison stands, allows his hand to be solidly squeezed, then released. "I will, of course."

"My secretary will show you out." Morgan ushers the other man to the door. When Edison is gone, he turns back to the wide bank of windows overlooking the street.

"Damn," he swears softly to himself—

And closes his eyes, thinking of what this latest news might mean. All his life, Morgan has understood the moral authority of wealth: the burden of responsibility for the public good that is conferred by his unique position. He has worked patiently to cultivate the garden of mankind's peace and prosperity: fertilizing here, encouraging there, judicious with his pruning shears when the need arises. But ever since damned Edison raised the possibility of time travel, the specter has haunted his nightmares. The vision of a world turned upside down, the orderly march of history and progress scattered to the wind, undermining the roots of everything he has struggled to accomplish.

More than once, he has tried to convince himself that these are needless fears, that the inventor's theories are nothing more than idle speculation. But although he does not have much faith in the wild daydreams of scientists—having been unimpressed by phrenology, psychophysics, mediumship, and similar cutting-edge intellectual fads—he knows by a hollow feeling in the pit of his formidable stomach that, on this subject at least, damned Edison is right. It is a gamble against the future: not a question of *when* a device that travels through time will be invented, but of whether it will ever be invented at all. And if there is one thing Morgan has learned, it is to avoid betting against the future. Which is why, more and more often, he finds himself unable to sleep, kept awake by the image of time turning back on itself, the serpent swallowing its own tail, of everything he has worked for unraveled and undone before it even began . . .

If there were someone else, Morgan thinks, who could take responsibility—but of course, there is no one. And so he has not spoken to anyone about his nightmares, and has endured the unprofitable conspiracy surrounding the subway-works, the maps and messages, the tedious evenings spent listening to Edison prattle about his latest bifurcated ratcheting steam-screwdriver . . .

In his gut he feels a pang: the same cramp that periodically throughout his life has stricken him with such agony that he has been confined to his bed for weeks. Silently he curses his decision to drink a second cup of coffee at Delmonico's last night and removes a silver pill jar from his pocket, swallowing two of the tablets that Dr. Tyng promised would help. He washes down the pills with a sip of brandy, seats himself once more at the desk, and begins to consider what must now be done.

PETER IS RECLINING in the shabby apartment's single armchair, an overstuffed secondhand monstrosity that leaks sawdust across the floor. Next to him, an iron stove glows faintly in the late-afternoon light, its many-elbowed chimney circumnavigating the two small rooms of the flat, providing heat. He is trying to read, a folded copy of the *Sun* on his lap—apart from walking through the city, this has become one of his great pleasures on his days off, studying the news for articles about faraway places. But today nothing in the paper holds his attention. He looks out the window, between the ragged edges of the burlap curtain.

Overhead the pale sky is hinging toward the early darkness of winter, the light thick and silvered as if permeated with dust. And she is out there somewhere, he thinks, in the vastness of the world. He remembers how they sat across from each other in the German restaurant, that first day: how she'd smiled tentatively at him. And now, he realizes, she might be smiling that way at someone else.

This wounds him for reasons that he can't really explain, as if the fact of her existence without him was a betrayal.

He knows that she is only a stranger who took momentary advantage of him. And the newspaper article about her arrest is the final proof that she is deranged. But even with this conclusion, he can't quite rest. It is not enough, a too-obvious answer that leaves him with the nagging feeling there must be something more. Some kind of hidden meaning that defies his efforts to pin it down. These thoughts circle through his head, like pieces of a jigsaw puzzle that won't quite fit. Tobias being led away by the guards; Paolo's gesture at the bridge; the shape of her back as she walked away—these fragments, and the memory of riding on horseback, his father in the lead, through the Idaho mountains along the edge of a wooded valley's rim.

A knock at the door startles Peter out of his recollections. He freezes for a second—apart from the landlord, no one ever visits, and rent for the week is already paid. He remembers stories of bandits who travel from room to room through the flophouse mazes of the Bowery, and his heart starts to pound. Another knock. Slowly, he gets up and grabs an iron poker from beside the stove, his knuckles whitening around the handle. Raising the weapon, he crosses the room and silently unbolts the door. Taking a breath, he jerks it open—and is greeted by the sight of a small man in a neat gray suit, a furled umbrella hooked over his arm, and pince-nez perched on his nose.

For a moment the two stare at each other. Finally, the man in the hall clears his throat.

"Mr. Peter Force?" If the visitor is perturbed by the still-upraised poker in Peter's hand, it doesn't show.

"Yes?" Peter lowers the weapon, feeling foolish.

"May I come in?"

Peter hesitates, glancing over his shoulder at the dim squalor of the apartment. "What do you want?"

"There is a matter of some delicacy that I wish to discuss with you. I have a proposition which I believe you may find interesting."

Peter briefly considers the possibility this might be a trap, then dismisses the idea. The man in the doorway is the picture of civility. He nods, stepping aside. Inside the apartment Peter's visitor looks around, taking in the bedraggled chair, the ratty cots along one wall, the rusting stove and half-filled rusty washbasin, with a single glance.

"Here—" Peter points to the chair and, after the slightest hesitation, the other man sits. Peter leans against a table and waits. The visitor looks back at him in silence, seeming perfectly content.

"So," Peter says finally, "something you wanted to ask?"

The other man nods. "Recently you were in the company of a certain lady—a lady who was taken into custody by the police in connection with an attempt on Mr. Tesla's life. Is this correct?" It is barely a question.

"Where'd you hear that?" Peter tries to keep his tone neutral.

The visitor shrugs. "She told us."

Peter hesitates, trying and failing to read the other man's face. The silence grows again. At length, Peter nods.

"Excellent. My employers have expressed an interest in meeting this lady. For this reason, I have been asked to contact you in the hope that you might be persuaded to use your acquaintance with the lady in question to influence her toward this end."

Peter blinks, trying to unravel this statement.

"If we arrange her release by the police," the small man says, sighing and fingering the handle of his umbrella, "will you bring her to us?"

"I—" Peter starts, then stops, feeling that he's flailing in waters too deep and wide for him to comprehend. "What do you want with her?"

"Conversation only, I assure you." The other man's expression is perfectly blank, an unreadable mask.

Abruptly, Peter feels a surge of anger—at this stranger's presumption in coming here, at his own powerlessness, at the fact that his life seems to be an open book. He suppresses the urge to seize this dandy by his neat mustaches and throw him out of the apartment. "If I say no?"

"Then she will languish in jail and a judge will find her guilty of attempted murder." The little man shrugs. "Or we will find someone else to escort her. However, she might find your presence more reassuring."

Neither says anything for a moment. Outside, engines cough and groan, traffic rattles past. Peter runs a hand through his hair. At length, the visitor reaches into his coat and withdraws an envelope from which he removes five ten-dollar bills, placing them on the arm of the chair. He returns the envelope to his pocket and takes off his pince-nez, polishing the small oval lenses with a very white handkerchief. Peter looks at the money, then away.

Fifty dollars is more than he has ever seen in one place before. Fifty dollars is more than three months' pay. Fifty dollars is enough to—

"Who's looking to meet her?"

The visitor settles his glasses on his nose. "Mr. John Pierpont Morgan." The name means almost nothing to Peter: some banker, he thinks, vaguely recalling a newspaper article he once read. The other man rises, leaving the bills on the chair. "Only consider," he says. "Her release, a pleasant dinner, an evening's conversation—not much to ask."

Peter opens his mouth, then closes it. Seeing this hesitation, the other man does not press his point. He crosses to the door. "I will return tomorrow for your answer."

Numbly, Peter nods.

"Thank you for your time." The small man executes a neat bow and is gone, the tapping of the umbrella's ferrule echoing in counterpoint to his steps down the empty tenement hall.

CHAPTER IX

THE POINT OF NO RETURN

DARKNESS, AND THE SOUND OF DRIPPING WATER.

It may be morning, it may not. The tiny, grimed windows near the ceiling let in the memory of light: a vague suggestion of the fact that, somewhere outside these stone walls, a day unwinds. She hears a shuffling of bolts and comes back to herself as if from a great distance, the gloom and stench of her surroundings coalescing by unwilling degrees.

For a moment she clings to the memory in which she has been taking refuge: the precise yellow rim of a teacup, on a table in the sitting room of her father's house, on a summer afternoon. Then she registers the fact that two guards have entered the cell and are staring down at her, and with an effort forces herself to return to the horror of the present. One of the guards, a tall thin man with scarred cheeks, smiles at her and licks his lips.

"We've a moment to spare, eh?" he asks his companion.

The other guard, shorter and rounder, shrugs indifferently and says nothing.

"After all, they don't come much prettier around here, do they?" the tall guard continues. He takes a step toward her, loosening his belt.

Looking up at the guard, she imagines lying back and simply spreading her legs for him. The weight of his body, sinking her teeth into his throat and feeling the hot gush of blood on her face—a vision that somehow both arouses her, and fills her with despair. But the foul thickness of the tall guard's breath as he bends forward brings her back to her senses.

"What"—she forces herself to meet and hold his eyes—"what is your name?"

"Quiet!" He raises his hand but somehow she manages not to flinch. For an instant, their eyes remain terribly locked. Then he straightens, spits on the ground, and turns to the other man. "Jesus, ye're no fun 'tall. Come on, then."

The two men grip her arms and lift her to her feet. They march her down the corridor to an armored doorway, where the shorter guard raps twice. She sees another guard glance through the little window before swinging the door open. They step through and all three take gasping breaths of fresh air, trying to forget the stink of mildew and latrine buckets inside the jail. The guards pull her down a narrow hallway, around a corner, and down another hall, and she struggles to keep up with them, her legs stiff after hours of sitting motionless.

And what will it be this time, she wonders? Most likely another interview, she thinks, sagging with fatigue. When they first brought her into the station, groggy with chloroform, she had answered their questions without thinking. During that muddled interval, she has since realized to her dismay, she told them a dangerous amount of the truth. At least enough, she suspects, for them to lock her up forever as a lunatic. And if they do . . . She shivers.

Since then she has clung to the insistence that she simply cannot remember what brought her to Tesla's chambers at the Waldorf. A story that, she guesses from these repeated interviews, doesn't sound any more convincing to the police than it does to her.

They turn another corner, and abruptly the yellow paraffin flames give way to a wash of silver brightness. She blinks, slowly focusing on the lobby of the police station and its doors opening to the outside world.

"Please," she asks the shorter of the two guards, "where are we going? What—"

"Quiet, you." The tall guard shakes her roughly, sending her head snapping forward. She falls silent, surveying the room and its bustle of bound suspects and bleeding victims. They lead her through the crowd toward the station clerk's desk, and then she sees the subway mechanic.

He is standing by the wall near the desk, hands in the pockets of his rough woolen coat, fear and determination written on his face. At this moment she thinks that she has never been so glad to see anyone, his presence here at once inexplicable and welcome beyond words. The guards stop and Peter nods at them, not even looking at her.

"What is happening?" she asks, glancing between the guards and the mechanic, her heart pounding with sudden, impossible hope.

"I'm here to get you," Peter says.

"Ye're free t'go," the tall guard agrees grudgingly. He pushes her forward, grabbing a handful of her bottom as she stumbles into Peter's arms.

"Come on." He is supporting her, since her legs seem to have given way beneath her. She feels stunned, rendered incapable of thought by this sudden turn of events.

"Come on," he repeats, more urgently. She forces herself to walk as he leads her through the lobby and out of the station.

They stagger down the steps, into the flow of foot traffic on the sidewalk. Her eyes water in the brightness of the winter sun, the clamor of the world overwhelming after the stillness of the cell. She clutches his arm, following blindly, fearing that at any moment a heavy hand will descend on her shoulder and a voice call out for them to halt. Finally they round a corner and he stops.

She looks up and around, gaping at the city. A scrawny leafless tree, the wheels of passing wagons, a painted wooden sign that reads APOTHECARY 2½ CENTS MIRACLE GOUT CURE—each of these things suddenly, impossibly beautiful.

"What—" She turns to him, struggling to put her thoughts in order. "How did you find me?"

"Saw in the paper you'd been arrested." He takes a step back, scrutinizing her. "You all right?"

"In the paper." She passes a hand across her forehead, trying to remember if any of the men who had questioned her during these last days might have been a reporter—but it's no good: already they have become an interchangeable blur of threatening faces. But if it was in the paper, she thinks, a crowd of nameless fears circling her like shadows, if everyone knows . . . She sways on her feet, unable to calculate what this might mean but feeling abruptly exposed to the glance of each passing pedestrian.

"Are you all right?" Peter reaches out to steady her. "They hurt you in there?"

"No. I am only tired." In fact, she realizes, she can hardly keep herself upright, the mechanic's hand on her arm the only thing that keeps her anchored to the world. "How did you make this happen?"

He shakes his head. "I'll explain later. Come on, back at my place you can eat something, get some sleep."

She wants to object, to force him to answer, but finds that she doesn't have the strength. Instead, she allows him to lead her to the corner and hail an omnibus; to help her up the steps when the vehicle draws to a halt, and drop coins into the fare box.

When they're seated on one of the wooden benches, he drapes his coat over her shoulders. She does not resist, grateful for its warmth and faintly comforted by the scent of his body. It seems impossible, she thinks distantly, that a week ago he was a stranger.

"Rest," he says. Glancing up, she finds Peter watching her. For an instant their eyes meet, and during this time she sees a crowd of emotions cross his face—then he turns away, looking out the window, as the omnibus lurches into motion.

"Rest," he says again. "Be there soon."

SHE LOOKS AROUND the dingy space of the apartment, the visions she'd had of a warm, clean bed vanishing. A diseased armchair, a clothesline hung with socks and undergarments draped between the chimney of the stove and the wall, a battered washbasin half filled with some brownish liquid.

"Roommates won't be back until late," Peter is explaining. "No guests allowed, but I'll think of something to tell them. Here, sit—" He ushers her toward the armchair. She falls into it, discovering that it's comfortable despite its tattered appearance. "You hungry? I'll get some tea."

She shakes her head—the idea of eating now makes her faintly nauseated—but he disappears into the kitchen anyway, and a moment later she hears the clatter of dishes.

She leans back in the chair and closes her eyes, letting fatigue overtake her. Staring at the patterns on the inside of her eyelids, she feels she is floating, unmoored from the laws of gravity. She thinks of how she has nothing left anymore—not a family, not a home, not even a name; as if all the variables and cross-canceled equations of her life have been returned to some primordial zero. But where the prospect of relinquishing these things seemed terrifying before, now she feels strangely untroubled. Even though abandoning these memories is a kind of death, she thinks, at least it is also an end to this uncertainty. A kind of peace.

When she opens her eyes—she realizes that she must have dozed off—Peter is standing in front of her with a cup of tea and a plate of bread. She accepts these things, setting aside the food and cupping the hot drink in both hands to inhale the fragrant steam. He sits on the floor with his back against the wall, searching her face.

"What happened?" he asks at last.

"I tried to speak with Nikola." She hears her own voice as if from a great distance.

"And then?"

"Then?" She draws a shaky breath. "He did not recognize me. And now, I wonder if I have not been mistaken." She closes her eyes for a moment and sighs. "These things I recall seem real. But now . . ."

Peter nods slowly. Hearing her say this, he feels a jolt of excitement. This is what he has been hoping for: her admission that this story of hers is impossible and can simply be left behind. Maybe now, he thinks, they can even talk about being together, simply, in the future. Recognizing something near sorrow in her expression, though, he tries to keep his tone solemn. "And now?"

She looks out the window at the city beyond. In the comforting warmth of the little room, against the lingering strain of her frayed nerves, she feels a surge of gratitude for all the mechanic has done for her and for the simple, reassuring fact of his presence. And it's possible that this, she thinks, is what the beginning of a new life might feel like. She turns to him. "To be honest, Mr. Force—"

"Please, call me Peter."

"Peter." She tries to smile but abruptly, with this familiarity, the recollection of her upbringing and social station returns, a chorus of hissing admonition. Because however she might wish otherwise— she admits, taking in the decrepit furnishings, the dirty laundry, and rusty washbasin—she does not belong in this place.

"To be honest, I do not know what I shall do." She looks at the floor. Through the flimsy walls comes the sound of a muffled oath from a neighboring apartment, the sound of glass breaking.

Watching the pained expression on her face, Peter thinks of what he has done to make this moment possible: a choice that seemed obvious at the time, but now makes him cringe inwardly. One more thing to outrun, he tells himself. Because, abruptly, more than anything, he finds himself wishing for an excuse to touch her.

"Don't worry," he says. "Just rest."

She nods faintly, chin sinking down to her chest.

"What about you?" she says.

"What about me?" Peter's heart starts to beat a little faster.

"How did you come to be here?" she asks, eyes still closed.

"In New York?"

"Mm."

Peter hesitates. As she slips toward sleep, he sees her fingers loosen around the teacup. He climbs to his feet, approaches the armchair where she sits, and leans over her to take the cup before it falls.

She opens her eyes to see his face a few inches away from her own, and the curve of his neck disappearing into the rough weave of his shirt collar. And in a flickering moment it comes to her that perhaps all her reservations and sense of propriety are beside the point: that whatever she feels in Peter's presence is something that perhaps goes beyond any manners or social nicety. And without giving herself the chance to reconsider, she reaches out to touch his unshaven cheek.

He freezes as if shocked, and she can feel him trembling. Peter closes his eyes, motionless, while she traces the line of his jaw. Then abruptly he pulls away, jerking himself upright, a red flush of something like shame on his face.

She looks up at him, wondering at what she has just done and wounded by his reaction. Perhaps, she thinks, he feels the distance between us as well: the burden of his own lowly origins. She opens her mouth, searching for some words with which to tell him that none of these things matter.

"Something I need to tell you—" Peter starts but she interrupts.

"It does not matter." She offers him a half-pleading smile. "Truly, it does not. After all that you have done for me——" She shakes her head and looks away, half shocked by this inner admission and unable to meet his eyes. "Thank you, Peter."

He nods, seeming at this instant very young and very lost. After a moment he seats himself on the floor again. She struggles to compose herself and rein in the welling disappointment in her chest.

"So, you were telling me your story?" she asks finally, needing to break the silence.

"What?" Peter blinks at her.

"About how you came to New York?"

He doesn't answer.

"You came here from Idaho?" she prompts, feeling a kind of desperation at the sullen line of his jaw.

"From silver-mining country." He takes a deep breath. Although it's a story he has avoided telling, and would rather leave unsaid, he guesses that—after everything that's happened—he can't exactly refuse to tell her. Peter's cheek still tingles from her touch as he takes a deep breath and squares his shoulders, trying to frame these things he's never really explained before into words.

IN THE WAKE of the gold rush, the Idaho frontier had more men than jobs, and despite his experience in the New Mexico Territory, Peter's father was unable to find work as a surveyor. Instead, James Force became a prospector, working for the Hercules Mining Company, a conglomerate that owned rights to thousands of mountainous acres around the town of Kellogg.

For his eleventh birthday, Peter received a woolen blanket and a huntsman's knife in an oiled leather sheath. But the real gift was that for the first time he was allowed to go with his father on a prospecting expedition.

On that first trip, they had hiked ten miles out of town, over a ridge and down into the dry gorge where a river once ran. Peter remembers scrambling over boulders after his father, the smell of wild mint growing along the riverbed, the feel of the ravine wall rough against his hands. At a certain point, James Force had stopped and chipped a fragment of rock loose from an outcropping with his hand pick.

As his son watched, he unbuttoned his pants and peed on the shard. Kneeling down in the riverbed, he motioned for his son to do the same.

"There." He pointed at the rock, where the urine foamed faintly green. "That's copper, you see? Antimony the same, except red."

Peter nodded.

"You know how to add and subtract?"

"Yes, sir."

"Know what right and wrong is?"

"The ten commandments?"

"Right's minding your own business and doing what you truly see as best. Wrong's telling somebody else what to do."

"Yes, sir."

"Here." James Force removed a collapsible telescope from his pack and handed it to Peter. "With this you can figure distances. See that peak?" He pointed to a mountain in the distance. "Here's how you tell how far."

That night they camped on the hillside above the gorge, unrolling their blankets on a carpet of pine needles. James Force boiled potatoes in a pot over the fire, sprinkling in salt from his pack and sage that Peter gathered. After they had eaten, the elder Force stood and carefully cut a series of notches into a tree trunk.

"Always blaze your trees." He turned to face Peter. "You know why?"

"To claim the water rights?"

"Yes." James Force nodded. "How they started that town, Kellogg."

"Sir?"

"Man by the name of Wardner. They'd just found the mine, Noah Kellogg and his partner, and started digging. Wardner was a storekeeper in another town, and when he heard about the mine he came up the mountain with some barrels of whiskey. Gave the whiskey to Kellogg and his crew, and they all drank themselves to sleep. While they were out cold, Wardner took an ax and walked around the valley, blazing all the trees."

"And then?" Peter had heard the story before, but it was one of his favorites.

"Well . . ." James Force spat on the ground. "When Kellogg and the others woke up, they asked Wardner what he'd been doing. He grins and says, 'I just staked out squatter's rights for this whole valley.'"

Later, as the fire dwindled to ember ghosts, Peter lay awake in his bedroll, looking up at the stars as his father snored a few feet away. The arc of Ursa Major and Andromeda, lonely and bright in the vaulted sky. He pressed himself flat against the ground, feeling dirt and dead leaves through the rough blanket and, further down yet, rock at the center of the earth. And he felt a pulse coming back out of the earth, a great slow steady throb in time with his own heartbeat.

Now, sitting in the New York apartment, this is what Peter remembers. But this isn't the story that she asked for, he thinks, watching her sit with her eyes closed in the shabby armchair. Realizing that he has been silent for too long, Peter clears his throat and says: "When I was nine, I started work with my father."

"In Idaho?" she asks sleepily.

"Idaho." He nods. "We worked together for twelve years."

"And then?"

"There was an accident." And this is where the real story starts, Peter thinks, the one she's waiting for. "We were out riding, collecting rock samples for silver ore."

They had been riding, in fact, some miles farther down the same riverbed where they'd walked during that first expedition, years ago. Peter realizes this, feeling a small sense of shock at not having registered the coincidence before. Closing his eyes, he pictures the ridgeline of the canyon above the river, the afternoon sunlight bright and golden against the evergreen forest of pine, manzanita, and laurel. The crunch of decomposed granite beneath the horses' hooves.

James Force had been riding ahead of Peter, the line of his back speaking of years spent in the saddle. At the crest of the hill where the ridgeline met the rock wall of the mountain proper, they had stopped. Around them the air was still except for the sound of distant running water and a woodpecker's drone echoing upward from the forest carpet below.

"Here," James Force says.

Peter dismounts, removes a pickax from his saddlebag, and bends to the work.

Suddenly a blast of air knocks him forward, smashing his face against the rock. He hears a cracking scream somewhere nearby, behind him, an inhuman sound that begins like thunder and scales upward into inaudibility so quickly that it's over almost before it began.

He rolls onto his back, the ax raised weakly in self-defense. His ears are ringing, his vision blurred. Looming upward he sees the dark, threshing shape of a rearing horse, his father astride, clutching the animal's neck—

Somewhere overhead a flickering of white light in the air, disappearing into nothingness. The tang of ozone. The world goes black.

An instant later he seems to wake with a start, sits up groggily and blinks away the blood that is running down from a cut on his forehead. His looks around in a daze, unsteady on his feet. Hearing a thumping sound from somewhere in the ravine below, he staggers to its edge.

The first thing he sees is the horse lying on its side, twenty feet down the slope, eyes rolled back in its head, one hind leg kicking rhythmically. His father's horse. He sees his father as well, but somehow this will not register in his mind. He looks at the horse, cursing its loss—two months' wages to buy another that's not half dead. His father lying ten feet beyond the horse down the hill, motionless, neck bent against a rock.

His mind will not register this.

And then he is skidding down the hill, faster than he has ever moved before.

He remembers sitting beside his father and shuddering as if a gear had broken in his chest, leaving him helpless and unstrung. He remembers laying his hand on his father's cheek.

He doesn't remember the ride back to town.

Near the mouth of a mine just outside Kellogg, he stops. He feels numb and made of ache. He is leading his horse, and the mare pulls at the reins, nervous—Peter looks at the corpse tied across the saddle, and then away. There is an engine near the mouth of the mine, shaped like an enormous potbellied stove, driving a conveyor belt laden with rock that crawls from the pit toward the water.

He looks at the engine, and then at the sky. A winter sunset— hills silhouetted below a firmament tinted fire orange. The clouds are small and high and profoundly still.

For a few days after that—after talking to the sheriff and the man from the mining company—he lies in the attic, looking up at the ceiling. His father's bed empty across the room. He feels strangely light, as if he had suddenly become weightless or limitlessly strong. At night he sleeps in snatches, dreams that always end with his father plunging over a cliff or being shot, that he wakes from with his heart pounding, barely able to breathe.

After about a week of this, Peter realizes that he can't spend another day in the attic without losing his mind. He goes outside and, because he can't think of anything better to do, heads to the nearest saloon and starts to drink. And at a certain point he starts to wonder: What really happened on that hillside? A bolt of lightning is the obvious answer; the storms that rage in the Idaho mountains are impossibly violent, tearing up trees by the roots and hurling them over precipices. When he was six, Peter's father showed him a boulder split in two—the smooth gray surface of the rock, worn by years of weather, and the shattered black inside, newly exposed to the sky.

"By lightning," his father had said.

His father now dead. He still can't think of it straight on—he takes a drink and squeezes his eyes shut, feeling the prick of tears.

It feels to Peter like someone else's recollection: James Force on the hill, the explosion, his head broken against a rock. But it *hadn't* been lightning, Peter decides in a sudden leap of intuition.

"So, was it an accident with your da, then, or not? What're you worried about? That someone killed him?" Two days later, Peter is still sitting in one of Kellogg's three saloons, and the man asking this question is named Camden Connors, an occasional friend of Peter's who, being in the insurance and confidence business, has taken a professional interest in the episode.

"Piss off," Peter mumbles, spilling his whiskey into his lap.

"Ah, I forgive you. A tragedy, no doubt—here, let me buy you another—"

Peter takes a sip of the renewed whiskey, hiccoughs, and starts to giggle miserably.

"What's so funny?"

"I just thought"—Peter wipes his eyes—"I'd ask him what to do. But I can't ask him anything . . ." He stares into his glass. Then suddenly, something Camden said clicks in his awareness. With an effort he sits up slightly straighter. "You think it wasn't an accident?"

"What?" Camden leans forward, digging in his ear with a grubby finger.

"But who——? Why——?" Peter clutches his head. Then suddenly it comes to him, in one of those moments of sublime clarity when the heavens of reason split open, banishing all uncertainty: Lucius Newton, the north diggings pit boss.

All the elements are there. Newton is a hard, angry man, known and despised at local brothels for his cruelty; a teetotaler, but drunk on his own bile. His father and Newton had ever been near blows. When James Force called Newton a fool for using an unshaped charge in a tunnel through shale, Newton had spat in his face—Peter had been present for this incident, one among many—and when the blast loosened a boulder that crushed a man's legs, Newton's stare at the elder Force had been poison. An explosion in the middle of nowhere—Newton had dynamite at his disposal; and that was the only way that made sense. Someone had planted a charge near where James Force had been sent to take samples that day, and set it off at a fatal moment. . . .

Peter explains his revelation to Connors, who seems unconvinced. "Well." He slides his hat back and scratches his head. "Maybe, I guess. But an explosion——? With dynamite——? Hell of a way to kill a man."

"Nah"——Peter Force shakes his head——"wasn't any accident, I'll tell you that. I know what I saw. Didn't look like any lightning."

Connors shrugs. "Like I say, maybe. Strange stuff happens out there. I know men've seen ghosts, glowing injuns, dogs with fire coming outta their eyes. Some even say the devil."

Peter nods, not listening. He has seen enough of anger, greed, and jealousy here on the frontier to understand what is possible, and even commonplace. The death of his father—there must be some rhyme or reason to it. The desperate optimism of the conspiracy theorist possesses Peter: that *some* kind of order must exist, even if it is that of scheming, hidden puppeteers.[*] He stumbles back to the widow's attic and, moving as if in a dream, withdraws his father's revolver from a drawer.

Around two a.m. he rips open the door of the hut where Newton lives in the mining company barracks. Newton spits and swears at getting woken, but quiets down when he sees the Smith & Wesson in Peter's hand and the crazed look in his eye. Peter marches Newton at gunpoint to the sheriff's house, and rouses the sheriff by hammering on the front door.

Muffled curses inside the house, growing closer, and then the door swings open to reveal the bulky figure of John Muncie, sheriff of Kellogg County, dressed only in a pair of boots and a holster

---

[*] As for the historical truth of what happened to James Force—really, I still don't have any clear evidence or answers. Still, I find myself haunted by a letter to the editors of the *Journal of the American Society of Electrical Engineers*, dated August 17, 1902, that I came across while researching Thomas Edison. In this letter, Edison (or more likely, one of his assistants) writes:

> *In our exploration of God's great workshop, it is sadly too often the case that the best of us may be lead [sp] astray from his responsibilities to society. . . . One example of this is Mr. Tesla's experiments in wireless power transmission, conducted near Colorado Springs from 1899–1900. . . .*
>
> *Residents of the town of Colorado Springs near Mr. Tesla's workshop reported erratic electrical phenomena around the building in which the workshop was housed. These included balls of fire, explosions of lightning, and regions of static discharge. . . .*
>
> *Indeed, while Mr. Tesla conducted his experimentation, explosions and spheres of lightning were reported throughout the region. Near Telluride, Colorado, a barn was leveled by a blast of lightning with not a cloud in the sky, according to the farmer who was witness. Near the town of Kellogg, Idaho, a man was killed by an explosion of lightning. Similar incidents abound.*

(*Journal of the American Society of Electrical Engineers* 12, no. 5 [September 1902].)

belt. In the puddle of yellow light cast by the swinging oil lantern above the door, the sheriff regards his visitors—Newton in his stained underwear like a pale, paunchy ghost in the darkness, Peter with his shirt unbuttoned, mud-smeared, and reeking of whiskey—and nods.

"Y'all better come inside, then," the sheriff says.

They stagger into the living room, where the sheriff lights another lamp. The bedroom doorway opens and Mrs. Muncie appears, clad in a frilly nightdress and clutching an iron skillet.

"Get back to bed, Trude," the sheriff says. She retreats, and he turns back to Peter and his hostage. "Now then, what's all this about?"

Peter's tongue feels like a dead thing in his mouth, the thought of explanations an intolerable delay before the towers of fury burning in his chest. Still, somehow, he manages to remember himself. "This man's the one killed my dad, sheriff." He tries to meet Muncie's eyes but the room won't stop spinning around him.

"Sheriff, I did nothing! Nothing, I swear, he's crazy!" Newton protests, struggling free from Peter's grip on his collar.

"What?" Without thinking, Peter jerks the pistol out of his belt, aiming it at the cringing pit boss. "Tell him or I swear, Newton, I'll kill you. Tell him what you said you'd do to my dad!"—this being the gist, at least, of the sentence he slurs.

"Please, Sheriff—"

"I'm warning you—he did it, Sheriff. He's got dynamite—didn't I tell you it was an explosion spooked his horse? And I heard him say he'd kill my dad, with my own ears." Which isn't the precise truth, but this nuance is unimportant in the present moment.

"All right now, Force, put it down." The tone of Muncie's voice brings Peter back to himself. He looks up to see the sheriff cock the hammer of his own revolver with practiced ease. "Put the gun down, boy." Somehow the fact that Muncie is naked, apart from his boots, only makes him more threatening.

Peter sways on his feet. Nonsensically, he pictures the night sky with its filigree of bright stars, arc'd over this wilderness and half-lit room—and abruptly his fury drains away, leaving only a sense of confusion and futility. "Listen, I've brought you the killer. Don't you understand?"

"I don't care what he did. Right now what's important is, you've drawn a gun in my house, and I don't let that happen." The sheriff starts to raise his revolver—but even drunk, an entire life lived on the frontier, scaling crags and handling a rifle, has left Peter alert enough to instantly level his own weapon at Muncie's head.

At this point in the story, Peter falls silent. Across from where he sits on the floor, she is motionless in the armchair and he realizes that she is asleep. He climbs stiffly to his feet and stretches.

Still, somehow, against his will, he finds himself remembering that night in the Idaho cabin. How he and the sheriff had faced each other across the room, each staring down the barrel of the other's gun.

Everything that had occurred next seemed to happen much too fast. Muncie's eyes had drilled into him, a gaze that—he'd known somewhere distantly—he was only able to meet because he was drunk. He felt like a finely tuned machine, sensitive to every fluttering of the other man's eyelids, finger ready on the trigger.

Then Newton tackled him and he stumbled, twisting and firing at the same time. Newton staggered away, clutching his stomach.

The glint of something like a frying pan flying through the air behind him—Peter staggered with the blow and the sheriff's fist smashed into his nose. His vision swam. Someone stepped on his wrist and he dropped the gun—and suddenly was lying on the ground, looking upward at Muncie's revolver.

Somewhere nearby, Newton was groaning softly. The sheriff kicked Peter's pistol away and crossed to the whimpering pit boss, prodding Newton with the toe of his boot. Peter glimpsed a dark stain of blood spreading across the other man's abdomen. Then Muncie moved back to stand over Peter.

"That man's always been a waste of skin," the sheriff had said. "Still, I think you best get out of town now, boy."

Standing in the New York flophouse apartment, Peter remembers these words and closes his eyes. Outside, the light has faded to blue, and then gray, shadows falling over the still lines of her face. She shifts in her sleep and murmurs something, a faint protest or demand.

After a time, he lowers himself to sit on the floor again. Holding a newspaper propped in his lap as an alibi in case she should wake, he gazes at her features and tries to lose himself in the moment. But despite his efforts, recollections of the western frontier and of the deal he made with Morgan's minion trouble his thoughts. So that gradually Peter begins to wonder, with a growing sense of dread, why—even after they have both decided to leave the past behind—that past still looms so near.

CHAPTER X

THE INNER SANCTUM

FROM THE NEW YORK POLICE DEPARTMENT
(2ND PRECINCT) BLOTTER, JANUARY 18, 1901:

Officers responded [to a] call from Morgan residence, interviewed Mr. Morgan [and his household] staff upon arrival.

Suspects identified [as] Peter Force and Cheri-Anne Toledo arrived approximately 6pm, met [with] Mr. Morgan [and] Mr. Edison in Dining Room. Following brief Conversation suspects became agitated. Force alleged [to have] fired [a] gun at Mr. Morgan before fleeing.

No injuries or items known
missing. 3 bullet marks verified [on
the] Dining Room wall. Suspects
described as . . .[*]

I am looking for a moment years ago, at the Pierpont Morgan mansion in New York: January 18, 1901, an evening at the heart of winter. The weather, according to the *Times*, is cold and clear, a wind from the north dropping the temperature below freezing. Piles of soot-stained snow line the streets. Icicles hang from the eaves of buildings and grace each doorway with a miniature portcullis, waiting to fall. Against the gas streetlamps, the branches of trees are monochrome, skeleton silhouettes.

A gleaming black limousine glides like a ghost through the

---

[*] New York Police Department 2nd Precinct Blotter, January 18, 1901, from an entry dated 7:20 p.m.—or at least, this is how the footnote ought to read. But in fact, the real story is more complicated (isn't it always?), the details more elusive.

According to the NYPD, the files that would contain this entry were lost during a fire in 1902. By an odd coincidence, the corresponding duplicate police records in the city archive can't seem to be located. In fact, the only remaining trace of these events is the entry reprinted in the "police log" section of the *New York Sun*, on January 20.

Only this one mention—and then silence.

No discussion of these occurrences can be found in Morgan's personal writings, and likewise none in Edison's. There are no newspaper articles on the subject (which, given the celebrities involved, should have caused a journalistic frenzy). Everywhere I've looked there is, simply, nothing.

What can a silence say? This is the question I find myself confronted with, reading this passage (and also, if I'm honest, with this whole history). Staring into these lacunae, I think of how Rossetti wrote about "God's word, which speaks in silence." But above the low burble of my television, or through the radio playing at the neighborhood café where I have my morning coffee, such subtle voices are beyond my hearing. So in the end, I suppose, this absence can only stand for what such pauses have always meant: nothing in particular, and everything still unsaid.

streets. In the back of the car she sits beside Peter on the lush velvet upholstery, sunk in private silence. She stares fixedly ahead, hardly registering her surroundings beyond the warring blindnesses of grief and fear.

When Peter had shaken her awake in the apartment and she had seen the neat little man standing in the doorway, when the mechanic led her outside and explained the bargain that he'd made, her first reaction had been disbelief. A feeling that remains with her even now, as she is still somehow unwilling to accept the reality of his betrayal. That all of his kindnesses have been empty gestures, and that there is no one at all left whom she can trust.

She tries to imagine what lies ahead, what may be demanded of her. And, thinking of the men she is being taken to meet, she understands clearly that the question is not one of whether she should be afraid, but of whether she is afraid enough.

In the limousine beside her, the mechanic shifts nervously.

"You were in jail. How is this worse?" he whispers. "They only want to talk."

She doesn't answer.

After a moment he turns away, unsettled by the stricken look on her face, to gaze out the window. The car pulls up in front of a massive brownstone situated on a corner lot, the manicured gardens surrounding the building now shrouded with frost. A murmur of disbelief escapes Peter's lips. The house is incredible, the kind of place men like him are arrested for walking too near.

Abruptly he realizes that, coming here, he has been operating on a kind of blind faith. But now he grasps, for the first time, exactly how far out of his depth he has ventured. These people could crumple him up and discard him without hesitating—this understanding is accompanied by a growing tendril of fear in his guts.

The door swings open and two hulking guards wearing Pinkerton Detective uniforms motion for them to exit the car. Having no option, they do. The guards trail behind as they climb the wide steps of the mansion.

They are greeted at the door by an immaculately dressed butler with a hooked nose and lacquered hair. He looks them up and down, instantly appraising their incomes, social station, and the exact degree of politeness necessary to the situation.

The butler nods to Peter, his smile radiating contempt. "Your coat, sir?"

Peter hesitates. He remembers sitting across from Neumann in the Suicide Hall, and the mechanic's words of warning, which had seemed paranoid at the time. But now, feeling the weight of his father's pistol in his pocket, hastily retrieved before leaving the apartment, he shakes his head. "I'll keep it. Thanks."

He looks around at the wood paneling of the walls, the intricate tilework on the floor, the framed pictures, potted palms, and china vases. It is a place unlike any he has seen before, the vestibule of another world. He glances at her, hoping to share a covert look, but she ignores him.

"Mademoiselle? May I take your wrap?"

She nods, handing the butler her tattered scarf. He accepts the garment with thinly veiled distaste. "This way, please." The butler walks away without waiting for them to follow. They proceed up a short flight of stairs, through the atrium and down a corridor, the Pinkertons trailing behind.

Rounding a corner, she recognizes a painting by Van Gröote that her father once showed her in a book and feels an instant of vertigo. The framed pastoral scene depicts a pair of young shepherds in an alpine meadow, a flock of sheep grazing in the distance behind them—and for an instant she imagines that she could step into the painting, her father's look of astonishment as she waves up at him from the page—

Abruptly, together with this reverie and the memory of her father's face, she also experiences a wash of anger. When her mother died, her father had worn that same look of stupefied disbelief; over the span of her childhood, he had retreated behind this expression, along with an ever-changing array of vague artistic pursuits, into a distance beyond her reach. In his absence, surrounded by the silent deference of the family servants who populated her world, she'd learned to rely only on herself, and on her studies—which, if not exactly comforting, were at least safe.

None of which, she reminds herself now, has changed. She glances at the mechanic, then away. Briefly she had allowed herself to imagine—

But how sentimentally stupid, she mocks herself, that hope had been. She should have known better: should have remembered that she can trust only herself. Only—her vertigo returns with such wrenching force that she nearly stumbles—she cannot even trust herself anymore.

The butler stops and opens a set of double doors, gesturing for them to enter. Peter hesitates, and after a moment she pushes through ahead of him. The Pinkertons follow, silently taking up positions on either side of the door.

The room inside is dimly lit, a single green-shaded electric bulb casting brown shadows over the walls. A round wooden table dominates the space, attended by armchairs upholstered in red leather. Pink marble columns rise in each corner, flanked by potted palms.

A huge, elderly man with angry eyebrows and a face like a bulldog is seated at one end of the table—this must be Morgan,

Peter guesses. Another man is sitting at the other end of the table, slumped over a technical journal in which he traces the words with his finger. The recognition is instant, but it takes Peter a long moment to digest the fact that he's in the same room as Thomas Edison—the combination of the bilious lighting, the red glow of the walls, and the silence making him feel like he is dreaming.

After a pause that is not quite long enough to be rude, but sufficient to convey an absolute sense of authority, Morgan sets down the newspaper that he is studying and looks up.

"Mr. Force," he rumbles. "Miss Toledo. Welcome to my home." He stands, towering over the others in the room, and offers his hand to Peter, who takes it, mumbling a greeting in reply as he feels the financier's fleshy palm envelop his own. Peter tries not to stare at the man's nose. Releasing Peter from his grip, Morgan bows to her; she acknowledges the gesture with a small nod.

"Thank you for coming to see me," the financier continues. "Please, sit."

Peter eases himself into one of the armchairs near Edison. The inventor is still absorbed in his journal, apparently oblivious to their arrival. Peter shoots her a sideways glance, trying to read her face for some sign of what she is thinking. But she looks like a photograph of herself taken from a great distance: features blurred, eyes dark and illegible. She remains standing.

Morgan sighs and shrugs, returning to his seat. This is not how he likes to do business—business is war, he knows, but that does not mean it cannot be civilized. He rings a small silver bell and the butler appears in the doorway. "Bring us coffee for four," he says. The butler nods and vanishes.

An awkward silence ensues.

"Mr. Morgan," she begins finally, "I appreciate your hospitality.

But you must understand if I am cautious, given that my presence here is not entirely of my own free will."

The financier fixes her for a moment with a penetrating gaze and then nods. "I understand, mademoiselle. The use of such methods is a thuggery that I abhor on principle."

"Yet you have employed them!" She stares at Morgan, and Peter can see that she is trembling. "Will you please explain your motives in bringing me here? For I cannot help suspect that you have some villainy in mind."

"Villainy is a complicated thing, Miss Toledo."

"You justify yourself, sir?"

Peter, who has been silently watching, flinches at this comment. Although he's still fumbling for some clue about what these men want, it seems clear to him that it's best not to make them angry. Strangely though, it is the financier who finally looks away from her gaze.

"Mademoiselle," Morgan says stiffly, "justification gets most of us through our days."

The door swings open and the butler enters again, carrying a tray laden with coffee service. He sets the tray down and ceremoniously pours four cups, a faint clatter of china and the warm scent of French roast relieving for a moment the tensions that crisscross the room.

"Thank you," Morgan says. "We will serve ourselves."

"Will there be anything more, sir?"

Morgan grunts and, taking this as a negative, the butler departs. The financier stands and takes a cup for himself, motioning for the others to do the same. Trying to seem at ease, Peter does, stirring in two generous spoonfuls of sugar before returning to his seat and deeply inhaling the aroma. The only coffee he has known is a harsh brew made from bark and grounds reused until they've nearly lost all flavor, and now he's embarrassed to notice the financier watching him with an amused smile. She ignores the refreshment.

"Miss Toledo," Morgan continues after a moment, "I will explain my motives, as you requested. But first——"

"Coffee?" Edison looks up from his journal, registering the presence of the two newcomers for the first time.

"Thank you for joining us," Morgan sighs.

The inventor doesn't react to this remark, but stands and holds out a chemical-stained hand to Peter, giving him an appraising look. "I understand you're a mechanical man, like myself." He nods. "Mr. Force, isn't it?"

Peter gapes at the proffered palm, dazed by the suddenness of his arrival in the presence of the man who invented the filament bulb, the talking machine, the bifurcated ratcheting screwdriver . . .

"Are you"—he manages to ask—"are you Thomas Edison?"

Edison shrugs noncommittally and crosses to pour himself a cup of coffee.

"You'll have to speak up, Mr. Force," Morgan says, rubbing his temples wearily. "My associate is a little hard of hearing."

Peter realizes that he is still staring at the inventor and, self-conscious, looks away. There are a thousand questions that he wants to ask this man, but all of them seem suddenly foolish. Tongue-tied, he looks down at the table and feels his cheeks flush red.

"Well, then." The financier leans back in his chair and sips his coffee, the delicate cup nearly disappearing in his massive grip. "I will explain myself as you requested. But first, allow me to ask you a question."

Standing in the middle of the room, swaying with exhaustion, she waits. His tone is civil, she thinks, his manner beyond reproach. So why, she wonders, am I still afraid?

"Where are you from, mademoiselle?"

She blinks at Morgan, hesitating.

"I read your story in the newspaper," the financier continues, "and wondered what sort of woman might say these things. I believe our origins play a great role in the development of individuals. Which is why I ask now: Where are you from?" He peers at her, waiting—and when she says nothing, he abruptly raps on the table with his knuckles. Both she and Peter flinch at the gunshot sound.

"In fact," she begins, drawing a breath, "I—"

"I'm from the Midwest myself," Edison interrupts. "Why, for a while we were practically neighbors. I was born in a little town called Milan, about a hundred miles outside Toledo. Used to work as a telegraph man all over that region. I remember one night in Port Huron when the telegraph lines across the St. Clair River froze up, I had locomotives pull up to either bank so we could signal Morse back and forth with their whistles! Another time—" The inventor rattles on, an artificial grin plastered to his face, and she realizes this must be a set piece, prearranged with Morgan to make her feel at ease. She ignores the inventor, her eyes fixed on Morgan.

At length, the financier stops the other man with a wave of his hand. "Very well, let me ask another question then. Mademoiselle, in what year were you born?"

She opens her mouth, and then closes it. Among all the people she has met in New York, the financier is the first who seems prepared to accept her story. And surely he could help, she thinks. At the same time she remembers her resolve to leave this morass of danger and crippling doubt behind. And this recollection, along with a sudden intuition of peril, makes her hesitate. She glances over at the Pinkertons standing by the door, then back at Morgan. "Why do you ask?"

"It says here"—the financier picks up the newspaper he was reading when they first entered—"that you told the police you have traveled through time. Is that true? I ask because if it were, that would be of great importance to me."

She tries to force her thoughts into some kind of order. The stillness of the room and the bloody hue of the walls, along with her own exhaustion, press down on her. Better to wait, she tells herself, remembering the men like Morgan who visited her father's house: how they made themselves seem like forces of nature while her father shrank and nodded helplessly, practically giving away the Kingdom before their demands. Better to wait, she tells herself, to carefully consider—

"To be honest," she says, "at this moment, I do not know. I have been imprisoned, and can hardly think clearly. I will be happy to discuss these things with you, but now I am tired. I have answered your question. Now, I must ask you, as a gentleman, to let me depart."

Morgan sighs.

"What was that?" Edison leans toward her, cupping his ear. "Didn't quite catch what you said, miss."

"She said," the financier says, "nothing."

The inventor nods and settles back in his chair, eyeing her doubtfully.

Morgan turns to Peter. "What do you think? I understand that you have some acquaintance with Miss Toledo."

Peter finds himself caught and pinned by Morgan's gaze. Seated at the table, he risks a glance in her direction but her eyes are closed. The other man's stare drills into him, and he tries to imagine what she might want him to say. Finally, at a loss, he falls back on the truth.

"Couldn't really say."

"Say again?" Edison shakes his head, then suddenly frowns and digs in his pocket, producing a battered ear-trumpet, which he screws into his head.

"Do you believe she is a madwoman?" the financier presses. "This appears to be the opinion of the authorities."

Peter shrugs again, painfully aware that he's in the middle of some negotiation he doesn't understand. "I don't know," he repeats. "She was sick. Nearly fainted when we were down in those subway-works."

"What's that?" A calculating look appears on Edison's face. "You were down in the tunnels?"

Immediately she stiffens and Peter realizes that somehow he has made a mistake. "I only wanted to show her." He tries to speak lightly. "I work there, you know. Didn't disturb anything."

The financier nods, fingering his mustache. "Tell me," he asks Peter, "what did she do while the two of you were in the subway excavations?"

"Do?" Peter glances at Edison, then back at Morgan. "Didn't do anything. Looked around a few minutes, then we left."

"And you say it was which tunnel, exactly, the two of you visited?" the inventor asks. Peter hears, or imagines, a sudden note of veiled excitement in his voice.

"Well, let's see——" he starts to stall, but she interrupts him.

"It was the Canal Street tunnel, Mr. Morgan." She draws a

breath. "So I have answered your questions. Now you will have to excuse us."

The financier is silent, his brow furrowed. "Mademoiselle, I am sympathetic to your plea," he says at length. "But I must refuse until we have discussed this further. Mr. Force, may I have a moment of privacy with Miss Toledo?"

"I—" Peter hesitates. It dawns on him that Morgan and Edison might be serious about her story and all these questions. That something like this audience is what she has been looking for all along, and that she might actually want him gone. His impulse is to stay, both to help her and make sure that she doesn't go back to her madwoman time-machine fantasies. But, again, she won't meet his eyes. He feels only slightly comforted by the weight of the gun concealed in his coat.

Beside the door, one of the Pinkertons coughs pointedly.

Halfway across the room from Peter, she feels rooted to the spot. Despite his betrayal, she finds herself silently hoping that the mechanic will refuse to leave. But beneath the twin gazes of Morgan and Edison, she cannot find a way to express this. Instead she closes her eyes and silently prays—to who or what, she doesn't know—*please*. And then hears the creak of leather upholstery as Peter stands.

"You need me," he says, "you just call." And the door clicks shut behind him.

"Now then, mademoiselle," Morgan says. "Will you tell us your secret? One way or another, we shall have the truth."

She closes her eyes for a moment. "Perhaps," she says, "I will have a coffee after all."

The financier nods and hands her a cup and saucer. She considers joining the two men at the table, but decides to remain standing, clutching to the small feeling of advantage it offers. She sips, trying to compose her thoughts.

"Mr. Morgan," she says at length, "earlier you told me that you would explain your motives. You have asked the details of my situation; now I would ask you in return why I was brought here."

The financier considers this. "Very well. That is reasonable." Morgan gestures at Edison, who has been following the conversation, aiming his ear trumpet at each speaker in turn. "My colleague Mr. Edison and I have been interested for some years now in the possibility of travel through time.

"Hell, more than interested!" Edison looks up at her, doubt and wonder visibly battling on his face.

"It is not impossible, Mr. Edison informs me," Morgan continues, "that men may someday find a way to journey to the past or the future. For a number of reasons, I believe that such knowledge would not be to the common good. Therefore I have taken it upon myself to follow cases such as yours."

She digests this statement, struck by its matter-of-fact nature. "How," she asks carefully, "do you feel this knowledge would be contrary to the common good? And toward what end do you gather this information?"

"Well, miss, personally it's a little hard for me to believe your story." The inventor answers first. "But the fact is, Mr. Morgan here has a pretty good nose. If he says we need to find out about you, I plan to take it serious. So we need to do tests, you see. Experiments, measurements, maybe look at how——" Edison abruptly falls silent beneath Morgan's gaze.

"In brief, my interest stems from the problems that would be created by travel through time," the financier says, turning back to her. "If one could travel to the past, carrying knowledge of the future, conquering nations and breaking banks would be child's play. One man might throw the world into chaos for his own gain. Similarly, if one could travel to the future, the foundations of history would be shattered."

As the significance of Morgan's words sinks in, she shivers. Abruptly she imagines a landscape of bridges melting away underfoot and buildings changing shape, whole cities unmaking themselves as their past is rewritten. The vision of a destroyed world, populated with orphans like herself, each tormented by doubt and struggling to find a home in the alien present. And picturing this, with a sense of horror, she realizes that the financier may be right.

Perhaps interpreting her silence as disagreement, he continues: "Of course we have, each of us, made mistakes that we would like to set right. Regrets that we imagine could be corrected." The creases in Morgan's forehead deepen and for a moment he glances at the portrait of a stuffy-looking young woman that hangs on the wall above the table——then shakes his head, as if banishing some private vision.

"But these are, in the end, irresponsible fantasies." The financier drains his coffee and returns cup to saucer with a faint chink of china. "Without regulation and careful study, we cannot risk the present for personal whim. Or notions of what might have been."

"Then what," she murmurs, "what would you ask me to do?"

"As Mr. Edison has mentioned, there are certain tests that must be performed and your story must be discussed at considerably greater length." Morgan pushes his chair back and climbs to his feet. Beneath the red glow of the lamps overhead, his face looks like an ancient, grotesque statue. "Although the accommodations at Menlo Park are not luxurious, we will try to make you comfortable."

She stands there silently, overwhelmed by exhaustion and uncertainty, each of her convictions—along with her desire for escape and the pull of the past—having canceled the others out. She closes her eyes. From some distant part of the house she hears, or imagines, the faint tinkling notes of a piano.

"Of course," Edison is saying. "I'll make sure. All my boys are trustworthy. . . ."

With a feeling of abstract wonder, like waking from a dream, she opens her eyes to the ballroom of her father's house. Around her a galaxy of candles glitter in crystal chandeliers, marble urns full of roses line the walls, and the sweep of music fills the space.

It is a Chopin waltz, she realizes belatedly, and she is dancing. Her partner is a tall young man with ginger hair and freckles, dressed in a black tailcoat; she herself is wearing a long ruffled gown. He must be some visitor in Ohio, she muses, untroubled by the fact that she cannot remember his name. Another of the would-be suitors whose company her father foists upon her.

They turn and glide to the measured notes. The young man says something and she nods. Over his shoulder she can see her father, Louis Toledo, chatting with two other men. As always, something strikes her as vaguely comical about his appearance. His dinner jacket is bunched and wrinkled on his stocky frame, and his protruding eyes, along with the wiry curls escaping from a gloss of pomade on his head, make her think of a friendly drunk, seized from his comfortable tavern and stuffed without warning into evening clothes. Seeing her glance, he waves timidly in her direction.

Deciding that she has had enough of dancing, she moves to disengage herself from the young man's arms. But when she does, the redhead's face hardens and his grip tightens around her.

"Sir!" she starts to protest. "Please—"

"Don't give me any trouble, eh?" The young man's voice is thick and strange with an unidentifiable accent. He looks down at her with cold eyes. "You come with me."

He begins to pull her across the dance floor. Suddenly Tesla appears, calm and collected as always, interposing himself between her and the other man.

She looks up at the inventor, relieved. "Nikola," she murmurs, "thank you."

"Come on," he says roughly. And with a start she realizes that it is the mechanic who is half dragging her out of the room. Peter pulls her roughly to his side. One of the Pinkertons rises from the floor, clutching his jaw, as the other guard circles toward them.

"What—" she begins.

"You were yelling," Peter interrupts. "Come on now." He backs toward the door, drawing her along with him. She feels as if she is floating in an eye of calm while around her feet a storm rages. The guards follow, crouched and sidling closer. Then suddenly Peter is holding a gun, its barrel aimed at where Morgan looms like a well-dressed monolith across the room. The two guards freeze where they stand.

"Easy," one of the Pinkertons wheezes. "Easy now, boy."

She sees these things as if remembering them long after the fact: as if on cue, the two guards beginning to reach into their jackets and the flicker of Peter's palm across the pistol's hammer as he fires. A cloud of shattered plaster blooming from the wall two feet from Morgan's head. Edison diving for the floor, the financier unmoving. The guards raising their hands and backing away. Then running beside the mechanic, pounding down the mansion corridors, through the door and into the night.

CHAPTER XI

THE SUICIDE HALL

AS OF THIS MORNING I'VE SOLD MY WORLDLY POSSESSIONS. A YOUNG homosexual couple is buying the antiques store: they will, I'm certain, do a better job of running the business than I ever did (their sheer enthusiasm leaves me exhausted). In an arrangement that my real estate agent calls "totally unusual," most of the proceeds (minus her commission) will be given to charity. At first I had wanted to donate the money to an orphanage, but since such places hardly exist anymore, it will be used to renovate the metal-shop classrooms for a number of local high schools.

We settled the final terms of the transaction last night at the antiques store. Standing in that little space, surrounded by relics of the past, I poured four glasses of whiskey and we toasted the agreement.

"So tell us," my real estate agent warbled, draining her glass, "what will you do now?"

"Take a cruise?" one of the new owners suggested. "Play some golf, maybe?"

I looked around the half-lit shop, at the clutter of artifacts that were no longer mine, searching for an answer.

Even though somewhere I'd always known it was a fantasy, the truth is that I spent years hoping some doorway might appear: a passage that would lead me back to you and the time we spent together. That if only I turned the right street corner, or wandered down a certain alleyway at the right moment, this portal would open.

Of course, it never happened. Decades passed, and I slowly tried to resign myself to this fact, to stop searching. I tried to stop, but of course I never really could. And then one day, in a way I'd never imagined, I stumbled onto my pathway into the past.

"Now?" I turned to my real estate agent with what I hoped was a smile. "Now I have a trip to take."

THE PHOTOGRAPH that I discovered one afternoon two years ago, tucked inside a magazine at the antiques store, is black-and-white, of course. It depicts three people, two men and a woman, sitting in McGurk's Suicide Hall.*

The two men in the picture could be a study in opposites. First

---

* According to the history books, McGurk's Suicide Hall

> was nearly the lowest rung for prostitutes, having taken over that position from the waterfront dance houses of the previous generation; hence the suicide-craze that gave it its name and, incidentally, its grisly lure as a tourist attraction. Figures are unreliable or uncertain on the total number of self-killings that went on there, but in just one sample year, 1899, there were at least six as well as more than seven attempts.

(Luc Sante, Low Life [New York: Vintage Departures, 1992], pp. 119–20.)

there is Nikola Tesla, elegant in his sleek black suit with a bow tie and white gloves. His dark hair is neatly combed, an expression of faint surprise on his face. A leather document folio sits on the table in front of him, along with his pocket watch.* Beside him, the impossibly young-looking subway mechanic is unshaven, his brown hair an unwashed mess, wearing a dirty shirt and a rough woolen coat. One of his hands, on the table, grasps a glass of beer; his other hand is out of sight, an angry look on his face. But of course, it's the woman in the photograph (it's you) that I can't stop looking at.

Studying this image, I'm struck by a kind of vertigo: the disorientation of an impossible point of view (like imagining yourself as a passerby on the street in someone else's life; momentarily seen and then forgotten). But let me be clear about this. At least, let me try.

The young woman who occupies the third seat is about twenty years old. Her skin is so pale that it glows. Her black hair haloes her features, stray curls escaping from a shoulder-length braid. On her face there is an expression of—what? I can't quite read it. Some intensity, some distance, as she looks past the photographer.

This is the photograph that I stumbled across by chance.

And, staring down at the monochrome surface, it feels to me as if I'm falling toward the scene it captures. That frozen moment and all the other moments, lost amid the blank spaces of history behind it: the hidden rooms and countless decisions that came together in this fragment of another life.

---

* Using a magnifying glass it is possible to read the time and day of month (registered in small rotating numerals) on the face of this instrument: it is the 19th, and the time appears to be just after eight o'clock.

·   ·   ·

THE HORSE-DRAWN OMNIBUS lurches to a halt, metal-bound wheels striking sparks from the icy cobblestones. Peter shoves his way through the crowd of passengers, half dragging her to the door and down the steps. They cross the street, swirls of falling snow illuminated momentarily in the lanterns of passing wagons. Then suddenly the city ends and she is stumbling behind him over hummocks of frozen grass, through leafless trees and forest undergrowth.

They stop in a clearing inside a thicket of bushes, their breath rising in clouds of steam. For a few minutes they stand there, recovering from their headlong rush. After a moment she tugs her arm free and steps away from Peter.

"Where you going?" He straightens, watching her.

She glares back at him, still panting with exertion. Gradually the terror of their escape from the Morgan mansion has begun to recede, replaced by anger. She takes another step away, almost tripping over a half-buried root, and shivers. "That is not your concern."

"Wait a minute." Peter sinks down to crouch on the ground, beckoning for her to do the same. "Please."

Silently she looks around. At the edges of the clearing is a tangle of undergrowth, bare except for a few ragged leaves. Above this, the branches of trees reach toward the night sky like skeletal arms. Farther away she can see the tops of buildings: a geometry of lit windows, pinnacles, and garrets that seems utterly disconnected from the woods around the two of them, a misplaced backdrop from another scene. Overhead, the stars are cold and bright and distant in the winter darkness.

She turns back to Peter. "What is this place?"

"Central Park." He shrugs. "I was thinking more about getting away than figuring where we should go. Seemed as good a place to hide as any."

"To hide," she echoes, the significance of these words sinking in. "You think the police are looking for us?"

"Could be."

She shivers harder. Looking down at the mechanic, and the wary expression on his face, she remembers his betrayal and with a sense of self-righteous injury wonders why she doesn't simply walk away. But, glancing again at her surroundings, she admits to herself that she has no clear sense of another destination to which she might walk. She sits on the opposite side of the clearing from him, drawing up her knees and hugging her legs against her chest.

Peter climbs to his feet and crosses toward her, slipping off his coat. He holds out the rough woolen garment and she looks away. A moment later she feels the weight of the thing wrap around her shoulders like a cloak.

"Here," he says. "Keep you warm."

She closes her eyes, trying to make herself hate the mechanic. But even now—breathing in the scent of his body, which clings to the fabric of his coat—she finds herself imagining his embrace. She bites her tongue, struggling to banish the image.

When she looks up again Peter has moved away. As she watches, he gathers branches from the ground of the clearing, then kneels and carefully constructs a scaffolding of small sticks, tucking dried leaves into the lattice. He pulls a box of matches out of his pocket and strikes one, and a moment later a little blaze crackles to life between his cupped hands. After adding more fuel and wiping his palms on his trousers, he beckons her closer. She hesitates, then moves to sit across the fire from him.

"Won't someone notice the light?" she asks.

"Not too likely." He gestures at the surrounding woods and she realizes, peering through the underbrush now that her eyes have adjusted to the darkness, that dozens of other small fires are burning on all sides of their own, each circled by a group of shadowy figures. Without thinking, she inches closer to Peter.

Watching her pale features in the firelight, he wonders about how their two lives have gotten so tangled together. A week ago, Peter reflects, he would probably have just walked away and left her to look after herself. But now, even if she'd rather see him gone—a fact that has been plain enough, ever since their encounter with Morgan—leaving no longer seems possible. So instead he struggles to find some kind of answer for the accusing look on her face.

"Listen," he starts, hesitatingly. "I didn't—that is, I never—"

As she watches him fumble for words she feels a kind of pity for the mechanic. Still, she sits silently and waits, remembering how she has been wronged.

Instead of continuing, though, he abruptly stiffens and clambers to his feet, staring at something beyond the light of the fire. She follows his gaze but sees nothing in the flickering shadows.

"You there," he calls. "Come out!"

She waits, heart pounding, and for a moment nothing happens. Then a small shape detaches itself from the darkness and moves toward them. It is a child, she realizes: a boy dressed in ragged, too-large clothes, his features smudged with grime and flaking scabs. The boy looks at them, picking his nose uncertainly, poised for flight.

"You want to earn a dollar?" Peter asks.

The boy hesitates, then nods.

"You know the Lower East Side?"

Another nod.

"I need you to go there, give my friend a message," Peter says. "You go there, then come back and tell us what he says."

The boy considers this. "Where's the dollar?"

Peter reaches into his boot and pulls out a crumpled bill. The boy starts forward, hand outstretched, but before he can take the money Peter tears the bill in two, stuffing half into his pocket and offering the other half to the boy.

"You get the rest when you come back."

The boy contemplates the torn paper in his grubby hand.

"Where's your friend live?" he asks finally.

She listens while Peter relays a set of meaningless directions, trying to decide whether this might be yet another betrayal. But even if it is, she thinks wearily, she cannot imagine what her other choices might be. The boy wipes his nose on his sleeve and disappears into the darkness, and Peter sits down again beside her.

"There's someone we can stay with, maybe," he explains. "Know him from the subway. Should be safe there, if he'll let us."

She nods, pulling the coat more tightly around her shoulders, and both of them stare into the flames for a time without speaking. All around them the hollow loneliness of night and things they haven't said. He half rises, adds another branch to the fire, then returns to sit beside her.

"I'm sorry," he says. "About Morgan. About all of that."

Some part of her has been waiting for him to say this, she recognizes. But strangely, with these words, her temporarily forgotten anger flares up again.

"It was a mistake," he continues clumsily. "I didn't mean——"

"A mistake? How? Did they pay you?" Even before he starts to deny it, she sees the answer on his face. "How much was it?" she demands.

"I never thought—" he begins.

"Are you really so naïve as that?"

He doesn't answer.

"How much did they pay you?" she presses. For some ugly reason, it feels important for her to know. "Tell me, how much?"

Peter hesitates. "A hundred dollars," he lies.

"A hundred dollars—is that all I'm worth, then?"

"I'm sorry. Guess that's all I can say." Peter turns back to the fire, his jaw set in a stubborn line. "Guess I thought it was better than you sitting in jail."

Without warning, the momentary blaze of her indignation collapses, leaving only a gray husk of futility. This wasn't how it was supposed to be, she thinks. None of this.

Peter is staring ahead blankly, turning a piece of wood between his hands. A meaningless gesture, the chunk of wood over and over, stray sparks rising from the flames into the darkness. Feeling suddenly very alone, she reaches out and touches his hands, stilling their motion.

"In any case," she says, "I suppose you did save us both, in the end."

He looks up at her and she experiences a moment of dizziness, seeing her own expression mirrored in his eyes. The same mingling of uncertainty and hope. Embarrassed, she smiles at Peter and drops her gaze.

"Tell me," she asks, feeling the need for conversation to fill the charged silence between them, "how was it that you became interested in mechanics, to begin with?"

He stares at her for another few seconds, then shakes his head. "Guess it was my father. Out there in the mountains, in Idaho, he was always tinkering with something." Peter glances at the chunk of wood in his hands before tossing it into the fire, fumbling as always for a way to put the thing into words. "It was a hard place. But something about those gadgets made me feel like maybe it was all for a reason. Like it all made sense somehow, if you know what I mean."

He shoots her a sidelong glance, and is surprised to find her nodding agreement. "How about you? Haven't met a lot of ladies who study math and science, all that." In fact, he silently admits, he hasn't met other ladies—not real ones, in the proper sense—at all.

Crouched inside the folds of his coat, she shuffles nearer to him, extending her palms toward the glowing embers. Tucking a stray strand of hair behind her ear, she smears a line of soot across her cheek, and it costs Peter an almost physical effort to keep from reaching out to touch the small black mark.

"I must have been eleven or twelve years old," she says, speaking slowly. "It was not long after my mother died. I had a tutor—Mr. Driggs—who was passionate about botany.

"He had given me a sunflower to study, and I remember counting the florets at the center of the flower. They grow in a spiral, and at a certain point I realized something about the number of florets in each ring. There was a shape to them, a progression to their growth: three in the first ring, then five, then eight, thirteen, twenty-one, thirty-four—"

"It's totaling up the numbers," Peter breaks in, "isn't it? If you add the first and second you get the third number, then the second and third numbers to get the fourth—"

"Exactly. The Fibonacci sequence, although of course I did not know it at the time. When I told my tutor he became very excited and gave me a book on mathematics." She shakes her head, eyes unfocused. "When I read those books it was as if I'd already known everything inside them, and had simply forgotten. As if I were remembering these things, rather than learning them for the first time. And I suppose the rest, as they say, is history. . . ."

She leans toward the fire, and as she does the pendant that Peter glimpsed in the subway workshop slips out of her dress. She reaches up, running her fingers over its surface, and Peter sees that it is shaped like a circle of leaves or cornstalks, enclosing a letter T.

"That stand for Toledo?" he asks.

She looks down, seeming to realize for the first time what her hand is doing, and nods. "It is the emblem of my family. The Royal House of Toledo. At least, it used to be."

He bends closer and she holds up the pendant for his inspection. Heavy silver, faintly tarnished, the green of some distant Ohio frozen in old metal. The warmth of her breath against his cheek.

For an instant Peter closes his eyes—then, becoming abruptly aware of his unshaven face and the sourness of his breath, pulls away.

"Royal House of Toledo," he repeats helplessly. "Guess all of this must be pretty different for you." He gestures, encompassing their makeshift campsite, his own dirty clothing, the world in general.

She begins to answer with an empty politeness, but stops herself. Instead she pauses, looking around at the frozen dirt and bare branches, at the concern and possessiveness on the mechanic's care-worn face.

It strikes her that, until these last weeks, she has lived in an impossibly small universe, willfully blinded to the vastness of existence outside of her chosen life. And perhaps, she thinks, this is how everyone lives. Perhaps it is exactly these blinders that the complacency and comfort of our days depends upon: we survive by shutting out the endless questions of what else might be. Only now—she glances at Peter again—that larger world, and all the strangeness it contains, has been made undeniably real.

Peter takes her silence as a kind of answer and gropes for a question—feeling somehow that if only he could find the right thing to ask, everything about this situation and her, about the two of them, would come clear. But he can't find, or isn't ready to hear, this final thing. So they sit silently for a time.

"You must miss Ohio," he says finally.

In fact, a week ago, she would have agreed without a second thought: all she had hoped for, in those first days of disorientation, was that lost world. But now she shakes her head. "My life there . . ." She gropes for words. "I was a kind of prisoner in my father's house. We had everything—servants and cooks. I think that I never once stepped into the kitchen. Garden parties, dinners, dances. That was the extent of my intended life."

"You were going to get married—be a lady and all that?" he asks, not wanting to hear the answer.

She registers the resignation on Peter's face and with an inward shudder remembers the endless, ornate luncheons with eligible bachelors she had been forced to endure. The tedious conversations with well-bred young suitors who had nothing to say apart from singing their own praises: the patronizing smiles and questions about whether she preferred needlepoint or embroidery. She looks away from the mechanic. "Something like that."

"And was there anyone—"

"Never," she interrupts violently. "There was no one, apart

from my father, who had any claim on me." Except, she thinks, for Tesla, recalling the warmth and intensity of the inventor's dark gaze, how he alone had taken her seriously and shown her the possibility of a different life. But even that attachment, she reflects, had been a kind of schoolgirl infatuation, although she did not know it at the time. Nothing like—

Looking at Peter's face in the flickering firelight, she feels a sudden pressure in her chest and shakes her head again. Her heart has no business doing the things it's doing now, she tells herself, expanding to fill her rib cage, fluttering in her throat—

Before she can find words to explain this, there is a rustling sound in the thicket and she looks up to see the ragged boy standing in front of them, panting hard.

"Saw your friend," the boy gasps, wiping his nose. "He says, you come now."

PAOLO'S APARTMENT is composed of three small rooms: the first, where she sits now at a wooden trestle table, functions as the dining room, living room, and laundry, a space cluttered with a decrepit secondhand sideboard, crude table and chairs, and a dented metal bathtub. Beyond this is the kitchen, which is also the pantry and the room where the children sleep behind the coal-burning stove. Past the kitchen is a windowless closet that Paolo and his wife call their bedroom.

She surveys this space, trying unsuccessfully to overhear the conversation between Peter and his friend as they confer in the hallway. Realizing that she is being watched, she turns to discover two little girls standing in the doorway to the kitchen, regarding her silently with dark eyes. She smiles at them, and is rewarded by a pair of tentative smiles in return—until Paolo's wife appears, scowling, to herd the girls out of sight with a stream of muttered Italian. Exhausted, she allows her mind to go blank, staring at the pattern of cracks in the peeling yellow-plastered walls.

"—set, then. Thank you." Peter's voice brings her back to herself, and she looks up to see him reenter with Paolo.

"Of course." Paolo nods at both of them, his friendly tone at odds with the strained expression on his face. "You want some wine, something to eat?"

"A glass of wine would be lovely," she says, "thank you."

Paolo ducks into the kitchen and Peter sits across from her. A moment later the Italian returns with a bottle and two mismatched cups.

She smiles up at him. "Won't you join us?"

"No, my wife—" Paolo shakes his head, seeming faintly embarrassed. "I must help her." He disappears back into the kitchen, and she watches Peter as he pours for each of them. She takes a cup and sips the bitter, tannic red.

"So," Peter says after a few silent moments have passed, "what happens now?"

She looks over at him, this simple question revealing in sudden sharp relief the depth of her uncertainty. A week ago, these answers were simple enough: vindication of her memories, proof of herself and the world that she has lost. Now, though, after the blankness of Tesla's face upon their meeting and Morgan's vision of destruction, these things feel strangely empty and irrelevant.

"I do not know." She shakes her head and stands.

As she turns away, her hip bangs the edge of the table, knocking over the bottle of wine. Cheeks flushing red, she searches for a way to stop the spreading flood of dark liquid: anything absorbent, some rag. Her eyes light on the overflowing ashtray near the center of table—which is perfect, she thinks, like blotting wet ink with sand, and dumps the contents of the ashtray over the spilled wine. The crisis averted, she crosses the room to stand beside the window and draw aside the rough curtain, gazing at the city lights and darkness outside.

"Do you know," she continues, oblivious to the disaster of the table, "I think that we are very much alike, you and I."

"What?" Peter gapes at her, then at the smeared mess of sodden ashes.

"I mean, we are both occupied by the same question: whether one can escape the past."

Not really listening, Peter takes a deep breath and starts trying to repair the damage before Paolo or his wife wander into the room. Gritting his teeth, he scoops handfuls of the dripping mess back into the ashtray.

"And even as we ask this of ourselves," she continues, "the question itself perhaps a kind of blindness, we each struggle in the grip of our histories."

Distracted, Peter shakes his head. "Don't know about that." He finishes collecting the last of the ashes. Wincing, he wipes his filthy hands on his trousers. "Not really how it seems to me, I guess."

"So you do not believe in fate?" She turns away from the window to face him.

"How's that?"

"Not mythic fate." She struggles to keep her voice level as the dimensions of their current situation become clear to her, carried on a wave of exhaustion and panic: pursued by Morgan, hiding in a flophouse apartment, more lost than ever. Peter's steadying presence, she thinks, is her last bulwark against despair. "Not mythic fate, but real, actual fate. The machinery of the universe, the laws of cause and effect, tell us that the shape of the future is written in the past. As the movements of a clockwork are visible in the design of its gears."

"Maybe so." He hesitates, considering this. Glancing up, his eyes fall on a murky photograph pinned to the wall: a snapshot taken by Paolo, depicting one of the little girls now asleep in the kitchen standing in front of the half-completed Brooklyn Bridge. He sees this and remembers how he'd felt after climbing that span above the river: a sense of meaning at once specific and impossible to define, urgent on his lips but never quite connecting with any possible words.

"Could be you're right about all that," he says slowly. "But everything in the past was once the present. And the present is always uncertain, isn't it?"

"Is it?" She stares at the mechanic, fighting back tears; defying him to contradict her, hoping that he will. "Is it really?"

Peter opens his mouth, then closes it.

"A man without choices is a man without a life," he hears himself tell her, startled by his own phrase and the sudden conviction that accompanies it.

She looks away, trying to absorb this statement. Trying to convince herself to believe him. And then, without meaning to, she reaches a decision.

What drives us to extraordinary acts?—she wonders; what leads us to abandon the safe, the reasonable? Maybe it is simply a sense of the scope of the world and the smallness of ourselves within it, she thinks. As if this awareness demands a protest and response, that we are significant and that our lives matter. This futility and strength.

"I will speak with Tesla," she says.

It takes Peter a moment to react. "No." He shakes his head. "No, that's crazy."

"He can help——"

"Listen to me." Struggling against a surge of frustration and dismay, he rises from the table to face her. "The last time you saw Tesla, what happened? Now, most likely Morgan has the police after us as well. It would be——" He takes a deep breath, trying to keep his voice level. "We have to leave the city. I have money, enough for two tickets to Chicago and some supplies. Blankets, change of clothes. From there——"

"All of that is true." She smiles sadly. "But still."

Peter stares at her. If she would just argue, he thinks, if she would rant and rave, then he'd at least be able to argue back. But in the face of her calm, he is at a loss. Thoughts of tying her up and forcibly removing her from New York flit briefly through his head. "This is crazy." He glances around Paolo's living room, wondering if there's any rope nearby.

"You are wrong." The edge in her voice dispels Peter's thoughts of abduction. "Do you think I want to be imprisoned or killed? Do you take me for a lunatic?" She stares at him, her lips compressed into a hard line, and he looks away—a silent acknowledgment that unexpectedly wounds her. Yes, of course, she tells herself, pushing ahead anyway. "Very well. Take me a for a lunatic. But still I must go."

"Why?" Peter's jaw is set stubbornly as he stares back at her. "Why does it matter?"

She wonders how to convey the realization that came to her with Morgan's warning. The image of a world in chaos, the simplest of events unraveling into a jumble of disconnected incidents.

The terror of this vision—and the possibility that she might in some way be responsible for bringing it to pass.

"You have seen it," she says. "For these men, this is more than a joke or fantasy. If we leave now, the secret may fall into their hands. Would you really give power over the past and future to Morgan or his partners?"

"You're talking about time travel?"

She nods.

"But time machines don't exist." Somehow, after all that has happened, this statement no longer sounds quite convincing, even to Peter.

She just looks at him.

"And besides, why're you upset about all this now? You're really so worried, seems like you could've just . . ." Not built the thing, he finishes the sentence in his head but doesn't speak the words, recalling the basic insanity of what they're talking about.

"I did not mean——" For a moment she continues to stare at him, defiance and anguish wrestling on her face, and then she drops her head. "As I told you, my intention was to create a device for transportation between one location and another. Not to travel through time. All of this"—she gestures—"is an accident. So, to answer your question, no. I had not considered the consequences."

Peter shakes his head. "Then why Tesla?"

She thinks of the inventor's face and looks away from the mechanic, at the warped floorboards of the apartment. From beyond the kitchen comes the muffled sound of Paolo and his wife, arguing in Italian.

"Why see Tesla?" Peter repeats.

She cannot meet his eyes. "Because"—she draws a deep breath, wondering if she really is crazy—"I believe he is trying to create such a device himself, and I must warn him of the danger."

"That doesn't make sense." Peter has to struggle to restrain himself from shouting. "And what makes you think he'll listen?"

"At heart, he is a conscientious scientist and a reasonable man. If he simply understood the risks"—she shakes her head—"I know that he would help. I will write a letter, one that he will not ignore."

"Help how?"

"To find a way of stopping all this." With an effort she meets his eyes. And to help make sense of what has happened—she thinks but does not say—to find a way of going back and restoring things to their proper place. Of undoing whatever damage has been done.

Peter shakes his head, looking away.

And of course, she thinks, he is right: in any rational terms this must be counted as a kind of madness. "Stay here," she tells him. "I will go to see him alone."

Paolo bustles into the room, laden with a pile of ragged blankets. "We should sleep now," he says, glancing toward the closed bedroom door. "It is late. We talk of what to do tomorrow."

AT THE WORLD CLUB, Tesla seats himself in an overstuffed armchair and orders his morning coffee, struggling to control his seething anger. Outside, on the steps of the club, the inventor had been accosted by one of Morgan's minions, a neat little man wearing pince-nez. Unwilling to invite the man into the sanctuary of the World, Tesla had been forced to converse with the financier's emissary there on the street—like a common merchant—while the little man made insinuating remarks about his monetary circumstances and the benefits of cooperation with Edison.

As in the past, Tesla had dismissed the man with a flat refusal—but still the suggestion enrages him. The notion that he might be pleased to "assist" Edison, that plodding dullard, is an unbearable insult—as is the idea of sharing the prize that he has pursued for so long. The very thought that his services could be bought, that he would come running like a lackey to the sound of a full purse! Even with the prospect of what he could accomplish with Morgan's riches, it is impossible, degrading, inconceivable—

A waiter deferentially approaches and places the coffee service on the end table beside the inventor.

"And my mail," Tesla murmurs.

"Of course, sir."

Lifting the first cup of coffee to his lips, the inventor draws a deep breath and tries to calm himself by contemplating the smooth curve of its rim, the contrast between the translucent bone-white china and the blackness of the steaming liquid, the ripples on its surface caused by the slight trembling of his hand. And slowly, his anger subsides. If one had time, he reflects, one could lose oneself in the beauty of these details: for even in such small things are all the perfections of mathematics made visible. The wave in motion describing a precise logarithmic function. The law of thaumaturgy: as above, so below. But of course, one does not have time.

The uniformed waiter returns and deposits a stack of mail at Tesla's elbow. On top of the stack is an overdue bill from the Waldorf-Astoria, and beneath this the inventor finds another bill, from his tailor, a bill from the club itself, a pamphlet for an upcoming conference, and, finally, a letter addressed to him in a neat feminine script. This last item, he notices, does not bear a stamp—meaning it was delivered by hand. This piques his curiosity; only the very rich, in this age, still use private messengers for their correspondence.

Setting the bills aside, Tesla opens the last envelope and withdraws its contents: a single sheet of paper. At the top of the page are a time, a place, and a date. Below this are two lines of mathematical formula.

Around him the world stops.

He stares at the symbols and numbers, digesting their meaning. At first, as is often the case, he grasps their significance more by a kind of intuition than through any rational process. He uncaps his pen and quickly scribbles a few figures on the back of the envelope, trying the equation for himself. It appears to work—unable to suppress a paranoid impulse, he glances over his shoulder, half expecting to find Morgan's minion smirking at him. But there is no one nearby—across the room, a pair of club members are trading quips about a minor society lady; a group of servants discreetly ignore his gaze.

He looks down at the letter again, wondering if he is dreaming. Rereading the page, he scrutinizes each word for hidden meaning. The handwriting, he thinks, looks strangely familiar, although he cannot place it. Folding the letter, he beckons to one of the servants.

"When did this arrive?" he asks, holding up the envelope. His voice is strained in his ears, but if the servant notices, he is too well trained to give any sign. "Who delivered it?"

"One moment, sir. I will ask." The servant backs away and Tesla unfolds the letter again.

It is a miracle, he thinks. It is impossible.

Studying the equation, he realizes that it is only a fragment of some larger theorem, a partial solution—but it is still more than he could have dreamed. He suppresses the urge to laugh out loud; with this one stroke he has more than Edison and all his lackeys, an affirmation that his years of effort have not been in vain. Already his mind is teeming with new possibilities, new experiments—

"Sir." The servant reappears beside Tesla's chair. "The letter was left at the concierge desk at the Waldorf-Astoria Hotel. I am afraid that no one knows who delivered it."

Tesla nods, not really surprised.

"Will there be anything else, sir?"

"No. Thank you."

The attendant retreats, and Tesla reflects that, of course, it could all be a trap. The letter is a request for a meeting—but what if I ignored that fact? he muses. As he thinks this, however, he realizes that, trap or no, he will go: as whoever wrote the letter must have understood.

And who, he wonders, could the letter's author have been? He decides that the handwriting is probably that of a secretary; there are only a few individuals in the world capable of such work, none of them women. Certainly it was not Edison or Marconi, Tesla thinks. The mathematics in the letter have an elegance foreign to both men. Maybe Ludwig Boltzmann, although he has not produced anything original for decades. It could be that young upstart, Max Planck—but this is not quite his style. In fact, Tesla realizes, the structure of the equation is very much like something he might have written himself. . . .

Tesla stands, shivering. Nearly oblivious to his surroundings, he pulls on his coat and departs the club.

He walks through the city, the collar of his long coat turned up and his head bowed in thought. He considers the letter, and the strange girl who appeared in his room a week ago, and wonders how these things might be connected. He thinks of Morgan and Edison, of how he might use this development to his advantage. Now, if he chooses, he is in a position to dictate the terms of their cooperation. Let them come crawling, if they want his help. Around him, the street bustles—he is dimly aware of the pleas of hawkers and beggars, the crush of the crowd that parts before him.

He thinks of numbers and electricity, reason and magic.

THEY SPEND the next day in hiding, emerging from Paolo's apartment briefly to dispatch her letter, along with instructions for its delivery, to a street-urchin messenger. Aside from the two of them, the apartment is empty: Paolo departed early in the morning for the subway tunnels, and his wife left with the children on some unspecified errand.

By early afternoon the space between the peeling clapboard walls feels to Peter like a cage of nerves and unvoiced frustration. He tries to pass the time by reading the newspaper—*"Defiance in the Philippines! U.S. Troops Set to Smash Spanish Resistance, as President McKinley . . ."*—but eventually admits to himself that he's too preoccupied to focus on the headlines. Each time she comes near, wandering from living room to kitchen and back again, he has to restrain himself from looking up at her, needing to speak but with nothing definite to say.

Because finally, Peter thinks, he now sees the depth of her obsession, its fatal pull—still present despite everything he has done, and whatever connection exists between them. And also that, in the end, nothing he can offer will change her mind. Remembering how she sat next to him beside the fire in Central Park, Peter experiences a surge of anger and despair. It seems to him as if part of his own heart has become an alien thing.

Pacing the length of the shabby space, she is feeling a similar sense of anguish. She glances at Peter's brooding face, then away, ashamed. Turning the situation over in her head, she understands clearly that what she is asking of him is impossible, that from where he stands, it can only seem like madness. Some part of her is even glad for his refusal, that whatever happens to her at least he will be safe. Still, she finds herself unable to bear the thought of leaving him behind, because the truth, she knows, is that Peter's presence has come to mean more than she can fully admit—yet at the same time, she feels equally unable to turn away from what must be done.

Finally, Peter puts down the newspaper and leans back in his chair. "Guess we ought to talk."

She forces herself to meet his eyes. "Is there somewhere outside we might go?"

He shakes his head. "Could be the police are still looking for us."

She nods, sighing, and sinks into the chair across from him. "I know. But being stuck in this place, I feel that I am losing my mind."

Peter bites back the sharp reply on the tip of his tongue. The cramped confines of the apartment weigh on him as well, stifling his ability to think clearly. And after a moment, he relents. "Thought I saw a scarf hanging on the kitchen door. Make you a little harder to recognize, maybe."

"Are you certain—?" She looks up at him.

"No," he says gruffly. "Not really. But let's go."

They leave the apartment together. He guides their steps east and they cross from the tenement mazes of Paolo's neighborhood through the chaos of the streets toward the humbler brick-and-lathe warehouses near the water. She keeps her head bowed, anonymous beneath the fringe of the scarf, and Peter ducks his head below the upturned collar of his coat. After her time in jail and the meeting at Morgan's mansion, they both feel like hunted fugitives. Around them the city is a landscape of potential danger, the passage of each patrolling policeman and the glance of every stranger laden with the threat of recognition.

As they turn a corner, a band of ragged street urchins stares at them. A filthy boy of nine or ten, dressed in a kind of tunic made from a burlap sack and smoking a cigar, mutters something and the others laugh. Peter glares at them, then leans closer to her.

"Anything happens," he whispers, "if there's trouble, you just run. We get separated, meet me at the Grand Central train station. In the main hall by the clock."

She nods silently and they quicken their pace.

Despite his fears, though, they seem to have become temporarily invisible, swallowed up in the moving crowds by the faceless-ness of poverty. No one else looks twice in their direction, and eventually they arrive at the edge of the city, at the bank of the East River: an expanse of snow-covered grass and leafless trees, the dark current and the repeated arc of bridges. The empty walkway, the darkly shifting surface of the river and a skyline of Brooklyn smokestacks beyond. They stop.

It wasn't far from here, Peter realizes, that they had first met—a week ago now. Standing beside the railing overlooking the water, he turns to her.

"That day you saw me here," he says, "what did you . . . ? " Not sure why he asks, or how to finish, or even if he wants to know her answer.

"I saw you looking at the birds."

"Don't remember that. I remember looking at the city." He gestures at the silhouettes across the river.

A silence, as they both search for what to say next.

"I am truly sorry for all of this," she says. "I never intended you to be involved in this way."

He looks at her; she is staring at the water.

"Guess I know that." And maybe it's true, he realizes: other than a place to stay, she hasn't asked him outright for anything. "But, still." He shrugs.

She turns to him, hoping the tearing sensation in her chest doesn't show on her face. "Peter, you should not concern yourself with this. You have already done more than enough."

He doesn't answer.

"I will go to see Tesla alone. This is my risk to take." She forces herself to smile, abruptly near tears at the thought of losing him. "You should leave, as you wish."

Peter nods automatically. He is thinking about what lies ahead of her: more danger and fear, without any possible gain or end that he can see. A lost cause; not anything worth calling a cause at all, really. Even so—

"Thanks. Not sure I can do that, though," he says, an admission as much to himself as her.

"Why do you say that?" She blinks, her eyes and nose red from the winter air.

Peter feels a brush of cold on his cheek. He looks up and sees that it has started to snow. A scattering of white flakes drifting downward, settling over the walkway and disappearing into the river. He looks at her face, the black tangle of her hair, stark against the white snow and pale gray sky.

Trying to think of a way to explain the things churning inside him, he is painfully aware of how he must seem to her: a country bumpkin, out of place in the world of privilege where she has lived, imaginary or otherwise.

"Guess I've started to like the company." He shrugs again, a sudden tightness in his chest.

"Let Folly smile, to view the names of thee and me in friendship twined." She murmurs this, looking down at the water and reaching out to rest her hand on his arm.

Beneath her light touch, Peter discovers that he is trembling. "What was that?"

"Nothing." She glances at him, a flicker of a sad smile. "A line from Byron that suddenly came to me."

"Byron. He's a poet?"

"He was."

For a time, they stand there without speaking. Their breath steams in the cold. The snow continues to slowly fall.

Peter tries to stand very still, a kind of dizzy urgency inside him.

None of this makes sense, he thinks. And there's nothing— couldn't be anything, really—between us, at least beyond these moments. Still, at the same time, it comes to him that maybe love is always this way, a long-shot gamble: a bet against the odds that some intangible connection—even one so strange as this— will outweigh all the details and triviality of the world that drive people apart.

He reaches up and closes his hand over hers. Neither says anything for a time, both of their awareness focused on this small contact, skin against skin.

"I'll go with you," Peter says, before he can reconsider. "I mean, when you go see Tesla."

"I don't—" She shakes her head, biting back the objection that politeness requires. "Thank you." She looks up at him, her eyes shining and wet.

He nods. His lust and longing and loneliness—and everything else—for a moment fallen away.

The bare branches of trees along the walkway, the silhouettes of the city. Barges drifting past on the current. Overhead, the cloud-blanketed sky is beginning to darken.

"If only," she finds herself thinking, "if only—" Not knowing how the sentence should end. She looks down, shaken by the intensity of her feelings, and pulls her hand away.

Peter takes a deep breath.

"Well, anyway," he says, "come on. Figure it's about time now."

SILENTLY they start walking again, across Grand Street, where escaped Chinese railroad-slaves sell fish and produce in sidewalk stalls. Looking over at the mechanic's mournful face, she feels a sudden, overwhelming impulse to kiss him. Because if not now, she wonders, then when? In the whirlpool days and danger of the world, the opportunity may not come again. Because finally, she admits to herself, the thing that exists between them goes beyond what may be ignored or explained away.

Turning a corner, she sees a uniformed police officer glance sharply in their direction. Clutching Peter's arm, she begins to move faster. He keeps pace, shooting her a questioning look. Peering over her shoulder, with a jolt of fear she realizes that the policeman is following, also moving more quickly. She stops abruptly, stepping into the shuttered alcove of the nearest store, and pulls Peter after her.

"What—?" he starts.

"Ssh." She leans against him, tilting his face toward her own. He frowns down at her—then his arms circle her waist. The warm pressure of his lips against her mouth. She closes her eyes. His breath, the rough stubble on his cheek, exerting a kind of gravitational pull.

For a long moment she surrenders herself to this, the world disappearing. Until, abruptly, it returns and she turns her head away, shocked by her own behavior. This is the first time she has kissed a man.

For the space of a dozen more heartbeats she stands pressed against him, eyes still shut. Somehow, without looking, she can tell that Peter's eyes are closed as well. His hands tracing abstract shapes on her back.

She finds herself wondering, through a fog of longing and frustration, why it has to be like this. Why, when it should be so easy between them, she needs to make it hard. It makes no sense, she thinks, the power of these dumb animal things, at a time like this: the dumb yearnings of muscle and bone.

She opens her eyes. Over Peter's shoulder, she sees the policeman walk past without looking at them. With an effort of willpower, she pulls away. Before she can, though, he cups her face and guides her back against him. This second kiss longer than the first, an urgency of warmth and yearning.

"No." She shakes her head, hoping that he can't see how she is trembling, suddenly afraid of what may happen to her, and the resolve that brought her here, if she allows the moment to continue. She takes a step down the street. "We have to go—"

Peter opens his mouth and closes it. Finally he nods, longing and confusion clearly written on his face. He follows her out of the alcove and they continue on their way.

She looks up at the passing buildings and the bright stone of the moon, pale and narrow as a scythe's blade. And she wonders what, of all this, she will remember years from now—if, indeed, "years from now" even has meaning anymore. Her memory seems like a landscape washed over by a flood: certain features remain the same but all the details are changed, entire new hills and valleys added where there were none before. Perhaps, she thinks, only this. Glancing upward in the frozen nighttime streets to see, for a moment, the crescent winter moon overhead, her heart pounding, still warm with the memory of his lips.

They cross the uneven cobblestones toward McGurk's Suicide Hall. Peter holds the door open for her and they enter.

Inside, the saloon is half empty. He chooses a table on the main floor, near the back but with a line of sight to the entrance. She fixes her eyes on the surface of the table. The other patrons glance at them, briefly curious about the newcomers, but their ragged clothes arouse little enough interest and these gazes soon drift away. When the waiter comes around, Peter orders two glasses of beer.

"You all right?" he asks. "You want anything to eat?"

She shakes her head, fighting the urge to run away. Out of all the strange surroundings she has wandered through since arriving in New York, none has felt more alien and threatening than this.

"Used to come here with Klaus Neumann," he tells her. "The mechanic I work with. He first showed me this place. That is to say, I used to work for him. All that's over now, I guess." He shakes his head. "Funny, isn't it? Keep thinking I'm still part of all that. The subway, I mean."

He gulps his beer, and she suddenly understands that Peter is just as nervous as she is. Somehow this realization calms her. She straightens and tries to smile at him.

"Do not worry," she says. "You will not need to do, or say, anything. I will handle Tesla."

"Well, I'm here." He forces a smile in return.

"And I am grateful for it." Her reply is automatic, but it's also the truth. At this moment, Peter's presence feels like the only thing keeping her anchored to the world.

"I'm glad we——" he starts. But at that moment Tesla steps into the bar, regal and incongruous in his eveningwear, and Peter falls silent, gesturing toward the door.

The inventor hesitates in the entrance, surveying the room with distaste. She raises her hand, beckoning. Seeing this gesture, Tesla crosses to their table and sits without waiting for an invitation. His expression is pleasant and neutral, and suddenly she remembers the inventor telling her how, in college, he paid his bills by gambling. Now, she realizes, he has his poker face on.

Tesla places a leather document folio in front of him on the table, and on top of that his pocket watch. The other occupants of Suicide Hall glance appraisingly at the expensive timepiece before turning back to their drinks; the three of them are a bizarre sight, but this is a part of town that deals in unlikely figures and improbable odds, anonymity its chief export to the better-heeled city that begins a few blocks away.

Sitting across from Tesla, Peter looks around—the whores in their pancake makeup and the sailors lounging by the bar all suddenly becoming figures of waiting peril. Inwardly he struggles to regain the feeling of abandon and extravagance in the face of danger—his unspoken gift to her—that he'd experienced by the river. Picturing his own rough clothes and unkempt appearance, he tries to return the inventor's coolly appraising gaze.

"Mr. Tesla," she says after a moment of tense silence, "I see that you read my letter. Thank you, and thank you for coming."

Tesla nods, revealing nothing. "Thank you for giving me the opportunity. Particularly after the misunderstanding of our last meeting." He rests a hand on the document folio. "I am to understand, then, that it was you who worked this out?"

"Then you believe it does work?" She blurts the question without thinking, her memory of hours spent studying with the inventor overriding her sense of caution.

Tesla glances at her sharply. "You do not know?"

"I—" She looks away. "I was not certain."

"That is very interesting." The inventor steeples his fingers, stifling a smile. His mind is racing as he tries to recall the details of their last encounter and to piece together how she might have escaped from the police. Still, he realizes already that all the cards here are in his hand. He waits until she has begun to answer and then interrupts briskly.

"But we will return to that subject. First, I must see where I stand: I expect you invited me here for a reason?"

She nods. Her recollections of Tesla superimpose themselves over the man seated across the table, forming a double-image that makes her stomach knot. "For several reasons. First—do you really not remember me? My family?"

The inventor begins an easy denial but then, struck by the grief in her voice, stops himself. Studying her face, Tesla feels again a flicker of something like déjà vu. He recalls the few unremarkable months that he spent in Ohio nearly a decade ago, and the shy girl with whom he had shared a laboratory—but this mental image bears no resemblance to the woman facing him now. In any case, he clearly remembers hearing about her death, and his memory, he thinks, has always been perfect.

"My apologies." He inclines his head a fractional degree. "But, as before, I truly do not know you."

"Then how——?" the words tumble out of her, fueled by outrage and despair. "It seems so much to me that I remember you, Mr. Tesla! How we studied together at my father's house. I remember your confiding in me that you solve mathematical problems to help yourself sleep, that you have always been terrified by germs. So many things! How can this be?"

Fidgeting uncomfortably in his seat, feeling useless and forgotten, Peter watches this exchange. He sees the flush of emotion cross her cheeks, the gleam of tears in her eyes, and the impassive calm of the inventor's face—and suddenly he wants to smash things. He clenches his fists beneath the table, squeezing the grip of his father's pistol in his pocket.

Tesla hesitates, studying his polished fingernails to hide his shock over how much she seems to know about him. For an instant, like a fragment from a dream, the image comes to him of walking beside her in a garden. But that is impossible, he tells himself. And she could have guessed or discovered all these things from any number of sources. Still—he concedes—behind the dirt, the gross flush of blood and the filthy condition of her hair, she is a lovely girl. And a remarkable mind, an intelligence nearly equal to his own, if she really—

"You must remember!" In the face of the inventor's silence she presses desperately ahead. "Think of your birthday, the tenth of July in the year 1893. How we dined together at my father's house. You cannot have forgotten that!"

"On my birthday that year, I was at the World's Fair in Chicago," Tesla interrupts. "I spent the day working on my exhibit there, and dined alone." In his voice, she can hear the truthfulness of this statement.

"But how——?" She shakes her head, fighting back the prick of tears. "How is this possible? You were with me, I remember. . . ."

A glib reply is on the tip of the inventor's tongue—knowledge is currency, after all, and he has always been a miser. But despite himself, Tesla remembers a moment from years ago, when he was a boy in the countryside of his native Serbia. A day when he had sat in the yard outside the thatched-roof cottage where he and his four siblings lived with their father, the severe Russian Orthodox priest, and their long-suffering mother. Kneeling in the grass of a mountainside meadow in Eastern Europe, building a waterwheel out of twigs in the little stream that ran through the yard . . .

"But that is always the case, is it not?" Tesla murmurs. "We all carry a half-imagined world inside ourselves, the world of our childhood and its lost wonders.

"However"—he clears his throat and straightens, annoyed with himself for permitting such a lapse—"in fact, I do not know the answer to your question. Were it not for this"—he taps the document folio—"I might say that you were deranged. Perhaps you still are. These equations, after all, are only a fragment of a whole—and indeed, out of context, they might simply be gibberish. Still, if I were to see that whole, I might be able to give you an explanation."

He waits, and Peter waits as well, holding his breath without knowing exactly why.

She hesitates. Then shakes her head.

"The equation I sent you was a by-product, an offshoot from

another direction of research." She smiles briefly. "And since I do not know you, even if I had the whole I would hesitate to show it, realizing that you could grasp its meaning. As Mr. Morgan was kind enough to explain, its misuse would be catastrophic."

He is not surprised by the financier's name, she notices, and a wisp of fear unfolds in her chest like smoke. She seems to see the inventor sitting across the table for the first time, abruptly noticing the differences between this Tesla and the figure she remembers: a degree of cold calculation in his expression utterly foreign to the conscientious, otherworldly man she knew.

"Mr. Morgan is a coward and a pessimist," Tesla answers mildly. "Besides which, if all you say is true, the only possible explanation is that somehow you traveled from one world, where you did know me, into this one, where you do not. Therefore, should you not trust me as you trusted my other self?"

She shakes her head mutely and the inventor shrugs. He removes a cigarette from his silver case and lights it, exhaling a stream of smoke through his nose. "Regardless of that, you said there were several reasons for which you wished to see me?"

Around them, the bustle and clamor of the dirty saloon. The door bangs open, admitting a gust of cold air along with a flurry of snowflakes. Someone yells for more beer. More beer or more fear, she thinks randomly.

She struggles to put her words in order and speak clearly. "Yes, there was another reason. Speaking plainly, I wish to warn you against what I believe you now seek."

"Oh?" The inventor raises an eyebrow. He is entirely collected again, his mind alive with calculation. If she has met with Morgan, he muses, most likely it was the financier who arranged her release from jail. Meaning it is also likely that she has spoken with Edison.

In which case, the crucial thing—Tesla decides—is to ascertain how much she might have told him. And then to discover what else she may know—or, at the very least, to ensure that no future conversations like this will take place.

"And how exactly," he asks mildly, "would you warn me?"

"Against the consequences of such a device." She leans toward him, and the inventor tries not to flinch from the heat of her proximity. "With such a thing, one man might throw the world into chaos."

Briefly, Tesla considers pretending ignorance and denying any knowledge of what she means—but gauging her expression with a gambler's eye, he realizes that somehow, impossibly, she understands fully what prize is at stake. The limitless power that would come with possessing such a thing. Which means—with a wrenching effort of will, he overrides his distaste at the idea—better to treat her as an equal, at least for now.

"I appreciate your concern." The inventor inclines his head solemnly. "But at the same time, imagine its benefits. The wars that might be averted, the cities evacuated before they were destroyed by some catastrophe."

She hesitates.

"Think of it," Tesla continues, warming to his subject. "The citizens of Pompeii saved, the Boer uprising averted!"

"No." She draws a deep breath, as if shouldering a great weight. "No, Mr. Tesla. It cannot be."

"No?" Tesla raises an eyebrow. "And why, pray tell, is that?"

"Perhaps you are right, in the best of all possible worlds. But you know what men are capable of. None of us is responsible enough for such power. The world would be torn apart—"

"To be remade as it should have been," Tesla interrupts.

She looks at the inventor, his unreadable expression and polished demeanor. But despite his charm and elegance, this Tesla is not the man she seems to remember.

Abruptly she recalls a classroom lesson from her time at boarding school. On that day, the teacher had exhibited a sphere of amber that enclosed a row of fossilized ants. Peering into the golden orb at the procession of tiny creatures, frozen on their way to some vanished destination, she had felt a wave of pity and horror at this glimpse of an alien world, a fragment of long-gone time torn from its rightful place and meaning. Those small shapes that had once been alive, now become an unmoving schoolroom exhibit.

She looks over at Peter, the tension and fear on his unshaven face, then back at Tesla.

"I am sorry." She bows her head. "I cannot. Even in the best of hands, it would be too great a power."

"I disagree." The inventor shrugs. "After all, any great advance may be used for the ill or the betterment of mankind. Electricity has brought us light, and may bring a great deal more. It has also created the electric chair."

"But this"—the words burst out of her—"this is different. It is something else entirely! You speak of electricity and its effects. But time is the very substance of cause and effect! Undo that foundation, and—"

"I see that you and Morgan are of the same mind in this regard." Tesla shakes his head. "But I have never been one who shrinks from the risks of what might be."

From the impassivity of the inventor's face, she realizes abruptly that whatever arguments she could offer would be in vain. The fear in her chest begins to tighten into a knot as she thinks of how badly she may have miscalculated in coming here. That she may have, in fact, actually helped him accomplish exactly what she hoped to avert.

"And did Thomas—I mean, Mr. Edison—agree with your dire assessment?" the inventor inquires. "I am certain he must have also, at the least, been interested in your formulae."

"I did not show Mr. Edison any formulas or proof," she says. "Nor did he ask."

"Well, then." Tesla leans back in his chair. He exhales a stream of smoke, running a hand through his hair—and abruptly, some perhaps-memory tells her that the inventor is satisfied by this answer. A fact that she wonders at, trying to understand what it could mean.

A few feet away, at the bar, two sailors burst into laugher as a trio of whores link arms and launch into a surprisingly graceful line dance, capering in drunken unison. The clash of glasses, swirling clouds of smoke above the crowd.

Peter clears his throat, and the others turn to face him.

"One more thing, Mr. Tesla." He winces at the roughness of his words alongside the other man's polished diction. "We figure that we've given you something valuable. You've admitted that yourself, coming here. So I'd say you owe us something."

She turns to him, surprise written across her face, but he pushes ahead anyway, improvising. "We need to get out of the city, Mr. Tesla," he continues. "We need train tickets and money."

The inventor shrugs, puffing nonchalantly on his cigarette. "Perhaps I only came here out of curiosity."

Peter's face hardens.

"But what you ask may be possible," Tesla continues. "Of

course, it is only reasonable that I ask something in exchange." He taps the document folio again with a gloved finger.

She opens her mouth but Peter answers first. "She already said no."

Tesla steeples his fingers. "You realize that as persons wanted by the authorities, your fates at this moment are somewhat, shall we say, tenuous."

Peter reaches into his pocket, fingering the cold shape of the pistol. "Maybe you'd better speak plainly, Mr. Tesla." His heart is pounding, but somehow his voice is almost level. "I'm not educated like you. Might be misunderstanding what you mean."

The inventor's bland expression does not waver. "I merely meant to suggest that cooperation could be to our mutual benefit."

Watching the other man's impassive face, the wild urge to smash things floods through Peter again and he grips the pistol tighter. "Well, you heard her."

"Perhaps," Tesla suggests, "she will reconsider after the two of you have contemplated your situation more thoroughly."

Now, Peter thinks. Now, or it will be too late. And hoping that she won't hate him for it, he seizes his glass and raises it over his head.

The other two stare at him, then turn as a general disturbance begins spreading through the room. She sees a man rise awkwardly from a table, his arms wrapped around a black box, and stumble past a burly longshoreman's bulk. The stranger starts toward them, trips over the legs of a chair and catches himself—and then he is standing in front of the table. Belatedly, she recognizes Paolo as he executes a small bow.

"Excuse me," the Italian says. The flash-rod in his hand goes off with a whoosh, momentarily lighting the stained walls and wretched furnishings magnesium-bright. The bar collectively staggers and tries to blink sight back into its eyes, recovering in time to glimpse the photographer disappearing through the door.

Tesla moves to rise but is stopped by Peter's hand on his shoulder and the gun pressed into his side beneath the table, concealed inside Peter's coat.

"What is this?" the inventor demands—her stare echoing the same question.

Peter smiles grimly. "Yes, we're criminals, Mr. Tesla. And you've just been photographed meeting with us outlaws. Might want to keep that in mind, when you think about our future."

A moment of silence. Tesla looks down at his pocket watch on the table. He opens his mouth and closes it. Then he bursts out laughing.

Peter gapes at him, along with her and most of the bar's occupants.

"This display is quite . . . startling." The inventor shakes his head, still chuckling. "And also, touchingly innocent." The laughter abruptly ceases.

"Your ruse with the photograph is ingenious, but also completely futile. With my reputation, excuses are cheap enough. Particularly, if you will forgive my candor, against the evidence of persons like yourself. And as for this"—the inventor nods minimally, downward toward the hidden pistol—"do you seriously think that the prospect of death frightens me? In my work, I confront such risks every day."

Tesla leans back in his chair, ignoring the gun barrel jammed against his ribs, and directs a gaze of glittering intensity at Peter. After a moment, realizing despite himself that the inventor is telling the truth, Peter looks away and lowers the gun.

From across the table, she watches this exchange and feels a kind of tearing sensation. She thinks of Peter's face as he walked through the nighttime city beside her. She remembers the look of satisfaction the inventor wore when she answered his question about Edison. And, abruptly, almost before it has started, the inner battle is ended.

"Of course you are not afraid of these threats," she says softly. "But consider this: as you have suggested, Mr. Edison may be interested in the formulae I have shown you. Those details, and many more—which he might learn quickly, if the police should happen to question us."

Tesla's expression momentarily darkens. "What is it you want? Money?" He stares at her. "I am disappointed, if that is the case."

She looks away and almost, then, an apology escapes her—but Peter interrupts.

"Yes, we want money. And you say anything about this meeting, we tell everyone what we know. Edison, Morgan, all of them." Peter bares his teeth, a cold fury building inside him at the faint sneer on the inventor's face.

Tesla pulls away from Peter, not quite managing to suppress a shudder. For a moment his fingers drift toward the trigger of the chloroform device hidden inside his sleeve—but this is an acceptable outcome, he tells himself. If need be, the mechanic can be dealt with another time, the girl tracked down. He nods.

"Very well . . . You need money for train tickets? You intend to leave New York?"

"That's right." Peter's heart is hammering, fear and adrenaline churning in his chest, but he tries to match the inventor's cool tone.

Tesla reaches into a pocket of his coat, withdraws his wallet, and pulls out a sheaf of bills. "This is all I have with me. Not quite a fortune." The inventor laughs humorlessly. "Alas, I did not plan on buying my life tonight. So you will have to sell it to me cheaply."

Peter takes the money and shoves it into his pocket, ignoring the brief sting of something like shame. He looks across the table at her. She is staring back at him, wearing an expression of disbelief.

"Regarding your warning, however," Tesla continues, "the nature of my research, of what I seek—these things are not open to compromise." He shrugs and directs a brief, contemptuous glance at Peter. "Although I would not expect a man like you to understand."

For an instant Peter's grip on the pistol tightens. Somewhere in the chaos of the bar, a man curses loudly and a woman starts to cry. With a wrenching effort Peter masters his anger and stands. "Come on," he tells her. "Let's go."

She hesitates, glancing at Tesla—but the inventor is staring into space, a slight smile on his lips. After a moment she turns and rises, taking Peter's hand.

"I trust your journey will be a long and safe one. Bon voyage," Tesla murmurs, not looking at them, "and good-bye."

CHAPTER XII

THE FALL OF THE KINGDOM

THE PSYCHOPHYSICAL PHILOSOPHER GEOFFREY SONNABEND ONCE wrote that "the world is the horizon of the Other; our memories are the slate of the Same."* But despite the philosopher's genius, I believe he got this wrong. The world is the landscape of sameness, of experience forced into the generic approximation of words and sentences. After all, it's easy enough to say what I see ("a typewriter on my desk, a framed poster, an empty apartment") and at the same time, impossible to see what I can't speak. When Columbus arrived off the coast of South America, the historians recount, those keen-eyed tribesmen couldn't make out the European ships at all, lacking any words or notion for "a floating island, made of wood, topped with towers of billowing white cloth." No, Sonnabend missed the mark: memory alone is the realm of *both* the other and the self, of a radical identity of sensations that are too nuanced for any telling.

---

* Geoffrey Sonnabend, *Obliscence, Theories of Forgetting and the Problem of Matter* (Paris: Éditions Jurassiques, 1939), p. 46.

And that's the funny thing about memory, isn't it? Nothing is so near, and nothing else so unreachably far. Even as our memories define the essence of our selves, they turn on us, flitting away toward vague forgetting, changing shape (each recollection a potential smiling Judas in the pay of time), and making us strangers to the past.

This isn't the first time I've tried to write down our history. During the first decade after I arrived in Los Angeles, more than once I sat down to record what happened. But with each effort, after a few pages I saw the words beginning to twist away from what I wanted to express, into a collection of irrelevant penny-dreadful details. (And what makes this time special? In the end, maybe it's only the awareness that I'm running out of chances that keeps me writing: the understanding that if I don't set these things down now . . . yes, all those maudlin old-man sentiments.)

But still it's such slippery stuff, these recollections. In my earliest memories, I've become an outsider to myself, watching from an impossible perspective as a figure who, apparently, was once me (a supposition that feels increasingly unlikely with each passing year) stumbles through a series of long-gone, poorly reconstructed scenes.

Of course, it wouldn't be fair to blame all this—the chasm between then and now, I mean—on the failures of memory alone. The shape-shifting, fickle present seems to me equally responsible for the distance of the past as any trick of forgetting.

This morning, for example, I rode the bus downtown to visit a counterfeiter of documents: my final errand before leaving the city. I had met Alfie shortly after I arrived in Los Angeles, and he supplied me with my first set of papers. Since then, official documents have become harder to produce, but Alfie's skills (and prices) have kept pace. Yesterday he called to report that my order was ready: using the amount I'd kept from the sale of the store, I had arranged to purchase a new passport, replacing the previous one, which was about to expire, and as an extra precaution a Social Security card to match.

In his anonymous skyscraper office, I sat on a black leather armchair and we made small talk for a few minutes before exchanging envelopes.

"Everything good in your world, Professor?" Alfie asked. "No trouble with the last set?"

"No trouble at all." I didn't know why he'd decided on this nickname for me several decades ago: he had never asked about my past or why I needed his services, just as I never asked about his.

"I'm planning to go away for a while," I said. "Thought I'd better be up to date."

"Good idea. The way security is these days, a man can't be too careful. But you'll be fine." Alfie winked and tapped the side of his nose. "Even the FBI wouldn't look twice at my work."

I wondered for a moment what he imagined my story to be— he probably assumed I was a retired criminal, if he wondered about such things at all.

"So, you traveling for business or pleasure?" he asked.

"A little of both."

"Well, have a safe trip. By the way, your name's Sabinsky now. Ethan Sabinsky."

We shook hands and, outside his office, waiting at the corner bus stop among a crowd of tired commuters, I wondered at the strange banality of this transaction. For the price of a small car, in the eyes of the world I had become a different person.

I suddenly remembered a television special I had seen the previous week, where an expert on quantum mechanics had explained a theory called "relative state formulation." According to the physicist, other universes may exist alongside our own: an infinite number of worlds, one for each possible variation on our own reality. In fact, the scientist had continued, with each decision of our lives a new universe may be created, branching off from our own: a world identical to this one, except for the outcome of the choice we have just made.*

Standing on the downtown sidewalk, sweating in my suit beneath the heavy Los Angeles sun, I closed my eyes. Another passport, another name, another world. And among all these endless, separate, branching worlds, I thought as the bus groaned to a halt in front of me, how can I ever hope to find the past I'm looking for, or find you?

THEY ARRIVE BACK at Paolo's apartment after a wordless omnibus ride from the saloon, the cold of the New York winter still clinging to their clothes and faces as they bustle into the living room. He peels off his jacket and she her shawl, and they both fall into chairs at the battered wooden table. A moment later Paolo emerges from the bedroom.

Paolo's children trail in behind him, staring wordlessly up at the intruders, followed by his wife. They exchange a few words in Italian and then the wife departs, herding the children with her.

---

* To the best of my (limited) understanding, this theory—now widely accepted among theoretical physicists—was first proposed by Hugh Everett in his paper "Relative State Formulation of Quantum Mechanics," *Reviews of Modern Physics* 29 (1957): 454–62.

"So." Paolo grins at them. "It was perfect, yes? Perfect. I love the look on that man's face, on all your faces. No one followed, did they?"

"No." Peter shakes his head, grinning back at the other man. "No one." He fishes the money out of his pocket and counts it—sixteen dollars in all—handing half the sum to Paolo. "Here. For the photographic plate."

"No, please. I cannot take this." The Italian shakes his head. "It was only a favor, for you. For Tobias. Because it was men like this who kill him."

At the mention of Tobias's name, Peter feels a moment of guilt as he realizes how little he has thought of the dead man, in the midst of everything else. "If you change your mind." He drops the bills onto the table, where they lie in a crumpled pile.

She reaches out and touches the money. "But why?" she asks, more sorrowful than angry. "And why did you not tell me?"

Peter looks at her, takes a deep breath and looks away. "Didn't think you'd agree. Didn't know if it would come to that, anyhow."

She doesn't answer, staring at the sodden bills and wondering, with a kind of abstract despair, how they have reached this point: as common thieves, in hiding, all her noble ambitions undone.

"Besides, I told you," Peter continues. "That Tesla is no friend of ours."

"And to blackmail him with a photograph—that was your plan?"

"Our plan." Peter glances up at Paolo.

"Stupid." She shakes her head, speaking as much to herself as the two men. "He would never have let himself be controlled that way."

"Maybe so."

"And for this?" She points at the money, her sense of outrage flaring momentarily. "To become a thief? Is that all?"

Peter shrugs. In the Suicide Hall, driven by rage and the need to break through the inventor's calm veneer, it had felt natural that he should demand something. Now, though, he is struck by the realization of how his actions might seem to her—and also how they seem to himself, if he's being honest. Still, he thinks, taking comfort in the fact, in the end he'd been right about the inventor.

"Guess I just wanted to even things up, somehow," he says finally.

She closes her eyes. In fact, she already realizes, this anger is only a façade. Because like the mechanic, she also felt the need to wrest something back from the world in exchange for all that has been taken.

The three of them are silent for a time.

"One thing I keep wondering . . ." Peter asks the question that's been nagging him since their escape from the saloon. "You said that you know Tesla. But he didn't recognize you." He shakes his head. "So what . . . ?"

"Yes," Paolo adds, settling into the chair beside Peter's. "What happened?"

"I did know him, although not as he is now." She looks around the dingy room, the peeling paint and the faces of the two subway men, and she thinks of the inventor's words: *another world.* Glancing up at Paolo, she hesitates, telling herself that, having relied on Peter's friend so far, the Italian might as well know the truth, whatever he may think of her after the admission.

"In fact," she says, "the Tesla who I called my friend was a very different man from the one we met tonight. And the truth is, I cannot explain it. Perhaps it has to do with my journey across time."

Paolo's eyes widen, but before he can ask the question forming on his lips she continues in a rush.

"This is, I realize, hardly an adequate answer, or one that permits easy belief. Yet the interest of men like Morgan and Tesla suggests that I am not alone in believing such things are possible."

"Across time?" The Italian raises an incredulous eyebrow. "But that is—"

"Hard to swallow, I know," Peter interrupts, seeing the look on her face. "But she's right about Morgan and Tesla. So I figure we ought to listen before deciding." He turns to her. "So will you tell us? How you got to New York, I mean? Don't think you ever really laid out the whole story."

"I can try." She draws a breath, gathering herself—because this is not something that she has ever considered as a story. And now, contemplating how an entire lost world might be expressed, she cannot find anyplace to begin.

"Let me tell you the history of it," she forces herself to say. "At least, the parts that I know.

"After I arrived in New York, I went to the library, hoping to learn what happened. However"—she shakes her head, struck again by the sheer scale of the cover-up that seems to have taken place—"I could find hardly anything."

Peter watches her, his expression giving back neither belief nor disbelief, and she feels a surge of longing to reach out and touch him, but restrains herself. Across the table, Paolo cups his chin in his hands.

"But," the Italian asks, "you know what happened, yes? Whatever the papers say."

She shrugs. "In a sense. But I hardly know where to begin. It might help if you simply asked me what you wish to know."

Peter nods. "So before you came here, you lived in that Ohio place? And your father was the king?"

"Yes. Although"—she shakes her head, as with the recollection she feels tears jump to the corners of her eyes—"he was not a king as you might imagine. My father was a lifelong dilettante, a romantic. He loved silly poetry and landscape painting. When his older brother, Claudius, was killed and my father discovered that he would have to assume the throne, he wept and tried to refuse the title."

Peter tries to picture her as a little girl, the childhood meaning of these words. "And when you came here—you said you were being attacked? Was it because of the machine? Was it Tesla? And how—?" He stops as she raises her hands against this barrage.

"These are all good questions," she says slowly, "and I will try to answer. But—" She closes her eyes, stricken by the thought of how much has been lost, how little can be explained or even fully remembered.

"The interest of the federal government, I have realized, was to prevent a public outcry. Since, I must believe, there would have been some outcry if the world knew what happened.

"As for my own experience, I never saw the face of the man who destroyed my home, my family, and my country. All I have been able to learn is his name, Captain John Harlan of the United States Army. And even Mr. Harlan was only a pawn in the hands of other men, whose identities I can hardly begin to guess.

"Still, somewhere, I imagine, in some office or drawing room, someone must have met and decided . . ."

IT WAS, in fact (I have learned from the sparse historical records) the morning of June 16, 1894, when a meeting took place between an army captain named John Harlan and a United States Senator, in a quiet back parlor of the newly constructed Officers Club in Boston.

Through the curtains of the room, pale afternoon sunlight filters across the thick green carpet, the rows of military portraits and the clusters of gilt armchairs. In one corner a group of junior officers play billiards, their voices low in deference to the captain and the diplomat.

Harlan, in his mid-thirties, is the younger of the two men. Decorated in the investigation of President Garfield's assassination, he is an up-and-coming officer with a proven track record. The Senator is from an old-money family; his father was also a senator, and his grandfather the first governor of Ohio.

The campaign for Toledo should have been—as the Senator puts it—"a pleasantry. A bit of long-overdue tidying up." He takes a sip of his whiskey from a cut-crystal tumbler and leans back in his seat. "These farmers *want* to be Americans."

The Senator's cheeks are pocked and swollen, pouches of weary flesh hanging from his face. His funeral-black suit makes Harlan's blue uniform seem dapper in comparison. Seated in an uncomfortable straight-backed armchair, Harlan nods and fiddles with his drink.

"You would, of course, agree?" The Senator peers at Harlan, who realizes that he has been silent too long.

"Of course." Harlan nods, then, lowering his voice, continues— "I have no reason to believe that you and I differ in the interests which we have at heart: that is, the interests of the nation."

"I am glad to hear that is the case."

"Yes, sir." Both men sip their drinks and Harlan listens to the faint clack of billiard balls.

"There may be those," the older man murmurs, "who romanticize the issue or, through idleness of ambition or want of patriotism, confuse our sovereign destiny with so-called humanistic concerns."

"Sir?" The captain allows the slightest surprise to edge into his voice, hoping to disguise his scorn for the Senator's little speech. Although it is seldom mentioned directly in either the official records or in polite company, everyone with an ear to Washington knows the powder-keg nature of the Ohio Problem, the old conflicts ready to flare up and shatter the delicate political balance.[*]

"I anticipate that the matter will be short and bloodless," the Senator says.

---

[*] In fact the "Ohio question" raised issues of nationalism both domestically (in the wake of the Civil War, ended less than a generation earlier) and abroad, which deeply divided the American political landscape at the time.

In Congress the week before this particular meeting, the Republican secretary of war, Elihu Root, had alluded clearly to the question of the Free Estate when he read a statement that began:

> *Mr. President, self-government and internal development have been the dominant notes of our first century: administration and the development of other lands will be the dominant notes of our second. God has marked the American people as His chosen Nation to finally lead in the regeneration of the world. . . . Pray God the time may never come when mammon and the love of ease will so debase our blood that we will fear to shed it for the flag and its imperial destiny.*

The next day, Senator William Jennings Bryan, the Democratic presidential candidate, had concluded his speech at his party's nominating convention to thunderous applause by directly contradicting the secretary of war, proclaiming:

> *Among all the threats which lie arrayed against the greatness of this nation and her peoples none looms so large as the possibility that in her haste to step upon the world's stage, America may forget the very ideals with which she began. . . . No greater injustice can exist than the subjugation of one people by another in the name of freedom.*

Harlan does not dignify this statement with a response. He has always known that certain difficult decisions must be made, that a man needs both friends and favor to advance in life. Growing up on a hundred-acre farm outside of Baltimore—an ancestry that he tries to skirt in conversation—John Harlan knows what happens to those without some means or connection, an observation that his time as an enlisted man has further solidified. Ordinary men are shot in mine strikes, burned in tenements, ordered to charge so that the enemy might waste precious ammunition. Ordinary men are tossed and torn by powers beyond their control.

But for those willing to make accommodations, to curry favor with the influential, Harlan knows, the world has its rewards. A captain's epaulets. A general's granddaughter waiting for him at home, whispers of greater things. But still, he cannot bring himself to take pleasure in this task he has been given—despite the fact that he has been searching for exactly such an opportunity as this: a chance for heroism, which has been in short supply since the Civil War.

"And the Toledo family?" Harlan asks, keeping his expression neutral. "What is the government's position with regard to them?"

The Senator winces slightly at the mention of this name, before waving the question away. "No different than our position toward any other citizens of the United States. The Toledos have done some great things by way of civilizing the Ohio frontier. Insofar as their prosperity has benefited this country, we owe them a debt of gratitude." He smiles humorlessly. "Only it must be made clear that no other flags, either Confederate or Ohioan, will fly on American soil." The Senator sips his whiskey. "Consider this expedition a reminder of that fact."

"Yes, sir."

"The best of luck to you." The Senator sets down his glass and stands.

"Thank you, Senator." Harlan stands and accepts the proffered hand. For a moment, it seems as if the old politician is going to say something more—but he turns and limps away, cane tapping counterpoint to his steps. The junior officers at the billiards table snap to attention as he passes.

Two MONTHS LATER, John Harlan sits on his horse, watching the perfect, pink Ohio sunset. The wooded hillsides outside the town stand black and silhouetted against the pale rose of the sky. In the valley below, the lights of houses are beginning to come on in the growing dusk, the guttering of candles, the yellow glow of oil and paraffin scattered around the Maumee River and through the buildings, an incantation against wilderness and night.

In the woods behind Harlan, two regiments of infantrymen are waiting. In their factory-milled woolen uniforms they sweat and sit in loose circles, drinking corn whiskey and throwing dice. They curse and laugh and try to think of anything but dying.

In the branches spiders spin their webs madly, trying to catch all they can before winter's famine; when the men remain still for too long, they find themselves tethered by tiny, shining strands. As the shadows grow, officers walk between the men, reminding them to stay awake—to drink if they need to, but stay steady enough to bayonet a man and move in a charge.

At the edge of the woods, on horseback, Harlan studies the peaceful setting. Toledo, the royal city, jewel of the Midwest. But although her factories and houses are well built, solid, and prosperous, Harlan also sees that nearly half the town is dark and deserted, the owners of those houses having fled to the hills when they heard of his approach—and of the bloody rout that had followed his clash with a group of armed farmers near the border of the Kingdom.

Looking down at Toledo, Harlan nods to himself and spits on the ground. He has seen enough battles to know a winning hand when he holds one. Strangely, though, this thought doesn't fill him with the same rush of excitement that it has on the eve of other engagements. If anything, he now feels an edge of sadness. Of regret, even. But he pushes these sentiments away and spits again. He is a soldier, he reminds himself, and at thirty-one has killed more men than he has lived years.

Shifting in his saddle, he tugs at his gloves, flexes his fingers inside the tooled leather, and glances at his new pocket watch—a gift left for him at the Officers Club by one of the Senator's secretaries. Almost time now. He leans from his horse to speak to the aide-de-camp waiting at his side.

"Get them ready. Quietly."

"Yessir." The aide runs off into the night and a moment later Harlan hears terse, barked orders, the rustle of packs and gear. It takes them only a few minutes to assemble, he notes approvingly, and then the man is at attention in front of him again.

"Sir, the men are waiting for your orders."

Harlan hesitates, drawing a breath and closing his eyes. Such moments always feel to him like the brink of a precipice, the mass of men and nerves straining for release. And his hand on the brake that will let them go.

"Sound the charge," he says.

At the heart of Toledo, the royal mansion stands silent and waiting. The house is modeled after a French chateau; in sketches and photographs it is airy and graceful with a column-lined façade and wide French doors leading onto rolling lawns dotted with topiary sculpture. It is not a fortress, and the hired guards—there has never been a standing army in the Kingdom— who are stationed at the perimeter of its gardens are painfully aware of this fact.

The avenues around the mansion are laid out like the spokes of a wheel, and the Royalist defenders have blocked off these streets with barricades constructed from overturned wagons, garbage, and debris. Behind these rough defenses they prime their muskets and wait.

The charge is heard on the hillsides outside the city. A bugle call and then another, the sound of horses' hooves growing closer. The defenders take aim into the empty streets. For a long time—too long, this wait unraveling the steadiness of hands and hearts more surely than any bullet—nothing happens. They spit on their muskets and climb to the top of the barriers, straining to see. Then all at once the air is murderous and alive with gunfire and flying metal.

Musket balls tear into flesh, men fall in twos and threes and the men behind them bellow and scramble forward. The army soldiers run toward the barricades with their shoulders hunched and rifles outstretched, and the defenders reload and fire and reload again until the streets reek of gunpowder and the barrels of their weapons grow so hot that the powder sometimes explodes as it is tamped down, blowing off fingers and hands.

The position of the Royalists is a good one, and the federal troops soon realize this. For the men behind the barricades, it is almost too easy: they fire at the exposed infantrymen in the streets and duck down again to reload. It's like a shooting-gallery game, and within the first few minutes of fighting the streets are littered with the bodies of soldiers, their blue uniforms staining to black with blood.

The defenders of the city each have their own reasons for being here. Some of the men believe they are fighting for their land, as rumors have circulated that the federal government will confiscate the farms that the Ohioans carved from the wilderness. Others are fighting for the payment that has been offered by the Toledos. Still others are here out of simple loyalty, to the family their grandparents followed to this frontier. And all of them, in this instant, feel invincible: they smile at one another's smoke-smudged faces and laugh, verging on hysteria.

Harlan's men take refuge. They hide in alleyways between buildings and behind abandoned street vendors' stalls, pinned down, sniping ineffectively at the barriers. Then the word comes, shouted from one island of safety to the next: fire the buildings. It isn't clear whether this is an order or simply someone's bright idea, but it makes no difference. For the men trapped in the streets, it is a matter of survival. Someone produces a bundle of hay soaked with paraffin, someone else a torch—and soon factories and houses begin to burn. The wind fans the flames inward toward the barricades, and now it is the defenders who must fall back.

Abandoning their makeshift ramparts, they turn and run, looking for new positions behind walls and piles of garbage. But no real second line of defense exists: there was no time to prepare one. With a roar, Harlan's men rush the fortifications and now men on both sides are falling. More houses start to burn and families run out into the street, mothers in nightgowns pulling their children from the flames. Gradually, the superior numbers and training of the federal troops begin to take their toll. Panicked defenders drop their weapons and run, while those who remain are forced to steadily retreat.

In the sitting room of the mansion, everything is quiet. The French doors are closed and the curtains drawn, oil lamps glistening behind crystal shades. In an armchair near the cold fireplace sits the king, Louis Toledo; around him are gathered his valet, two bodyguards, and the old family butler, Nonce. Across the room, on a burgundy velvet sofa, the princess, Cheri-Anne, sits fidgeting nervously.

Watching her father, she is struck by the thought that for once he looks dignified, even regal. Louis is dressed in a dark suit; the royal purple sash is draped across his chest, the silver Toledo crest pinned to his lapel. When news of the federal troops' approach arrived, he had ascended to his chambers and then reappeared, perfumed and clothed in this finery. Calmly, Louis had read a passage of Byron to the assembled militia. And now, as he stares at the empty living room fireplace, fingering the silken sash, she wonders at the sudden transformation of his normally overwrought character. Through the lace curtains over the French doors, the evening sky has begun to glow red.

"Sire."

Louis Toledo looks up at the wizened butler. "Yes, Nonce?"

"We should go, sire. It is time. If we wait much longer—"

"I won't be going."

"Sire?" Nonce's eyebrows bristle. "As we discussed, your carriage is waiting."

"I know." Louis climbs to his feet and crosses to a mahogany sideboard, pouring a glass thimbleful of cognac. He turns and addresses the room. "I—I have changed my mind. Though I have failed as king in some respects, let no one say I failed here. A king should live and die by his kingdom. This"—he gestures, encompassing the room, the house, the countryside beyond—"has been my life. By God, I shall not forsake it in its hour of direst need!"

For a moment, shock and disbelief drive all other thoughts from her mind as these words sink in. It must be some kind of horrible joke, she thinks, one of his stupid pranks—

"Sire!" Nonce hesitates for an instant, then rushes angrily ahead. "I have served three generations of Toledos, and I tell you that this is not what your father would have wished. If you think you do a noble thing, you are mistaken. Flee! What will it benefit your family if you are cut down or arrested like a criminal?"

"Enough!" Louis stares unsteadily around the room, mopping the sudden sweat on his forehead with a handkerchief. "My mind"—his voice cracks—"my mind will not be changed."

"Father! This is madness!" She stares up at him with a growing sense of despair as she realizes that he is serious. If Tesla were here, she thinks irrelevantly, if he hadn't moved back to distant New York, he would have some answer to this insanity. Then abruptly she remembers the untested machine that waits in the basement laboratory, and her heart begins to race.

"Daughter." He returns her gaze, a brief confusion crossing his face—the same incomprehension with which he has always watched her. "The carriage will transport you to safety. But my fate is here."

Like an image snapping into focus, understanding comes to her then. His calm demeanor, his sad smile: all of it makes sudden, terrible sense. Because all of his romantic heroes, the poets and novels that he loved, were training for this moment, she realizes. For him, this is not about politics or business, but rather the wheel of fate and the fall of empires, the chivalrous last stand and the noble death. Glimpsing the terrible equation of her father's obsession, she shakes her head. *Unless you act now,* some inner voice whispers. *Unless now, at last—*

"Do you wish so much to leave me an orphan?" She stares at him, this strange man whom she loves and has never really known. "I beg of you. This is only a senseless, romantic insanity."

A musket ball thumps into the front door with the sick sound of splintering wood. No one moves.

"Sire." Nonce's voice is low and urgent. "We still have time. Will you reconsider?"

A stillness descends on the room, then, an instant of balanced forces, as if each of their decisions—king, princess, butler, valet—has canceled the others out. A window breaks somewhere, glass tinkling into silence. The moment of anticipation when the dropped object seems to hang motionless, waiting for gravity to arrive. And then it does and she feels something tearing in her chest, pushing her to her feet as she thinks of her hours of study and effort, now crystallized as signs pointing to this moment, of what can still be saved.

"Then if you will do nothing, I shall!" She whirls in a white blossoming of petticoats and runs out of the room.

"Damn." Louis Toledo sets down his glass, mopping his forehead again with the handkerchief. His hands are trembling, he notices, and to hide their flutter he draws the small pistol that he had concealed in his pocket.

"Make sure the carriage is ready," he tells the butler. "You and the princess must escape. See to it that she is not harmed. Take her to Boston, as we discussed."

For a moment, it seems as if Nonce might object—but he does not. Bowing his head, he shuffles out of the room. The valet follows with relief.

The king adjusts his sash and positions himself in the center of the room, facing the doors. The two bodyguards move to flank him. Outside, the sound of fighting is very near now.

"The king is dead," he says softly to himself. "Long live the king."

The front door bursts open with a crash, showering splinters into the room.

Somewhere downstairs, her heart pounding, Cheri-Anne throws a switch.

A moment later, the world explodes into fire and light.[*]

SITTING IN Paolo's nighttime apartment, she finishes this story and for a moment all three are silent, lost in the skein of what has been

---

[*] The only account of this event seems to be that recorded by the Amish historian Daniel Yoder, who collected various oral histories of the Ohio region. In his volume *An Account of the Ohio Region Told by the Common People of That Area*, he writes:

> The son of one land-owner, Jacob Marse, who claimed to have been among the city's defenders, fondly recounts his father's tale: "He got his gun and went with the other men to the city. Louis Toledo came out in front of his house and read the men a poem. Then my father went and hid behind a cart with another man in an alleyway. When the enemy came [my father] started shooting and the man beside him was shot dead. Suddenly there was a loud noise that knocked him down and broke all the windows nearby.
>   "My father dropped his gun and went out into the street. All the other men had gotten knocked down and no one was shooting anymore. He looked at the Toledo mansion and it had disappeared. There was a cloud of smoke that covered half the sky. For a week after that, the weather was strange and nobody's compass would work. It took [my father] a year to hear right again."

(Yoder, *An Account of the Ohio Region* [Milwaukee: Barlow & Sons, 1908].)

said. She looks over at Peter, expecting to see incredulity or some harsh judgment on his face, but he is staring out the window at the darkness beyond. Paolo methodically smokes a cigarette.

"It is a good story," the Italian murmurs at length. "This is how it seems for me too, when I remember Italia—so long ago now, it is like a fairy tale." He sighs. "So this is how you come here?"

She nods.

Peter knows that he should say something, but is at a loss for how to respond. He feels that in some way, with this story, something has changed. He thinks: *like the easing of a knot*, but then doesn't know exactly what this image might signify.

How to find a place for the inexplicable in the world, he thinks, to make room for what defies all common sense? But then, he reflects, studying the solemn lines of her face and remembering the touch of her lips, maybe it's always the inexplicable things that matter most. He reaches out, covering her hand where it lies on the table with his own. She squeezes his fingers for a moment before glancing up at the Italian and drawing her hand away.

"Thank you," he says. "For telling us, I mean."

"You are welcome."

"And now——" Peter starts.

"Now we sleep," Paolo interrupts, yawning.

"Sleep," she echoes. Abruptly the long shadow of the day before, its recesses of tension and fear, envelops her in exhaustion. "Paolo, you are a genius."

And they do: she on a cot behind the kitchen stove with the children, dreaming of her father, who melts and transforms into an unrecognizable stranger before she can reveal some essential thing to him. Peter, restless on a folded blanket on the living room floor, dreaming of a house, and Tesla's face in flames.

CHAPTER XIII

THE DOOR IN THE EARTH

AT LAST I'M ON MY WAY. SEATED ON A JETLINER HEADED EAST, I look through a porthole at the vast landscape of clouds and sky. My neighbor in the next seat, an overweight woman wearing a hideously purple sweat suit, tries to strike up a conversation by asking if I think we will arrive on time.

"We will come to claim our cast-off bodies," I tell her, *"but it would not be just if we again put on the flesh we robbed from our own souls"*—which, as I'd hoped, puts an end to our acquaintance (Dante seems to have that effect on people), leaving me free to study the passing clouds. Ten thousand feet below, beyond the citadels of white cumulus, forested mountain ranges spread like gnarled roots across the distant countryside. Watching them pass, a sudden sense of familiarity prompts me to flag down the nearest air hostess.

"Excuse me," I ask, "can you tell me where we are?"

"We should be passing over Coeur d'Alene, right about now." She smiles blandly. "Is there anything else, sir?"

"No. Thank you."

She wheels her cart away and I turn back to the landscape, recalling how once—lifetimes ago—I sat on a river outcropping, somewhere in these mountains, gazing up at the sky. As a boy, I remember wondering what it might feel like to be a bird, wheeling above the clouds and mountain landscape. Back then, the height of a hawk's ascent seemed as unreachable as the moon.

Now, flying over the Idaho wilderness, I think of this past and the impossible chasm of years that has made that young man seem like a third-person stranger, and find myself wanting to laugh and cry. It's moments like this that leave me feeling like the punch line of some ridiculous, cosmic inside joke. Because certainly I couldn't have foreseen, or chosen, any of it: not the things that chased us like criminals through New York, or these strange shipwrecked years of living without you, and most of all not the consequences of my terrible choice, on that terrible final day.

PETER WAKES to the clatter of cheap earthenware on wood. Opening his eyes, he sees Paolo's wife—he can't remember her name—setting down a plate of toasted bread and a teapot on the living-room table. He sits up, blearily scratching the stubble on his cheeks. She gestures silently at him and then the food.

"Thank you." He smiles at her. "And for letting us stay. Won't be much longer now, I guess."

She stares at him with dark, expressionless eyes—then turns away, disappearing through the kitchen into the bedroom. A moment later she emerges with the children in tow and, with another silent glance at Peter, leaves the apartment.

He climbs to his feet, stretching, stiff from spending the night with only a blanket between himself and the floorboards. Pulls on his clothes and laces his boots, shivering in the morning cold. He pours a cup of tea and gulps it down, standing in the middle of the room. The weak, early sunlight, the warped floorboards, quiet, and the cracked yellow plaster of the walls.

It's over, he thinks, it's time to go.

Standing in the chill living room, he waits for the sense of relief that this realization should bring: a chance for safety and escape. Maybe even a happy ending with her by his side, if such things are possible. And the relief is there, all right, but also with it, strangely, a wash of diffuse sorrow at the sight of Paolo's shabby apartment in the morning light. The echo of some imagined moment, years from now, and its ghostly, far-flung distances: that this may be the last time he sees this place, this city.

Stepping into the doorway of the cramped kitchen, he realizes that she is still asleep on one of the cots beside the stove. Eyes closed and unmoving, gripping the blanket with one hand, he is shocked by how young she looks, the intensity of her waking self stripped away. She stirs and opens her eyes, peering up at him, her dark hair a tangled halo around her face.

"What . . . ?" She takes in his coat, hat, and boots. "Are you going somewhere?" Her words blurred with dreams.

He nods. "Going out. I'll be back in a few hours."

"Where are you going?"

"Buy us train tickets."

She looks at him and then nods before burying her face in the pillow again.

For a second, standing in the doorway, Peter feels an urge to cross to her side, put his arms around her, and who knows what could happen from there. . . . But some voice of caution stops him, murmuring not yet, time enough for all that when you're both safe.

He hesitates, and then turns away. Pocketing a piece of bread from the table in the living room, he strides out of the apartment and down to the street.

Outside, the jangling movement of New York, the cries of pedestrians, jostling traffic, the high blue stillness of the winter sky. Along the crooked streets lined with decrepit buildings where Paolo lives, across the refuse-laden expanse of Washington Square, then north along the meridian of Fifth Avenue. He boards an omnibus, watching through the windows as the buildings grow taller and more ornate, stone façades replacing swaybacked lathe-and-plaster. Half an hour later, he disembarks across the street from the vast bulk of Grand Central Station.

Standing in the doorway of a shop, trying to make himself invisible, Peter surveys the crowd of passengers who pass between the pillars flanking the station entrance, the stalls of vendors, knots of beggar children, and shouting porters with their mountains of luggage. Before coming here, he'd imagined—felt a sick certainty, in fact—that Tesla or Morgan or the police, or maybe all of them, would have lookouts posted near each likely point of departure from the city, waiting for the two of them to appear. But after half an hour spent watching the building's entrance, he decides that the train station isn't guarded—or else, guarded in ways too subtle for him to see.

Teeth chattering from standing in the cold, he gathers his courage and drifts up the steps of the station. His heart catches as he passes through the door, half expecting a heavy hand to descend on his shoulder—but no one notices. Invisible among the crowd of travelers, Peter makes his way through the enormous open space of the lobby to the ticket booths on the far wall—where, waiting in line, he tries to keep his eyes fixed on the floor and his expression blank. Still, he can't stop himself from glancing over his shoulder every few seconds. Then, abruptly, he is standing at the counter and the clerk behind the wrought-iron cage is asking for his destination.

"Chicago," he says, throat tight and dry. "Two tickets, one way. Third class."

"Forty-two."

Feeling utterly exposed, Peter extracts the roll of crumpled bills from his boot. The clerk passes back the tickets and his change. Peter takes them, turns away. And then somehow he is outside on the street again. The slips of paper that mean escape in his pocket: a minor miracle. He staggers away, drunk with relief, fighting the urge to break into a run.

He boards the omnibus back toward Paolo's apartment. All that's left now, he thinks, are a few final preparations. Buy a suitcase for appearances' sake, maybe, even though they have nothing to put inside. A good meal, and then catch the evening train. Nothing more. Except—it strikes him suddenly—for the matter of good-byes. When he'd left Idaho, it had been a rush without a single proper farewell, but this time—

For a moment he debates riding the omnibus to its final stop, near City Hall, and walking to the river as some parting gesture to New York itself. But there isn't time, he reminds himself. And whatever the city was trying to tell him—the almost-meaning he'd felt at the sight of its buildings and bridges—is a secret he will never understand, or will only discover somewhere else, in another form.

The horse-drawn tram creaks to a halt. They are near the Canal Street subway-works—and these good-byes, Peter decides, can't be ignored. Shouldering past the other passengers, he jumps off the omnibus and starts toward the excavation site.

Walking down the streets in this part of the city, looking up at their disconnected details—the tangle of wrought-iron fire escapes, hurrying pedestrians, the painted signs of stores—he thinks of how it has all changed since his arrival, a few months ago. All these things, that were once embodiments of his own loneliness, have now become familiar, already layered with remembered moments. On a break from work, smoking newspaper-cigarettes with Michael, Tobias, and Jan. Silent walks with the older mechanic, Neumann.

He turns a corner. Down the street, he sees two figures outside the wooden fence around the excavation site—and stops abruptly, a sense of danger registering before the fact of recognition. Tesla, in his usual eveningwear, is standing beside the neatly dressed little man who visited Peter's apartment. Peter ducks back around the corner and presses himself against the brick wall of a building.

From this vantage he watches as the two men talk and gesture at each other. After a moment they walk off together in the opposite direction from his hiding place, and he realizes that he has been holding his breath. He straightens, heart hammering, and tries to consider what this might mean.

A hand descends on his shoulder.

Peter whirls, fists clenched—and finds himself staring into a pair of bloodshot eyes. For a suspended instant, time stops. Then he recognizes Josiah Flocombe. He takes a step away from his old subway-crew foreman, nerves twanging with adrenaline.

"What—" Peter forces himself to draw a breath and smile at the other man. "How are you?"

"Can't complain." Flocombe shrugs. Although his tone and

expression are casual enough, Peter imagines a tension between them. "Haven't seen you in a while. Been keeping yourself busy?"

"Guess so."

"Well, then."

"Well."

They stand awkwardly regarding each other, and for an instant Peter is oddly reminded of his first day at the subway-works—that initial glimpse of Flocombe, sitting on a pile of rubble.

"Well," the foreman says gruffly, "I expect you'll be going now."

"I thought—" Peter begins.

"Might want to take your portrait with you." Flocombe pulls a crumpled sheet of paper out of his pocket and offers it to Peter, who accepts without thinking. "Take care of yourself," the foreman says. He nods, then turns and walks away, back toward the construction site.

Left off balance by this exchange, Peter watches him go before unfolding the scrap. On the page, he finds his own likeness looking back at him—a sketch of his face, next to a sketch of hers. With detached fascination he reads the text beneath: "Suspected of Sabotaging Subway Lines . . . Wanted . . . Reward . . ."

Feeling suddenly lightheaded, he looks up. Down the block, Peter notices for the first time that two hulking guards are standing outside the excavation site gate, heavy truncheons strapped to their wrists—a different species entirely from the bored, slouching company watchmen who occupied this post before.

Concealed around the corner and pressed against the building wall, Peter is thinking furiously. Something isn't right here, he realizes. The unwatched train station, the now heavily guarded subway-works—what's happening doesn't make sense. Doesn't come close to adding up, unless—abruptly he turns and starts running, back toward Paolo's apartment.

To MAKE herself feel useful, she has decided to sweep the living room floor of Paolo's apartment. In theoretical terms, the broom that she found in a cupboard, and the dust-scoop that accompanies it, make perfect sense. In practice, however, the sweeping project is one problem after another.

The implements are unwieldy, the broom knocking her in the face with every gesture, and the dirt refuses to stay still, the piles of debris she gathers from beneath the furniture scattering before she has a chance to deploy the scoop. Housekeeping, she has decided, is harder than calculus.

Still, she perseveres, telling herself that one way or another, these are things that she will have to learn. They are leaving the city to start a new life: this is the realization she has been grappling with since she woke in the Italian's kitchen. And when she pictures Peter as a companion, the idea of finding a place in this world feels almost like what she has been searching for, without knowing it, all along.

And with the mechanic by her side, she can almost believe that anything is possible. A chance to begin again, she thinks, for the kind of freedom and happiness, together with Peter, that the strictures of life in Ohio could never permit. If only she can master the countless everyday things she has taken for granted until now, like the trick of sweeping the floor. Then the door bangs open as Peter enters, and with a sense of relief she abandons her task.

He sits at the table, out of breath, cheeks flushed with the cold, and she crosses to stand near him.

"How are you?" she asks. "Where have you been?"

"Train station. Then the subway-works."

"Oh, really?" She says this brightly, trying to sound like—she stumbles mentally, then pushes ahead—an ordinary woman, from his world. "What happened?"

Peter doesn't answer, staring at the surface of the table.

"I'll make you some tea," she announces, bustling into the kitchen.

In preparation for his arrival, she has all the necessary equipment laid out—tea, kettle, cups. Dumping a few fistfuls of the dried leaves into the kettle, she sets it on the stove and waits. Nothing happens. Of course, she realizes, there should be a fire in the stove. After a brief rummaging she locates matches and coal, in the bin next to the washtub. The coal streaks her hands black when she scoops it into the stove, but she wipes the smudges off with the hem of her dress.

Now, though, the coals are not lighting. Which makes sense, she realizes, given the low air-to-fuel ratio in the little chamber of the stove, plus the relatively high adiabatic combustion temperature of the coal. Glancing around the kitchen, she sees a pile of newspaper and a bottle of some brown liquor on a shelf. She crumples the paper and sets it on the smoldering coals, then nestles the bottle in the newspaper—which will evaporate the alcohol, she thinks, which should burn hot enough to set the coal ablaze.

She touches a match to the paper and, after counting sixty seconds, uses a spoon to knock the cork out of the bottle. This produces the desired effect of releasing the combustible reactant, igniting the coals at a high temperature and causing them to burn nicely.

Shielding her face with the spoon, she nudges the stove door shut. Some scraps of newspaper have fallen to the floor, smoldering from the initial blast of flame, and she carefully stamps them out. Noticing that the fire licking through the grate is beginning to die down, she approaches the stove again. A moment later, as she'd expected, the liquor bottle explodes in the heat, sending glass shrapnel pinging against the iron walls. She crosses her arms and waits for the kettle to be ready.

Suddenly the mechanic leans in through the doorway, startling her.

"You all right?" he asks, a strange note of concern in his voice.

"Of course. Thank you for asking." She smooths her hair with her fingers, realizing that a few stray curls are singed.

He stares at her, then shakes his head, grinning. "Guess I'll have to explain a few things about cooking, one of these days."

She looks back at him and feels a sudden, overpowering yearning for a future filled with moments like this one. "I'd like that." She returns his smile, and they stand silently facing each other.

Then the front door bangs open again, Paolo entering, and Peter turns away. She remains in the kitchen, listening without really paying attention, as the two men converse in the other room.

". . . early?" Peter asks, muffled through the wall.

". . . changes. All of us assign to different crews," she hears the Italian answer. "Tomorrow I start . . ."

She stares at the dark iron belly of the stove, thinking of how she has always imagined some future greatness for herself. How she has always seen herself as destined for some role that will change the world. But why, she wonders now, is that needed, and for whom? And for myself, shouldn't happiness be wherever I can find it? And with this thought, abruptly, she experiences an almost giddy sense of relief: like the answer to a problem she has been wrestling with for years, suddenly falling into place, or the lifting of an unseen burden.

The kettle begins to rattle on the stove and she lifts it off, pouring two mugs full of unexpectedly brackish tea. She carries them out into the living room, handing one to Peter and then, belatedly, offering her own to Paolo, who accepts with a brief smile.

"So." Peter turns to her. "You ready to leave?"

"Yes," Paolo adds. "He says you will take the train to Chicago?"

"I bought two tickets."

She takes a breath, looks up at him and nods. "Yes." She tries to smile. "I am ready."

"Well, then," Peter says.

He runs a hand through his hair.

Closing his eyes, the image that comes to Peter is a small log cabin somewhere in the woods. A stream running nearby, the two of them living together, evenings spent in conversation. Some flickering movement and faint laughter among the daffodils growing by the porch that could be the shadow of children to come. With sudden clarity, he sees that beyond his aimless days in New York, this is what he longs for.

Except that, for no reason he can understand, Tobias's face returns to him, hanging between himself and this vision. The memory of his friend being dragged away by the drilling company guards, of Tesla and Morgan's minion smiling together outside the subway-works. Of John Muncie, the sheriff of Kellogg County, staring down at him beyond a gun barrel. And with these images an abrupt, unreasonable anger.

"It's a funny thing, though," Peter finds himself saying, almost against his will. "Seems like that's what they want too."

She frowns. "What do you mean?"

"Wasn't anyone watching at the train station." As he says this, Peter feels the reasonable, cautious part of himself slipping away. "No one stopped me when I bought those tickets, either. But they had more guards at the subway tunnels. They were waiting for us there."

He pauses and, when she doesn't say anything, continues. "That looks like a message to me. 'Get out of town. That's fine. But don't go near the subway-works.' What it seems like they're saying." Peter stares at her. "So what're they looking for down there?"

She shakes her head, clinging to the sense of clarity and release she felt in the kitchen, unwilling to answer.

"It just doesn't make sense." He sits down at the living room table.

"It is true," Paolo says. "They are looking for something in the tunnels. As well as your picture, there are new men, not workers, who go into the tunnels." He shrugs. "And we find some strange things down there. Old pipes made out of wood, part of a ship, old bones, some different kinds of rock. But none of these, I think, are what these men look for."

A silence. Dust filtering slowly downward, in the late-afternoon sunlight. She sinks into a chair beside Peter.

"I know what they are looking for," she hears herself murmur, wondering at the same time why she doesn't simply remain silent— these words coming from some part of her that still clamors for vindication, despite what she has decided. "They are looking for the mass anchor."

"The what?" Peter frowns at her.

"The mass anchor," she repeats, speaking half to herself. "The device we built used a large block of mass to connect its origin and destination points. An object that would exist in both places at once, creating a conduit for travel between them."

"And . . . ?" Peter prompts.

"It did not have to be very large since, as we built it, the mass anchor formed the apex of a conic projection. But"—she looks up at him—"it had to be embedded in the earth itself, underground."

She stares down at the table. How will I ever be free, she thinks, how can I escape this history?

"When you first came to New York," Peter is asking, "when you first woke up, what's the first thing you remember? You see this mass-anchor thing?"

"I woke up in the Battery Park." She remembers her initial wheeling disorientation, the terror of being unable to assemble a chronology. "But I did not see the anchor. Still, it should have been nearby.

"You see"—her words start to come more quickly as the excitement of the equations overtakes her—"the anchor marked the center of a spherical magnetic field, within which objects could be translocated. A region perhaps"—she closes her eyes—"perhaps fifty feet in diameter."

"But what—" Peter gropes for the right question. "What would it be? What would it look like?"

"Like nothing special. A wooden door, about four feet wide. It was a door in the basement of my father's house. Although—if it did exist, it would have been there for seven years now. It might have been destroyed."

Paolo shakes his head. "I haven't heard something about a door in the tunnels."

"Nothing near the Battery Park?" Peter glances at the other man.

"As I said, only some different kinds of rock."

All three are silent for a time.

And then it's over, Peter thinks. His relief strangely edged with disappointment, as he starts mentally assembling a list of supplies they'll need for the trip to Chicago and whatever lies beyond. An ax and a compass, blankets and a change of clothes—

"In the South Ferry tunnel," Paolo continues, "at first it was only granite. But now there are lots of little holes in the rock. Holes and cracks."

In a long-disused part of Peter's memory, something clicks with these words. "Little holes in the rock?"

Paolo nods.

"Round holes, like bubbles in water?"

"Just like that. They make the drilling hard. The bits twist and break."

"Why do you ask?" she asks.

"It's just that . . ." He hesitates, remembering long-ago nights spent in the Idaho mountains. Sitting crouched by a campfire in the dark immensity of that wilderness, listening to his father talk about geology and the language of the earth. The days spent exploring old mine shafts with his father, so many hours underground that he'd learned how to traverse those caverns almost by intuition alone.

"It's just that those kind of bubbles usually mean a fissure or cave nearby." He pauses. "Aren't many caves under Manhattan, least not around there."

"I see." She fails to hide the tremor in her voice.

"That tunnel is almost under the Battery," Peter says.

They turn to each other.

Peter feels, all at once, a sense of both sinking and rising. The downward pull of peril and conspiracy he has struggled to escape—but also, a beam of improbable hope. Because—the sudden, glittering possibility strikes him—what if everything she has said is true? An overwhelming vertigo of new choices. Because maybe, he thinks, even if the past can't be escaped, it can still be set right.

Abruptly then, reaching the end of the caution and reserve he has clung to and fought against his entire life, he looks at her and decides.

"We'll go down there," he says. "Tonight. We'll find a way."

"Tonight?" She stares at him.

After everything else—the dread, uncertainty, and hope of the previous days, and all the decisions and reversals—I still can't really guess what passed through your mind at that moment. But finally, you looked up at me and nodded.

"Very well. Tonight."

THEY WAIT in the early darkness, beside the high fence of rough boards surrounding the subway construction site, their breath steaming in the leaden winter evening. The last of the men from the excavation crew are filing out of the tunnels, each slack-faced with fatigue, glancing in puzzlement up at the sky before dispersing to wander away through the streets.

"Now?" she asks. Her teeth are chattering.

"Almost." He peers into the burlap sack he's carrying, which contains the simple machine on which their plan hinges. "Not long."

After spending the evening gathering supplies, the device that Peter inspects is mainly a product of her ingenuity. It is, as she'd explained, a crude smoke bomb: a candle with saltpeter and sugar mixed into the wax, it should smoke profusely for a few minutes after being lit. That is, he reminds himself, if it doesn't explode or go out first. If I haven't lost my mind completely here.

More minutes pass. The streets begin to empty and the sky darkens further. Trying to ignore his second thoughts, Peter peers through a chink in the fence and sees a small light go on inside the night watchman's shack, the dim silhouette of the watchman as he bars the construction-site gate.

He draws a shaky breath. "Now."

The placement of the candle, he thinks, should be just across the fence from the shed where the dynamite and blasting caps are stored. From the watchman's position, it will look like the shed itself is on fire—at least that's what he's hoping, and what he's told her.

He passes her the box of matches. "Wait until—"

"Until you are in position," she interrupts. "Then light the device, and signal when I see the guard coming. I remember. Then we meet at the gate."

He nods. They look at each other, a conspiratorial glance. Peter starts to speak and then stops himself—too much, he thinks, everything and nothing, and it's not the time for words anyway. He hands her the sack of supplies and walks away.

Around the corner and halfway down the block, he stops outside the barred entrance to the subway-works. The gate is twelve feet tall, built from massive planks that loom over his head. Still, he thinks, it's not so much taller than boulders he's leapt over while scaling crags in the Idaho mountains. But it has to be done all at once, he knows, without any second thoughts or doubt. All at once, or not at all. Heart pounding, he clenches and unclenches his fists, and waits.

Nothing happens. Silence, the *cloosh-cloosh* of horses' hooves through icy slush somewhere in the distance. Maybe the device didn't work, he thinks. Then he sees the cloud of black smoke rising in the evening air, hears her whistle.

Before he can reconsider, Peter hurls himself up onto the gate. Straining his entire body upward, he catches the rough top edge of the boards. For a moment he hangs there. Then, with an impossible effort, heaves himself up and over.

He lands hard, twisting his ankle. Ignoring the pain, he fumbles with the bar across the gate. It sticks at first but then gives under his weight. The gate swings open with a metallic screech. A moment later, she slips through.

"Which way?" she whispers.

Peter fumbles to re-bar the entrance, scanning the piles of rubble for the mouth of the tunnel. "There." He points.

Somewhere across the construction site he hears mumbled curses and running footsteps. Ignoring this, he limps as fast as he can toward the pit.

Unlike most subway sites, here the tunnel starts abruptly. From the surface, a hole descends vertically for twenty feet to the excavation proper, spanned by a wooden ladder. Peter climbs down first, moving awkwardly on his injured ankle. She tumbles down the ladder behind him, falling over the last rungs into his arms so that they both collapse onto the rocky floor. Painfully, they climb to their feet.

The place they have entered is far different from the lamp-lit chaos of the tunnels where Peter worked on the digging crews before. Here, after hours, the darkness and silence of the underground passageway are final and absolute. Even directly below the entrance Peter can hardly see his hands in front of his face, and ahead of them the excavation is a rough corridor leading to utter blackness.

They move slowly into the dark, supporting each other and tripping over outcroppings of rubble. Within minutes both of them are bruised and bloodied from banging against the unfinished walls. Groping their way around the first bend in the tunnel, they stop, clinging to each other.

Gradually they catch their breath. Still they remain pressed together, eyes closed.

Some unknown span of time passes. She breathes in the scent of his body, the universe shrinking briefly to the diameter of his arms. Finally, feeling him shift nervously, she forces herself to step away.

"Here," Peter whispers. "I'll light the lantern."

"Are you sure it won't be seen?" A hissing echo of her words coming back to them from unseen rock walls in the distance below.

In response, he takes the burlap sack from her and fumbles inside, pulling out the small paraffin lamp purchased that afternoon—along with a compass and a few other supplies—by Paolo's wife, with Peter's dwindling savings. She strikes a match and their shadows flare hugely for an instant before he shortens the wick. The flame through the glass illuminates only a few feet around them.

They continue downward, into the pit.

A hundred feet later the tunnel branches to the left and right, and they stop.

"Which way?" She looks at Peter. He pulls the compass out of his pocket. By the guttering lantern flame, he studies the instrument—then shakes it, and shakes his head.

"What is wrong?" she asks.

He holds up the compass. The needle swings right, pauses, swings left and then right again, refusing to come to rest. "Broken."

She nods, struck by the thought that the problem may not be the compass but what lies ahead in the underground darkness. North, the compass says. West, south, west, north. She shivers, not only from the subterranean chill.

"What now?" she whispers. "Can you find our way without it?"

Peter frowns. The directions that Paolo gave him through the tunnels were vague at best. South and then east, almost under the river, the Italian had said: not much to go on in these unknown diggings. And really, he thinks, the reasonable thing would be to turn back now.

He looks up and sees her expectant expression in the flickering light. And for no clear reason, the image of his father's face comes back to him.

"Maybe." He nods. "Stay quiet."

He waits until the echoes of these words have died away. When they do, the silence of the tunnel is unsettling. During Peter's months in New York, the white noise of the city has become what stillness means—so that now, this absolute absence of sound feels like something else, heavier and more threatening.

Closing his eyes, he snaps his fingers and listens to the series of fading clicks down the tunnel. He snaps his fingers again, trying to visualize the city above, the shape of the branching rock walls around them. He opens his eyes.

"Half a second to the first branching. Can you remember?"

"Why?"

"The echoes. A trick my father taught me."

Abruptly the puzzlement on her face shifts to an expression of wonder, as realization—and with it, a crowd of questions and possibilities—floods her mind.

"Of course—like Archimedes, measuring the displacement of water!" She steps toward Peter, grasping his arm. The idea of using echoes this way, substituting sound for light—the notion takes her breath away: a whole new kind of vision, a means of mapping the unseen corners of the world. "Tell me, is this done often on the frontier? Has anyone built a machine for the purpose? And why snap your fingers instead of, for example, whistling? Do you find that lower sounds echo better than a higher pitch? Because I would think—"

"Ssh," Peter interrupts, glancing back toward the mouth of the tunnel, and she realizes that she'd nearly been shouting. "Later," he whispers. "We need to keep moving."

She nods, chagrined, and follows him down the left fork of the tunnel, descending deeper into the earth. As they walk she snaps her own fingers and slaps the cave walls experimentally, trying to correlate the reflected sound with this underground geography, until he asks her to stop—and they move onward in silence.

Darkness and more darkness. After a time, she cannot tell whether they have been walking for minutes or hours. She feels as if she is going blind, the small puddle of yellow lantern light around them revealing the same scene again and again: dull rock on all sides, repeated to infinity. Twice they arrive at dead ends and she feels the beginnings of panic, imagining the two of them wandering sightless until they die of cold or starvation. She tries to ignore the weight of unseen stone pressing down on all sides, to focus only on her footsteps, the next breath, and the next. Finally, after an eternity of this, he stops and holds up a hand.

"Here," he says. "See?"

She blinks and scrutinizes the spot where Peter is pointing. At first it seems identical to every other part of the excavation, a rough tunnel of gray stone. Studying the wall more closely, though, she realizes that the tunnel is riddled with tiny indentations and hairline fissures.

Looking at the pitted granite in the flickering lantern light, she feels a faint tug, as from a distant magnet, from somewhere beyond the rock wall.

She turns to him. "What now?"

In answer, Peter takes a rock hammer from the sack and presses his ear to the stone. He taps delicately, moves the hammer, and taps again. Lowers the hammer and looks at her. "There's a cave," he says. His voice echoes strangely in the lifeless underground air. "The wall isn't thick. Another six inches, maybe, they would've been inside."

"How big is it?"

"Hard to say. Not very, I'd guess."

She shivers, imagining a teeming of unseen presence in the air around them, a soundless whispering. Abruptly, her heart is pounding in her chest. "Can you blast the wall? Is it possible to get through?"

"Maybe." He considers. "Dangerous, though. Could bring the whole tunnel down on us. Or could be a pocket of gas behind that wall—kill us just as quick."

She does not say anything, only looks at him. Peter returns her gaze. In the inhuman silence, this meeting of eyes carries the intimacy of a kiss.

"Peter——" she starts.

"I brought two blasting caps," Peter interrupts, doubting his own resolve and unready to hear what she might say. "So we'll have a second chance." Without waiting for her response, he presses his ear to the rock.

The first thing every miner learns is to never blast inside a tunnel without cross-bracing. Even a small explosion can cause the fragile arch of an excavation to collapse, so that seasoned rock men won't even stand inside a tunnel when dynamite is involved. Peter remembers this clearly, along with all his father's other warnings. And now, he has nothing to reinforce the tunnel, not even clay or wood to direct the explosion. Trying to ignore these facts, he closes his eyes and concentrates on the stone reverberating beneath his hammer, its secret flaws and hidden volumes. Somewhere he knows this is craziness, but the fact is oddly untroubling to him. In fact, he thinks, there's almost a reassurance in giving up on the idea of living as if the world made sense.

Finally, when he has found the place where the wall seems thinnest, Peter removes the box of blasting powder from the sack and surveys the rock surface.

Despite the underground cold, his palms are sweating. He sets to work, chipping out a channel between the three largest bubble-concavities in the granite. When this is done, he fills the hollows with blasting powder and uses all his strength to tamp down a layer of dirt above the explosive. The blasting cap goes into the topmost depression. Finally, the fuse——looking at it, his heart sinks.

At Paolo's apartment, the roll of magnesium-laced cord that the Italian had smuggled out of an excavation site looked substantial enough, but now Peter realizes that it's less than ten feet long. The tunnel runs for at least fifteen feet before it bends——so even without saving any of the fuse, he thinks, it won't be enough to get away from the blast.

He looks up at her. Around the two of them, the lantern casts a fragile globe of light, a few illuminated feet amid the miles of underground darkness. His heart catches.

"Get around the corner," he says. "Put your back against the wall, plug your nose and ears." He shows her how, and she nods. "I'll be there soon."

"Thank you," she says. "Thank you for everything, Peter." She rests her hand on his arm. The ghost-lightness of her fingertips carrying an electric charge that rushes through him.

A surge of recklessness and longing takes hold of her, and, ignoring the inner voices of lifelong restraint, she leans forward, pressing her lips to his. His arms go around her and she closes her eyes, the looming weight of subterranean night and peril irrelevant for a moment as something seems to pass between them, a wordless message like a promise of everything that can never be put into words.

Shivering, she pulls back, looking up at him, naked beneath his gaze.

"Go," he tells her.

Abruptly self-conscious, she nods, turns, and walks away.

Peter watches her retreating shape, his head spinning. He takes a breath, trying to focus on the task before him, and surveys the packed charges of blasting powder. He mentally reviews the layout of the tunnel, the exact series of motions that his body will need to perform next. Gripping the end of the fuse, he lights a match, noting dispassionately that his hands are shaking. Touches the flame to the magnesium-laced string. He hesitates for a fraction of a second to make sure it has caught—then launches himself into a run.

The force of the explosion catches him mid-stride, lifting him off his feet and hurling him forward. For an instant, he sees the tunnel wall rushing toward him with incredible clarity. He sees a particular small depression in the rock, its dark texture and grain.

Then darkness. The touch of her fingers on his face.

Peter tries to open his eyes but his eyelids are sticky, and even when they seem to be open he sees only blackness. He tries to sit up, but dizziness overtakes him. He lies back down. A wave of nausea hits and he vomits helplessly onto the ground.

"What—?" he croaks. "Can't see."

"Can you speak?" she asks. "Can you hear me?"

Peter realizes that he must have lost consciousness. He takes a ragged breath, manages to nod.

"Can you hear me?" she repeats, her voice edging closer to hysteria.

"Can't—" His mouth is full of blood and he spits, clears his throat. "Can't see," he rasps.

"The lantern went out." With the sound of her voice, all at once Peter's sense of the world returns, and with it the weight of remembering. The terror of where they are at this moment, of the fact that something has gone horribly wrong. For a moment he longs only for oblivion, to just close his eyes and—

"Are you hurt?" she asks.

"Don't know."

She helps him lean against the rock wall of the tunnel and he sits there, gasping, for a few moments, trying to regain his breath. Every part of his body hurts, most of all his left leg. He feels blood on his face, tastes blood in his mouth. Painfully, he tries to move and discovers that—miraculously—all of his limbs still work.

"Can you stand?" she asks.

He nods.

"Can you?" she repeats, more urgently.

Belatedly, Peter realizes that his gesture is invisible to her in the absolute darkness around them. "Think so." He coughs, tastes more blood. "What about you? You all right?"

"I only had the breath knocked out of me. But you—"

Peter feels the flutter of her hands against his shoulder, his cheek. He closes his eyes, but when he does so a wave of dizziness hits him. He forces himself to sit up straighter and fumbles the box of matches out of his pocket.

"Need light." He tries to strike a match but his bruised fingers are too clumsy for the task. He holds the box out toward the sound of her breathing. "Here, light a match."

She gropes through the darkness and finds the small box. A moment later, the scrape of the match and the whiff of sulfur— and both are blinking at each other in the brightness of the tiny flame.

Her hair is a tangled mess, soot smeared across her cheeks. As for Peter—she tries not to wince at the deep cuts and fragments of rock embedded in his face and hands. She looks away, over her shoulder, toward the pile of rubble where the blast went off. The match starts to burn low and she drops it.

Darkness covers everything again.

"The lantern," Peter says.

"Yes." She gropes at the rough stone floor of the tunnel, un- steadily rises to her feet. "I will find it."

Peter hears the shuffling of her footsteps. Abruptly, with pain- ful clarity, he recalls the spot where he put down the lantern. "It was by the wall, where I set off the powder. No way it could've survived the blast."

Another match flares blindingly to life and he looks up to see her silhouetted a few feet away, gazing toward the loose rock that clogs the excavation's width.

"I don't see it."

"It's gone," he says.

The second match goes out and she lights a third, cupping it in her hand as she returns to where he sits against the tunnel wall, lowering herself beside him. The match burns low and she blows it out.

"Careful," Peter says. "How many matches left?"

The lisping sound of the box being opened.

"Eight, I think."

"I need to think," he says.

He is silent in the dark and, abruptly, she feels a knot of panic growing inside her as she registers their situation. Sightless and freezing, lost in an underground maze, likely to be arrested, or worse, if they are discovered—she bites her lip, struggling for calm.

Peter says nothing.

Something begins to happen in the blackness around them. By slow degrees, she feels the darkness solidifying. As if it were more than the simple absence of light, but a substance with its own weight and thickness. A curtain of blindness beyond which, she images, something is beginning to stir and wake.

"What shall we do?" she whispers, trying to suppress the growing pressure of hysteria that she feels. "What should we—"

"I need to think," he says.

Peter tries to consider their options. Maybe, if he can walk that far, they could find their way out of the tunnels using feel and echoes alone. But in the darkness, more likely they'd end up lost, or worse: easy to stumble into an unseen crevice and break an arm or a neck.

He feels lightheaded and drowsy, struggling to concentrate. Distantly, he suspects these are the effects of his collision with the rock wall. But somehow, between the heaviness that fills his body and the warmth of her presence beside him, he can't find a way to put his thoughts in order. Better to stay here, he thinks.

"We'll wait," he says. "Shouldn't be more than three or four hours until the crews arrive."

"But the police—"

"I worked with these men. More than a few hate the law." He closes his eyes, waves of something like sleep lapping at the edges of his consciousness.

She draws a shuddering breath. The black of the tunnels is so intense that it appears lighter when she closes her eyes and catches the stray motes of imagined vision.

"Could we—" Her mouth is dry. "Could we fashion a torch of some kind?"

"Not without oil or paraffin."

A silence, punctuated by the faint echoes of their breathing.

"We should at least look," she whispers finally. "Now that we are so close."

Something in her voice, a note of barely suppressed panic, prompts Peter to open his eyes and brings him back to himself by a few degrees. Still, the ache of bone-deep weariness remains with him. He shakes his head in the darkness.

"If it exists, then"—her voice cracks—"perhaps we could escape that way. We could go back and change all of this."

She listens to the dying echoes of her words in the cavern silence and shivers, hearing aloud the possibility that, until now, she has not permitted herself to consider.

At this moment, he is too numb to really register the significance of her words. Instead, again, it's the tone of her voice that moves him. Gritting his teeth against the protests of his body, Peter climbs to his feet.

She lights a fourth match and they link hands. Slowly, they limp toward the pile of rubble.

Chunks of rock litter the ground around where the charge was laid. As they approach, in the flickering light of the small flame, Peter sees that the wall of the passage is scarred and uneven, a gouged-out crescent curving from waist-height up to the ceiling. She stumbles and he almost falls beneath her sudden weight. She drops the match and it goes out.

"Did you see anything?" she whispers.

"Don't think so. You?"

She squeezes her eyes shut and tries to visualize the ruined tunnel wall. The dark streaks left by the blasting powder on the dull gray rock, the debris and puddles of mud on the ground.

She feels him shift, unseen, beside her. "Then we should—"

"Wait," she interrupts, groping blindly to put a restraining hand on his arm. "Perhaps I did see something. I am going to light another match."

Peter silences the objection that starts on his lips and a moment later light blooms through the cramped underground world.

Blinking against the sudden brightness, she points. "There, on the wall—you see? A darker place?"

He peers and then sees it: one of the gouged fissures in the rock that looks infinitesimally different from the others, a deeper shadow to its darkness. Peter half falls toward it.

"What do you see?"

"There's an opening."

Peter hears her draw a sharp breath. His heart is racing as well, his earlier drowsiness vanished. "Give me the matches," he says. "I'm going in."

The fifth match sputters out.

Gingerly, he fits his bruised body into the fissure in the tunnel wall. The jagged opening is hardly wider than his chest and as Peter pushes farther into the narrow space, his coat pocket catches on an outcropping. He pulls at the fabric but it holds fast, his arms wedged helplessly against his sides by the rock. He becomes abruptly aware of the mass of stone around him, the tons of blackness pressing downward on this fragile pocket of air. The crushing weight of granite—

A wash of terror hits him, and he stifles the urge to scream. Beyond the verso of the unending subterranean night, he can feel something growing closer, some kind of presence, hungry and poised. With a burst of panic-born strength, Peter frantically jerks again. With a tearing sound the snagged pocket gives way and he tumbles forward, crying out as his aching body lands on jagged rock.

"Are you all right?" she calls.

He stands. "All right," he croaks, hardly recognizing his own voice.

Shakily he lights a match and holds up the flame to the crevice in the cave wall—which is suddenly reduced in scale to a few difficult steps over a rocky ledge. She is standing in the outer darkness of the tunnel, her arms wrapped across her chest, squinting against the light. He holds his hand toward her, helping her through—then raises the match, and together they survey the space.

The cave is the size of a small room, a dozen feet across and the same in height. The walls and floor are dull gray granite, flecked with quartz. The stone is molded into uneven arcs as if shaped by gas or water—a space that has been here, he thinks, since before the city and before all of us, unknown and waiting. And in the wall, opposite where they stand, is a small wooden door.

For a time, both of them simply stare.

The most disturbing thing about the door is its utter ordinariness. It is made of old, unpolished wood, reinforced with three horizontal iron bands. Five feet tall and three across, it is set directly into the sheer rock wall of the cave without any visible frame. It is the most unlikely thing, here in this impossible place, Peter has ever seen.

And everything, all of it, was true. This is the thought that hits him, the realization accompanied by a wave of dizziness that nearly makes him stumble beside her. Her story, the journey through time—all of it. He shakes his head, stunned by the wealth of sudden possibilities.

Some letters have been carved into the center of the door. C-R-O-A-T-O-A-N, he reads. She starts forward but he grips her arm, holding her back.

"Wait," he says. The match burns his fingers and he blows it out.

In the darkness that descends, neither says anything. Half-formed thoughts are leaping at the edges of her awareness: threads of hidden meaning, each leading away into the warp and weave of things unseen. She tries to remind herself that now, more than ever, it is essential to be careful and scientific. But at the same time, unthinking, the door seems to pull her closer. On her arm, she can feel that Peter's hand is trembling.

"What does it mean?" he asks. "Those letters?"

"I do not know." Her throat feels constricted and tight. "I saw this door and the letters in the basement of my father's house. I never thought about their meaning. The mark of the carpenter, I supposed."

Again, neither speaks for a time. The darkness and silence around them broken only by the faint sounds of dripping water and their breathing.

She reaches out and touches the dry, rough wood. Lets her fingers drift across the letters, down to the door's iron handle. Silently he does the same. In the dark they are standing almost cheek to cheek.

"What now?" he whispers.

She closes her eyes. The alternation of absolute blindness and sudden light, together with the swarming murmur of underground echoes, prevent her from thinking clearly. She pictures the green vistas of Ohio, the landscapes that haunt her memory. The quiet rooms of the house in Toledo where she grew up, the order of her basement laboratory with its racks of polished instruments, the look of hopeful confusion on her father's face—

All this comes to her, an abrupt longing that takes her breath away. And now, all these things are possible and within reach. This, and even more: perhaps she could travel back even further and prevent the invasion of Toledo, to save everything that was lost. To be reunited not only with her father, but with her beloved, long-dead mother, whom she can hardly remember—

She sways on her feet, shaken by the images. When she had first arrived in New York, the demands of survival had obscured any speculation about what might be possible if she could find or reconstruct the device—daydreams that had seemed, in any case, shadowed with the threat of madness. Later, after their encounter with Edison and Morgan, she had determined to ignore such hopes. But now, standing in front of the door, they come crowding back more urgently than ever.

And even if beyond the portal is only fire and death, she thinks, in the last moments of the exploding mansion—even so, it would at least be certainty.

Beside her, Peter shifts nervously in the darkness.

"So, now . . ." he starts, then trails off, not knowing how the sentence ought to end.

His mind is racing as he grapples with the reality of what they have found. He thinks of his father, half shadowed across a night-time campfire. The sky and the dark evergreen forest and the rearing horse, its forelegs churning. His hours here in New York, beside her, all their misunderstandings and accidental betrayals: all the things he could've said and done better. Only—the realization strikes him—there's something that feels strangely right about their time together, despite everything, awkwardness and all. That we even met, that any of it even happened, he thinks. Maybe that's enough.

"But think of Morgan," she murmurs in the darkness beside him.

"How's that?" Peter shakes his wandering thoughts away.

"Think of how he or Tesla might employ this device." She draws a breath. "If we use the door, they will find it and follow us through. Even if I were to destroy the device itself on the other side, it is possible the portal would remain open."

"So, then . . . ?"

She closes her eyes.

This should be—she expects it to be—a terrible decision: between everything she has loved, and her responsibility to the world in which she finds herself now. But strangely, with Peter beside her, it hardly feels like a choice at all. Because maybe the past only exists, she thinks wordlessly, to make the future possible.

She opens her eyes and straightens.

"Will you light a match?" she asks.

Peter feels inside the little box with his fingertips. There are four left, he is pleased to discover—although what good four moments of sight will do in this vast darkness, he realizes, is hard to imagine. He fumbles out the match, and strikes it.

The flame is dazzlingly bright in the small space of the cave, exaggerated shadows leaping across the stone walls. They squint against the light, at the ancient wooden door, a fragment from another world juxtaposed into this alien setting.

"Can you destroy it?" she says.

"The door?"

She nods, fighting the urge to cry. "If the mass anchor is destroyed, the portal should collapse."

Peter looks up and around, surveying the space. Small cracks run through the arched stone of the roof, the fragile hollow of the cave already weakened by the rift in the tunnel wall. Even so, he realizes, it will be dangerous—maybe even more risky than the first blast.

As the match sputters into darkness he meets her eyes again: her face smudged with dirt, her nose dripping from the cold, a tightness of held-back tears around her eyes.

The match goes out.

He stands very still, hearing her breath and feeling the warmth of her unseen presence.

Inexplicably now, Peter remembers the sense of invisible power that once pushed him up the span of the Brooklyn Bridge. Maybe this—it strikes him—is what the city, with the nameless urgency of its buildings and bridges, has been telling him all along: not any one meaning, but something about why things mean at all. Which is that if things were certain, they wouldn't mean anything.

If it were certain, it wouldn't be love.

"Yes," he says. "It's risky for us. Very risky. But, with luck, yes."

Utter darkness.

"Climb back into the tunnel," he instructs. "I need rocks to shape the charge."

She nods, wresting down a momentary doubt about the door. Because this is the only way, she reminds herself: for the sake of history itself. For the sake of everything. To put the past aside, and by doing so to make the future possible.

She gropes her way along the wall of the cave until she finds the fissure and pushes herself into it, a wave of claustrophobia descending—and then she tumbles out into the wider excavation beyond.

"I am outside," she announces.

"Good," he calls back. "Toss the rocks through."

Fumbling on the tunnel floor, she feels her fingernails break as she lifts chunks of debris and pushes them through the crevice. Despite the pain, she is grateful for the distraction from the suffocating weight of darkness on all sides. Inside the cave she can hear the tapping of Peter's hammer and the faint exhalations of his effort, echoing in the tomblike stillness. Then the sound of his hammer stops and he mumbles a curse.

"What is it?" she calls, straightening. "Is something wrong?"

"Not enough fuse left."

"Then"—her heart catches—"you cannot destroy the portal?"

"Not without destroying us along with it." He groans, a shuffling sound as he shifts his weight. "Fuse won't reach out of the cave."

Both stand silently in the dark for some unmarked span of time.

There must be a way, she thinks, clinging to her earlier sense of conviction.

"Could we—" Abruptly, in the darkness, a spark of inspiration comes to her. "Perhaps we could use cloth from my dress."

"Wouldn't burn hot enough."

"If you dust it with blasting powder?"

He falls silent and she waits, holding her breath.

"Maybe," he says. "Could work, I think."

Crouched inside the cave, Peter hears the sound of ripping fabric.

"How much of this do you need?" she calls.

He tries to visualize the space of the cave, at the same time trying to ignore all the things that could go wrong. "About fifteen feet."

The ripping continues, then stops. "Do you need more rock?"

"No. Got enough here already."

He hears her shuffle, slip, cry out softly, and then she tumbles through the crevice to half fall against him.

"Here." She presses a coiled strip of cloth into his hand, and then he feels her move away. Clutching the makeshift fuse he kneels by the base of the door, where he has chipped out a channel in the rock. He opens the bag of supplies and gropes for the powder box—then feels inside the matchbox. Three matches remain. One match, he has promised himself, he will save, even if he isn't certain exactly why.

"Take the matches." He holds the box out toward where he can hear her teeth chattering. A moment later her hand finds his own in the dark. "Strike one, and step away."

She does, and squinting against the light Peter glances in her direction to find himself looking up at a breathtaking expanse of exposed leg, below the torn hem of her dress—

Struggling to focus on the task at hand, he dips his fingers into the powder box and runs them down the length of the cloth. The remaining blasting powder he pours into the channel below the door, fitting in a blasting cap at one end and tamping down a layer of broken rock above.

The match gutters out.

She climbs back through the fissure into the tunnel. He follows, trailing the makeshift fuse.

"Here," he says. "Sit with your back to the wall. Plug your eyes and ears, like last time. You remember?"

"I remember."

He lowers himself beside her.

"You have the matches?"

"I do." She presses the small box into his palm.

He removes their next-to-last match from the box and draws a breath. This time, strangely, he is hardly nervous at all. He feels larger than himself, filled with some beginning or end. He reaches out and squeezes her hand; she squeezes back.

"Are you ready?" he asks.

"I am," she says, pressing herself against him.

He draws a breath and strikes the match, touching it to the fuse. As the cloth begins to smolder they regard each other in the brief, flickering brightness.

The rumble of falling rock.

And a moment later, the world explodes in fire and light.

CHAPTER XIV

THE RETURN

SUMMER IS IN ITS LAST DYING PAINS WHEN THE AIRPLANE TOUCHES down at my destination. After retrieving my luggage I stand in line at the taxi stand, sweating in the humid air beneath a low belly of gray clouds that hangs overhead, pregnant with the threat of thunderstorms. Finally I clamber into a foul-smelling yellow minivan and give the driver directions to my hotel, then collapse against the sticky vinyl of the seat, exhausted, to watch the smokestacks and weed-filled parking lots pass outside.

The hotel is a tall cinder-block cube, nearly identical to the buildings on either side. When I check in, using my new passport, my room is similarly featureless: the white-walled space, the molded plastic ashtray on the bedside table, the dingy telephone and the blank face of the television, all feel interchangeable with thousands of other rooms in dozens of other cities. Lying on the stained sheets and trying to ignore the shooting pains in my chest, I stare up at the ceiling and think of how, in this place, I could be anyone, anywhere.

Strange how it's only the most intangible of things, the battered sheaf of my memories, that sets me apart from all the previous occupants of this room.

Closing my eyes, I remember the terror and dislocation that I'd felt during those first days, after waking to find myself on a beach I had never seen before, wet with the surf of a foreign ocean. Then, looking around the dark shore, lit in the distance by the glimmer of countless electric lights, I was struck by the thought that I had died and wandered into some strange heaven.

It was only after a stranger told me that the ocean was called the Pacific, and that the year was 1954, that I began to guess what might have happened. How the blast in the subway tunnels must have transported me, in the same way it had hurled you from the Ohio of your childhood into the New York where we'd met. Either that, or I had simply lost my mind.

The first thing I did, of course, was start looking for you. Sleeping on park benches, bewildered and struggling to comprehend my surroundings—the buzzing helicopters and gleaming superhighways—I searched for you. At any moment, I expected, I'd find you waiting for me. Together, I told myself, we would make sense of what had happened and set things right, or simply begin a new life together. It was nearly a year before the social workers found me living as a vagrant and began their project of rehabilitation, and before I admitted to myself that you weren't going to appear around the next corner.

I found a job washing dishes at a restaurant (the only place that would hire me without proper papers—since, as far as the state was concerned, I was dead) and took a room in a boardinghouse. I spent my mornings before work reading the newspapers and trying to understand the new world in which I found myself. And as soon as I could afford the ticket, I boarded a cross-country bus for New York.

I lived there for eight months, working odd jobs and walking and rewalking the streets we had passed down together. The Morgan mansion was a museum now, I discovered, and the tenement where Paolo lived had been demolished decades ago, replaced by a row of smart townhouses. Everyone I had known was dead or disappeared. And again, you were nowhere to be found. Finally, I rode the bus back to California—which wasn't home but where, at least, my heart didn't break at the sight of every half-remembered boulevard and building.

Two years later, I visited Toledo. Amid the factories and slums, I searched for some hint of the kingdom you once told me about. Picturing you there as a little girl, in scattered places—while looking up at the old oak trees in a park or the crumbling façade of a warehouse near the lake—I sometimes imagined that I felt a flicker of the history you had described. But nowhere did I find any hint of your living presence.

Now, lying on the hotel bed, I remember this: standing beside an empty factory in Ohio, amid the fast-food litter and used condoms, looking out at the blue surface of Lake Erie. Imagining that once, maybe, you had stood in this same spot, contemplating the same horizon . . .

When I wake up on the morning after my arrival in New York, I discover that I've mistakenly taken someone else's luggage from the airport. Enormous brassieres and jogging clothes fill the space where my folded shirt and trousers should be. Pulling on the gray suit that I'd worn the day before, and borrowing a (hopefully) clean pair of athletic socks from the suitcase, I stop at the deli next door to the hotel for a cup of coffee before starting through the clamor of the streets.

It's been more than twenty years now since the last time I was in New York, and at first the experience is overwhelming. It's not just the traffic, or the noise, or the endless towers of glass and steel (in fact, all of these things are far less chaotic than the Manhattan I remember, although hugely magnified in scale)—instead, it's simply the way that everything here is so *fast*. As I walk down Broadway, leaning on my cane, stylish young men and women jostle past on either side, making me feel like I'm moving through another, slower world that is superimposed over my present surroundings: an indistinct metropolis of memory, its landmarks the settings that once framed our time together and your face.

It takes me until early afternoon to make my way through the maelstrom of Times Square and past the sleek boutiques of SoHo (where Tesla's laboratory stood until it burned down in 1904), to Battery Park on the southern tip of Manhattan. There, finally, I let myself collapse onto a bench, trying to ignore the unsteady hammering of my heart and the ache in my hips.

Relatively speaking, it's quiet here. Along the margins of the park vendors sell postcards and T-shirts to the strolling crowd of tourists. A breeze kicks up small, choppy waves on the surface of the bay. The clouds have cleared overnight and the sky is a high, pale blue overhead. In the distance I can make out the warehouses of Brooklyn and, farther out yet, a lonely weather-battered woman, her arm raised in a gesture of defiance and hope, silhouetted against the horizon of the Atlantic.

The expanse of water, the shabby trees and park grass, the

white noise of the city. A few hopeful pigeons gather briefly around me, then disperse as they realize no crumbs are forthcoming.

I close my eyes, hoping for some kind of clarity.

During my years in Los Angeles, in your absence, our time together became more and more like a dream. Even while your memory haunted me, and while I continued to scan the sidewalks for your face, I started to believe that maybe I had invented the whole thing and simply convinced myself it was real.

Searching for some kind of certainty, I became a student of the past. I enrolled in community college courses and started to read obsessively: most of all I read Byron and Dante, the poets you had loved, and history books. I spent my nights after work hunched over library texts, slowly making sense of the last six decades and hoping to find clues about what happened to the world I remembered—and (most of all) about what happened to you.

Some of the answers were easy to find. I learned how Morgan died like a king, lonely and surrounded by admirers, while Tesla's last days were spent hungry and penniless in a fleabag hotel room. Absence itself provided other hints: the terrifying repercussions of time travel, which you had feared so much, were nowhere to be seen. Instead, the forward march of history continued just as inevitably (and perhaps more horribly, with the two World Wars, Vietnam, and the rest) as ever before. So in this sense, at least, it seemed that we had succeeded (at least, if I hadn't made the whole thing up). But despite my efforts, the crucial things—the facts of your life, and of our time together—eluded me.

Oh, I found a few scattered bits of evidence: the details about a young man named Peter Force, who was born on the frontier and moved to New York, emerged after months of searching, even if I had no way of proving their connection to my present self. In occasional brief footnotes I'd find some mention of the Toledo family and the Kingdom of Ohio, references to books long out of print, or dry asides based on rumors and hearsay. But beyond this, either the records didn't exist—or in the vastness of all the words ever written, the traces of our passage were too insignificant for me to see.

Gradually, after each year of failure, the moments I remembered started to seem like a kind of fairy tale: an imperfectly recalled story that still shaped my days, but which I couldn't really believe. And eventually, between the demands of the world, the arguments of common sense, and the weight of uncertainty, I decided that the only thing I could do was to try to forget.

So I tried. By that time I had a new identity, a regular job, and an apartment of my own. I bought a pair of acid-washed jeans and a denim jacket (this was in the 1980s), signed up for a dating service, and started listening to popular music—Michael Jackson, Genesis, Huey Lewis and the News.

It didn't work. Despite my efforts, this newly invented version of myself felt like an awkward disguise. Most of the time I managed to hide my sense of unease, and the women I met for dinner and a movie seemed unaware that it was just a façade. But it was a futile attempt. Some part of me understood this from the beginning—in the same way that, remembering your face, I knew that I would not fall in love, in that way, again.

And in the end, I gave up trying to find a home in the present. (Except, that's not quite right: what I really mean is that I gave up trying to imagine a place for myself in the future. After all, if we strive in the present it's for the sake of some landscape we yearn to someday reach, a destination I could no longer imagine.) That was when I opened the antiques store, which I intended to be my refuge from the world. I reduced my existence to the morning bus ride to work and the evening ride home, the television, and the microwave. Occasional customers and trips to the grocery store. Sitting in the park and watching the sun sink over the Pacific Ocean. A modest life, fenced with careful oblivion.

Until one day, I found your photograph—the picture Paolo had taken of us sitting in the Suicide Hall with Tesla—and everything changed.

It was all real. At that moment, looking down at the image, I understood that everything I had denied, everything that I'd made myself ignore and forget—all of it had been true. This was the realization that left me sobbing and helpless in the antiques store. All these things returning like a flood, and with them, an abrupt, desperate urgency.

Everything had changed—but still, at the same time, my situation remained stubbornly the same. It was true that, despite my doubts and despair, I had never completely given up looking for you. After all, how could I? My memories of you, and our time together, were the things that defined me: I could not stop searching for you any more than I could forget to breathe. But despite this, the facts were still facts. I was still an old man, living alone in Los Angeles. You were still gone, and I still knew nothing more than before about what had happened to you.

So finally, because I couldn't think of anything else to do, I started to write.

Now, sitting in Battery Park, I remember the first time I saw you near this river: that cold afternoon, a century ago. The gray clouds blanketing the sky and the dark mirror of the current, the foghorns of barges and the leafless trees. How you fell, and for no clear reason I decided to help. The lines of your face against the monochrome winter world. Pale skin, dark curling hair, a shabby antique dress. My surprise, and the distance in your eyes: two strangers thrown together, briefly facing each other in the endless rush of days.

I shake my head, blinking the present back into focus. I could spend (and have spent) days wandering through these memories, but that's not why I came here.

So why did I come to New York?

When I bought the airplane ticket I told myself that I was returning here to search for you one last time, equipped with the results of my studies and the urgency of my failing heart. But writing these pages, some part of me has always understood that my recollections might be mistaken and that, in the end, my searching hasn't really answered anything. Heaven only knows, for that matter, whether the Kingdom of Ohio ever existed as you described it to me, or as I've tried to piece it together.

Although I've tormented myself for years with the need for some clear truth about what happened to us, and what happened to you, I'm not any closer to certainty than I had been at the beginning. And maybe, I tell myself, that's simply the way life is: maybe the past is always, ultimately, unrevealed and unknowable. An endless series of "what if" questions whose answers never arrive.

Maybe that's why, if I'm honest with myself, the truth is that I really came to New York to say good-bye. To stand in the place where you might pause and glance up on your way through the vastness of the world, this final point of shared passage between us.

In front of me, small waves on the surface of the Atlantic reflect fragments of late-summer sunlight; behind me the city begins in a gleaming wall of skyscrapers. I think of how we stood here together. And I hope—if such wishes mean anything, or have any power through the barrier of time—that somewhere you have been, or will someday be, happy.

Finally, ignoring the protests of my legs and back, I climb to my feet and start walking again. Past the neoclassical fortresses of Wall Street and the quiet avenues of Tribeca, I make my way north toward Canal Street.

Although the buildings have changed, the bustle of Chinatown remains the same. The sidewalks are still lined with vendors hawking their wares, and I recall the smell of rotting fish and charcoal smoke in the air. But when I try to picture the excavation site, Paolo and Tobias and the others amid the piles of machinery and broken rock, I can't bring the image into focus. Against the backdrop of my present surroundings, the ranks of garish advertisements (*Best Electronic Deal! All Brand Name Rolex, 90% Discount . . .*), and the swarm of pedestrians crowding the sidewalk, my memories of that time seem irrelevant and unreal.

From almost the moment I started walking, my heart has been pounding and I feel uncomfortably short of breath. At the end of the block I see an entrance to a subway station and hurry toward it, clutching my cane, thinking that I can't stay in this place. But when I reach the stairs that lead down to the subway, I hesitate.

The first time that I returned to this city after my "accident" (the wrong word; but if there's a right one, it escapes me) I had visited the subway. Stepping into these passageways—excavations that I remembered so vividly, but which had become utterly alien in their tile-lined, fluorescent-lit modern shape—I felt such a wave of disorientation and fear that I had to scramble back toward the surface, gasping and nauseous. After that, on my subsequent visits to New York, I'd avoided the underground railroad. But now, clutching the handrail, I take a deep breath and descend into the tunnel.

And this time, standing in the subway station, all that comes to me is a vague sense of sadness. The flow of commuters through the turnstiles and the electronic ticket-vending machines are empty of threat or significance. Instead, these things are only more reminders of the impossible distance that separates the present from the vanished places I remember.

I board the subway and lower myself into one of the scarred plastic seats. As the train lurches into motion I study the faces of other passengers: polished professionals in expensive suits, tired shop workers slouched behind tabloids, knots of gossiping teenagers. A random gathering of lives, each oblivious to the rest. Myself among them, an old man in a world that doesn't make sense, wearing a stranger's socks.

I close my eyes, swaying with the motion of the train. It's over, I tell myself. This is how the story ends.

I realize that I'm holding my breath, waiting for . . . something. I don't know what. But nothing comes: only the white noise of the subway rushing through the tunnels, accompanied by a pang of weariness.

I open my eyes again.

Above the graffiti-scarred windows opposite me are a row of brightly colored posters: advertisements for tourist destinations, dentistry services, and bunion cream. One of the signs depicts a Native American, wearing an elaborate headdress, talking to a pilgrim with an awkward hat and wide-buckled shoes. Glancing up, I notice the caption above this image. *Croatoan: Artifacts and Art of Early American Colonies*, it reads.

As I look away, at the subway floor, I feel a faint sense of familiarity that I can't quite place. I look up at the advertisement again, trying to pinpoint the source of the sensation. Then, abruptly, the memory clicks into place, and the world stops.

Croatoan.

That was the word I saw carved into the door we found in the subway tunnels, the same word printed on the sign I'm staring at now.

For an instant, I feel a shock of numb disbelief. But really, I tell myself, this is just a coincidence: another of fate's practical jokes. This is exactly the kind of false clue that I've been chasing for decades now, on an endless futile search that I've come here to leave behind.

Still, I can't help climbing to my feet, stumbling as the subway jolts around a bend, and pushing my way through the crowd of commuters toward the sign. Ignoring the scowls of the other passengers, I study the fine print at the bottom of the advertisement. The poster is promoting an exhibit at the Museum of Natural History, I realize, a special event that will be ending the day after tomorrow.

The subway slows, pulling into a station. And then, before I quite realize what I'm doing, I'm shoving my way out of the train and up the steps, waving at a passing taxicab on the street.

The Museum of Natural History is a rambling castle built of red stone, with crumbling turrets and a sagging slate roof, across the street from the green expanse of Central Park. As I approach the entrance a column of schoolchildren, walking in pairs, emerges from the building. I stand aside as they jostle down the wide steps, filing into a row of waiting yellow buses. As they do, a young girl—

maybe seven years old, with blond hair and a grubby T-shirt—stops and peers up at me.

Looking at her, I imagine that there's an unspoken question in her gaze. And what can I possibly tell her—I think, as our eyes meet—what message can be conveyed from where I stand? Maybe just the strangeness of the way our lives are shaped by the past: even the things we imagine to be lost. Because all of it stays with us, always, shading the light of our days until there is no longer any difference between it and us and the glimmering scene reflected in the mirror-surface of the present.

The little girl frowns, and, at a loss for words, I stick out my tongue. This seems to satisfy her—she laughs and turns away, skipping down the steps. I close my eyes. I understand that I am sick with the chasm between this world and the things that I remember. But if I can't forget, and can't find any kind of certainty, what is left?

The schoolchildren finally pass and I continue climbing the steps. At the ticket booth, the blond twentysomething attendant looks at me skeptically.

"We're closing in half an hour, sir," she says, after I ask her for one senior-citizen admission. "Maybe you want to come back tomorrow?"

I shake my head and she shrugs, counting out my change. My hands are shaking as I stuff the crumpled bills into my pocket, and I feel lightheaded, dizzy.

"Enjoy your visit," she calls after me. I nod back at her, nearly stumbling over my cane as I hurry into the museum.

As quickly as decency will allow, I make my way through the dimly lit galleries, the dinosaur bones and silent dioramas depicting fragments of other landscapes: a series of stuffed birds against the painted backdrop of a sunset lagoon, extinct buffalo gazing out from a prairie of dried grass, carved totem poles in a forest. Finally I find the exhibit that I'm looking for, at the end of a silent corridor.

My heart is hammering as I step through the door and look around.

Coming here, I didn't really know what to expect—but it certainly wasn't this. The room is lined with displays that contain an assortment of neatly labeled artifacts: old-fashioned muskets, crude iron pots and pans, wooden dolls. Near the center of the space, a glass case exhibits a model of a few log cabins inside a rough wooden stockade, surrounded by trees.

Crossing to the nearest display I scan one of the informational placards. *British colonization of the Americas began in the late 16th century, and reached its peak toward the middle of the 17th century*, the text begins, continuing to explain the challenges these early settlers faced. Nothing that has any connection with my memories, or with you.

I shake my head, the wave of disappointment like a physical blow. And with it, an irrational surge of anger—as if I've been the victim of a cruel joke. For a moment I close my eyes, trying to push away the sense of frustration that makes me want to cry.

I take a deep breath, and with an effort look around again.

Beyond this first area of the exhibit, doorways open onto a series of smaller spaces that display artifacts related to the same historical period. And at the very least, I console myself, one of them might offer an explanation of the word from the sign on the subway, even if it's only a coincidence. Inside the next room I find a collection of objects almost identical to the ones outside: carved forks and spoons, a painting of a sailing ship, etchings that depict life in the American colonies.

A third room also reveals nothing about what I'm looking for. A bored gallery attendant, wearing an ill-fitting museum uniform, wanders in and glances at me indifferently. He is about to turn away when, out of desperation, I limp toward him.

"Excuse me." My voice is too loud, echoing in the empty spaces, and he scowls at me. I try to speak more softly. "I have a question."

The attendant glances at his watch. "We're closing in fifteen minutes, sir. What's up?"

"The name of this exhibit, *Croatoan*. What does it mean?"

"Oh, that? Something to do with the settlement at Roanoke." He shrugs, indicating a direction with his head. "Explains about it all the way in the back, over there."

"Thank you." I shuffle in the direction that the attendant indicated, through a passageway that leads me to a dimly lit space with no further rooms beyond. I stop, looking around.

Unlike the rest of the exhibit, there aren't any artifacts on display here. Instead, opposite from the entrance where I'm standing, is a single black-and-white drawing: a pattern of abstract lines maybe six feet tall. In the center of the image, written in crude letters like a child's penmanship, is the word that brought me here.

Several other pictures are also on the walls, but I hardly register their presence. Staring at the image in front of me, I experience a moment of déjà vu that makes me feel like I'm falling toward those rough letters. It's a dreamlike sensation, suspended between wonder and disbelief. Without quite realizing what I'm doing, I cross the room and run my fingers over the drawing.

Gradually, the rush of recognition fades and I turn my attention to the text that accompanies the images on display. *The Lost Colony of Roanoke*: *An American Mystery*, the heading reads. I try to focus on the words, to focus on what they mean.

The placard describes one of the first British attempts to colonize America, an expedition organized by Sir Walter Raleigh in 1587.

In the summer of that year, I read, a fleet of three ships carrying 121 colonists departed England for the wilderness of Virginia. The expedition was commanded by a man named Captain John White, and only two members of his crew had ever seen the New World before.

Shortly after setting sail, the smallest of the three ships disappeared in a storm off the coast of Portugal. The remaining vessels arrived in Chesapeake Bay at the beginning of autumn, and the colonists disembarked on Roanoke Island to begin their new settlement. Among them were Captain White's daughter, his son-in-law, and his infant granddaughter. Before departing, White told the colonists that if they needed to move, they should carve the name of their destination on a conspicuous tree. If they left under duress, he said, they should also carve a Maltese cross. After giving these instructions, Captain White sailed away, promising to come back in six months.

When White arrived back in London, however, tensions with Spain had escalated into war, and Queen Elizabeth called for all available ships to be used for the protection of England. By the time the Spanish Armada had been defeated in 1588, Lord Raleigh had turned his attention to other projects, and as a result Captain White was forced to raise money for a fleet of his own. It was not until February of 1590 that he was able to set sail for Virginia again, three years after he had told the colonists he would return.

When he reached Roanoke Island, the settlement was deserted. The huts and stockades built by the colonists stood empty and abandoned, but still intact. Captain White and his crew discovered no evidence of violence, no bodies or graves. The only clue about what had happened to the colonists was the word *CROATOAN*, carved on a tree. Along with this word White found a Christian cross, but not the Maltese cross that the settlers were told to carve if they left the island in distress.

While his fleet was anchored offshore, a storm blew up and two of the ships' anchors were lost, forcing White to depart for England. Unable to find backing for a third voyage, Captain White did not return to Virginia and never saw his daughter, or granddaughter, again. Their fate—the placard concluded—like that of all the Roanoke Island colonists, remains a mystery to this day: a false beginning to the history of an America that never came into being.

I finish reading and sit down on a bench in the middle of the room, trying to think about what this means.

The word that you and I found on the door in the subway tunnel, a portal we destroyed in order to keep it from the hands of Tesla, Edison, and Morgan, was marked with the same inscription that had been carved on a tree in the Virginia wilderness: a hidden message at the birth of another America that vanished without a trace. Clutching my head in my hands, I struggle to guess the significance such a coincidence might have.

Around me the museum gallery is dim and silent. I imagine that I might be the last visitor in the building, alone with these artifacts in the windowless white-walled space. From a hallway in the distance, the muffled sound of footsteps grows nearer and then recedes.

For no clear reason, I find myself thinking of what Tesla said to you in the Suicide Hall: *"The only possible explanation is that you traveled from one world, where you did know me, into this one."*

I remember this, and also what you'd said after we first met: *"Our goal was the construction of a device to transport men instantaneously from one place to another."*

Abruptly I'm struck by an idea that jerks me upright on the bench. It's an intuition that comes out of nowhere, but that has an urgency I can't ignore. And really, I think, it's not impossible. Neither you nor I ever actually stepped through the doorway; both of us were simply nearby when the explosion happened. And what—I wonder—what if we had been wrong about the portal? That instead of creating a passage through time, the doorway was somehow actually a link between different worlds.

After all—it occurs to me—if free will exists, it's a decision that we make between futures. In which case, as many different versions of the future might exist as there are human choices. An infinitely branching set of parallel worlds in which our memories, both of what happened and what we wish could have happened, map out a single life's path.

I shake my head and stand. For some reason, accompanying these thoughts, I feel a strange sense of certainty—but, really, I remind myself, my imagination may only be running away with me: and in any case, I will never really know. Crossing to the black-and-white image, I scrutinize it again.

According to the caption, it is a drawing of the inscription found at Roanoke, made by Captain White. Looking closely, I realize that the lines around the word *CROATOAN* are not an abstract pattern but instead are the patterns of tree bark.

A moment later I notice the carved cross that was described in the placard for the first time. It's etched into the wood above the word itself, an asymmetric symbol inside a faint circle. In fact—this occurs to me—it looks like the pendant you once wore: a letter *T*, enclosed by a ring of twining cornstalks.

I open my mouth and then close it, blinking. Looking at the blurred lines, I feel suddenly dizzy. I feel as if a bridge has unfolded out of the air in front of me, a pathway into the impossible past; as if I've just glimpsed your ghost. A tingling chill that makes the hair on the back of my neck stand up. I shiver and turn around, convinced that someone is watching.

There is a wooden door in the wall behind me.

It is roughly made, out of place against the blank white plaster of the museum. Carved into the door, halfway up, is the same word from the photograph of the tree. Something seizes inside me, my heart seeming to turn over in a somersault. The sharp pains in my chest that have been with me for these last years seem to recede, along with my awareness of the gallery around me, these things fading into unimportance as I stand motionless, staring.

My first thought is that the doorway was there all along, part of the exhibit that I didn't notice when I first entered. I close my eyes, trying to remember, but I can't be certain. It's possible the door wasn't there the last time I glanced at the wall. Instead—this suspicion slowly grows in me—maybe it appeared the instant before I turned, through some hidden mechanics of time and fate.

In a daze, I cross to the door and reach out toward it. The handle turns easily beneath my hand, the old wood swinging silently away from the wall. Peering through the crack I see a wash of white light, a blinding brightness.

Some part of me is thinking that all of this is impossible, a fantasy from which I'll wake up at any moment. But these doubts—along with my surroundings, and all the uncertainties and longing that have been with me for so long that I've almost come to think of them as myself—all these things are suddenly unimportant.

Hesitating in the brightness of the doorway, I think of what I might find on the other side. It could be the empty forest where the Roanoke settlement began, a wilderness at the beginning of a world where everything was different. It could be a portal to the city of Toledo, in a version of history where your kingdom and family survived and thrived, where we would be reunited. It could be anything.

For a moment then, I feel a pinch of doubt. But really, I tell myself, maybe this is how the stories that we live finally end: with the blankness of a new beginning, beyond the maps of memory and history.

I take a breath and think of your face. Then I step through, and begin again.

ACKNOWLEDGMENTS

I'm grateful for the friendship and support of everyone who read this novel in its nascent state. In particular, I would like to acknowledge the patience and insight of my wonderful agent, Stephanie Cabot; Amy Einhorn, editor extraordinaire; Joel Elmore, Lindsay McClelland, E. A. Durden, Ethan Bernard, and Daniel Meneley, aka The Cabal; and most of all the incredible faith, understanding, and undeserved blessing of my *bashert*, Jessica; my sister; and my parents.

ABOUT THE AUTHOR

Matthew Flaming was born in Los Angeles and studied philosophy at Hampshire College. He currently lives in Brooklyn.